THE GREAT CARRIER REEF

PHIL GREEN

Published by Peagreen Publishing

Copyright © Phil Green

All rights reserved.

ISBN-13: 978-0-9928779-0-3

To my girls, Sophie, Mocha and Snickets.

I miss you.

Writing seems like such a solitary process. It especially is if you isolate yourself in a Scottish Castle – a long story. I would suggest always remember the real world as well as your imaginary one. Interaction with real people is invaluable, something I forgot along the way.

I apologise to my true friends and especially my family for becoming reclusive. A big thank you to those who intervened, bringing me home and back to reality, which has been a difficult but worthwhile transition.

1

The family plot contained seven graves. The addition of two more was particularly tragic as the family lineage was now left in the hands of one man – Daniel Morris. The setting for the graveside was beautiful, overlooking the warm and tranquil deep blue Florida sea. Dan had never truly appreciated the natural beauty; he had only ever associated the view with death.

The open graves stretched beneath the elongated shadow, perhaps appropriately, of an old battered weeping willow, its branches wistfully touching the ground with fatigue. A synthetic luminescent fake grass, often found draped across the tables of flower sellers, covered the freshly dug mounds of earth. Its intrusive colour seemed highly inappropriate against the picture postcard setting. Two solid oak caskets, containing Dan's only remaining family members, levitated above their impending final resting place.

Dan was eight the first time he stood on this hill overlooking the sea, at the time he had not fully understood nor appreciated what was happening. He thought his Mom was asleep and one day she would simply wake up. It took many months to realise the finality of what the golden coloured oak casket truly meant. His mother had chosen her final resting place many years before. How she knew at such a young age where she wanted to be buried puzzled him immensely; she was younger than he was now when she died.

As a child she had played on a rope swing under this very weeping willow. Her father, his grandfather, had tied the rope to one of the overhanging bows and attached an old cross-ply tyre which provided the seating. A trick he also employed when Dan had come to live at the family home after his mother's death.

His tree was within the orchard closer to the house where, as kids, they had lovingly built their den. Granddad had never done things by halves. The rope had long since rotted away but Dan could see the gnarled intrusion on the branch, the braided strands of hemp remained, where the friction of his mother's swinging motion had visibly worn into the bark.

His memories of his mother were somewhat hazy, he knew the jumbled images he remembered could not truly be his; they were associated through his Grandparents' storytelling and countless retelling. In many he could not have even been born, yet he had so many distinct visions imprinted in his mind's eye. He could visualise his mother seated on the swing, no older than he was when he came here, cascading long blonde hair, a white dress with blue polka dots, matching blue sandals and ankle socks. She was staring intently towards the distant horizon watching the bejewelled sunset. Instinctively he knew these memories were not his own but even so, they felt real. They were vivid but ultimately gleaned from the stories and family pictures atop his Grandma's roll top desk.

His mother's grave was the first beneath the willow, her dying so tragically young. His Grandparents also decided to be buried in the same spot after their death, which was appropriate, as they loved this place too. Grandma had always tended his mother's grave. As time took hold and as his Grandma's hip had started to wear, the curved wooden bench, hugging the willow's trunk had been positioned so she could sit in the shade and idle away the hours updating her on all of the local gossip and family news, good or bad. By default, through the addition of his Grandparents to the site, it had become the family plot. Dan believed it was a gruesome idea but it was a tradition which transferred from their original family roots in Scotland. Dan may have classed himself as an American but his ancestors were far more colonial. It seemed ironic he returned to the motherland with his own career.

There were no upright gravestones, something his Grandmother had insisted on, thus not disturbing the panoramic vista from the house, or the look of the ancient willow. Each grave was marked instead with an individual granite slab, black for the male members of the family and grey for the female. Uncle Mike and Aunt Susan's open graves were dug side by side, laying between his Uncle James', Aunt Pat's and his Mother's. An entire Morris generation rested directly beneath his Grandparents. Even worse, his cousin's graves, who were his childhood best friends, were marked by their own individual stones behind where he stood; now resting directly beneath each set of parents.

If you could view the family plot from above, it would look like a hierarchical family tree of death. Laid out by birthright and colour coded according to sex. All that was missing were the connecting lines tracing the history. There was room to the right for him and if he eventually married; his wife. Would he carry on the Morris family tree? Ultimately only time would tell.

What the hierarchy and coding could not indicate from the surface, was that four of the coffins were empty. Uncle James and Aunt Pat, along with both of his cousins, Matt and Ashley, were tragically lost to the sea, none of their bodies ever recovered. It was deemed the right decision to bury four empty caskets in memory, alongside the rest of the family.

He and Lizzie had taken a boat out after the ceremony and floated a wreath close to where the family yacht had been discovered. They both had agreed this was far more fitting and appropriate than the empty burial. The family's love of the sea was what brought them all together and kept them close. It was also what made Granddad buy the land and run down house, because it was situated next to the water, just like his Granddad's ancestral home in Scotland.

Lizzie was stood directly opposite, alongside her father, Charlie, who was probably the oldest and closest friend of the family, he was also their family lawyer. Dan looked directly into Lizzie's eyes. Between them it seemed, they had shared an awful closeness to death, it was what brought them together and also these last few years, what had driven him away. When his Grandparents died it was extremely hard to go through the motions, he was very close to his Granddad, having never ever known his real Father.

Matt, Ashley, Lizzie and himself had also been extremely close growing up, in fact inseparable, along with Bowie the family dog. His eyes swept over the small grave, also buried in the family plot. A larger than life character, Bowie had been a red boxer with so much energy and love. He was really Dan's but very much the family pet, his remains now only marked by a small granite stone.

University finally split the four of them, burgeoning adulthood suggesting they should partially grow up. Lizzie stayed at home, mainly for her father, although she was the string that bound them together, always keeping the lines of communication alive.

Many people from the local town had come to pay their respects; a few faces he recognised as parents of the kids they had been to High School with. All four of them were in the same year, something that could never have been planned, considering the age differences between their respective parents. Three cousins all in the same school year. Aunt Susan had been the High School secretary up until a few years ago so had known many people locally. They all looked at him with pity and sorrow; he hated this now-familiar look. He knew what they were thinking, how could such torment befall such a family? They had been so well liked within the community. He, along with the rest of the community, had trouble digesting what had happened.

Reverend Biggs' voice suddenly drifted back into Dan's consciousness. The service was coming to an end. Charlie nodded at him, realising any second he would have to step forward to lead the mourners. When they buried his Mother, Granddad had insisted on burying his daughter the way he grew up back home. In Scotland the men traditionally lowered the coffin into the grave. Up to eight men, close family and friends, were invited to *'take a cord'*. Each individual was called to the graveside by the funeral director, taking an end of four cords running under the coffin and through the coffins rings. They then lower the coffin into the grave.

His Mother's funeral was a simple affair but when his Grandparents were buried, having two coffins complicated matters slightly. They needed sixteen people to each take a cord. At this point Scottish tradition was slightly overlooked, as the women were also asked to take a cord. Dan vaguely remembered through his tears that he had stood next to Aunt Pat and Uncle James at the head of his Granddad's coffin. He could not even recall who was there, let alone who else took the remaining cords.

The last family funeral was horrific, four empty coffins lowered by a plethora of people Dan hardly knew. All he vaguely recalled was the numbness he felt as he was called to stand at the head of Matt's coffin. Lizzie had taken the cord at the head of Ashley's, Uncle Mike took Uncle James' and Aunt Susan took the head of Aunt Pat's. Dan shook the memories from his head as his name was sympathetically spoken by the funeral director, along with names Dan did not recognise except for Charlie, Lizzie and Mary, Aunt Susan's oldest friend.

They positioned themselves on boards, perilously close to the edge of the grave. Each held a black cord which ended with a decorative tassel. On top of Uncle Mike's coffin Dan placed a folded Scottish flag. His Uncle had returned to Scotland to study history at a famous University. St Andrews was Scotland's first university and the third oldest in the English-speaking world, founded in 1413. It was also where he met Aunt Susan who was studying to be a teacher. Everyone had loved Aunt Susan, for all the years she lived in America, she had never lost her eccentric Englishness which had made her so popular.

Lizzie stood at the head of Aunt Susan's coffin, on which she placed a box of Yorkshire loose-leaf tea. Yorkshire Gold had been her most recent favourite, 'it suited the Florida water', or so she said. Heaven forbid if you ever made a cup using a teabag, it was sacrilege. She could tell from ten paces. To her, herbal teas were the stuff of floggings and tea was served in a fine bone china cup with only one ginger nut biscuit per brew.

As the last person took his place, the funeral director directed the cord bearers. "Let the cord slip through your hands." The wooden poles holding the coffins were removed as the pallbearers, standing behind, took the strain. The mourners individual cords were just a gesture, they let the silk braid slip through their fingers as the coffin was lowered into its final resting place by the pallbearers. "Drop your cords into the grave and carefully step away." The director finally instructed.

Reverend Biggs then proclaimed. "Having given thanks for the lives of Michael William and Susan Emily Morris, we commit their bodies to be buried, earth to earth, ashes to ashes, dust to dust, through our Lord Jesus Christ." During which he threw several handfuls of dirt onto the coffins. "Go in peace; the blessing of God, the Father, the Son and the Holy Spirit be amongst you and remain with you always. Amen."

The congregation all spoke Amen in unison, except Dan who stared defiantly into the graves. He no longer believed in God. His faith, not that he had much left, finally was lost along with his entire family. Dan stood as the mourners filtered past offering their individual condolences; each squeezed into their obligatory black suits, the ones specifically dusted off for funerals, long out of style and well overdue replacement.

He shook hands, nodding his appreciation, hugging every woman until the black parade eventually passed, heading back towards the house. Charlie and Lizzie waited dutifully behind. Charlie approached Dan, purely by instinct Dan stuck out his hand to shake, which Charlie took, looked him in the eye pulling him into his arms. Dan finally cracked, half collapsing, sobbing uncontrollably into his shoulder. Lizzie wrapped her arms around the pair of them, hugging them both as the three of them cried together at their loss.

2

Dan, Charlie and Lizzie were the last to get back; they took their time, regaining their composure for the guests, walking in silence back down the hill to the house. The front doors were open. The guests were milling around in the drawing room to the left of the entrance hallway, chatting and making polite conversation. They all seemed a little lost as they apprehensively eyed the buffet table. For an American what was on offer would look extremely alien, the spread was not your traditional funeral affair.

What was being served would traditionally be known as 'High Tea' in Britain. A selection of finger sandwiches, cut into triangles, which in truth had no mystery, the pots of homemade jams, or fruit preserve, as an American would recognise it. Alongside, clotted cream, which at first glance had the look of curdled milk, with freshly baked scones which would certainly confuse; an American would traditionally refer to them as a biscuit. The whole platter would certainly not be seen as funeral food, if indeed any of them had seen it before.

A cream tea was the Morris family greeting and if you had never been for one, you really did not know what you were missing. Freshly baked scones with lashings of clotted cream and jam was a traditional family favourite, served with copious amounts of hot fresh tea. Lizzie was very familiar with the tradition and only ever had it when up at the house, she really missed this particular Morris ceremony. Aunt Susan always baked the most amazing selection of scones, mainly plain but some with currants or cranberries, which were her favourite.

They were nothing like the hard biscuit affair Americans offered, many sections of the population pronounce it as "sk'on", to rhyme with gone and the rest pronounce it "sk'own", to rhyme with cone. The latter pronunciation is more popular in Scotland, thus the Morris family cream tea was a skown served with Aunt Susan's homemade jam and of course, Cornish clotted cream. Lizzie, as ever, was the first to the table taking a side plate and napkin, placing a scone on the plate, cutting it in half, spreading a good serving of strawberry preserve on both halves and then spooning a dollop of clotted cream on top of both. The smell of the warm scones with sugared fruit was intoxicating. The mourners, as if taking their cue and suddenly understanding the protocol, started to make their way to the table. They scrutinised Lizzie's plate to make sure they used the correct etiquette, not that there really was any, except in the case of the Morris family which was to consume as many as you could without being sick, or until they were all gone.

Looking at Lizzie by the table, it dawned on Dan that this was the first time he had seen Lizzie in a dress since their high school prom. All their lives she had been very much the tomboy but today, of all days, she looked unassumingly beautiful. Her chocolate hair, usually tied back, was allowed the unusual privilege to be free. Naturally straight, it parted and flowed down over her bare shoulders, its lustre stood out against the formal black fitted dress, which in turn accentuated her toned and athletic body perfectly.

Lizzie was a rare gem who genuinely did not realise her good looks, let alone use or abuse them for personal gain. Her face rarely saw makeup and her pale skin exuded a rosy glow in her cheeks, topped with freckles, it gave her a mischievous fresh look. Her clear honey glazed eyes exuded such warmth they instantly put anyone at ease with a disarming manner. Coupled with this was the fact her mouth turned up slightly at the corners, giving the outward impression Lizzie was continually smiling. Only her lips had the faintest hint of makeup, a lipstick two shades darker than her true natural colour, although even this element was more function over fashion because if you were not careful the Florida sun would dry and crack your lips.

As she crossed back to where Dan and her Father stood, impatiently she took a bite from the first half of the scone. The warmth of the scone had liquidised the preserve and cream; it made a break, running down her chin. Realising the cream was heading south to settle on the front of her new dress, without thinking she instantly used her fingers to catch the jammy trickle.

"Here." Dan slid the napkin out from under one half of a fully loaded scone on Charlie's plate and thrust it at Lizzie. "It's nice to see the little black dress holds no more affection than one of your old T shirts!"

Lizzie stood licking the jam and cream from her fingers. "I purposely bought it knowing full well it would be high tea. The dress isn't dry-clean only you know, it's functional."

Charlie piped up from behind, "Unlike my suit!"

Dan turned and Lizzie peered round him to see Charlie had succeeded where Lizzie had failed, dribbling a mixture of blackcurrant jam and clotted cream down the front of his suit, looking startling like a sixties tie dye project. As Charlie tried to look down to survey the damage, awkwardly he raised both arms, tilting the plate in his left hand slightly, the other half of the scone slid off and tumbled to the ground, abiding the laws of buttered toast, landed clotted cream side down, spraying the cream in a three hundred and sixty degree arc.

This scone was fully loaded, which shot the sticky concoction up both Dan's and Charlie's suit legs. Fortunately Dan took the full force of the cream napalm attack and Lizzie's long legs were left unblemished, which was good as they were bare and her black suede open toed sandals would have been completely ruined. They all laughed, which lightened the mood slightly and the whole morbid proceeding seemed to change gear with a little light laughter.

Dan started to mingle and talk to the mourners, putting names to faces as he chatted to everyone and to thank them for coming. His biweekly Sunday evening conversations with Aunt Susan over trivial local gossip made the process easier because he could find something to talk about, matching unfamiliar names to Aunt Susan's idle chatter.

He also broke out his Uncle's favourite Scotch whiskey, Glenmorangie and also a Scottish gin, which was his Aunt's favourite; Hendricks, which she insisted was served with tonic over ice, dressed with cucumber, the suggested way of serving. Of course there was coffee for those who needed sobering and who truly did not like a proper cup of English tea. As the afternoon progressed to early evening, the house gradually emptied, finally leaving only Charlie, Lizzie and Dan. Lizzie started to clear the table.

"Leave that till later Liz, it'll give me something to do." Dan looked at Lizzie as she scraped the plates and separated the last of the scones. He gently touched her arm, "Please, I'd rather you left it, Aunt Susan would be mortified."

Lizzie realising he was right, stopped and viewed the table. "Well I'll just stack these plates in the kitchen then." Lizzie went through leaving Dan and her Father alone.

Dan turned to Charlie. "Thanks for sorting everything out Charlie, you have no idea how appreciated." Charlie was holding his crystal whiskey tumbler to the early evening orange sunlight streaming in the window. Watching the refracted colours through the bottom of the amber liquid, completely lost in thought.

"Don't be silly lad, Lizzie and I ..." he coughed, "... that is, you are the closest family we have." Charlie paused again as if trying to clear his throat. "I'm so sorry, I just, I just can't believe what has happened, it makes no sense. Your Aunt and Uncle were harmless, it's such a waste and so young." He bowed his head as his voice trailed away realising he may have said too much. Dan walked across placing his hand on Charlie's shoulder looking him in the eye, Charlie nodded in understanding.

Lizzie waltzed back into the room, instantly lightening the mood and snatching the glass from his hand. "Right you old fart, you've certainly had enough of the whiskey and I believe you aren't even supposed to drink on your tablets."

"Yes Doc." Charlie mocked and wobbled his head in agreement, Lizzie gave a disapproving look. Dan pushed the half empty bottle of Whiskey into Charlie's other hand and winked as Lizzie ushered him towards the front door, linking her arm through his.

Charlie spoke over his shoulder. "Don't forget I need you to drop by the office and sign some legal papers, how long are you planning to stay?"

"Well I'm in no rush, I'm on leave so intend to be around a while. I'll pop by tomorrow if you like?"

Lizzie lit up. "That's great, are we going to get a coffee at Java's?"

"My God, is old Mrs Itchen still running that place, she was ancient when we were kids."

Dan marvelled. Mrs Itchen ran the best coffee shop in town, in fact the best he had ever known. She knew everyone locally and treated the kids with a kindness and acceptance many of the other establishments simply did not. Therefore she remained the firm favourite with the kids and locals alike to hang out in. More importantly though it remained profitable and open, where-as many incomers opened and closed in very short timescales in such a small community.

"Still no influx of Starbucks?" Dan ventured, knowing the truth. You could not compare Java's with Starbucks but it certainly did offer coffee to die for. Java's, as locally known, was originally a Java Joe's franchise but did not do very well and closed pretty quickly, setting the precedent, which is probably why no other franchises ever hit town.

Mrs Itchen ran the sweet shop next door but owned the building which incorporated the section housing Java Joe's. After leaving unpaid bills including rent, they left all of the equipment behind which Mrs Itchen claimed through the bankruptcy and with little or no investment, she gained her very own coffee shop. Owning the building meant there were few overheads; this allowed her to be competitively priced and had since done really well. She also launched a local competition at the local schools to name the coffee shop and get some exposure and thus 'Java the Hut' was born, playing on a whole generation of Star Wars fans.

Dan smiled, Lizzie noted it seemed a little forced. He also seemed to be operating on autopilot but under the circumstances that was understandable. Charlie fished his keys from his suit pocket and threw them to Lizzie. "Here, you'd better drive, I'm sure I'll be over the limit and don't want a DUI." Lizzie hopped into the driver's seat and started the car.

Taking her sandals off, she threw them over her shoulder and onto the back seat. Dan knocked on the window, Lizzie lowered it and he leant in kissing her gently on the cheek. "Thanks for today, like always, I don't think I'd have been able to do this alone."

Lizzie looked into his eyes, a little flustered as her hand nonchalantly touched where he kissed her. Charlie managed, as ever, to bring her back to earth. "Come on gal, put your boot down woman."

She smiled and drove off down the gravel path watching Dan in the rear view mirror as he waved, then put his hands in his pockets, he walked into the empty house; she tooted the horn twice as she turned onto the road heading for town.

3

When Dan was running, he truly felt at ease with the world. Maybe it was a remnant of his youth but he loved the freedom cross country allowed, just the elements and accumulated miles under his feet gave him security. He also loved to run first thing in the morning, it worked for him on so many levels, clearing his mind, jolting his body from slumber and ultimately setting him up for the day. In fact he was one of a rare breed who felt worse without some form of exercise to start his day. He liked his training, it was the one thing he had relied on throughout his life. It was his down time and also his own personal addiction. Many spent their time supping a six pack; Dan took pride in chiselling one.

It certainly paid off handsomely. Dan looked as though he had stepped from the cover of a men's fitness magazine, genetically gifted, he exuded every part the poster boy model but never displayed any form of arrogance with his good fortune.

He hid his physique well with fitted clothing but his musculature was impressive, his six foot stature kept everything in proportion. He was also blessed with a beauty many men learn to hate, high cheekbones, a strong rugged jaw line and purposeful five o'clock facial hair. The only trait, which would worry many at Dan's age, was that he was starting to gain speckles of grey in his dark hair. At 28 he felt it gave him an older much more appealing look, which in his profession was good because he was far younger than many of his colleagues. His salt and pepper hair aged him appropriately and gave him a maturity beyond his years.

This combination of brawn and good looks bred a certain amount of mistrust. An excess of muscle or beauty stereotypically endows an assumed low level of intelligence. Dan however was exceptionally intelligent, which was why he was promoted within New Scotland Yard at such an early age. Unfortunately this all encompassing package seemed to frighten many from getting close. He rarely dated and found it difficult to mix with the guys, as he had little to nothing in common. Many men felt threatened, so rarely asked him out for a drink with their partners and his few friends hopped on the revolving wheel of love; going steady, engaged, married and then ultimately divorce. Dan always seemed to be the one sidelined, until the ejection from the marital home but he was always there to help pick up the pieces and lend an ear, without question or judgement.

A psychiatrist would suggest this seclusion further drove his exercise addiction because it was his most reliable friend and ally. The gym was always there when trouble stirred. It never stood him up and it never ever had a cross word with him about being late. Many would say it was unhealthy but his chosen lifestyle did feed into the other parts of his life.

Most of his friends or prospective partners over the years had either been from the gym or work, so they fully understood he much preferred a workout to a get together, or a protein shake as opposed to a pint. If a training session clashed with a social gathering, his true friends just accepted he would be a little late, the ones who did not would see the friendship fade. The rare few who did befriend him grew to love him for these traits and realised it was just the way he lived and ultimately how loyal and trustworthy a friend it made him.

Running was his first love, followed by the gym. He had already used the multi gym at the house this morning, which was originally his from high school. The low weight had not satisfied his lust, his muscle tone compared to his teenage years had come on leaps and bounds, needing a much higher resistance. Without enough weight it felt a little futile so he headed out for a run.

Dan liked to run topless. The weather in London did not always give him the opportunity. He had noted there was always a slight jealousy towards someone in shape, something he could never understand about the British culture. They took serious pride in their slovenly nature, talking about the effort or indeed the financial commitment they had invested into their beer gut.

This morning he wore a pair of dark blue compression shorts to run in, which to the untrained eye looked more like a pair of revealing swimming shorts. However after the pain and surgery of a double hernia at 20, putting him out of action for many months, these shorts supported him a lot more than a jock strap and basic shorts combination ever did and, if supported properly, the hernia would never return. In London he would also have worn a pair of loose shorts over the top but here he felt enough freedom not to care. A Y-back racer vest was tucked into the back of the shorts in case he stopped and cooled but the early morning sun felt really good against his pasty anglicised skin. Just a pair of athletic fitted socks and running trainers effortlessly propelled him along the cliff top pass.

The low sun bounced off the sea, concentrating its early morning rays, as if reflected from a constantly shattering mirror. The cliff top path to overhang point was just over two miles and the path back down the other side to home, was a further three. A quick five miles before the day started and then a nice hot shower, to wash away the grime and sweat.

He loved this route, much of the path was still on the family property and although private, many people walked their dogs here. The coastal path was something his Granddad was adamant should be used by everyone because he insisted. *'We may have paid for the land but ultimately we are only a custodian.'* It was a good philosophy, obviously he could see why his Granddad had been like it, when he was running in Britain many footpaths had fallen into disrepair and frighteningly you would be harassed by the alleged owners for running or walking across, what was in effect, a public right of way. Only constant use kept these paths accessible and open, plus who would want to stop anyone from experiencing this view?

Dan felt free but was troubled, he was trying to comprehend why his Aunt and Uncle had been murdered but nothing really made sense. After everyone had finally left last night he had commenced the horrible task of sifting through their personal belongings. The events simply did not add up, for a bungled burglary all his alarm bells were ringing.

There was no sign of forced entry and from what he could tell nothing was missing, not a single antique, computer, appliance or, in fact, anything had been removed. It looked as though Aunt Susan's copious jewellery collection had been left totally undisturbed and in their bedroom on the dressing table was roughly $400 in cash. These are the opportunistic things to take, plus the bodies were left undiscovered for approximately 48 hours, plenty of time for the burglar to return and take anything he, or indeed she wanted.

What was ultimately worrying him was that he was unable to find any of the keys to the safe. Not a single one remained in the house, or at least not that he could find. He was hoping they would be amongst the personal effects found on their bodies when they were removed by the coroner. The Sheriff said he would return them as soon as possible, although the Sheriff seemed perfectly happy with the idea his Aunt and Uncle's death was a burglary gone awry. He however was not so sure.

Too many questions were left unanswered. His career and training made him question these things. Why were all the external cameras transmitting static at the same time? The power was still operational and the LED indicators were still illuminated green at the base station. If the power was severed by force, the LED would turn red but each camera also has a backup life which would run for approximately 36 hours. Plus it would sound the alarm to indicate a power failure or that a camera had been tampered with. The base station had not indicated any of this. Each camera was transmitting an independent wireless signal picked up by the base station, including the one on the front gates. None were hard wired, an intruder could easily cut the power but the cameras could and would continue to transmit an image.

If this was a burglary then why was there no sign of forced entry? Did it indicate that his Aunt and Uncle knew the perpetrator or indeed the perpetrators? If this was something as simple as a robbery, what had gone wrong for them to both be killed? Ultimately and finally, where were the missing safe keys? He could answer some of these questions with the keys in his possession, his own set ominously, were also nowhere to be found in the house.

As he ran back down the hill, traversing the kissing gate, he turned left back onto the main road running adjacent to home. Coming towards him was the Sheriff's patrol car, he obviously could not have seen it was Dan running up ahead of him. The Sheriff indicated and disappeared from view, entering the driveway. With the amount of people going backwards and forwards to the house in the last few days, the electronic gates had been disabled and left open.

Dan picked up his pace and turned into the drive. As he got to the gate he stopped, studying the camera. The power cable was internal, running down through the arm connecting it to the brick pillars. It was carefully positioned at the head height of someone sat in their car. This camera was mounted on a motorized arm, controlled by a joystick on the base station allowing you to move the camera and view anyone from the house, such as someone making a delivery in a high truck for instance, before letting them in.

Dan instinctively ran his hands over the external surface of the camera shell and then underneath, he felt something. On the underside of the camera housing, was what looked like a piece of clear tape, which seemed a little odd. He dug his nail under the edge peeling it from underneath; it came away easily leaving no residue. Had it been there a while it would have been a lot more difficult to remove, he touched his finger against the tacky surface, it was sticky but not with the direct adhesive nature of sticky tape.

He held it to the light and through the clear plastic he noted lots of tiny wires, inter crossing throughout its structure. "Hmm odd." He spoke aloud to himself as if to break the silence, it was not the sort of packaging tape he had ever been familiar with.

Remembering the Sheriff, he ran on up the driveway as the Sheriff was just getting back into his patrol car. Spotting Dan he stopped and stepped away from the car.

The Sheriff was your typical small town officer; slightly worn around the edges giving the outward disposition that everything was just far too much trouble for him. His grey hair matched the grey handlebar moustache, the worn out feeling crossed to his voice giving an air of boredom within its monotone.

"Mornin', I was just popping by to drop off the personal effects of your Aunt and Uncle, as you asked. Apologies for swinging by so early." There was a slight pause as his eyes swept up and down Dan's semi naked body. Dan took his cue, grabbing the vest tucked in his shorts and put it on. The sweat instantly soaked through the cotton material. He then stuck out his hand, which the Sheriff took and shook.

"Hi Sheriff, thanks, much appreciated. I've some filter coffee on the go, would you like a cup?"

"That'd be mighty kind. It'd save a stop at Java's on the way through to the office."

Dan walked up the steps, followed by the Sheriff and they went inside. On a chair just inside the hallway was a small envelope, the Sheriff picked it up handing it to Dan as they headed through to the kitchen following the alluring smell.

Dan tipped the contents from the brown envelope onto the counter top, a couple of Aunt Susan's rings; her wedding ring, watch, an antique pendant and her much loved Father's monogrammed signet ring. For Uncle Mike, there was just a watch, house keys and his wallet. The safe keys were prominent by their absence. This was worrying because his Aunt and Uncle never left them lying around anywhere. They were far too valuable.

The Sheriff eyed Dan and coughed apologetically, raising his eyebrows and studying Dan's face. "Have you discovered anything missing?" He paused searching for the right words. "Have you found anything missing so far, or can you think of anything which would suggest a reason behind the burglary?"

Dan tried to hide his dismay about the safe keys. "No, as far as I can tell nothing has been taken at all, not even cash?"

"What do you mean cash?" The Sheriff sounded shocked.

"There was about $4oo dollars on Uncle Mike's dressing table left untouched, surely if this was a burglary they would have taken that?" There was silence, the Sheriff found this kind of situation awkward. He had known the lad since he was a kid and there had been more death associated with his family than any other he knew.

"I don't know Dan. If they got disturbed the burglar could've just fled, maybe he even spooked himself?" The Sheriff was convincing, at least in his own mind. "Can I make a suggestion?" He looked very seriously at Dan, "Lock the doors, especially with recent events."

Dan looked up surprised. "Oh okay, sure but up until now I haven't been able to, well, not without locking myself out." He grabbed a set of keys from the pile of personal effects from the envelope and jangled them on his forefinger in front of the Sheriff.

The Sheriff forced a smile. "Oh, I'd have thought you'd have had your own keys?"

"I have but I forgot them. They're in London. I've not been back home since the burial of Uncle James, Aunt Pat, Matt and Ash to be honest. Work has kept me busy. Aunt Susan came and visited a couple of times in the UK but as for getting back, in truth there is not that much to come home for these days …" His voice trailed off.

"Yeah, I'm sorry. How long do you intend staying in town?"

"I've taken some leave. I need to get a lot of things in order as you can imagine, I don't really know yet." Dan picked the filter coffee machine off the stand grabbing two mugs from the cupboard. "Do you take milk or cream?"

"Black, two sugars please." The Sheriff looked at Dan glancing over his shoulder at the monitor and camera base station in the corner of the kitchen. "I see the security camera is working on the gate, what was the problem?"

Dan turned; the top left quarter of the security monitor was now working fine and displayed the view from the camera at the security gate where he was a few minutes earlier. Dan stared in disbelief at the image, yet the three other cameras still showed only static. "I've not done anything." Unclasping his hand, he stared in disbelief at the balled up tape in the palm of his right hand he had just removed from the underside of the entrance camera.

4

The Sheriff and Dan stood side by side staring blankly at the monitor in the kitchen. All four security images were now working correctly on the display. Using the base station you could view each individual camera, or all four simultaneously plus using the joystick allowed movement on each camera independently.

Camera one, the gate camera, was out of position focussing on the opposite side of the main road. Camera two was directed down the drive, so you could read a car's licence plate coming up or down the drive. Cameras three and four showed the front and back of the house respectively so you could see exactly who was entering and leaving the front or back entrances.

The base station had four strips of what seemed like innocuous sticky tape attached side by side, whatever these things were though, they were far from innocent. Dan showed the Sheriff the tape and explained he had literally removed it from the gate camera as the Sheriff had driven in. Between them they checked the rest of the cameras; each had a two inch strip on the base. Upon closer examination of the tape, each had tiny wires transposed through the core, the same effect could have been seen in the heated windscreen of an expensive car.

Dan, purely by accident, stuck the first strip on top of the monitor for safe keeping while they went outside and checked. The monitor was an old CRT screen and when they returned it had caused the area surrounding to form a rainbow effect, which suggested it radiated a magnetic field of some kind.

When each individual strip was removed from each camera it miraculously sprang back into life, when reattached the camera transmitted only static. They concluded this was what was causing the cameras' fault but why was it there? Was it intentional or simply a coincidence? Dan, through his career, was not a believer in coincidences. The Sheriff however was far more open minded or, at least, less pessimistic than Dan.

After the initial gruesome discovery of Dan's Aunt and Uncle, the Sheriff had had a security firm check the cameras over; their direct connections were fine. This tiny element, easily missed, explained why the connection through the wireless transmission was lost with the tape attached underneath.

"Right then." The Sheriff finally broke the uncomfortable silence. "I don't even know who to send something like this to for analysis. I'll drop in to the security firm who checked the cameras and see what they make of them. Not sure what else to do right now. All we know is if we stick it back on they stop working."

"But Sheriff, whoever did this have taken nothing from what I can tell, except two innocent lives, what was their motive?" Dan had tried to sound professional and remain neutral from his personal loss; however the Sheriff could plainly see the pain in Dan's face and hear it in his voice.

"I don't know but I'd hoped you'd maybe have more of an insight but I do intend to find out before this happens again."

Again? Dan suddenly felt as though the Sheriff was holding back and not being one hundred percent truthful about the incident. The Sheriff was baffled; it was beyond the realms of his experience. It was something akin to a spy novel, not for a small backwater town like this.

They both stared at the monitor deep in thought. The Sheriff picked up and drained the last of the coffee. Even though it was cold, they had finished the pot between them. He turned to leave. "I suggest you lock the doors if and when you leave the property Mr Morris, and make sure the security gates are closed. Can I ask if you know the code to open them?"

"Yes I remember it, but I may just change it before I head off into town."

"Probably a good idea, I'll take a couple of these strips to see if I can get them analysed somewhere. Call me if you find anything else out of the ordinary." With that the Sheriff was gone.

Dan sat and stared at the monitor, bewildered by what had happened and the discovery of the tape. In his line of work he had heard of such clever technology but never actually encountered it. It was quite shocking to see it in reality, especially when it was attached to the cameras surrounding his family home. If work was not such an issue back in London, he could easily have called a few people in the UK and gotten some answers instantly but right now he was a little bewildered as to what to do as that avenue was closed.

Looking at the kitchen clock he realised it was over two hours since the Sheriff arrived. He picked up the phone and stabbed at the buttons for Lizzie's cell. It seemed a little odd not putting a country code in front. He decided to pop into town and sign whatever Charlie wanted and hopefully go for that coffee with Lizzie.

As he held the phone to his ear, it was strange the line was silent. He waited and after a couple of seconds of nothing, he pressed the button a couple of times then realising the phone line was dead. This was no ordinary burglary; there was something far more sinister going on. The phone line had been cut.

A cold chill ran through Dan, his hairs stood on end, suddenly feeling naked and very alone within his family home. A feeling he was not used to for a man who had lived on his own for so long. He realised he was still in his running clothes, the sweat had long since dried so he headed upstairs to take a long overdue hot shower and rinse the dirt from his body, but only after first making sure the front door was indeed firmly locked.

The realisation his Aunt and Uncle's safe keys were truly nowhere to be found unnerved him. With them in his possession he may actually be able to make some sense of this mess. The family safe held the answers and he needed access, but how?

5

The one thing Dan loved most about growing up in Florida was the weather. More than that, he liked to be able to drive a car along Ocean Drive in the sunshine. It was true; many American cars handled more like a comfy couch with the added afterthought of a steering wheel and engine, but with such great distances to cover you needed comfort and a sense of domain.

An American car provided this without candour or apology. You may arrive quicker in the UK with higher speed restrictions in a more refined quality car but in America you arrived in comfort, not to mention many Americans needed the full couch to themselves.

Granddad had had a love of many things but as someone so stoically dedicated and proud of his roots, he had an unmitigated soft spot for American cars. The underground garage beneath the house, added as one of the many improvements during the extensive rebuild of the house after a fire swept through, housed many rare specimens.

Today though Dan chose to use the one car his Granddad would not let anyone drive. A 1948 Tucker Sedan, one of only 51 cars ever made. Granddad would not let him even breathe on this car, let alone take it for a run. The family operated a *'you bend it, you mend it'* mentality, which allowed them all to drive any car they wanted. They were not precious about a hunk of metal, except for the rare few Granddad kept under lock and key.

Dan smiled to himself hoping his Granddad was not looking down on him as he took the number eight key from the wall mounted cabinet, meaning bay eight. He felt like a naughty school kid as he left the underground garage gunning it down the driveway. He could hear his Granddad's words echo through his ears. *"You fill it up before you bring it back, it don't run on empty ya' know!"*

Cruising down the short stretch of road along the beach front before town, he had to admit this was something else, in Waltz Blue, it was beautiful. The car was innovative and fresh for its time but what had interested his Granddad so much was the invention within its structure.

Many of the then revolutionary improvements are now familiar in modern day cars but many are still not. The car was rear-engined and rear wheel drive. A perimeter frame surrounded the vehicle for crash protection, as well as a roll bar integrated into the roof. The steering box was behind the front axle to protect the driver in a front-end accident.

The instrument panel and all controls were in easy reach of the steering wheel, and the dash was padded for safety. The windshield was designed to pop-out in a collision to protect the occupants. The car also featured seat belts, very much a first in its day. The car's parking brake had a separate key so it could be locked in place to prevent theft. The doors extended into the roof, to ease entry and exit, the list was endless.

Dan marvelled at the ingenuity, for the time, 1948. He could see why Granddad was so fascinated with it, considering he had also been a man of engineering firsts. Dan's favourite feature of the Tucker was the directional third headlight, or Cyclops eye, which turned in conjunction with the steering when cornering, to light the car's path at night. The distinctive look it gave the car was second to none, he found it odd many states had laws against more than two headlights!

Probably the reason he loved it so much was the passion his Granddad had had for it. When he was passionate about something he wanted to know everything about it. This passion was ingrained in the whole family no matter what they did or started, it was to the highest level of commitment. His Granddad, much to his detriment, had pushed that through the psyche of every Morris family member.

Up ahead, just before the main strip in town was The Pumping Station. A combination of diner, filling station, and auto shop. At the rear was the Marina where you could get a boat moored or put in dry dock. Run by Joel Hazle and family, his wife ran the ever popular diner, which suited and welcomed everyone from high school kids to truckers passing through.

The place was also a constant source of employment for the local kids. Everyone growing up around Santa Rosa hung out at The Station. Java's during the day. The Station at night, it was an unwritten rule. There was never any trouble as it was very family oriented; couples shared their first date here, proposed here and eventually it was where they took their kids for a burger. It was a place where everyone knew someone and always felt welcome.

Dan pulled up at one of four gas pumps, which were something left from the early fifties. The Shell domes on top of each pump looked faded and old. He took the battered nozzle and stuck it in the gas tank after unscrewing the cap. He flipped the handle and the digits on the pump lazily reset back to zero, all slightly off centre from the wear on their gears. Pressing the trigger they started whirring. The pump still had a small dial that counted off the pints as they whizzed round, one to eight and then back to zero, incrementing the gallon, an antique maybe but it looked fantastic.

When you filled the tank, or at least roughly reached your goal, give or take a couple of cents, you'd make your way inside. To the right was the diner, to the left the bathrooms and in front was the pay station. An old antique till faithfully continued the look inside, the operator hand pressed the digits to correspond to the correct price. The Station had always operated on a good will gesture, people faithfully reported what they had filled, paid their dues and left.

However Dan could see that, disappointingly, the 21st century had crept in, which saddened him somewhat. A monitor behind the old till showed a camera was trained on each pump. The dials could now be read from inside, or ultimately catch the licence plate of a splash and dash. A credit card, point of sale machine sat next to the till, the juxtaposition of technology was somewhat ludicrous. However the rest remained faithful to the place he remembered, especially the smell.

Dan pressed the button to call the assistant. In the back of the work shop he could hear the old style tring as the bell announced his intention to pay. A lone voice could be heard. "Two shakes, I'll be right there."

Joel Hazle was a big bear of a man, possibly the most hairy man on earth, yet completely bald on top. He sported a biker moustache that blended into a goatee and disappeared amongst a hairy barrel chest which was permanently on show. Although very unlike the unattractive skinny, open shirted 70s polyester look, it was forced by the sheer size of this man's chest, disappointingly medallion free but somehow the look suited this grease monkey.

Joel's family had moved to Santa Rosa when he was twelve, originally from Brooklyn, the accent was every bit gangster but the personality, Mother Teresa. Joel had been the same age as Uncle James and they had become great friends over the years, mainly due to a love of wreck diving.

As he walked into the office, head down, wiping his paw like hands of grease, he looked up to face Dan. Taking a deep breath his chest looked like it would burst through his overalls, he lifted the hatch sweeping Dan up into a vicelike bear hug, Dan's feet forcibly left the ground having been caught a little off guard with the move.

"Whoa Joel!" His voice squashed to a wheeze, as Dan's lungs forcibly exhaled by Joel's grip.

After a few moments Joel gently lowered Dan back down, gripping him with both hands on either shoulder, looking him directly in the eyes and in his Brooklyn drawl managed. "I'm so sorry."

Dan was still trying to take a breath and could only nod his thanks. "How you doin?" Joel asked. "Under the circumstances?"

"Not really the way I wanted to breeze back into town to be honest, but hey I'm dealin'."

"I saw the Sheriff earlier, he said he'd been up to the house. Are there any clues or suspects?"

"No, not really." Dan felt as much in the dark about the whole affair as the town did, although he was unaware how much unrest it had caused. A burglary gone wrong, two locals dead, no suspects, no apparent reason, it was a small town's worst nightmare.

"I was going to come by yesterday but I never really knew your Uncle Mike all that well."

"It's all right, don't sweat it, never really the greatest event to catch up with anyone anyway; at a funeral."

Joel forced a weak smile. "Follow me through, the family account is out back. I was going to pop by tomorrow and fill the tanks, so it's great you called in. By the way does your Granddad know you have the Tucker?" He nodded in the direction of the car sat in all its shining glory next to the 50s pump, which as a picture post card, with a sepia tone, would have looked perfect for the age.

Dan grinned. "Nope, he'd have a fit if he knew. I might even light up a doobie in it before I take it home."

Joel belly-laughed as they headed to the back workshop. This part was where the 21st century definitely took over. The shop was immaculate, clinical in fact. Dotted round the walls were computers of differing degrees of technicality; used for technical readouts, fault diagnosis, tuning and many other duties. Two bays stood, each with a car hoisted up on elevated ramps. The floors were immaculate and a light was shining under the rear wheel of a Dodge Viper, obviously the car Joel was working on. Two young guys, who Dan did not recognise, were unsuccessfully trying to fit a silencer to a Chrysler of some generic description.

Joel continued to walk through and headed to the office overlooking the Marina. The office joined a second workshop which was equally as spotless; except for a number of outboards lining up along the wall, plus a number of filled diving tanks and unknown apparatus awaiting collection by their respective owners. The marine workshop opened out on to the Marina, where a floating gas station serviced the plethora of craft on the Marina. This area was run pretty much by his two sons, J.J - Joel Junior and Niles. Niles was the same age as Dan; they had gone to school together. He was out on the dock with a dismantled jet ski, he smiled and waved, Dan waved back.

Joel had an envelope on the desk which he picked up and handed over. Dan opened it, scanning down through its contents. Joel asked before Dan had time to work it out. "I wondered whether you wanna carry on with the account, or let it go? I didn't know whether you were going to hang about or head back to London?"

"I'm not sure yet. I don't think I'll let the house go, so if it's all right with you I'd like to keep it open and you can invoice me, or we'll set up a debit."

Dan scanned through the list of items on the invoice. The fuel bill for filling the boat house tanks at home were expensive and seemed to be done every month without fail. He did not realise Uncle Mike was taking the cruiser out these days. After the loss of the rest of the family to the sea, he supposed time had been a healer. The family had the boat house rebuilt to house a cruiser and a small speedboat they all used to water ski from. The cost of mooring the cruiser on the marina was expensive especially as it was used very little. His Granddad decided with modifications to the existing boat house, it would be used more often and ultimately pay for itself, which in fact was the case.

The work was also instigated around the time of the fire. The foundations and sea bed were excavated deeper to accommodate the depth of the keel, which meant removing a considerable amount of bed rock. He remembered the area was out of bounds for a long time and was permanently covered. The boat house was quite beautiful when finished. It looked like a floating garage from the sea and housed a large open plan room above with bi-fold doors opening onto a panoramic sea view balcony.

The final item on the invoice made Dan instantly cold. Looking up at

Joel. "I didn't realise the yacht was still here?"

"Did you not? It's in dry dock sat out the back. It has been ever since the accident. Your Aunt Susan wanted it sold. In the end they decided to leave it. In truth I just don't think your Uncle Mike could part with it. It's pretty much exactly as it was left after the investigation, although it's looking a tad sorry for itself these days."

6

There was something indelibly evocative about a wooden schooner, representing a far gentler and somewhat more civilised age. Hand built by the most skilled shipwrights, distinguishing and separating an age of refined skills against androgynous, generically designed GRP. 'Hydrous' was one of the most imposing yachts on the Marina in its day. Today she looked a little sorry for herself and rather desolate, standing alone in her cradle.

Like everything Granddad had purchased, there was always a story behind its beauty or origin, Hydrous was no different. The interiors and decking were made from rare Dahat Teak, so rare it is now endangered. No one knew the true history or identity of the schooner but the workmanship was second to none. It had been abandoned and towed in to the marina where Granddad first spotted it. The fact it had no one to cherish its beauty was enough but when it was condemned to be stripped and destroyed, this prompted him to buy it, welcoming the yacht to the bosom of the Morris family and thus having the boat lovingly restored.

The interior was sympathetically updated with all the mod cons you would need to circumnavigate the globe. The decks and rigging were altered to allow single-handed sailing, which was a hefty engineering feat to achieve. Dan's cousin Matt had undertaken the work when he first set up his engineering firm. It was designed and implemented so as not to detract from her elegant beauty, it worked brilliantly. Even Dan was able to sail the schooner. He was never the greatest sailor but when he first finished high school he took it down to Cuba on his own, although this was not popular with his Grandparents when they eventually realised. Lizzie and Dan had always secretly planned a trip to Cancun but never ever seemed to find the time.

Dan had always found it hard to believe how things could have gone wrong. Hydrous sailed effortlessly with the GPS auto helm Matt installed. Whatever happened that night at sea, when the family disappeared, was a total mystery. Initially there was talk of a kidnapping by pirates, even drug connections but eventually as no bodies were found or a ransom issued, death by misadventure was lodged and the tragedy that had struck the Morris family became yet another unsolved aquatic statistic.

To see the boat in dry dock was a bit of a shock. The red teak deck was dulled by the Florida sun and the pastel blue paint unkempt and neglected. Blue is considered unlucky for sea bearing vessels throughout folklore. Maybe it seems foolish, if not irresponsible, to ignore the superstitious practices of our forebears. This vessel had certainly seen its share of sadness and desolation.

Out of the water the boat looked imposing and a lot larger than he remembered. Like an iceberg, you never realise how much of a boat's hull is under the water, Hydrous was no exception. She looked bottom heavy but in reality was very nimble and easy to sail.

There was a ladder placed against the starboard side of the vessel. He climbed up, swinging himself into the cockpit. The chrome to the self-steering gear was dull and uninspiring, a lot like the craft in general, a far cry from the love it had been bestowed since becoming a member of the family. He pushed the wooden deck cover back and opened the doors to descend into the snug interior. It smelt musty with a salty wooden over tone, although the smell of teak never fades, its essence felt homely.

The galley was to the right and a dining table to the left, a small door separating the living areas. Immediately beyond was a walk-through cabin which slept two singles, one either side leading to a room separator, housing a small toilet, sink and shower and then through to a secluded double cabin in the bow. Above the cabin you could slide a portal cover and get out on deck or simply stare at the stars from the mattress. It was beautiful.

Dan walked through and looked in the small bathroom, a few items such as shaving gel and toothpaste were scattered in and around the sink. The double bedroom did not seem to have anything packed away, in fact it was suspiciously empty. If they had gone away sailing for the weekend, or to dive, where were their personal items? Not a single shirt, pair of jeans, or anything of worth anywhere.

Dan checked the stow-away cupboards below the single bunks. They housed the life jackets and other emergency items, first aid box, flare gun, even an emergency locator; all were present and complete. There were a few clothes, the families battered Cluedo, even an old jacket of his. Dan considered what he was looking at. It seemed there were no personal effects left behind, if there had been an emergency, surely something would have been missing or used?

It puzzled him. The boat was effectively empty, nothing suggested it had even been away. The caddies usually held coffee, tea, sugar and whitener, they were all empty. Even the cooler was devoid of anything, which after a trip away would have at minimum held the discarded empty bottles of wine or several beer cans. After a weekend on the boat as a family, they always laughed about the standard trip to the recycle bank on the way home.

On the dividing wall between the galley and the sleeping quarters Dan reached up, sliding a small silver lever. In turn he slid a teak wall panel down to reveal an LCD monitor. This displayed the GPS system from the cockpit and doubled as the entertainment screen for DVDs. Below the screen was the boat's radio and satellite phone. When the panel had reached the bottom of its travel it folded down, resting neatly on the kitchen table. The inside of the panel was covered in glass and underneath was the nautical chart for the Gulf Of Mexico, folded to reveal the Pensacola coastline.

Surveying it closely, marked in china graph pen on the glass it had the position of dive wrecks, several he recognised having dived them, the others he assumed the family had visited. However written in red marker under the glass was a set of coordinates; GPS coordinates N30:02.6, W87:00.4 and 30*02'38"N Lat, 87*00'25"W Lon. Why would those particular coordinates be scrawled on the map? Dan unhooked the retaining edge strips holding the glass in place, removing the chart.

He stared intently at the coordinates as he walked through to the cockpit. He stabbed the on button of the GPS, it momentarily flashed into life and then died, the battery must have been dead. He stared at the chart for a moment trying to think what they could mean. He somehow recognised the writing but could not work out whose. It was not Matt's or Ash's but still very familiar. He carefully folded the chart making his way back to see Joel, tucking it in his back pocket.

Niles was in the office. He smiled broadly as Dan entered. "Gonna take the old gal out for a sail while you're in town then? I know she looks a bit tired but she's still in great nick."

Dan was broken from his trance. "Actually yeah, I think I could go for that. How quickly do you think you could get her back in the water?"

Joel walked in the office overhearing the conversation. "A little TLC and she'll be good to go. Only really needs the chrome polished, a bit of a scrub and the deck oiled."

"That'd be great, although I have a favour to ask first? Do you think you could repaint the hull from that pastel blue, I think she's seen her fair share of bad luck."

Niles looked up. "I have some yacht paint in the back for a job that never happened. It's black but I think she'd look stunning in that."

"That'll be fine; in fact I also think she'd look good in black, especially against the chrome and the warm colour of the teak." Dan smiled. "Right I have to go, I'm supposed to be meeting Charlie."

Joel followed him out to the pay station, as he passed one of the old style fridges Dan grabbed a bottle of Coke. "You can add that to the bill."

"Nah that's a freebie, you can have that on the house." Joel grabbed the bottle from Dan, rested the edge of the cap on the counter and banged it savagely with the back of his bear-like hand, popping the top off, he handed it back.

"Thanks but have you never heard of a bottle opener?" Dan smiled, taking a swig. "See ya."

7

Like any seaside town, Santa Rosa had a somewhat weather-beaten and bleached exterior. Shops and office fronts all seem to have been picked from the same pastel palette, like the varying muted shades found throughout British seaside sticks of rock. Somehow it worked as a cohesive unit but no one would intentionally sit down and design the colour scheme from scratch. The look grew organically over the years, each owner adding eclectic eccentricities which gave a worn and faithful feel, slightly rough but endearing to the locals and tourists alike.

Charlie's office was located towards the top end of the high street, conveniently opposite Java's. The façade of the office was freshly painted in a pale sage and the woodwork complemented it in a shade of mushroom, a dusty grey. It may have been fresh but it still looked like it had been that way for thirty years or more. The office had previously been a small florist and boasted an ornate oval window, above which, mirroring the curvature of the window line, an elevated brushed stainless steel and understated font reading 'C. H. Price Lawyer, Charles Henry Price'.

Inside, the front reception was tastefully decorated in white oak. On the right wall stood a floor to ceiling bookcase, housing a vast selection of legal tomes covering a wide range of subjects, from divorce law to boundary disputes. They were graded by colour throughout the bookcase, looking uncannily more decorative than functional for legal precedence or reference. An antique library step chair sat in the window, in case you needed to ever reach the top shelf, also looking unused.

By the window sat a green antiqued leather two seater Chesterfield couch with a roll top desk completing the look. Strangely the trappings of modern business looked totally out of place against all the wood; a fax machine, telephone and laptop all looked rather estranged in comparison.

Two doors led from the reception. The right door led into a small kitchenette and on to a bathroom. The left was to Charlie's office. Just as Dan entered Lizzie came back through with a face like thunder carrying a bundle of papers. She lit up as he stood in the doorway, throwing the bundle on the roll top desk.

"I'm gonna file this lot in the bin," said with venom, Dan almost believed her. She glanced over her shoulder and shouted through to the office. "Dad, Dan is here."

Lizzie fell into her seat next to the desk and swung it round to face Dan. "So what's your plan, other than taking me for coffee?"

"Well I have some time off. Was thinking of taking the yacht out for a sail, how about Cancun?"

"The yacht?" You could see this information caught Lizzie off guard, Cancun hardly registered.

"Yeah, I didn't realise but it's in dry dock down at the Marina. I asked Niles to give it a lick of paint and get it in the water. He's going to paint the hull black for me?"

"He doesn't change does he?"

Before Lizzie could start to reminisce about their teenage years, Charlie came shuffling through in his usual attire of an ivory linen suit which looked as though it had seen better days. A far cry from the pressed crisp black number he wore to the funeral yesterday, this was far more Charlie, crumpled and comfortable.

Charlie was unbuttoning the jacket as he appeared, seemingly forever disorganised and bumbling; this disarming parody hid a sharp mind. His nature gave an endearing quality and separation between lawyer and friend. Charlie had presence, not in stature as he was only just five foot six, but warmth that was fun to be around. When you spoke to him, he had a knack of looking totally rapt, even if he was thinking about the tip on the two o'clock horse race.

Charlie should have been a big shot lawyer in a big city; however his passion for an easy life and his beautiful wife's artistic fervour led him to a sleepier and much more idyllic town; Santa Rosa. How he ended up here in Santa Rosa Dan never really knew. Kind of like how many locals surmised how his grandparents moved here, to have a slower way of life and more time with the kids.

"Thanks for coming Dan. We have a few financial formalities to sort out first. Most of it is pretty self explanatory but some detail will need to be made, depending on what you want to do with the estate."

Charlie was trying to be professional and formal. Dan could tell it was a chore as he had known him since he was a child; in essence he was more father figure than lawyer.

"It's all right Charlie. I know there are going to be lots of financial things to go through, much of which I'll never understand." Dan was resigned to this. He was the last Morris and therefore all the assets and family holdings would come to him.

It was actually weird to think in less than five short years the entire family had pretty much been wiped from the face of the earth. The family money had very much been something of a myth. He never really knew what the family was worth but also he never believed all of it would be his. One of the main reasons he left for England was the chance to make something of himself from scratch, without help or financial assistance. In fact his trust fund had never even had so much as a dime taken from it after he left home.

Lizzie was hovering. "Do you want a coffee or tea? We have proper tea leaves and I don't very often get the chance to make a pot."

"Actually, I don't suppose you have a Coke?" Lizzie looked at him disapprovingly.

"Don't look at me like that. I was at the Station and had my first bottled Coke in years. You rarely get it in the UK, only cans and it just tastes so much nicer from the bottle. I'm sure it's psychological but hey, I'm home and would love another."

"I'll have to pop over to Java's for Coke; it's not something we serve our clients."

"Well maybe you should, being as I am one." Dan laughed and Lizzie cuffed him in the shoulder.

Charlie lit up. "Well if you're going over to Java's, can I have one of those syrup latte things? What's the special this week?" Charlie looked almost pleadingly to Lizzie, then at Dan. "She has me on a diet, look at me I'm practically wasting away."

Charlie stood sideways and forcibly pushed the excess gut over the top of his belt slapping the flesh through his shirt, which visibly swayed beneath the cotton. Lizzie screwed up her face, picked up her purse and flounced out the door. Charlie motioned towards the office. "Come on through Dan."

Charlie's office had the same white oak panelling against the far wall, but the rest of the office was painted white, which was crisp and contemporary. His desk was an expansive partner's desk. This allowed a friendlier atmosphere, opposed to the impression of a formal interview desk so many environments portrayed. The top was inlaid with green leather, not dissimilar in colour from the carpet which ran throughout the entire building. The only item on the desk was a grey box file with the name William Morris. The penmanship was intricately scribed in black ink, the name of his Granddad.

Charlie took his seat, sliding the box towards himself placing it under his hands, waiting for Dan to take the exact same seat opposite. "You may or may not be aware that other than your trust fund and Matt and Ashley's, which were set up to fund you all through University or whatever you chose to do, all the family's finances basically came from one large smelting pot." This was not really news to Dan as they all had cards which accessed the central bank account. The idea was when they reached 25 they were issued with one.

However the exact amount of the pot had never been openly discussed, at least not that he was aware of; it was just something as a family they never discussed. To discuss it openly, albeit within the family, was frowned upon and considered rather crass.

Charlie continued in his more professional tone. "Sadly, as the last remaining heir from the lineage, all the family assets finally come to you. This includes all financial and business acquisitions and of the latter there are a fair number. Your central monetary fund is constantly accumulating due to the family leasing land, on which many oil companies are operating from. This was where your family made its money in the first place."

Dan was silent taking in this new information. "You mean, in effect, I'm an oil baron?"

"No, in effect you're a landlord."

"Oh, that's disappointing." Visions of shoulder pads, donning a cowboy hat and attending the annual oil baron's ball vanished in an instant.

"Not really. Your family has had all the financial stability and accrued wealth, without the actual risk and uncertainty of prospecting for oil. Or at least you do until the day the oil runs out." Charlie started to laugh at the latter part of the sentence. "Not something I think you need to ever worry about, well, not in your lifetime or at least not for several more generations."

Dan sat in stunned silence; he was not sure what to say. The idea of the family wealth coming from oil contradicted the whole engrained family ethos. At least this was the ideal his upbringing had been founded on, his Granddad's work and consequently his Uncle James',

Aunt Pat and Ashley's continuance certainly belied. Although maybe the essence of their work, funded by the oil industry, was recompense or at the very least ironic.

8

"How much are you worth then?" Lizzie bounced back in the office carrying a cardboard holder with two Java cups and a bag in one hand, the other held Dan's coke. Where she had crossed the street in the warm air, vapour had condensed on the cold bottle and small beads of water clung to the outside. As she banged it down on the desk the water slid in tiny rivulets to the base forming a water ring.

"Enough. It would maybe stretch to buy you dinner over a coffee at some point, if you fancy it?" Dan was still shell shocked at the number of zero's on the printout he held in his hand and this was just one of many accounts.

Lizzie smiled pulling a necklace hidden under her top, out over her head. On the end of a silver chain was a small penknife, rather like a Swiss army knife. However this was much smaller, with tortoiseshell fascias, consisting of a large blade, a small blade, a corkscrew, a button hook, a nail file and, more importantly, a bottle opener.

She flicked open the bottle opener and took the top off the coke. Dan lit up as he saw the penknife and fumbled in his pocket. He pulled out a set of keys to his London flat on which his own penknife was attached. His was slightly bigger and differentiated itself because it also contained a Philips screwdriver and a wire stripper. Both Lizzie and Ashley had been given tortoiseshell versions. Matt and Dan's were in black Onyx.

Dan opened the large blade and engraved on one side was the name 'Apóllō', written in Greek script – Απόλλων, which out of context looked extremely odd. Lizzie duly opened the blade on hers to reveal 'Hestía' - Εστία. When they were growing up Matt, Dan, Ashley and Lizzie were inseparable. During one of their many long summers together Ash become obsessed with Greek mythology, christening each of them after a Greek God.

Matt became Dionysus, God of wine, parties and festivals, madness, civilization, drunkenness and pleasure. Ashley chose Athena for herself, Goddess of wisdom, warfare, strategy, heroic endeavour, handicrafts and reason. Dan was Apollo, God of music, healing, plague, prophecies, poetry, and archery; associated with light, truth and the sun. Lizzie was Hestia, virgin Goddess of the hearth, home and cooking. Bowie, Dan's beloved dog became Cerberus, a multi-headed hound which guarded the gates of Hades, to prevent those who have crossed the river Styx from ever escaping.

At the time they allowed Ash to have her way because it was far easier than arguing with her when she started campaigning for something. All of them liked them as well, giving their gang an identity, if not a little more academic than Matt, Dan or Lizzie would have chosen but the names stuck, becoming part of family folklore and a part of the Morris family history.

Their last night together before they all started high school Granddad had asked permission to come into the den, which was duly granted. He bought lemonade, tea and ginger biscuits as a bribe. He sat on the pillows and idly talked of family and friends, of mysteries, greater truths and just causes on which to place hopes and dreams. High school was the start of their journey, an adventure if you will, to the start of their adulthood.

None of them really knew or fully understood at the time, he was trying to help them understand how important family truly was. When the tea was cold and the biscuits all gone, or at least fed to Bowie who snored loudly with his tongue sticking out, contented in the corner on his bed, Granddad took out five small packages. Each had a hand written tag in red ink, Dionysus, Apollo, Athena, Hestia and Cerberus. He handed the packages to them, which were unwrapped with eagerness.

Each contained a single ornate pen knife. Bowie's was a dog tag, personalised and engraved with his Greek name as well as his real name on the outside. The penknives were personally individualised, along the main blade of each knife their Greek name was engraved, much to Ash's delight using the Greek alphabet. After Granddad had left, they made a pact to always carry their penknife with them, wherever and whatever they were up to for the rest of their lives. Each of them felt they were special; it was a good luck charm, a totem of their childhood which bonded all of them together, even in adulthood.

On Dan's key ring was also the old dog tag of Bowie's. Lizzie picked it up. It had the same black Onyx on one side and a stainless steel tab with

Bowie's details engraved on it. His real name, house address and telephone number. Rotating the steel tab underneath it had his Greek name Κέρβερος, Cerberus engraved.

"It seems funny to think we were given them nearly fifteen years ago. How much time has passed and sadly how much has changed."

Dan was a little subdued but kind of elated Lizzie still carried the knife. The bond and memories they shared he had with no one else on earth. They had both suffered immeasurable losses. It was the first time he had seen Lizzie in this light, as someone more than a childhood friend. He saw deeper than the freckles, pig tails and the missing front tooth. The girl standing before him was a woman. Both suddenly awkward, it was the first time they had ever felt like this in each other's company.

Charlie as ever, managed to bring the mood back to the present in timely fashion. "Watch the water from that coke; it'll stain my leather desk." Lizzie picked up a napkin and as Dan picked up the bottle, she wiped away the water ring as if wiping away a tear they both shared.

9

After their short coffee break and idle chat, Charlie turned lawyer. "Do you mind leaving us now Lizzie?" Dan did not really know what was going on but looked at Lizzie, he wanted her to stay, it felt right she should.

"I don't mind Lizzie staying." He turned to Lizzie who was getting up to leave. "You can if you want to, in fact I'd like it if you did." Lizzie sat back down, like a petulant child in defiance of her father. He half expected Lizzie to poke her tongue out.

Charlie was not flustered. "Okay, I don't mind, in fact, I don't really know what this part of the meeting will entail as I have no idea what the following will be, or in fact what the following actually is." Charlie withdrew a padded envelope from the top drawer of his desk and handed it to Dan who looked at it and then back to Charlie. On the front was Dan's name written in Aunt Susan's unmistakeable balloon scrawl.

"It was given to me by your Aunt a few months ago. She asked me to keep it safe, which I have. I don't know what it is and she never told me." He said shrugging his shoulders.

Dan wielding his pen knife slid the blade under the gummed flap and sliced open the top, slipping the contents on to the desk in front of them. A second slightly smaller envelope sat on the desk; it had been sealed with Aunt Susan's family crest pressed into red molten wax, a trick she loved to deploy for birthday cards and other family fun. Although in this instance, for some reason, it seemed slightly more sinister.

The crest was passed down to her from her father in form of a reversed gold monogrammed signet ring, which Dan had been given earlier by the Sheriff within Aunt Susan's personal effects. On the front of the envelope was written 'Daniel Morris' and underneath his birth date.

He pulled at the flap breaking the waxed seal and upended the envelope. A burned DVD slid across the desk and finally, much to his relief, the safe keys which he had been desperately searching for. These were in fact his own set of keys which he had given Aunt Susan to look after when he left for the UK.

Charlie pushed the items together into the middle of the desk. Dan looked in the envelope and pulled out a folded piece of paper. He unfolded it like a map and placed it on the desk between the three of them. On it were the architectural plans of the family home. The A1 sheet read 1 of 5. Lizzie, Charlie and Dan studied it somewhat puzzled.

Charlie finally broke the oppressive silence. "OK, I have two questions. One." He pointed to a small rectangular room in the middle of the house. "What the hell is that, I've never seen a room leading off the study." Charlie stabbed the sheet and his finger traced the outline of the small room. "And two, I can see that this key," holding the smaller of the two keys up before them, "is obviously a safe key, as I've seen plenty of them over the years dealing with wills and such things, but what the hell is this?" Charlie picked up the second key. At first glance it looked like a standard Chubb mortice lock key but instead, it had what looked like a USB flash drive attached to the end.

As Dan studied the plans, he spoke quietly. "That room is a Panic Room. It's what Uncle James and Granddad designed when the house was rebuilt after the fire. It is supposed to be burglar and fire proof. It also has a satellite phone inside, which obviously can't be cut off. I've searched the entire house for Aunt Susan and Uncle Mike's keys since I got home but haven't been able to find them. I'm assuming the burglar kept them. The first key operates the safe, that key …" He pointed to the key in Charlie's hand, "… operates the mechanism, which in turn opens the Panic Room."

Lizzie looked pale. "I don't understand. If your Aunt and Uncle's deaths were part of a bungled burglary, then why are only the keys missing and nothing else?"

"That's what I don't understand either." Dan filled the pair in about how he had discovered why the security cameras were not working and also the final discovery the external phone line was disconnected, or cut. They all sat somewhat alarmed by this latest revelation.

In Dan's mind he was relieved he had his own keys. What he withheld from Charlie or Lizzie was each of the USB keys only worked with them individually, even with Aunt Susan's or Uncle Mike's safe key the burglar would still have been unable to gain access to the Panic Room but what he had hoped was his keys would be inside the safe.

Now he had his own, he would be able to find out a little bit more. The Panic Room had its own secrets within, certainly not revealed on this drawing and only known by the immediate family. At the minute, until he had opened the Panic Room he decided to remain silent about what was hidden inside.

After an age of silence, all in their own way trying to understand these revelations, Lizzie picked up the disk and walked over to the TV and DVD player, she placed the disk in the slot closing it. Nothing happened, they patiently watched as the DVD players logo bounced endlessly round the TV screen, until finally it displayed the message 'no disk'.

"Oh great." Dan said falling back into his seat. "It's broken."

"Do you reckon your Aunt made this on her DVD camcorder?" Dan stared at Lizzie with a blank expression. "You remember when she came over to you last year for the vacation? Well, she gave me a disk to watch when she came home. The camcorder she used, she bought it while over with you, it was British, hang on."

Lizzie disappeared back into reception, Charlie and Dan looked at each other not following, she returned with her laptop. Tapping away, she threw the remote at Dan. "Turn the DVD player off and back on again." The screen went blank momentarily and then promptly returned to the prompt of no disk. "Right, now press button 3." Dan did as he was told. "Followed by 1, 4, 1, 5, 9 and now 2." The display changed and read power on, the disk started whirring and a picture appeared on the TV screen.

Lizzie looked triumphant. "The camcorder was bought in England. They encode DVD's differently, America is region 1, Europe, Region 2 and so forth. We just used a DVD hack from the net to force the player to play European disks. I had to do this last year with Aunt Susan's holiday video to make it play at home." Charlie and Dan tried to look unimpressed. "By the way you look very hot in Speedo's." A mischievous grin spread across Lizzie's face and as she winked at him, Dan shifted uncomfortably in his seat, knowing exactly the incident she was referring to.

The camera had not been level when it was turned on, there was a whirlwind view of the ceiling in Aunt Susan's bedroom as the camera gently righted itself and was placed on a steady surface. The auto focus finally concentrated on the bedside cabinet. It must have been evening. The camera image had a warm glow due to the bedside lights giving a synthetic orange tinge to the recording.

The lens focus shifted slightly as a woman's backside blocked the view; the backside turned and sat down on the bed facing the camera. Aunt Susan stared into the camera lens.

In every family there is usually someone who holds them as a unit, every family has a lynchpin; the one who brings everyone together, the one who organises the birthday parties or anniversaries, the one who cooks for Christmas or Thanksgiving. The one who keeps everyone in touch with the constant round robin of phone calls; they are the family encyclopaedia who connects all the drudgery of day to day life, taking pride in this essential role. So many families fall apart or simply lose connection when something happens, good or bad. When the latter, Aunt Susan was always the one to make the call and smooth over any rising tension, she was the proverbial family glue.

Seeing her physically on screen was the first time Dan truly felt a sense of loss. Aunt Susan was so calming and always spoke in a motherly and caring tone; she had also been as much a mother to him as she was to her own son, Matt.

"Hello Daniel." Like a mother, Aunt Susan was the only one who insisted on calling him Daniel, but then Ash was always Ashley, Matt was always Matthew and Lizzie was always Elizabeth. Heaven help the person if they ever called her Sue.

"I made the decision to make this DVD and give to Charlie for safe keeping. In the envelope you'll find your set of keys, I'm sure you'll recognise them." She paused as if looking for something more positive to say, fumbling slightly. "I decided, in the event of anything happening to us, you should have them and the best way for that to happen is through a lawyer. If there are any unforeseen problems, then whatever happens, they will find their way back to you through law." Aunt Susan seemed to be struggling to find the words, which was never usually a problem for her; she could talk for England and so often did.

"With everything that has happened, much of which you are not aware of with you being so far away, I need you to understand the items in the envelope are extremely important. You know how to use your keys. There are answers in the safe and I'm sure you'll know exactly what to look for, it will show you the way." Aunt Susan seemed to glance over her shoulder towards the door situated off screen, there was a muffled noise, turning back to face the lens, leaning in and lowering her voice a little.

"Remember Daniel, we all love you very, very much and we are all really proud of you." She got up blocking the camera lens as she turned it off, the screen went blank.

10

There were many questions the DVD posed. Why did Aunt Susan make it? Why did she make sure Charlie had it in his possession? Did Uncle Mike know? Did she foresee future problems and if so, what? Why were there only his safe keys plus an architectural drawing of the house? However the biggest question the DVD raised which puzzled Dan more than anything, what did he not know about and ultimately what was puzzling, was her turn of phrase at the end of her recording.

When you sign off or say goodbye you would normally say 'I love you' or even 'we love you' to include Uncle Mike. However Aunt Susan had specifically used the term 'we all love you' and 'we are all really proud.' All refers to several, all means more than 'I' or 'we,' what or whom could she have meant?

Apart from the initial search in the study for the safe keys, Dan had been consciously avoiding the room. Although the blood had been washed away, you could still see the faint tinge to the woodwork on the floor. He was sure he could smell old blood as it broke down, like the unfettered smell of a butchers. It unnerved him and in his mind he could see their lifeless bodies stretched out on the floor. The study seemed normal, nothing having been touched from what he could tell or remember from his last visit, although it had been a few years since he was last in here.

He crossed to the family portrait, it struck him how they all looked so young, carefree and happy. It had been taken a few years before he had moved to live with his Grandparents. It was the last time they were all together as a family, for Granddads birthday. It was also one of the only big family portraits to survive the fire. Everything around it had been blackened and reduced to ash but beneath the glass they all stood, forever smiling, not knowing the future events which would eventually befall each of them.

The portrait was a survivor of the fire; it was also the rebirth and symbol to many family secrets. The innocent smiles belied the truth hidden behind the glass, photographic paper and wood; you would never guess the portrait was the entrance to something so secret.

Dan reached beneath the solid wooden frame sliding a hidden latch to the left. This simple latch alone would not budge the portrait; a solid silver plaque engraved with the Morris coat of arms at the front had to be depressed like a button and held, the latch unlocked a mechanism, which in turn allowed the plaque to be depressed. Dan gently caressed the silver, fondly running his thumb over the beautiful engraving. It depicted a shield with a lion rearing on its hind legs. Above the shield was a knight's helmet and all around the outside were flourishes of acacia leaves, which through heraldic symbolism meant eternal and affectionate remembrance. As he pressed the silver engraving, with a click and smooth movement, not unlike the smooth automatic drawer openings in an expensive car, the picture gently swung open to reveal the family safe.

The front of the safe was level with the wall; it was not huge but served its purpose. Dan slotted the safe key into the keyhole. Turning the key he exhaled deeply, worried about what he would find. He swung the door open. Inside, the contents surprisingly still looked to be there and untouched, he had honestly expected them to be gone. There were many documents but the contents of the safe were carefully considered, mainly to throw off the scent of its true nature. It held some cash, gold jewellery; even several untraceable bearer bonds which would have been handed to a thief if opened, worryingly these were all still present.

Dan reached in, removing the contents and placing it on the desk. Everything seemed to be accounted for, from what he could remember. When the safe was finally empty, removing the key from the front of the safe and fondling around towards the back he located a second key slot in the roof, inserting the key. The safe was fitted lower than you would expect and unless you carefully looked from beneath, or literally stuck your head inside, you would never spot the second key hole.

This time Dan rotated the key counter intuitively, anti-clockwise. After a click, the back of the safe fell forwards, softly rapping him on the knuckles. Removing the key allowed the false back to fall to the base, fully revealing a bizarre looking device hidden behind.

Reaching in with both hands, he grabbed a handle either side of the device pulling them towards the front of the safe. The device was an iris scanner. State of the art when fitted, it was programmed to work with an individual key and linked only to the key holder's eyeball scan. This was why he would have been unable to gain access with either of Uncle Mike's or Aunt Susan's keys, because they were programmed to work with their individual iris scan. Pulling the device into the cold light of day, Dan recoiled in horror, a sign he prayed he would not find.

The top and bottom of the device had an indent to rest your forehead and chin. This simple control aligned the person's head and eyeball with the scanner. Around the plastic, there was blood. Someone has forcibly been in the Panic Room. This was obviously something more than a robbery gone wrong. He had to find out what they were looking for, what had been taken and more importantly by whom?

Taking a deep breath, slightly hyperventilating, Dan inserted the USB key from his pocket, into the slot by the iris scanner, turning it clockwise. A little LED illuminated and started flashing red. Dan forced himself and pressed his head up against the dried blood. The squeamish part of him wanted to be sick knowing one of his family members' blood was smeared on the plastic.

A sequence of light flashes hit his right eye and the LED stopped flashing, indicating his eye scan has been read successfully. Turning the key anticlockwise, the LED turned green. With a low audible click, to his right a small section of the bookcase, along the wall held firm by an electro magnet, gently popped open revealing the hidden Panic Room.

11

The small monitor unexpectedly blinked to life. The camera feed was operational. It sounded a small warning alarm. The man through instinct, began to assess the operation. The monitor was now receiving a signal, it had been dormant for too long. The waiting and constant vigil was over, finally the end game begins, or so he presumed.

He was beginning to think he had played the wrong hand or at least been too quick in his earlier dealings, believing through his actions, the underground assignment had gone back to sleep. For years the case had been left, however now seemed the right time, for him at least. The last couple of days though had been uneventful. He was beginning to suspect Daniel Morris was a pointless mark. Having lived in London, disconnecting his life from the Morris family, he was beginning to believe Morris was unaware of the family secrets; that was until this very second when his tiny camera blinked to life.

The Panic Room was exceedingly well shielded. The signal was instantly lost when he had closed the bookcase door after his initial investigation. Now it was open, maybe he would discover something he missed, or at least Daniel might lead him in the right direction or possibly a different direction entirely. He had always been extremely thorough, however the last operation had taught him an invaluable lesson. One could always better himself and one's craft. It paid not to be so quick willed on some occasions.

What had he missed? Was there anything? Would Morris lead him towards the goal? He had swept the property for a heat signature finding nothing out of the ordinary. The only anomaly was a small hidden device behind the bookcase. He probably would have dismissed it as an induction pipe for the central heating had it not been for the way the sad old man challenged him in the study, instinct had told him there was more. The old man may still have even been alive if he had not been so foolish. He killed them far too soon.

This was an error of judgement on his part, another one in a chain of many recently but he would soon repair his standings. For now it was damage control which meant Daniel Morris was going to be of use, whether he knew it, or not.

This operation had a strange chequered history, very difficult to follow through the case notes dating back to the fifties. Handed down through countless hands, it had been asleep for many years and was one of the longest running on file. He had been involved at an early age, a memory he treasured with fondness, he was so young back then. It had left an indelible mark in his memory. It was amazing how paths crossed time and time again, like fate, if only he truly believed in it.

While investigating his last assignment he had, by accident, discovered Daniel Morris and his family again. As a matter of course, he had researched the neighbours of his previous job. It was not unusual in this field to discover friends or acquaintances who had their own file, mainly through association with the underworld or other agencies. This however was not your typical case file. It was not retribution or disclosure. This was a control case, extremely rare in its own right, going right to the top. If he could finish this after all these years, he would be more than welcome back to the inner sanctum.

His mind wandered to the situation which had led him here, sitting in a hot sweaty van on surveillance duty. He had become blasé. It had led to his mistake. A mistake which should never have happened. The girl should have been alone; he never left anything to chance. Enough, the past was just that, he had been sloppy. There would be time for introspection over the job after reaching the conclusion of this one. If he could achieve what so many others before him had failed, then maybe at minimum he could regain operation status.

Right now he was off the grid. Working alone, it was the way he liked to work but this operation was not sanctioned. He was operating outside of any agency or direct orders and without back up, it could go horribly wrong. In truth, he desperately wanted to dispose of this Daniel Morris. He hated him but that was a highly unprofessional feeling. In truth he should not feel anything towards him.

Unfortunately, for now, he was resigned to the fact he needed him, he was now the last remaining link to this operation. He stared intently at his monitor, grateful of something finally happening. Watching the wall of the Panic Room fold back as Daniel pulled back the bookcase, illuminating the inside of the Panic Room and entering.

12

The bookcase door was counter balanced, swinging effortlessly on its hinges, fully loaded with books and made of solid cherry wood. It was extremely heavy but felt like a normal door to open or shut. At the top of the bookcase was an intricately carved coat of arms inset into the elaborate dark wood, mirroring the silver engraving on the portrait. The shield was elegantly carved and the detail picked out. The lion was brushed with gold leaf, the knight's helmet was brushed with silver leaf and the acacia leaves around the outside were hand painted a dark emerald green.

The coat of arms signified so much to the family, the Knight's helmet signified guiding the body; a man's journey through life. The Lion represented the dauntless courage on their quest and the shield represented the defence of the family. As a whole, the coat of arms represented their rebirth.

Inside, the Panic Room was comfortable; it was small but perfectly formed to fulfill its function. As you entered, to the left was a small couch, spanning the width of the room. Directly in front of the door, on the opposite wall was the ventilation and electrical components servicing the room. The major device being a satellite phone and the alert buttons were pre-programmed, directly connecting to the Police and Fire service.

On the right was the eyes and ears of the house, the family affectionately referred to it as the womb. The womb in essence was a high tech observation booth, permanently watching the entire house. A bank of three identical monitors positioned side by side for the operator were attached to the wall. Two of the monitors constantly polled the feeds from the hidden cameras positioned throughout the home. The left monitor displayed the downstairs cameras and the middle monitor the upstairs. The right tapped the external wifi cameras, mirroring the monitor in the kitchen; this feed could also be viewed on any TV in the house.

Dan sat down at the desk; he first wanted to check all the cameras were working correctly. Using the computer mouse, a menu appeared on the central screen changing the outputs accordingly. The left screen continued monitoring downstairs, the central screen was now the operator screen and the right was adjusted to monitor the upstairs cameras. Dan scrolled the outputs to read thumbnails. The screens slowly refreshed to show a numbered thumbnail from each feed, sixteen thumbnails on each monitor, totalling thirty two cameras, over two floors. Three of them were not working, 17, 23 and 32. They however were in spare bedrooms and the loft space, so not a major problem. It could even be something simple just blocking them or their view.

Dan accessed the database manager to confirm each camera was on loop record, date stamping and continuously overwriting the imagery on the hard drives. The database recorded in two week blocks or eventually looped over a 14 day rolling period. It could be more but the compression hit compromised the detail, making the imagery useless for analysis. He double clicked the folder 10 days previous, the day of his Aunt and Uncle's death. A sub folder dropped the camera feed folders, all 32 of them. Folder 9 contained the video feed to the study. He double clicked on the video file, the hour glass ticked away, nothing happened. He double clicked again impatiently, still nothing happened.

"Bollocks." Dan loved this English turn of phrase. It seemed highly appropriate right now. Turning the shuttle controller, still nothing appeared, then a warning box appeared on screen, 'unable to locate media'.

"Fuck." Dan slammed the controller down on the desk and flung himself into the back of his seat. As his chair rolled backwards and to a halt, he could see under the desk. The cabinet was opened, his heart sank. Whoever had been here really knew what they were doing; he could tell even from this distance. The hard drives had been removed. He crawled under the desk and opened the doors; every module was missing.

After the fire, the whole point of the Panic Room was to capture another event; the family had never truly believed it was an accident. This was the sole reason the Panic Room was built, to survive and record everything. If the equipment missed or lost the data, then it was a fruitless exercise. Inside the basic wooden structure of the house, the

Panic Rooms floors, ceiling and walls were made of poured reinforced concrete. If the ventilation broke down, the room had its own internal air supply and scrubbers, submarine technology reducing carbon dioxide build up. Dan himself had designed and built the security surveillance to the standard of the Panic Room itself, over engineered, like everything the family did. He prayed the killer had not realised just how clever.

Dan had hidden extra hardware within the computer casing. The database and contents had been mirrored internally, in case of complete failure. If the external disks were removed from their individual caddies, the data mirroring stopped. Theoretically though, the mirrored disks would still have the original footage up to the point of the originals' removal.

Dan crawled closer to the unit, using his feet for leverage and his back against the wall. He pushed the heavy computer racking under the desk, shifting it sideways. He ran his hand over the carpet which had no other indentations. When a heavy object is on a carpet it leaves an imprint. Running his fingers over the pile he doubted it could have been moved and then shifted back into exactly the same position, it would be almost impossible in these cramped conditions.

Sliding the side panel off the machine, he sighed heavily with relief, the mirror drives were still in place. Finally the fucker had made a mistake. Carefully Dan removed the drives and placed each of them in a spare caddy, individually inserting them in the disk enclosures. As they each plugged in, the drive caddy illuminated and whirred into life.

The computer sensed the drives were connected. After an initial hardware check, it showed four drives individually appear on the desktop, one by one. The database controlled the footage date stamps and organised the imagery in order, however the mirrored drives simply recorded an endless stream of data 24 hours a day, 7 days a week. The problem and known limitation with this type of backup was that the four drives were treated as a single unit, basically striping the data across all of the four drives. If incorrectly reconnected, the data would appear corrupt and useless which was another useful security measure.

Having built the system from scratch, Dan was more than aware of this protocol with four drives; it was how he purposely designed it. Each drive could only be used once giving a possible 24 different combinations. Flicking the system from record to play on the controller, he re-linked the player to the recovered database, manually reassigning the drive letters correctly. It was this kind of minute detail he remembered so well. It was what had made him so good at his job. Dan sighed with relief as the thumbnails started to appear on the monitors, each individually assigned to their camera number.

When the thumbnails were all available Dan clicked on folder 10, followed by 9, and then finally double clicking on the video file. The hour glass ticked away momentarily and then an image appeared with the time of '00:00:00' in the bottom right hand corner.

The image of the study looked distorted, showing a panoramic view of the entire study, because it was being viewed through an infrared fisheye lens. The study had obviously been empty at the time of the recording, more than likely his Aunt and Uncle had been asleep. Using the controller and the step button, he stepped through the footage in increments of 10 minutes until day break changed the image back to colour and the whole room was illuminated. Dan was still rather pleased with the detail of the imagery. The cameras had been expensive but worth the extra cost.

At 09:20:00 he could see someone sat at the desk. Stopping and examining the frame Dan realised he was now looking at unseen footage of his Uncle. Fast forwarding from this point using the jog shuttle controller, a sped up re-enactment visually paraded on screen. Uncle Mike made a comedy phone call around 09:24:00, slamming the receiver down. Aunt Susan came in giving him a drink and Uncle Mike gulped it down. As soon as it was finished she promptly whisked it away, then came back, sat down, picked up her book, crossed and uncrossed her legs several times. They both left and came back in, many normal mundane day to day activities passed on screen in quick succession.

Then at approximately 10:59:00 Aunt Susan slammed her book down on the reading table, in real time it would look like she placed it carefully, taking note of the page. She got up and after a delay returned followed by a third person. Dan stopped and froze the action. Here he was, of course he had assumed the person was a he and here he was!

Linking the camera to time, he double clicked on the hallway's camera, folder 1. With the reference the camera sprang open at the same spot. Aunt Susan went to the door and opened it. A man was stood in the doorway with a clip board and pen. Aunt Susan obviously asked for identification and he handed it to her from around his neck. She then stepped aside and the man finally came into view.

"Damn it" Dan cursed as he saw that the man had been wearing a baseball cap; keeping it low to hide his features. Aunt Susan and the man headed for the kitchen. Dan re-linked the time stamp to camera 6. They could be seen in the kitchen chatting away like old friends, but

Aunt Susan had been like that with everyone. The man had his back to the camera and was fiddling with the external camera monitor and controls. Uncle Mike then entered and they both prodded at buttons on the monitor, polling through the individual feeds. The man unhooked each feed from the controller and the static disappeared; then reappeared. They all chatted a little more and the man headed back outside. Dan linked back to camera 6.

The man heads through the front door and after several minutes passed, came back in carrying a toolbox. He reappeared back in the kitchen. Aunt Susan gave the man a cup of tea, obviously tea as it was in one of the guest cups. All three chat momentarily, Aunt Susan leaving followed by Uncle Mike. The man started pulling the control box apart. Several bits of kit were attached to cables and removed circuit boards from the box.

Dan started to lose interest; the guy certainly looked to be testing everything fully. Dan sped through the footage again and the man continued to invest his time in the external camera feeds. He then packed up and left, presumably to chase the fault on the external cameras. Dan went back to searching through the footage in the study. There was a long gap and then suddenly, he stopped.

Creeping into the study was the camera repair guy. The man systematically surveyed the room, with a definite look of intent. What had he been up to? The guy turned and faced the camera, stopping the recording on a single frame. What the hell did he have in his hands? Dan leaned into the monitor staring at the image… it can't be! Why would a repairman have a thermal imaging camera? Dan realised in an instant what the man was looking for as he swung back around, facing the camera directly at the Panic Room.

13

He had removed the drives and was now feeling rather smug. They were piled in his van on top of a stack of empty greasy fast food containers. Ultimately though they would have revealed very little. He had been trained to keep his head at a certain angle, with the two dimensional spherical nature of the lens in a security camera, it made automated facial recognition and general viewing quite difficult to pick out a person's features. The baseball cap happened to make the task even more difficult. The point of taking the drives was more about removing any incriminating evidence.

That said, he never expected the sophistication of the internal monitoring system. The surveillance was very progressive, something he had never seen within an alleged domestic home; that was the key of course. It obviously hid something far deeper than what the family portrayed; it was this which was the key to the whole conundrum. On a sweep of the property it would be very difficult to find the secondary system, especially with the cheap domestic one in plain view. It was clever and would certainly be enough to throw a layman off the scent.

He smiled to himself; on his screen Dan threw the controller across the desk. He had discovered the drives were missing. Dan slouched back into the chair, rolling away from the surveillance camera fixed to the right edge of the left viewing monitor. The camera was state of the art, almost naked to the visible eye and invisible in the gloom of the Panic Room.

Daniel disappeared from sight, sinking below the desk. He had obviously gone down to look at the computer drives. Foolish boy. He idly reached up and took one of the drives and looked at it, stroking across its exposed electronic circuitry. All in all, he had to admit, it was quite a sophisticated system but with a little research and understanding anyone could build one like the Morris household. The cameras were not cheap though, especially for their intricate size and coupled with the infra red lenses throughout the house. Tiny fibre optic cables had linked each feed to the base computer. The computer would have needed an exceedingly high specification to handle the masses of data coming in from so many different feeds. He did not take a considerable look at the internal workings but at a guess, at least a quad core processor was controlling four independent modules of eight separate cameras to each drive.

"I wonder if you can purchase the software off the t'interweb?" He idly mused to himself about it, tapping his right hand on an invisible air keyboard. "It's probably shareware."

Dan's hand suddenly appeared briefly from under the desk and placed a small rectangular silver box on top. A minute later a second box appeared next to it … what was he doing? Then a third appeared, he leaned in closer to his monitors to look at the boxes on screen and then at the hard drive in his hand; surely it could not have been that sophisticated, could it?

He leaned in to the screen, any closer he would fall through watching and shaking with rage as Dan took the clearly visible drives from the desk and placed them into spare caddies, then returning back under the desk. His anger started to rise, he had made yet another mistake. Without thinking, he viciously threw the redundant drive across the van; seconds earlier he had caressed it with all the fondness of a lover.

With more luck than judgement, the drive struck the other three sending all of them crashing to the floor in a polystyrene frenzy of cartons, soggy lettuce, tomato ketchup and mayonnaise. One of the electronic circuit boards broke from the disk, skidding across to his foot. He stamped on it with a hefty size 10 sole.

His anger somewhat diminished and sated at this outburst, he pulled the monitor towards him to assess the new situation. Daniel was using the controller to shuttle through the footage but he could not see what was on the surveillance screens, his only view was Daniel Morris' features.

"Fuckin' hell." Slamming his fist on the table, his monitor rocked. "I should have placed the camera behind the desk!" If he had placed the camera overlooking the operator's shoulder he would not have been blind to this new development because he would be able to see the monitors and what Daniel was looking at. For now, all he could do was watch and wait.

Several minutes passed as he watched Daniel operate the video controller. Daniel slowly sat back in the chair... what was wrong with him? Daniel started to cry; wiping his eyes with the back of his hand. He stared into the monitor, with quiet satisfaction spoke again to himself. "You are weak. You are pathetically weak." Smiling and cracking his knuckles together towards the monitor.

Daniel suddenly looked directly into the camera, leaning forward towards the screen. "Shit." He believed his camera had been spotted as Daniel's hand struck out for it. The camera went blank as it was covered, he jabbed his finger at the screen. "Maybe I have completely underestimated you, again."

However the camera did not go dead, it continued for a few minutes to transmit the image of a dull blank surface, without definition or any discerning feature. What was Morris doing? The camera had not been found, as it was still transmitting. Daniel must have moved it aside. Cursing himself again, "Bloody stupid place to put it."

Wait, what is that? He stared at the image on screen. Was he mistaken? Was something happening. The transmitted foreground moved slowly from right to left on screen. The image pushed from grey to black as the lens on the tiny camera automatically tried to adjust to the darkness.

He could not believe what he was seeing. He stared at the screen, blinking in disbelief. The camera was looking directly through the gloom at a handrail, a handrail for a set of hidden stairs heading down, beneath the Morris family home.

14

On the thermal imaging camera's sensor held in the repair man's hand, Dan could quite clearly see the thermal signature of the equipment in the Panic Room. It was not really hot but was visible to question what it was. He watched as the man suddenly changed momentum. He reached behind, retrieved a gun tucked in the back of his jeans and walked out of the room. Panicked by what he had just seen, Dan started randomly jabbing at folders to access other footage from other cameras. In his alarmed state he could not remember what folder linked to which camera.

A multitude of windows opened footage to the garage, hallway, a spare bedroom and then the landing. Dan watch helplessly as the man took giant strides across the landing, the gun in his right hand, purposefully heading for the master bedroom.

In the master bedroom Aunt Susan was making the bed. Obviously startled as the man entered, she spun round to face him. He caught her with the back of his left hand, smacking her with considerable force across the cheek. Aunt Susan fell on to the bed, consumed by the billowing duvet cover. Her glasses were resting at an awkward angle over her face; he grabbed her hair, dragging her out of the room.

On the landing, he pulled Aunt Susan back down the hallway. She was bent over trying to prise her hair from his hands; the pair descended the stairs and disappeared from the camera view.

On camera 1 Uncle Mike must have heard the commotion as the man and Aunt Susan descended the stairs. He ran from the kitchen but before he reached the bottom step, he raised his hands and started to walk backwards. The man's legs came into view as he descended and then gradually his entire body, revealing the gun levelled at Uncle Mike's head.

Words were exchanged and the gun was shook sideways motioning for him to return back to the study. Uncle Mike went first, with the gun pointed at the back of his skull; Aunt Susan still being unceremoniously dragged by her hair, followed behind.

Dan switched back to camera 9, the study feed. Aunt Susan hurtled through the door into the room landing in a pile on the floor. The man shook his hand and clumps of her hair fell to the floor. He kicked Uncle Mike in the back of the legs and he collapsed forward to his knees in a heap next to Aunt Susan. Dan watched as Uncle Mike tried to comfort his crying wife and then angrily turned to confront the man who moved closer, pressing the barrel of his gun against Uncle Mike's forehead. Unfortunately he stepped in to the view of the camera and hid what happened next.

When he backed away, there was a three way conversation back and forth between them. At one point there was a disagreement and the gun was pointed at Aunt Susan. Uncle Mike hastily back tracked holding his hands up and shaking his head. He visibly sighed and took the safe keys from his pocket, the ones Dan had been searching for, giving them to the man and Aunt Susan did the same.

The man then grabbed Aunt Susan from the floor throwing her into her reading chair. Uncle Mike got off the floor revealing the safe under the portrait. The man waved the gun in his face and he stepped back, standing behind Aunt Susan and putting his hands on her shoulders. Uncle Mike must have started to say something because the man stepped away from the safe after he had opened it.

He waved at Uncle Mike to empty the safe and as Uncle Mike started to do so, he turned with the cash and pleaded with the man, it seemed nothing would stop him. Uncle Mike threw the bundles of cash to the floor at the feet of the man and turned back to the safe.

Without warning Uncle Mike flung himself round holding a pistol, a new addition to the safe obviously, something Dan had never seen, however Uncle Mike never even got his arm round level to take the shot. The man fired, hitting Uncle Mike in the chest.

Although it all happened in milliseconds, Dan saw the sequence of events in slow motion. Uncle Mike's chest erupted in a sea of crimson, a look of surprised pain and terror etched across his face. Dropping the gun, he fell to his knees and then face first into the carpet. He never moved of his own accord again.

Aunt Susan looked stunned, paralysed with fear, eyes wide open in terror to the horror happening before her. She gripped the arms of her chair, her knuckles whitening as her mouth fell open wide in a never ending scream. Dan could hear it through the silence of this very room; he could feel its very essence in the images that were unfolding before him.

Aunt Susan had just witnessed the most brutal killing anyone could. The person she loved and adored more than anyone, killed before her in cold blood. The man however did not falter. His arm moved silently sideways as Uncle Mike's knees hit the ground. A second shot fired, hitting Aunt Susan in the centre of her forehead. Her mouth continued to scream as her head fell forward, Dan could hear her and it would be something he would hear for the rest of his life.

Bursting in to tears, it was the second time he had cried in as many days but this was far more painful than burying their bodies, he had just witnessed their brutal murder. Dan had expected to see it but nothing had prepared him for something so vivid.

For work, he had witnessed images like this before but had never been attached personally. He quietly hoped the Sheriff was right, that the murder was an opportunistic crime which had gone tragically wrong making the perpetrator flee from the scene. This would have at least explained the reason their personal effects still being in the house.

This however was premeditated, discovering the man had looked for and found the Panic Room was unnerving. The more he watched, the more it became apparent the man seemed to move with deliberate efficiency. Dan watched as the video rolled, resigned to a strange kind of morbid voyeurism and fascination. The man pulled the iris scanner to the front of the safe examining it carefully.

He then flipped Uncle Mike's body onto his back, using scotch tape from the desk, he held his eyes open in a forced unblinking stare. Picking Uncle Mike up under the arms, the man grappled with his considerable bulk. It was like watching someone playing a sick party game. Uncle Mike's head was forced into the embrace of the iris scanner, held there by the killer's own forehead pressing into the back of Uncle Mike's skull, as he operated the key.

The scenario took a considerable amount of time and trial to get right. The man dropped Uncle Mike's body twice before the bookcase finally opened, exactly as it had for Dan not more than 15 minutes ago.

Dan knew the rest, although he watched until the image stopped at 12:04:22. Uncle Mike and Aunt Susan went to their graves protecting the family secret. At least he had the mirrored drives; maybe this guy is not as clever as he had thought. Dan switched the player off and wiped his tears away. He had seen more than enough.

Reaching for the left monitor and pulling the screen towards him, it swung to face the blank wall. Directly behind the monitor, in the wall, was yet another key slot, however this was just operated by the USB key. Dan inserted his key releasing another hidden magnetic lock. The side panel of the Panic Room dropped away by about an inch and then slid effortlessly on its track to reveal an inner sanctum, with a small stairwell going down. The only illumination into the gloom was from the open door of the bookcase and the monitors themselves.

Taking a deep breath Dan tentatively stepped down onto the first step, it was very dark. Removing his cell from his pocket and stabbing at the buttons, Dan descended into darkness, illuminated only by the feint glow of the screen.

15

The plans of the house, taken from the package Aunt Susan left with Charlie, clearly defined an internal room depicting the Panic Room. What it hid within its carefully designed dimensions of the poured concrete walls, was a stairwell.

The stairwell descended the equivalent of three stories, making two U-turns before it reached the bottom. Dan had been up and down this stairwell hundreds of times but somehow this felt like he was descending towards hell, albeit a somewhat chillier version. Most subterranean temperature levels remained constant because the surrounding earth maintained a uniform level. The poured concrete foundation received little direct sun light, not heating the super structure and therefore the ambient temperature remained cold.

Unsure of what he would find, Dan's subconscious made the stairwell feel oppressive and it smelt musty, as though it had been unused for a very long time. Blindly moving downwards, the darkness closed around him. The small amount of light from the Panic Room above did not help. Only his sense of touch and the familiarity of his territory stopped him from falling head first down the stairwell. Dan's breath was heavy and although cold, he was sweating heavily. Following the hand rail downwards he had not been counting the steps and his leg jarred hard on the concrete basement expecting another step.

Dan shuffled along the corridor in the cloying darkness, hugging the wall, a salty smell hung in the stale air. The corridor seemed longer than he remembered as he desperately fumbled for the light switches. Using the illumination from his cell again he found them, slightly higher on the wall than standard lighting, he flicked them on. Looking up, nothing happened, he expected a hum as the overhead fluorescents kick into life, but instead started to panic in the silent darkness, unsure of what he would find down here.

He could see through the lighting diffusers in the ceiling, every second ceiling light, an LED was illuminated inside. The power from the main house was powering the emergency lights. For some reason the lab's secondary electrical circuits must have been either dead or disconnected.

To the right of the switches, on the same panel, was the emergency lighting over ride. A special key usually operated the switch to check their longevity in case of power failure and the need for evacuation. Unfortunately Dan was clueless as to where this key was, so using his coveted pocket knife, Dan inserted the screwdriver. Fiddling around he managed to flick the emergency lighting switch and they slowly sprang to life. The lab illuminated before him in a dull incandescent light. The emergency battery cells although working probably would not last a long time. The massive steel door was already open.

The lab was designed and built by Uncle James and Granddad after the fire. Everything about the house was rebuilt on a much bigger and grander scale, to the families' own specifications and needs. While digging the new foundations, it was discovered the old house was originally built on a mound of sand, too soft for the proposed newer bigger building. As it was excavated it was found to be rather deep but eventually they hit bedrock. However instead of refilling the hole with hard core they decided to build the underground garage and, at the deepest section, they built the lab. It was constructed from poured concrete, with incredibly thick reinforced walls. Its walls were far more utilitarian, suggesting an underground car park but having the look of a nuclear bunker from the cold war, with all the technical equipment in place.

The decision to hide the lab was something Dan only really grasped in his later years shortly before he left home. All he really understood was that he was never allowed to discuss it with anyone outside the family, not even Lizzie. Not totally agreeing, this had always caused him a little discomfort, because he saw Lizzie as family but he had respected his families' wishes. Even now they were all dead he felt compelled to keep it secret but he had the overwhelming urge to show Lizzie the underground lab.

His Granddad, before coming to America, had worked covertly for the British Government's military divisions, mainly within revolutionary submarine technology. In effect he was never supposed to continue to develop ideas for his research but his Granddad had elaborate ideas, especially when he could see huge humanitarian uses for his technology. Uncle James had followed in his footsteps and together they had quietly continued to develop them, which was why the families' oil connections seemed so far removed from their research.

The underground lab was more of a precaution to protect this research. A second, more open lab had been built away from the house; the sole purpose was to throw anyone snooping off the scent as to what they were really up to. Aunt Patricia mainly used it as a studio for her art work. That was as much as Dan knew or cared to know in truth. The less he knew, the less likely to accidentally say something or unconsciously blurt it out.

However stepping through the steel door came as a shock; the lab was more or less empty apart from the free standing stainless steel cupboards and drawers around the perimeter. All of the elaborate scientific equipment which lined the walls and all available space, none of it was there. The centre island, on which used to sit several high tech computers, was also bare. Every surface throughout the lab was devoid of buzzing machinery.

Dan wandered slowly through the lab which now just resembled the look of a bare stainless steel kitchen. The feeling was strengthened by the far left hand corner of the lab. It was piled with all sorts of items and food products; reams of paper, printer cartridges, several hard drives, batteries, a couple of torches as well as tins of chilli, soup, tomatoes, dried fruit and other food stuffs inherently having a long shelf life. On top of the pile was what looked like a small shopping list in Aunt Susan's and Uncle Mike's writing, batteries, sugar, coffee; all reading like the basic mid-week shop for essentials. Dan picked up one of the torches, absent-mindedly switching it on, the beam bounced off the shiny steel surfaces.

He opened the drawers randomly in the units and all were empty, the cupboards were also bare. At the far end of the lab was a massive set of architectural drawers which were used to hold detailed plans and technical drawings. Dan opened the top drawer, he knew what was here; it held the rest of the plans to the house, parts two to five were left untouched. These showed the elevations, engineering and technical details of the underground lab. Dan pulled out the sheets, laying them on top of the central island.

Flicking through, as far as he could tell, there was not any further useful information on them, none he could see was of any relevance anyway. The last sheet clearly showed the service tunnel heading out from the underground complex at forty five degrees, leading to the boat house. Another reason the boat house was excavated deeper was to supply sea water through this connecting tunnel. He had forgotten about this. Once when it was empty, the three of them, Matt, Ash and himself had used it to escape and meet up with Lizzie after being grounded. Ultimately it had led to them all being grounded for a further month, one very long month. Dan smiled to himself at the memory realising he could now tell Lizzie the truth. The three of them had made up the most elaborate cover story as to how they escaped unseen.

Half-way along the service tunnel was a special two way valve; designed by his Granddad, built by Matt, it was unique in the way it functioned. If the tide was too high it would keep the water level at the correct height within the lab, so it would not flood. If the tide was too low it would keep the water higher to maintain the correct level. Venting the tunnel was interesting, which was why it was separated from the rest of the lab by a clear acrylic wall; a complete fail safe if the valve ever stopped working. Behind the plexiglass, it could fill completely still not flooding the lab and its precious equipment.

Dan still did not understand. Why had Aunt Susan only put part one of the plans in the envelope, what did she want him to discover? From what he could understand the plans did not show him any more detail that was missing. Dan slid open every drawer, each was empty until he reached the bottom. In the bottom drawer were countless sheets of engineering drawings, he took them out, spreading them alongside the house plans.

There were in effect two different sets of plans. One set labelled 'Marion Hyper Sub', a carefully detailed engineering specification which looked, according to the scale, very much like a miniature submarine. It could have been something his Granddad was working on.

The second set of plans had Matt's engineering firm logo on the top; which was titled 'Wet Lab'. The difference with these plans, unlike the Hyper Sub plans which were on standard A1 draughts paper, were that they were drawn on to a form or transparency, not unlike tracing paper but certain details were missing, such as dimensions and the usual engineering detail from a technical drawing, which were obvious in the complete submarine technical drawings.

They were also labelled overlay two of four A, four of four A, then two of four B and so on, but what did they overlay? More importantly why were all the odd overlay sheets missing? What relevance were they? At the back of the drawer was a drawing tube. Dan carefully rolled the two sets of plans up, gently slipping them inside.

16

The van was stifling. A black van was not one of his smartest moves. He dare not have any of the windows open, plus running the engine for the air conditioning might arouse suspicion while parked up.

He had been in town for supplies, looking like a travelling tourist. The locals' main topic of conversation wherever he stopped was the apparent murder of the much loved Morris family. Anything around the family home could and would look suspicious. The Sheriff's department would be far more vigilant than normal after the event. You could have abandoned a nuclear missile carrier in the car park before the incident and no one would have batted an eyelid at its presence.

He was parked in a small picnic area just off the main stretch into town, close enough to pick up the signal from the camera within the Panic Room. More importantly, it was on the coastal path which led into the property so that, if the need arose, he could easily get on to the Morris property undetected.

He had watched on the monitor as Daniel descended into the gloom of the stairwell. Several minutes passed and he was surprised when the whole stairwell illuminated from below. Although the lighting was weak, the camera instantly corrected itself for the new conditions. The stairwell was very functional; it was not overly detailed or ornate, none of the delicate wood panelling lined the walls, which at a guess he would assume from the image, was simply poured concrete. Certainly not a cellar that had been forgotten.

Wherever this stairwell led, it was an intrinsic part of the house, certainly something to investigate further. The question he kept playing through his mind, did he wait until the house was empty before going in again? The potential trouble he faced was if Daniel closed the Panic Room, because without the bodies of the Morris couple he would not be able to gain access again. Right now Daniel Morris was too valuable to kill. He needed to gain access to the room and stairwell to find out what is down there. It may simply be a wine cellar or an elaborate fallout shelter. William Morris did work for the military, maybe he built it for a future holocaust?

Time ticked by, Daniel had been gone several minutes and he did not seem to be returning any time soon. He picked up his gun, inserting a clip into the chamber and then screwed a silencer on to the front.

"Ah fuck it, let's go see what the Morris family's been hiding in the basement."

He opened the back doors to the van and jumped down, pressing the gun into the back of his jeans. Running at full pelt along the coastal path, it was not far but within thirty paces he already felt out of breath.

17

Dan slung the carrying strap from the tube over his shoulder, putting his hand against the Plexiglas wall to steady himself. The acrylic wall stretched the full width of the lab, from floor to ceiling, recessed into the concrete. The acrylic was 1.25 inches thick and bulletproof, not that those properties were inherent in its use.

The chamber was divided into two. A door led to the left lock out chamber and then a second water tight door into the second chamber. This inner chamber had a six foot square well in the floor.

He turned on the torch, opening the left door entering the compartment. The smell of salt water in here was very strong but it was not fresh, it smelt as though it had been empty a long time. Grabbing the door handle to the second water tight compartment he pushed, expecting resistance because the door used to be difficult to open as it was hermetically sealed but it swung in easily with a slight audible sucking on the seals around the door edges.

Swinging the torch beam across the square pit in the floor, usually full with salt water to approximately six inches beneath the level of the lab floor, it was empty. In the water pit, his Granddad's technical equipment was usually submerged; the water fed the intricate machine keeping it cool. It could be raised on a track out of the pit for monitoring, any updates or repair work. Primarily though it remained submerged most of the time, from what he remembered.

However not unexpectedly, along with the rest of the lab's equipment, the pod, as the family referred to it, was missing and the well was completely dry.

With the door open, Dan felt a slight breeze against his face; fresh salt air was blowing down the service tunnel into the musty lab. He stood on the edge breathing fresh air and directing his torch down into the well. The sides and wall in front were vertical drops but the drop directly at his feet had a wooden ladder descending approximately ten foot down to the bottom. The water line was clearly defined around the edge of the well by green algae when wet, the steps were exceedingly treacherous, but it had long since dried.

Dan swung his torch around the pit floor noticing debris in the bottom, which was unusual as it was always kept immaculately clean, it had to be with all the sensitive equipment. As he passed his torchlight over what looked like a discarded empty water bottle, a reflection flashed in the beam. Dan could see a small silver object with black sides sticking out from under the edge. What was that? Turning round, grasping the ladder he descended into the well, the breeze and smell was far stronger down here.

At the bottom, he turned and kicked at the bottle, underneath Dan was shocked to see the familiar shape of a pen knife. Crouching down to pick it up, it was unmistakeable it was the other black handled pen knife. It was Matt's pen knife! Dan could not believe it. Picking it up he flicked open the long blade, not that he needed confirmation but inscribed in the same script as his own knife, was the unmistakable script Διόνυσος, meaning Dionysus, Matt's Greek name.

Dan's mind started to race. Matt should have had his knife with him when he was lost at sea, they swore to the pact to always keep their knives with them which they all did, even Lizzie. Why was it here? Dan put the blade in his pocket, squeezing the knife in the palm of his hand, a feeling of warmth spread through him. He had found something that was Matt's. It was something he never thought he would ever see again, it felt amazing.

Turning off the torch, he turned to climb the ladder, the service tunnel stretched off to his right and into the distance; there was a muted light at the end of the tunnel. Why was that, it should have been in darkness? He ducked down and crawled into the tunnel. Moving on all fours he crawled down the tunnel, towards the light.

18

By the time he reached the front door of the house his breath was wheezing, his chest was tightening and he felt like he was going to have some kind of asthma attack, or worse, a heart attack. Trying to breathe slowly, he put his head between his knees. His chest felt like a cushion was trapped inside his lungs, stopping him from taking another breath. The feeling was not new but every increasing attack caused him to panic.

He tried to calm himself, having an asthma attack on the Morris doorstep would not be the best way to reintroduce himself, considering the circumstances. He took shallow breaths and the pain started to subside slowly, enough to stand up and alleviate the chest pain. A light headedness followed and his vision in front sparkled as he saw stars flash in his vision, he stood up maybe just a little too fast.

He reached for the door and pressed down on the handle, hoping the cool interior of the house would settle his vision. The door handle did not budge.

"Shit." He had not thought about Daniel locking the door, but then it would make sense to lock the door now. He fumbled in his jean pocket and pulled out a set of keys. One of two sets Daniel had been searching for unsuccessfully since he got home; he had taken them both from Susan and Mike Morris.

On each set were the safe keys and three other keys. He knew two of the keys would open the garage door and the separate exterior lab, built away from the main house, he had checked both before leaving. The Panic Room was a shock and certainly not what he was expecting to find in the house.

As he inserted the gold key in the lock, he heard the rumble of a car pulling across the gravel driveway behind him. He knew whoever it was would be in view in seconds. He twisted the key opening the door, just as the bonnet of Charlie's BMW swung into view. Praying he had not been seen, he dived through, slamming the door shut and locking it behind him.

He did not move, pressing his back to the wall, beyond the door. He heard the car come to a stop and the engine die. In his mind's eye, he could see the scruffy lawyer open his door, get out and slam the driver's door. He obviously then opened the passenger door to retrieve something as that promptly slammed shut. He heard the gravel crunch under foot as he walked towards the front steps; all of the sounds were in sync with the vision in his mind.

He knew what Charlie looked like as he had been watching him for a couple of weeks and could recognise the car instantly. He pressed himself against the wall harder with his gun drawn up to his chest, the barrel pointed at the ceiling. The door handle creaked but did not move and the door was pushed rattling the barrel in the lock; a long friendship and an open home dictated nothing less. A moment or two passed, which felt like an eternity and then the old school bell rang in the direction of the kitchen announcing a visitor.

There was silence, a deafening silence which seemed to last for an eternity. A package was pushed through the letter box and landed on the mat. The stuffed A4 manila envelope lay flat on the floor with 'Daniel Morris' neatly written in ink by hand.

The footsteps walked away from the front door but instead of heading back to the car, the creak of the wooden floor boards could be heard heading around the porch to the back of the house. What the hell was he doing, why was he not leaving?

19

The service tunnel seemed to stretch off for miles into the distance. This was an optical illusion enforced because the concrete shaft gently curved heading towards the boat house. The light Dan could see when he entered the tunnel had disappeared as he had crawled further in, it was puzzling him.

Nearing the half way point, covered in a foul smelling, algae infested primordial soup, Dan could now see the two-way valve was missing. It had been removed from its locking bay, leaving a stainless steel manifold impregnated into the concrete surface.

What Dan had probably seen was the reflection on the stainless steel bouncing light from the small pools of water still in the tunnel. The breeze coming up the tunnel was rippling the water's surface and iridescent beams shimmied across the bland grey walls.

In its absence, the valve left a large void conveniently allowing him to continue crawling through the tunnel. With the valve in place, he would have needed specialist tools to manually tilt it to gain access. When in situ, the valve could be hydraulically controlled via computer allowing the tunnel and pit to be drained or manually tilted for an inspector to squeeze through the gap. During low tide the sea entrance tunnel could almost be empty depending on the time of year. The valve would stop the water in the pit from emptying, keeping it full.

He crawled onwards, knees aching with the effort. His jeans were soaked through and were looking rather unpleasant. He reached a dead end. Above Dan's head was the boat house deck, it looked solid but like the picture in the study, a small latch secured a hidden trap hatch allowing an escape from the tunnel.

The wall to the side of the tunnel worked like a sluice gate to a canal lock, water tight when closed stopping the sea water from the boat house flooding the service tunnel. Presently it was fully closed which explained why the tunnel was dry and empty. The walls were covered in the same dried uniform algae as the rest of the tunnel but the stone steps leading out were scuffed, as though something had been pulled across the surfaces scratching patches of algae away. Dan ran his hand over the grooves, it could be recent but difficult to tell, certainly made since the tunnel was emptied as the deep scratches did not contain any algae residue.

Opening the hatch, from beneath and sucking in a lungful of fresh sea air, he felt like he had surfaced from a deep sea dive, squinting in the bright light. Dan ascended on to the decking, looking out across the water of the boat house. He dropped the section of deck back down into the flooring, which ran around the inside wall of the building. The door closed back into the recess hiding the service tunnel, with immaculately chamfered teak decking.

It was a rather imposing building, rather excessive in truth for its use but the first floor gave beautiful views off the veranda overlooking the sea. Dan always had visions of living in the boat house when he was older. He believed the hero from a novel would live in a place like this, it seemed fitting.

The boat house walls above the water had been built with ornate granite blocks imported from the UK, exactly the same as the exterior lab and feature walls of the house. The bifold doors overlooked the horizon and stepping out on to the veranda gave a beautiful view. The interior however was outdated slightly, having most of the contents salvaged from the old house after the fire, especially the kitchen, but somehow this look befitted its character.

Beyond the exquisite exterior and craftsmanship above ground, hidden below the surface the boat house foundations were more than extraordinary. Anyone looking at the plans, now tightly rolled in the artist's tube slung over his back, would surely realise the entire subterranean lab had a purpose. It was obvious that it was not an ordinary installation, the opulence hid more. Dan was starting to marvel at the ingenuity of the complex construction, he had never really understood how it all connected together, until today.

The tide was high and the water lapped gently against the inside of the solid granite walls. The boat house door was down and the waves could be heard slapping gently against the outside, inside the water surface was only punctuated by the slight breeze coming through the external oak louvered door towards the open sea.

The interior was sheltered from the elements and hidden from view externally by a large overhead electric garage door sitting low in the water. The door moved on metal tracks by a motor, eventually laying flat against the ceiling. It was a little excessive but extremely useful. The same style door was fitted to the garage beneath the house, each car had a remote control door opener, the same could be said of the families' boats.

Dan scanned the empty boat house. Where was the cruiser and the speed boat they used for water skiing? The boat house was completely empty. Dan pressed the keypad located next to the door and the garage door shunted into life. The electric motors whirred overhead, grumbling apologetically and straining against their cables before gradually pulling the heavy door into the ceiling.

Across the door was a dried dirty water mark, a good three feet above the present water line, giving the impression of a dried tidemark around a bath. The door only rose about a foot before it exited the water. There used to be a good four feet submerged beneath at high tide. Even at low tide the door remained above water level. Someone must have adjusted its submersion depth, why was that? The door rumbled up rolling along the greased tracks into its final resting position, revealing the unspoilt sea view.

Dan walked out through the louvered door along a small jetty, expecting to see the cruiser or ski boat moored to either of the two spare orange buoys anchored just off the coastline, they were both empty.

Dan's mind raced back to earlier in the morning at the Station when Joel asked him about filling the diesel tank for the boat house. If the cruiser is no longer here then what had been using the fuel? The diesel tank was around the back for easy access, so Dan walked round to check the gauges. It was filled last month and yet they read almost empty.

He was suddenly snapped from his thoughts as he heard a car coming up the driveway across the angry snap of the gravel. He set the boat house door in motion as it slid effortlessly down its track, sliding back beneath the water line. Closing the oak door behind him he headed back up the gradual slope towards the house. The higher level adjustment on the door puzzled him, along with the missing family boats, and who, or more importantly what was using the fuel?

20

One of many things they do not teach, or convey to you through law school, is the amount of bad news you always seem to be privy too. It is rarely a pleasant job when a lawyer is involved; a messy divorce, a criminal court case or ultimately, to inform a relative of the unfortunate news that, after a family death, they have been written out of the will, which in some instances, could be fun. It was very interesting, the considerable blame heaped against the deliverer and bearer of such bad news.

A lawyer is supposed to remain diplomatic and unattached, without moral or ethical judgement toward a particular client, while remaining professional and fully impartial. However this was a tall order when you took into consideration the locale and affectionate nature and regard he held towards so many of his clients within this welcoming town, particularly as, more often than not during a case they became good friends.

Charlie was a good lawyer and understood the intricacies of law to the letter. What he was not good at was distinguishing the business from this ever increasing circle of friendship. It was not to say he did not do well, he was in real terms extremely well off but it was sometimes difficult to differentiate the client from a friend. The Morris family had been his oldest and longest served clients. He had sorted their affairs since the day they had bought the house 'Sea View,' and renovated it.

The house was originally part of an older estate which was left unoccupied for many years. The family who had inherited rarely visited and it fell in to disrepair, becoming somewhat of a town folly. The house was ramshackle and rather forlorn but after Daniel's grandparents, William and Mary Morris had walked along the coastal path hand in hand on vacation, they had fallen for the beautiful vista and unrivalled setting.

Purely by chance they stumbled into his pokey little office on his very first day of business. Freshly out of law school, a late graduate, wet behind the ears and hoping to make a living in a very small town, William Morris, became his very first client. With a little research he had discovered who owned the property, ultimately leading to the purchase of the house and surrounding land.

It had been a very fortunate accident for Charlie, because the Morris family were non domiciles, it created a lot more paper work and ultimately for him a good financial return for handling the transaction. William paid Charlie a lump payment and with that, C. H. Price, the practice, was born. From then he became the Morris family lawyer for all of their financial and legal needs; which turned out to be an extremely lucrative challenge. The Morris family were a very wealthy client and eventual friend.

After the house's first restoration, William and Mary had moved in along with the youngest daughter Deborah, Daniel's mother. James and Pat, their eldest son and his wife moved into the expansive house after both graduating from university. A couple of years passed before Mike and his then fiancé, Susan, also returned to the family home after both graduating from St Andrew's University in Scotland.

They were an incredibly close knit family, welcoming Charlie and his wife with open arms. Charlie assumed it was because they were also outsiders within the tiny community of Santa Rosa but he also realised it was because he was discreet, did not gossip locally and did not ask questions about their background.

James and Charlie eventually became best friends due to the same love of Scotch Whiskey and wreck diving. Diving was something of a local passion, which engrained them further into the local community. Deborah had been a late addition to the family, a good nine years after Mike was born. She was unexpected but the icing on the cake for Mary who had always wanted a daughter.

Deborah, like her older siblings, had been exceptionally gifted and had left home to attend University and from there, gone to work for the FBI in Washington. It was the events leading up to this career and lifestyle choice which had separated a once harmonious family. They never really spoke of the rift but Mary always seemed to suffer the hardest.

It was somewhat ironic all three of their grandchildren came along in the very same year, Matthew, Ashley and Daniel. Daniel was a bit of a shock to the family, he was born out of wedlock and the father was never revealed or known. It was even more ironic that Charlie and June, his wife, after years of trying also had a daughter, Elizabeth.

Cruelly though, complications during the birth had taken June from Charlie. It was this event that sealed the bond between the families, Morris and Price forever. Mary had stepped in as Mother and Grandmother to Lizzie, which cemented the friendship, akin to blood. Later, as Lizzie grew, it was Susan, Matt's mother who she turned to for motherly advice.

Over the years Charlie had learnt many things about the family. As lawyer he was bound by client privilege confidentiality, he was however very worried about recent events. Until Susan had come to the office with the envelope for Daniel, he had genuinely forgotten about the background of the Morris family. He saw them as true blue Americans with nothing to hide, but the fact was, they were hiding many secrets. Just how many was beginning to play on his mind; he had been a party to many deceptions.

Charlie was heading towards Sea View in his trusty BMW, on his way and ordered by Lizzie to check if Dan was okay rattling around in the house all alone. Plus he had compiled a final break down of the companies the Morris family had invested in over the years. It was his indirect way of not looking too clingy or as if he was worrying. Many of these investments took care of themselves and paid the family a healthy return, not that they truly needed any.

Originally the idea was to offer small but considerable funds to start-up companies, to invest in research for untested new technologies, a form of private venture capitalist. However some of the companies had thrived making extremely good returns, others simply ticked over; very few it seems had failed over the years. The point was to provide capital many banks or investors would simply not risk. The list was quite extensive and the technology interesting in its own right. It would be impressive under any portfolio but considering this was from a single private source, made it even more so.

Charlie was lost in thought as he drove; he had managed the portfolio for many years. A couple of the companies had continual investment because they were revolutionary, or something William or James were passionately interested in. After their deaths Charlie and Mike had continued to fund the research in these companies, in their memory. The investment return folder was worth in excess of $68 million, which was extraordinary considering they started it with a paltry fifty thousand dollar injection. He was hoping Dan would continue to do the same, as it was something he found quite exciting and surprisingly enjoyable.

The only problem was a couple of the investments simply never repaid a dime, in fact over the years the family had sunk millions in with no return. William was an optimist and wholeheartedly believed revolutionary technology needed many years of development, if not decades, to perfect it and many private investors did not allow this timescale without a significant return. One company in particular had swallowed millions and after compiling the profit and loss sheets stretching back several years, it seemed financially this one was a white elephant.

As Charlie spun the car in to the driveway, out of the corner of his eye he thought he saw the front door of the house closing. Killing the engine and jumping out, he opened the back door grabbing the envelope containing the freshly printed portfolio and slammed it shut. After all these years the BMW still sounded like new, the build quality was far superior to the last car he had. He always laughed at how William loved American cars and Charlie had fallen for the elegance and refined design of a European car.

Walking across the gravel Charlie bounded up the steps and tried opening the front door. The door handle resisted the turn, expecting it to be open as the house always was, it came as a shock when it stayed firmly shut. It seemed alien and somewhat distressing the Morris family home was now sombrely closed.

Charlie could vaguely see through the pearl window on the front door, which obscured the hallway in an opaque crystalline stretched effect. He pulled the old antique bell, the kind you would see on the outside of a stately home. He could hear the muffled butler bell announcing a visitor; he waited. Through the glass, he could see no movement and no one approached the door. "Oh well." He mused out loud, lifting the letter box he pushed the portfolio through, hearing the thud as it hit the wooden floor on the other side.

Charlie turned to leave, it was such a beautiful day, he did not fancy going back to the office just yet and headed to the side of the house. The porch stretched round the exterior of the house onto an ornate veranda looking out towards the sea. Under the kitchen window was a set of wicker furniture, Charlie sat down. As hand woven furniture, the seats were extremely comfortable. It had been several years since the last time he had sat in this chair but it felt like it was yesterday.

James and Charlie used to drink on the veranda into the early evening; both enjoyed good conversation, a whiskey or two and the occasional stogie. It was interesting as they had gotten older, the pair of them never felt the need to talk, just sit together and enjoy the silence, fine whiskey and the plume of hazy blue cigar smoke around their heads. It was like an old contented marriage.

However one of their last times together was on his mind. James had been a little melancholy but something he said always stuck in Charlie's mind. *'Promise me, whatever happens, you'll look after everyone for me.'*

It was a line that haunted him; it was as though he had foresight of the impending accident. Charlie felt powerless over the events of what had happened to Mike and Susan, a guilt gnawed away at him. It felt like a broken promise by letting something so truly horrific happen to them.

Now all he could do was make sure Dan was okay but even then he felt pretty powerless. Since his grandparents' death, Dan had distanced himself from the remaining family, he would, whether he realised or not, always be like a son to him.

The steps on to the veranda creaked. Charlie had been lost in thought and was startled; he turned to see Dan stood on the veranda covered head to toe in green algae.

"You look like you've just crawled through a sewer?" He gave the look of a disapproving parent.

Dan did not want to explain about the lab, not just yet, thinking fast. "I was down in the boat house; I was going to take one of the boats out and was checking the diesel tanks."

"I take it they're a little green then?" Pointing to the green knees of Dan's jeans.

"Yep, it's a little bit stagnant down there but neither of the boats are in the boat house, or moored out on the buoys. I was at the station earlier this morning and Joel never mentioned having the cruiser or speed boat down at the marina."

"Maybe your Aunt Susan managed to finally convince Mike to get rid of the cruiser? I think he sold the speed boat after you guys blew up the engine out at the lake water skiing, but she never mentioned the cruiser was gone. Without you lot around to take them out, I guess it was a bit stupid to keep them. She never did like the sea though your Aunt, I can only remember a very few occasions when she ventured out, actually maybe only once."

This was true but considering the diesel bill Dan had seen this morning, it seemed odd to him that both of the boats were gone. Like many things he had forgotten about destroying the engine on the speedboat.

"Anyway what are you doing here?"

"I just compiled a list of the companies the family have invested in; it didn't take much. I thought you might like to see and wondered whether you wanted to continue the portfolio along the same lines? I posted the document through the letter box as you had locked the front door. I was truly not expecting the old house to be locked, odd really ..." Charlie's voice trailed off, lost in thought again.

Dan suddenly realised the house was locked. He had left all the keys inside and the only way in was back through the service tunnel and through the lab. He started to panic; there were too many secrets right now for Charlie to see, time for him to go.

"I'll take you through it, if you like; there's one company I'd like to show you."

Without thinking or waiting to be asked Charlie got up and headed for the back door. Pulling his keys from his pocket, he inserted one in the back door and unlocked it. "Your Aunt Susan gave me a key just in case there was ever a problem and she locked herself out. I think Lizzie has a set too." Dan looked a little dumb founded but could only follow in a slight panic.

21

Remaining pressed against the wall by the front door, listening intently for any external sounds, the blood in his ears seemed deafening as he strained for an indication of the direction Charlie had taken. Charlie had disappeared from view and his footsteps had faded round the back of the house. He could be anywhere on the grounds, around the extensive garden or down on the sea front.

Either way, his position could be compromised. If Morris headed out of the Panic Room, he needed to form an escape plan if needed, or find somewhere to hide until the coast was clear.

The hallway silence was broken as a clock quietly chimed the quarter hour from the study. It was the second chime since he had entered the house, far too long. Morris could head back at any minute. He had been making some very stupid mistakes. Why was he rushing everything, making rookie mistakes? He was better than this.

From his present position he could not be seen, but neither could he see anyone approaching. After what seemed like an eternity had passed, he leant forward checking the front door, there was no one at the front of the house. The study was quiet; the Panic Room door was still ajar, *'take your time Morris, take your time'*. He headed for the kitchen, elegance in his stride and an arrogant confidence. "Steady", he said quietly to himself.

Maybe he had gotten complacent, too many jobs without consequence, was this his penance for what he considered perfection? He was getting above himself and life was bringing him back down. The gun in his hand gave him the feeling of a godlike power and he relished the respect it gave him. Maybe that was his problem?

The kitchen was contemporary in comparison to the rest of the house, it was fresh and new. He crouched low, just in case anyone was looking in through the kitchen window, his back resting against a stainless steel dishwasher. The appliances looked like they were hardly used, or maybe immaculately maintained, a lot like the whole house. In front of him the security monitor was polling through the cameras, he could see they were working again.

Morris must have found the signal jammers he placed on the camera bases. The camera paused for several seconds on the front door, the image changed to the view of the back door and veranda.

Charlie Price was slouched in one of the chairs; it looked like he had his eyes closed. The image disappeared glowing white and warping sideways as it changed, re-materialising and fading to the front gate. Keeping low, he crossed the kitchen, pressing the buttons on the base station till the image of the veranda remained static on the monitor. Charlie sat up in his chair continuing to talk to himself.

He strained to hear through the walls at what he was talking to himself about. He could hear the low mumbling, but not enough to pick out coherent words. How many people, in their solitary moment and believed seclusion of their home or work, had he seen talk to themselves out loud? It was a consistent trait he had witnessed throughout his career in surveillance. However the mumbling remained constant, Charlie's mouth was closed and the conversation continued. 'Shit' was there someone else was out there?

. Starting to panic again; was this a trap? Had he been too quick to rush into the house? Had he been set up? Spinning wildly in the kitchen he looked for any signs of the internal cameras. Had he rushed in too soon? Was Daniel recording again? With his new found impatience, he had forgotten his training; his face would clearly be visible from any angle.

Jerked back to reality while admonishing himself, a key rattled inside the lock of the back door, they were coming in. He was totally exposed but definitely could not be seen.

Adrenalin surged through his body, propelling unresponsive limbs forward launching himself from the cover of the dishwasher, he ran back into the hallway. The back door swung open, he just disappeared from view as Charlie entered, followed by Daniel. He sprinted wildly down the hallway. There would never be enough time to unlock the door and retreat. Slipping on the hall rug and careering, uncontrolled with more luck than judgement, he raced into the study. Without any thought or plan he plunged through the bookcase and half fell into the Panic Room. A dead end, he was caged like an animal.

Charlie strolled into the hallway from the kitchen, absently stopping to kick the edge of the upturned rug back into place with his foot. Walking to the front door, he picked up the envelope turning to follow as Dan passed him quickly in the hallway slipping into the study rushing to the open Panic Room. The room was still as he had left it only a few minutes earlier.

Dan turned the key behind the monitor; the sliding door silently returned on its rail closing the stairwell from view. If Dan had been more observant and not concentrating on his own illicit actions, he would have seen his Aunt and Uncle's killer quietly disappearing into the gloom, backing down the stairs, gun drawn, aimed directly at the back of Dan's head.

He removed the USB key and the wall silently slid back on its runner gently secured by the electro magnet. He folded the monitor back into position just as Charlie appeared at his shoulder.

"Nice." Charlie looked stunned as he surveyed the small Panic Room. "This is some set up, I certainly never expected this."

22

Charlie had a sick look across his face. Perched on the couch at the back of the Panic Room; his usual rosy cheeks had drained to match his grey flannel suit. His eyes rolled back in their sockets with the disoriented look of someone just about to pass out, throw up, or both in unison.

Dan had just shown him the footage to the brutal killings of Uncle Mike and Aunt Susan on the internal recordings. Regaining his sense of self composure, breathing deep, Charlie tried to regain an exterior calm.

"We need to show the footage to the Sheriff, he needs to see this. Its evidence, not that it explains much or that you can see who the guy is."

"I know but there is more at stake here, they died protecting …" Dan's voice trailed off. "… I don't know what yet but Aunt Susan's DVD envelope has all, or at least part of the answer."

"You can't withhold this Dan, it's a murder investigation. You need to disclose this now and the sooner the better." Charlie unsteadily rose to his feet, clutching the wall for support. "I need a drink and I don't think caffeine is quite going to hit the spot."

Charlie headed from the confines of the Panic Room to the drinks cabinet opposite the bookcase. He took a bottle of scotch, pouring himself a large shot. Tipping the tumbler to his mouth he downed the contents in two gulps and filled the glass a second time almost to the brim. As he raised it, it visibly shook in his hand. Dan hovered in the Panic Room doorway watching how unnerved Charlie had become by the imagery.

Charlie, with a little Dutch courage inside, turned to face Dan. "Look, I don't know what you think you're protecting. I understand you only got your keys earlier but putting my lawyer head on, just for a minute, says to me you've also been withholding evidence. You knew the house was rigged with internal cameras. Why didn't you tell the Sheriff's office this vital piece of information straight away?"

Dan could see from the outside withholding evidence looked bad. He sighed and crossed to the desk, removing the tube still hanging around his back. Dan slid out the engineering drawings. Rolling them out across the desktop, he placed various stationary instruments from the desktop at the corners to stop them from curling back up.

On the desk, discarded earlier, was the folded architectural drawing of the house from Aunt Susan. Charlie recognised the sheet as Dan unfolded it and spread it over the rest of the drawings.

"It's obvious what these are of. It's the overall plan of the house, displaying the basic outline of the house. What you pointed out this morning is the inner hidden Panic Room." Dan motioned in the direction of the bookcase. Charlie took another hefty swig from his glass, nodding and stepping closer taking a second look at the plan with refreshed and open eyes. He was still in shock from what he had just witnessed, the whiskey calming his nerves only slightly.

Dan removed the folded sheet that Aunt Susan had given to Charlie, revealing the second drawing in the sequence; a plan of the grounds. Charlie studied it for a moment getting his bearings and nodding, recognising the aerial view. The rear of the house faced south towards the ocean, the boat house was along the sea edge and the outside external lab was away to the south east of the house, hidden from view by the orchard. It was pretty self explanatory, Charlie shrugged at Dan.

Dan removed the second sheet to reveal the third plan. This one was familiar like the second but had more and yet distinctly different detail. Charlie leaned closer to understand what he was looking at, placing his tumbler on the desk. What he saw on this plan did not make sense. On this sheet, the perimeter of the house was marked in a dotted line.

However there was a bold line outlining another floor, which had approximately half the floor coverage as the house footprint, with what could only be described as a small corridor connecting to the boat house.

Charlie looked up at Dan. "I don't understand what this is. What is it? A proposed extension to the house?"

"No, not a proposal Charlie. It exists!" Dan tried to humour Charlie a little, waiting for this to sink in.

"What exists? This outbuilding exists?" As Charlie spoke he traced the outline of the new building and then followed the service tunnel down to the boat house.

"Yes it exists, you're standing above it"

"You mean the garage?"

"No, if you think about it, the garage sits at the front of the house; this is beneath the rear and stretches beyond towards the boat house underground."

Charlie was having trouble grasping the concept. "What, like an underground bunker?"

"Kind of but it's not a bunker. It's an underground lab."

Charlie was not fully sure whether Dan was being serious but could tell from his face he was at least telling some kind of truth. Charlie grabbed the tumbler and took another large gulp of whiskey. Dan removed sheet three to reveal a side elevation of the mammoth excavation project that housed the lab. The ground level could be clearly seen, from which protruded the two normal levels of the house.

The basement below ground level was the garage, which Charlie was more than familiar with. However what was intriguing was the structure beneath the house, much deeper than the basement, connected via a vertical shaft, the stairwell hidden by the Panic Room.

The ground level fell away from the main level of the house down to the boat house, which in turn was connected to the lab via a corridor running perfectly horizontal to the excavated base of the boat house. As Charlie lifted the sheet, he could see the final plan of the lab with all its technical details and depths, and although he did not fully understand, the design structure and detail was impressive.

"So let me get this straight ... you're saying this lab exists several stories below ground, where we're stood right now?" Dan nodded in agreement. "You're joking, right?"

Dan could see how sceptical Charlie was. It seemed farfetched even to him and less than 15 minutes ago he had crawled on his hands and knees through the service tunnel. Dan motioned for Charlie to follow him. They went back into the Panic Room; Dan folded the left monitor towards him reinserting the USB key.

The sidewall slid away in its runner for a second time. Charlie's mouth dropped open; instinctively the glass filled the void as he drained the last of the whiskey. He stared in to the gloom at the stairwell heading into the depths. Turning around he headed back to the drinks cabinet reaching for the whiskey bottle again, filling and emptying the glass for a third time.

"I just retrieved these plans from a set of drawers down in the lab; I knew they were down there when I saw the first sheet at your office. There were also these plans in the cabinet."

Dan placed several large transparent sheets on the table, flicking through them, none of them having any particular coherence to anything. "I know Matt's firm's logo." He pointed to the logo on the transparencies. "I can understand why these plans would be down there, although as of yet, not what they are but have you ever heard of a Marion Hyper Sub?" He removed the transparencies uncovering the plans of the Hyper Sub.

Charles looked at Dan with a look of bewilderment. "Did you say Marion?"

"Yeah, it says Marion Hyper Sub, look; it's watermarked on every inch of the drawings. Although you'd call them blueprints really, I've never seen anything so detailed."

Charlie was no longer listening; he was ripping open the envelope he had carefully prepared for Dan. He pulled out the contents, spilling the A4 sheets on top of the plans. Shuffling them round, he located the final page summary he wanted to show Dan, the whole point of the drive visit.

"Listen, the reason I came over was to give you a breakdown of the businesses and companies the family had invested in, their profits, returns, losses etcetera. There was one company that was a pet project of your Grandfather's for many years."

Charlie thrust the paper into Dan's hands and pointed at the figures. Dan read through the names suddenly realising why Charlie was so excited. Next to several payments made over many years, one little over two months ago for a considerable sum, was the company Marion Reynolds.

"Marion Reynolds." Dan repeated looking at Charlie in bewilderment. "I need to go see this company and talk to the owner. He might be able to shed some light. Aunt Susan has directed me to these plans for a reason, I need to know why." Dan was looking at the business breakdown Charlie had given him. "Matt's old engineering firm is also on here, why is that?"

"What do you mean?" Charlie took the sheet back and looked; it was true there had been investment in the firm several years ago.

"Why would there have been investment in Matt's firm. They were not what you would have called, 'innovators in technology'." Dan almost laughed at the thought.

"I don't remember the details of all the transactions, there have been so many over the years. You're right though it does seem odd, especially when Matt would have been funding the company privately,

I'd certainly have assumed so anyway"

"I'm gonna go and see Marion tomorrow, is this the correct address for the company?" Dan pointed at the address on the sheet. Charlie pointed to the blueprint.

"Looks like it." Charlie looked uncomfortable. "Dan, we really need to get the Sheriff out to view the CCTV footage?"

Dan had been waiting for this inevitable statement. "We can't, not yet."

"Why not?"

Dan felt uneasy about answering the next obvious question. "Well, they are going to want to know why the family has such elaborate hidden security measures for starters and then they'll want to know why there is an underground lab. Those are just two questions that instantly come to mind and right now I don't have an answer for them. Not one that makes any sense, not even to me."

Dan needed to deflect the latter question; what is the lab for? "As my lawyer, you tell me; I have primarily withheld evidence from the police because until today I did not have access to the Panic Room. How would you play it?"

Charlie looked concerned scratching his chin, contemplating the predicament, he could see the problem. "Another 24 hours is not going to make a difference. The Sheriff is still convinced it's a burglary gone wrong. However I suggest you hand the hard drives to me and I'll lock them away for protection. If at the end of tomorrow we've not found anything else, we'll hand the drives to the Sheriff for full disclosure. I can do that within the law before obstruction of justice comes into play, plus I can say I instructed you to do so."

"Okay, that seems sensible."

Both Dan and Charlie seemed to deflate simultaneously with the weight of what was bearing down on them. They both knew many family secrets were hanging in the balance and Charlie knew a few that Dan still did not.

"We need to sit down tomorrow and work out how to fully approach the situation after you've been to this company, Marion Reynolds. It's going to get complicated, especially with the disclosure of the lab. I can't see how we can hide it." Charlie sighed. "Dan, you do realise your Grandfather was effectively on the run from the British government. He came to Santa Rosa to drop off the grid and I helped him do that. I knowingly helped him create a life here in the United States, even though there is no paper trail. It wouldn't take a genius to trace your family roots back to Britain and when they do, who knows what'll happen. I'll tell you one thing though, it'll definitely get a hell of a lot more complicated."

John McAdams

Political targets were notoriously difficult to silence due to allies asking too many questions, or having direct links with powerful friends who could easily undermine or halt a mission.

The Minister embroiled in the latest scandal had recently upset too many in his quest for open dialogue with the Prime Minister over certain underground military funding. Somehow information had come into his possession which could be highly damaging to the country, especially when viewed within the political landscape, or by the rest of the world. Great Britain stood on a knife edge of acceptability within the European community, the information would be extremely damaging.

McAdams had been studying the Minister for several weeks, plotting his movements and social calendar. Making the usual background checks on everyone he had contact with, including his business acquaintances, neighbours, friends and even his family.

Deleting a high profile MP was not without risk, certain political manoeuvring and high risk strategies could see the highly sensitive information they were trying to halt released without warning within the public domain, which could damage more than just a career.

MP Edward Stephens annoyingly was not a creature of habit and he was, unfortunately, as far as politicians go, whiter than white. The material in his possession had been given to him in good faith, it was a political hot potato, a case of he without sin cast the first stone. Unfortunately for those protecting the Prime Minister, the information had finally fallen into the hands of someone who was without sin and Edward Stephens was looking to use it to correct a wrong.

Usually some other form of persuasion could be found to deter a Minister from going public, however Stephens was intelligent enough to realise the information would not benefit the country by entering the public domain. Therefore he was making noises and rattling the top brass. It was how far up the chain of command the filth rose before action was taken, obviously it had gone far enough for him to be given this assignment.

He found a copy of the data in Stephen's personal safe and another in his office safe, which was the first part of his mission. However he did not know how many other copies had been made and whether the confidential data would be redistributed, or worse, released if anything happened to him.

John McAdams decided a simple elimination was not the correct procedure for this mission. The chain had to stop; threats would not deter, only strengthen this crusader's resolve.

His attention had shifted from the main target. McAdams had been watching the Minister's daughter for several weeks. She lived a rather secluded life, far removed and away from her father's public figure, mainly due to her sexuality. He had subtly pressured Stephens, suggesting the information about his daughter would be made public.

Instead of taking the news quietly and ducking for cover, he held a press conference with his daughter's blessing. Announcing to the world she was in fact gay and due to some unscrupulous political posturing about important security information in his possession, his private life and that of his daughter were being threatened with disclosure.

It was a calculated risk, unfortunately one in which Stephens was reaping huge political reward because it strengthened his case and his public profile. If anything happened to him now, serious questions would be asked, the public demanding full disclosure of the information in his possession and why he was being targeted.

McAdams' superiors were extremely unhappy with the recent outcome. His assignments always went according to plan and so they never interfered, the extra pressure had made him careless and sloppy. He had not expected this turn of events and was angry with himself. Up until now, his record had been immaculate.

The room was like any other interrogation room he had ever been in, windowless, uncomfortably warm and slightly claustrophobic. All designed to give a feeling of unnerve, strangely this comforted him. This was his territory, he completely understood the game. His refusal to speak to anyone but Daniel Morris would also unnerve the arresting officers. He knew there would be total confusion outside this room. No one would know what to do with him and no one would take responsibility, not yet anyway.

He had already made his phone call, direct contact putting the wheels in motion for his immediate release. The call was untraceable; it simply flagged his capture, enabling the right departments to get everything in order, contacting the relevant people. At the very latest he would walk from here in 24 hours and promptly disappear, maybe for a little play time.

At worst he would be suspended from duty for six months while they cleared up the mess and allowed the dust to settle, then he would return back to work, back to another job no one else had the balls to deal with.

Looking into the mirrored glass, he surveyed his reflection. He was looking slightly peaky, maybe it was time for a jaunt to the Caribbean, Puerto Rico would be nice and quiet this time of year. He ran his hand through his thinning blond hair and nonchalantly placed the tip of his manicured fingernail against the reflective surface. There was no gap between his fingernail and the reflected image, he smiled knowingly and returned back to his seat.

Behind the glass, Dan's boss was staring through the two way mirror at the suspect in his interview room.

"What the fuck is he smiling about? You caught him bent over the lifeless body of Miss Stephens who had already been the direct target of some political foul play. He's got fuck all to smile about. We got him bang to fuckin' rights, especially with the hypodermic in his hand."

Andrew Harnell had been a hard copper in his time. He had survived the many political correctness overhauls within the Yard as more paper work took over. He was just slightly obsolete in his attitude and antiquated morals. However his instinct and bravery kept him at the Yard. If he had had more subtlety with his approach and more respect for authority, he probably would have gone further but the job was everything, being a yes man was not, his position suited him. Those who worked beneath him were loyal and most of all they asked to work with him, that kind of respect was rare within the Yard.

Daniel Morris on the other hand was an outsider, an American. He was here because of the tenacity within his department and his data analysis skills. He followed protocol and the correct procedural way of doing things, to the letter.

To Andrew, Daniel made things complicated because he was quiet and unassuming without gut instincts. He methodically joined the dots in the background, which was why he was excellent at his job, admittedly, bloody good. Andrew though found him hard work.

Daniel was an oddball, he had never covertly been on the streets, he had graduated directly into Special Operations because of his skills and he worked exclusively within the NIS or National Identification Service. If the Yard had trouble tracking someone down, Daniel had a way of finding them. He could cross reference data streams like no other within Special Operations and see patterns within, most simply would not.

However that was the trouble, no matter how much the other guys tried, Daniel never really fitted into the team. He was a loner, a fitness fanatic, he did not drink or smoke and he never really gelled with the lads. Plus a lot of the sarcastic banter and in-joking seemed to pass him by, possibly because of his American background.

He had never been on the frontline forging those irrepressible bonds between colleagues. Only real work could do that and he did not interact with the guys outside of work and on the streets that sometimes got men killed. Andrew liked and respected Daniel but he never really warmed to him.

Of course, these faults aside, he had discovered and apprehended the man sat before them in the interrogation room. Taken him down single handed and calling for back up, that deserved huge respect and Daniel was maybe more than just the paper pusher Harnell loathed with such passion.

This man in front of them was obviously dangerous but what worried him most was when he asked for Daniel Morris by name, this led to trouble internally and someone always fell foul to the system, usually taking a fall.

"I don't like it. I don't want you goin' in there alone, the situation stinks." Andrew spun on the spot whirling like a top, his arms raised to the heavens energised by rage and small significant details that shat on protocol from a great height. He ranted at no one in particular. "How the fuck do you remove your fingerprints without scarring?"

Dan faced Harnell calmly, his back to McAdams through the two way mirror.

"Well basically it's done over months. You simply use an abrasive surface, a pumice stone might do it, and over the course of days, maybe even weeks, it will sand your prints clean away without bleeding or pain, leaving your fingertips as smooth as glass, but like a haircut, it's not permanent. The methodology is much better than mutilating yourself, plus if you ever need to integrate back into society they will eventually grow back."

"So you're saying he did that to himself?"

Dan turned back to look through the glass. "Yep. He's a spook, working for God knows who. Maybe we need to get the MP in here to see if he recognises him as the one who intimidated him?"

Harnell was out of his league for the first time in nearly thirty years and was mildly annoyed by the feeling. "So why does he want to talk to you? No offense Morris but you're a white-collar worker, you're a paper pushing nobody! No offense son."

"None taken! Look the guy's a pro. He just checked the bloody mirror with his nail to see if he's being watched. He would have done his homework. If this was a hit, he will have watched me because I was her neighbour. He'll know I work for Scotland Yard and he'll be using that to bide his time. We know little or nothing about him. Maybe he'll be more open to talk to me, who knows? If he gets released though he'll disappear without trace and we'll have nothing, except having to somehow explain to a wealthy and prominent MP that the man who killed his daughter escaped unpunished. We'll look like idiots and the press will have a field day."

Morris was annoyingly right on all fronts. They had nothing except the bastard in the room. They had already taken a call from someone high up the chain of command who knew this man was detained but how did they know? A leak within the department? That pissed him off more than the smug cunt through the glass; heads would roll if he found out whom.

"Okay, I'll let you go in but if I feel the man is making a cunt of us, I'll pull you out. You got that?" Dan nodded. "We'll be watching and we'll record everything that goes on. We only have a few hours before we have to charge him with something and to be blunt, it'll be his word against yours in court because there are no fingerprints, no forced entry and no CCTV footage. Frankly I don't fancy the chances of even getting the bastard to court."

John McAdams' Interview

Dan had been seated for little over two minutes since he entered the interrogation room. He did not look directly at the man seated in front of him, instead keeping his head bowed. He could see the man was not intimidated in the slightest by his presence. Dan watched him carefully, trying to look uninterested as he perused through the paperwork in front of him which had nothing of note to say, as they knew very little.

The man's head moved from side to side, cocked on a jaunty angle, the way a chicken looks at you through its beady little black eyes weighing you up. They were the only real point of interest on his otherwise bland instantly forgettable face.

His pallid features all blended together. He was someone you would pass in the street without so much as a glance, blending to any background and disappearing without trace. His eyes seemed lifeless, yet they stared right through you, boring into your soul. This anonymity made it hard to judge his age. He could pass for a man in his early thirties but his thinning hair and lines round his empty eyes suggested he was older.

Dan finally closed the paper work, looking up to stare back at the black eyes before him, empty but with a certain amusement in them. This was just a game. Dan placed both forearms on the table, clasping his hands together on the paperwork and leant forward.

McAdams did exactly the same, mocking his movement. He was trying to intimidate him. Strangely Dan felt very calm under the circumstances, considering this was the first interview he had ever personally taken. He cleared his throat to begin, sipping from a polystyrene cup containing a cold black liquid which resembled the look of coffee but was more chemical than caffeine.

"I think it would help both me and our investigation if you would cooperate and tell us who you are, or at least who you work for?"

McAdams casually leant back in his chair, the palms of his hands face down, squealing as he dragged them backwards, working against the friction of the laminated surface. He never blinked, never did his eyes avert from staring deep into Daniel's.

In the apartment they had fought savagely, the man reacted like a cornered animal leaping at him with such ferocity upon his discovery. It was only Dan's physical strength and basic pure luck that over powered him, plus an offhand backwards swat from his laptop across the side of the head, flooring him.

Dan's mind wandered back to the limp lifeless body of Sophie sprawled across the floor, totally naked as he found her. She was beautiful, hauntingly so, even in death. He discovered this man sitting directly opposite, crouched over her with a small insulin syringe in his hand, as if leering over her young tender body. He knew he had to stay objective but inside he seethed with anger towards him, dealing with death was never Dan's strong point.

Sophie had become a very good friend, one of only a handful he could count on since he came to London. They often walked the short distance from their apartment block to the gym and went to the movies together at the weekends when they had nothing better to do. Although his initial intentions were not so chivalrous, he had noticed her one morning during the early birds swim dressed in a miniscule bikini, embarrassing himself by asking her out.

They went on what could be considered a single date where she confessed she was gay. He always believed she had weighed him up before confessing her secret, wanting to know whether he was worthy of her friendship. If he was not, she would never have confessed her secret and they would never have gone out again, friends or otherwise.

He would have been none the wiser but instead they became close. She reminded him a lot of Lizzie. He was convinced it was due to her similar tom-boyish nature, fabulous physique and obsession with the gym. The memory stirred absolute loathing. His friend had been murdered and this bastard was completely nonchalant about the whole affair. An innocent life was lost and he was oblivious to the pain anyone was or would be feeling.

He knew rational or conventional conversation with this man was going to be fruitless. He would be trained to be evasive or simply not speak at all. Dan surprised even himself by what he suddenly attempted. Totally out of character and also very much against interview protocol, he grabbed McAdams by both wrists.

This was completely unexpected, he tried to pull away, the amusement in his eyes turning to rage at being touched. He had already discovered how much stronger Dan was than himself during their tussle in the tiny apartment. Dan pressed his thumbs into tiny pressure points on the inside of the wrists pushing a number of nerve endings, just above where you would wear a watch strap.

The manoeuvre was not painful but gave enough leverage to move an opponent's wrists into a locking position if needed. However this was not Dan's motive but it did throw his slick demeanour off, which was his intention.

He twisted McAdams' wrists against his will, for a moment he could see anger in the seething black eyes. His palms faced upwards and Dan looked at the fingertips as if what he had casually done was by invitation, like a palm reader and then looking directly into his eyes, this time also forcing himself not to blink holding the man's stare.

"Nice work! I was just discussing with a colleague, hypothetically, how long it would take to reduce your fingerprints to nothing more than flat stumps. What have you used, a pumice stone? How long would it take? Days, possibly weeks, but ultimately the question on my mind, is how long would we have to keep you locked away before your fingerprints grew back and we'd be able to find out who you really are."

McAdams wrenched his hands away from Dan slamming them face down back on the table leaning menacingly towards Daniel. A malicious grin spreading across his face. Lines formed around his black eyes, which remained unblinkingly fixed.

"The thing is Daniel Morris, who I am really is inconsequential and worrying about my true identity is quite futile as I'm a nobody. Ultimately I believe you should be worrying about who you really are." Small droplets of saliva exploded through his mouth as he spoke, splattering Dan's face. McAdams continued through gritted teeth and with convicted venom, but his initial outburst came under control dropping back into a far more jovial patter.

"It should be somewhat ironic that through no fault of their own Miss Stephens randomly had the cause of her own death chosen in effect by a stranger and who happens to be living next door? Her gym buddy." He paused for a reaction from Dan but there was none. Dan was a little lost as to the direction he was heading.

"Tell me Daniel, have you ever questioned your family about the cause of your Mother's death?"

Dan was winded by the mention of his mother. How could this man possibly know anything about the death of his mother?

He spluttered. "I can't see how the death of my mother has any bearing on the killing of Soph ... err, Miss Stephens."

"Daniel ... Daniel." He shook his head. "So naïve! Your background file was what gave me the initial idea and subtle means I was looking for to erase Miss Stephens. Your family is rather well documented over the years. Of course, the drug is a little outdated in truth, far more traceable these days but it was a very popular method around the time your mother was killed."

Dan sat in silence, hoping his face would not belie the shock he was feeling inside. He was trying to understand what had been said. The words floated in his brain, his mother had been killed?

He was eight when his mother died. He was the one to find her lifeless body in their apartment on his return home from school. She should have been at work and did not usually return until at least five but on that day he found her naked body on the living room floor.

At the time he was too young to understand the implications. His whole world imploded as he was forced to leave his Washington apartment, his friends and went to live with his Grandparents. Many questions he had growing up were met with thoughtful reassurance that it was just an accident. He never questioned anything they told him, he never felt the need. However the whole family were very careful never to discuss his mother around him; that he knew for certain and now his world was crashing down round his ears, again. A total stranger had just told him his mother had been murdered.

Dan pushed it to the back of his mind. The man was trying to get a rise, he was baiting a hook, making connections was easy, he did it every day. Anyone could have researched his background and discover what happened to his mother, twisting the information to fit any fictional story they deemed fit. However Dan felt a certain disadvantage, he never worked blind, he always garnered all the information before cross checking and verifying. This guy was off the grid and therefore he certainly had the upper hand, especially with alleged data which was unverifiable.

McAdams looked smug, he had thrown him a curve ball and of course the kid never knew his mother had been killed. No one did. Only his Grandfather was informed, it was the only way of controlling the Morris family, which it had done very well for many years.

Dan was running through the last few moments in his mind, his emotions needed to be kept in check, deciding to ring fence the information about his mother. Without any form of confirmation it was purely speculation and circumstantial, he would deal with it later. Dan may have never interviewed anyone but he knew how to sift through the bullshit, only utilising relevant facts from the many transcripts he had read of interrogations over the years. He straightened in his chair, his composure restored.

"So you've researched me? I feel somewhat at a disadvantage and also kind of privileged. I know absolutely nothing about you. You've done your homework, but then I suppose it's the least you do before murdering someone. You never know what threats exist, do you? Research their background, including everyone in contact, such as everyone in our small building. It's not difficult to do is it? It's what I do every day. It's my job, using intelligence to piece together disparate facts. Often simply overlooked or mismatched. A person's identity and background is quite easy to assimilate with access to the correct information, or lack of it!"

"You are quite correct in your assumption! It is very easy when you have the correct information available to you, as you know. Your lack of history was the interesting part though, which made me delve deeper. Easy if you have security clearance as high as mine, your family history is quite unique; reaching back several generations. It certainly makes for excellent bedtime reading."

Dan shifted uncomfortably, he never expected this. He knew he needed to understand where this man was heading. His own background seemed irrelevant to the investigation but why would his family history have such a high security clearance level? That puzzled him. He had looked up his own file out of curiosity when he first joined his department, kind of like looking up your own name on Google, but there were only bullet points of interest. He had always assumed it was because he was of American birth and there was little known.

"Okay, I'll bite and pander a little, purely from a professional interest you understand. I'm intrigued to know what data you could possibly have available which I don't, especially with my own high level of clearance. What information are you privy to which you believe gives an insight into some deeper conspiracy concerning my mother? More importantly, what relevance is it here, right now?"

McAdams smiled feeling at home, this was going to be fun. His confidence exuded and his charisma shot up a level. Dan was sure women would find this confidence erotic and quite charming; he found it somewhat disturbing wanting to hit the guy again, although his laptop lay in several shattered pieces from the first attempt. His fists would have to do this time, smash his smug expression to the other side of his face.

"Yours is an interesting story. If not, rather tragic!" He almost seemed whimsical in his storytelling as he started the preamble of his story.

Dan was repulsed as the man's demeanour changed, a complete reversal from the angry flash just a few moments ago. He was now in control, it was like he was settling in for the night with a good book and a warming cup of hot chocolate.

"Your Grandfather was a rather intelligent man, an understatement I suppose – a modern day genius, a mad man, possibly? Top in his field, probably throughout the world, never surpassed in his field then, or even now. Except maybe by his first son, James, who, I don't know about you but I'd say simply stood on the shoulders of his father?" McAdams looked at Dan for a reaction who chose not to give one, these details were not news to him. He knew the family history but the walls had ears. They were recording the conversation and Dan knew he would also be aware of this.

"Your Grandfather was the linchpin to many highly secret projects conducted for the M.O.D and the British Government. He made some startling discoveries; one in particular was going to change the face of warfare forever, but your Grandfather was a pussy!"

The venom instantly returned to his voice, he sneered at Dan, over articulated the word, practically grinding the word 'pussy' with his teeth.

"He never saw, or even cared it would make Britain great again. He chose a different path, only he knew what and he ran. He disappeared and along with it the greatest mind and possibly one of the greatest discoveries ever." He stopped for effect, he wondered whether he should elaborate further, there was no need really. Only a few more details and this little miscreant's career would be destroyed, his reputation would be in tatters ending his tenure at New Scotland Yard. That would teach the bastard for capturing him.

"Your family disappeared off the face of the Earth. Many thought your Grandfather defected but nothing came of the technology. The scientists he worked closely with couldn't make it work. They didn't understand what he had created and gradually the project was shelved as the only test where it worked was when your Grandfather was in charge and it was never successfully repeated, ever! That was until an academic paper was released many years later following the same experiment, not to the letter but it was similar enough for the establishment to recognise its worth and who was the author. Yep, you guessed it, your Uncle, James Morris."

Dan was listening intently, he knew this story. It was family legend. He had always assumed it was only within the family home that it was known. He suddenly felt like he was indeed listening to a folk tale, one he had heard many times but only a certain portion, bits had been elaborated for effect or missed entirely through its retelling. He needed to redirect the conversation away, at present there was no problem with the story, what his Grandfather and Uncle had done was no threat to him.

"Intellectual property, as far as I'm aware Jon." Dan felt the need to call this man something, to familiarise him, root him. Jon Doe was always used when an identity was unknown in the states. The man however flinched, he seemed unsettled as he called him Jon, it was duly noted.

"I'm sorry but I felt the need to give you a name, to ground your ego slightly. Apologies, so for now, if you don't mind I'll call you Jon Doe. As an American, you may be familiar, it's what we call a suspect whose name we don't know and as we don't know your real name it seems fitting, unless of course you'd like to give it to me now?" Dan looked at him for some kind of answer, none was forthcoming and although he expected none, there was an uncomfortable silence between them before McAdams spoke.

"Yes Jon is fine by me; it's very apt you know."

Dan continued. "Intellectual property, as far as I know, remains with the inventor unless someone else has recreated, or eventually surpassed the work and patented the next logical idea, step or product?"

"This is true, however some ideas are never patented because they are far too valuable a commodity in their own right. Governments move heaven and earth to retain their assets Daniel. The British Government owned your Grandfather's research, it was theirs. However your Grandfather was far too valuable to terminate. He'd already done one moonlight flit taking the research with him and he was affluent enough to do it again. The risk was too great."

Dan slumped in his chair, he could feel the blood draining from his very soul, an uncontrollable anger was rising within and he visibly shook.

McAdams was on a roll. He wondered how many were listening behind the two way mirror, rapt to the story unfolding. Well the finale was coming, hold on to your seats lads, it is a great twist. It was a shame Dan had his back to the mirror, if only they could see the pain on Morris's face, he was ready to explode.

"What nobody expected was the black sheep of the family doing something stupid. The shunned daughter making a play! Yes, Deborah Morris, the single parent. Your mother threw her hat in the ring and made the stupidest of mistakes by making an enemy of the British Government. She played them for fools and betrayed the family's trust by hawking the scientific data and whoring herself to the highest bidder!"

Without warning Dan launched his entire body across the table. His chair shot backwards hitting the mirror behind. As it smashed in to a million pieces, it fell like rainbow confetti to reveal Dan's bewildered colleagues listening through small speakers to the conversation in the interview room. Andrew Harness, mouth open, stood transfixed as he watched the spectacle unfold before him.

Dan lent across the table, his hands tightly gripped around McAdams throat, his continuing forward momentum, tipping his chair backwards. They both uncontrollably slid towards the hard floor as gravity took effect. Dan's grip, tightening around his throat, was unceremoniously dragged along for the ride. Dan's chest rested on McAdams' knees as he flailed helplessly through midair, crashing against the floor and smashing his head.

The impact sent shockwaves through the pair. Dan was slightly winded but managed to claw his way over McAdams' knees and the chair. Dropping his considerable weight on his chest, pinning him to the floor, his knees on either arm, still in his seated position, now horizontal. Dan raised his clenched fist to beat it into the calm smiling face of John McAdams, whose eyes remained unblinking.

The interview room door burst open. Andrew Harness grabbed his balled fist, while two officers pulled him from McAdams, wildly kicking. As he was dragged backwards, Dan managed to plant a well aimed heel into the side of his ribs, a satisfying snap echoed round the room as the attack eased and he was forcibly removed.

McAdams rasped through gritted teeth, clutching his broken ribs. "The bitch was taken out, deleted, terminated. She pissed off the wrong people Daniel. Chances are, when a colleague of mine turns up at your door, you've upset the wrong fuckin' people. She paid the ultimate price, along with your family!"

He bellowed the last four words as Dan was dragged backwards from view into the corridor.

23

On a sliding scale of distance, Marion Reynolds was surprisingly close to home. In terms of American distance, this was a short drive. Dan had taken Aunt Susan's Range Rover; it had taken him just over six hours to reach Kingsley Lake. Driving was something which never fazed him. Living in the UK, travelling highlighted yet another cultural difference between the Americans and the British.

It was interesting how the British truly believed anything above and beyond a thirty minute drive was a long journey. Their idea of driving was not the same as an American. He was never sure whether it was in part due to the extortionate cost of fuel, or because distance was viewed under an entirely different scale. In fact if he had left London and been on the road for the same duration, he would probably have entered an entirely different country; Scotland, his ancestral home.

The UK may have an aversion to driving long distances but they more than made up for it with their infrastructure. Dan still marvelled at the railway network and local buses. The country, nationwide, complained about it but compared to the States it was simply fantastic, maybe a little over priced for the distances covered in his humble opinion. To get anywhere in the States you needed to be mobile and the car was the ultimate expression of freedom, hankered for by every teen across America.

Dan drove with the windows fully open, the warm air filling the car. His car in the UK did not have air conditioning. It had become a habit driving with the windows down. It was only recently aircon had started to come as standard in the lower end market British cars and not as an optional extra.

Many cars had the luxury of a tilt and slide sunroof, which had since become the optional extra, or if you were exceptionally brave, you could choose a convertible. Ironically with Britain having the worst weather in Europe, the ratio of convertibles was inversely proportional to the number of sunny days.

As he drove the familiar route, Dan remembered fondly his very first summer living with his Grandparents. Granddad had driven them all out to Kingsley Lake, one of Florida's premier recreational lakes, famous for its clear waters, water skiing and fishing. That year Granddad drove them all in an old GMC Vandura, towing behind was a rigid inflatable Zodiac bought for fishing which had very little previous use.

Granddad had hoped learning to water ski would give it the use it deserved and also give them the love of the water the rest of the family shared. Fishing had been an unmitigated disaster as they all found it so boring, plus Granddad had not been impressed, much to their amusement, when they had coaxed Bowie to dive off the boat after his rubber ring scuppering any chance of catching an elusive fish for supper, as after that Bowie spent more time in the water than on the boat.

The trip had worked on many levels, they all learnt to ski really well and Granddad was able to fish quietly while the five of them, Matt, Ashley, Lizzie, Bowie and himself went looking for adventure. It was his first family holiday which was why it held such fondness in his heart but it was also the defining moment that cemented their commitment to each other.

Previously as an only child, living alone in Washington and growing up with a single mother, he had never experienced the family camaraderie and bonding on that level. The trip was etched into family folklore, repeated many times over the years as a family and later, alone in their teens.

One of his many memories of the lake was a story his Granddad told while they were sat around the camp fire one evening. According to legend, Captain Kingsley was surrounded by Indians on a trail south of the lake; his only way of escape was to swim his horse across to the west shore. The horse was said to have dropped dead from exhaustion and the lake had been called Kingsley ever since. A great yarn for the camp fire but Dan remembered Lizzie discovering many years later, it was actually alleged the lake was in fact named after a Zephaniah Kingsley, a wealthy slave owner but could not fully remember the sketchy details. He much preferred his Granddad's story, which was far more endearing.

Florida is a massive state, although in comparison to the largest, Alaska; it was a tenth the size, ranking number 22. Many of the Morris family investments were within Florida. Maybe it was only word of mouth which drew people to the family, or maybe it was simply the type of industries and technologies they invested in, breeding a tight knit group, all seemingly topographically drawn to the sunshine state.

Dan had his own theory. It was his families' bizarre excitement and trepidation of the unknown, which he did not share, towards the research and development phase, and ultimate realisation of a new revolutionary product. His family, obsessed with technological break-through allowing smaller independent companies to approach them for funding. Their enthusiasm towards innovative technology and obvious financial gravitas gave them the kudos to help where many private investors would not.

Marion Reynolds, he had since discovered on entering reception, was an entrepreneur with an exciting ideal. One in which, after perusing the walls, Dan could fully understand why his Granddad had invested in the company. The connection was obvious even before he had spoken to or met the owner. He was a visionary and a man after his Granddad's and family's hearts.

The walls were carefully organised with images of detailed design sketches and probable pre cursors to the blueprints Dan had discovered in the lab. From the outside it was an unassuming building giving little away to what secrets lay inside, only the beautifully framed technical imagery hinted at the company ethos.

The receptionist had rung through announcing his arrival. Within seconds of her replacing the phone, the door to the left was flung open with such exuberance; Dan was taken aback and physically jumped. The man entered in high spirits with a smile that exuded confidence but on seeing Dan, it faded with a quizzical look. His step notably faltered with Dan's presence. Dan could see he was not the man he was expecting, so he stuck out his hand to introduce himself.

"Hi, I'm Daniel Morris, nephew to Michael and Susan Morris."

The confident smile returned, thrusting a strong sea farers hand into Dan's, shaking it warmly. "Hello Daniel, Marion Reynolds." Marion replaced the plain baseball cap on his head which was held in his left hand, covering a closely cropped receding hairline. "I was expecting your Uncle for a visit at the end of next week." This statement was more of an uncertain question.

"I know …" Dan lied. "… which is why I'm here." Dan explained to Marion about his Aunt and Uncle's recent funeral, leaving out many of the massive and niggling uncertainties within his story. As far as Marion needed know it was a burglary with tragic consequences. Reynolds listened with a look of sheer horror, the smile disappearing from his bronzed face leaving a subdued, thoughtful yet caring look.

"I'm so sorry for your loss, please accept my condolences. I have known your family for many years on a personal level ... I just can't believe it." Shaking his head. "It's truly shocking. Please come on through." Marion directed Dan through the door; he had only moments before bounded through with countless energy, which had been subdued by the tragic news.

Dan entered a small square windowless office with a table located in the middle and four chairs surrounding a conference telephone situated in the middle. Expecting to take a seat Dan was surprised when Marion opened the through door and indicated to follow.

"As I mentioned to your Uncle last month on the phone, the works would be finished and ready for delivery at the back end of next week." Marion continued to walk on through the main office which was obviously the technical drawing room.

Blueprints and CAD diagrams littered every available work surface. Varying incarnations of cross sections and technical elevations were pinned to every wall, all with the same feint watermarks in the paper, 'Marion Hyper Sub', exactly like the plans taken from the lab.

Marion stood in front of a set of double doors, gripping both handles; he opened them together like the genial game show host revealing the prize, he pushed the doors outwards stepping aside.

24

Dan walked through the double doors into a massive workshop, a warehouse hidden by the relative comfort and normality to the façade contributed by reception. The warehouse had the appearance of an aircraft hangar; motorised winches were suspended in the roof along reinforced steel joists allowing easy movement of heavy or awkward objects.

Hung around the corrugated walls were the remains of a myriad of assumed test panels, mainly made of fibre glass but some were of other plastics such as carbon fibre, judging the composition and finishing. From their arranged nature along the walls, it was more likely a chronological history or timeline of the way the Hyper Sub metamorphosed from concept to product.

Dan remembered seeing a submersible dive on a TV documentary many years ago where they had taken a polystyrene cup attached to the outside to demonstrate the extreme pressure. The cup came back to the surface about one tenth its original size. Some panels had this strange shrivelled look, like the passing of time on a person's face; others were ripped, shredded or torn by unknown forces. Rigorous testing of old and trusted materials, against new unknown had obviously led the development of the project.

A section separated by a wall of benches, overloaded with cabling, complicated electronics and navigational monitors was built along the left hand wall. At the far end adjoining the electronics booth was a large fabrication workshop. All kinds of machinery, of which Dan had never seen before, dedicated to cutting, drilling, joining and welding filled the space, much of which he could only hazard a guess at their individual uses.

Along the right hand side were all manner of key mouldings for different GRP panels. That side of the workshop was obviously dedicated to the laborious task of layering the fibre glass panels and fitting the internal reinforcement structures.

The centre of the warehouse was divided by a set of black railings running across the front of a pit, erected to stop anyone from inadvertently falling in. As Dan approached and put both hands on the rail, he could see down in. The entire warehouse had been built over a dry dock leading out to the lake. The hydraulic doors were closed and the dock was empty, however slightly below eye level because of the removed water, Dan breathed heavily in amazement, glistening and shining in the dock was the unmistakeable vision from the blueprints – the Hyper Sub.

Looking down on the sub, from first glance you would be forgiven for thinking it was a specialist speed boat. The sleek bow had a V shaped hull, the cock pit gave the impression of a fighter pilot's seating position although having a much higher, panoramic and unobstructed view. It continued the full length of the craft, but unlike an aircraft, the cockpit did not taper towards the rear in glass, instead finished in a white tapered cowl.

Through the clear acrylic there were only two seats positioned one behind each other, for the pilot and co-pilot. The back of the cockpit looked empty. Dan remembered in his detailed set of blueprints there were five seats arranged one behind the other, for the addition of more passengers.

Situated at the stern, unlike a traditional aeroplane where the tail would usually have a single vertical stabilizer, the back of the fuselage on the sub had two, placed either side of the passenger cockpit and linked across the top, giving the impression of a spoiler.

Marion stood next to Dan along the rail, a wide grin spread across his face as if admiring an expensive sports car for the very first time. "Come down and take a look." Marion hopped the barrier, followed by Dan, descending iron steps fixed against the wall of the dry dock. As Dan slowly followed he glanced over his shoulder, the structure was resting on a giant cradle suspending the sub above the floor of the dry dock. At the same level as the bow, the view of the structure was startlingly different. The bow was divided into three sections giving the distinct look of a trimaran hull, but the usual individual hulls were integrated giving the front an imposing and unique look.

Marion was on the floor of the dry dock looking up at Dan. "The water line sits slightly lower in Hyper 2 at cruising speed, compared to the original. We haven't had time to adjust the ballast to change the height as of yet. We may be able to before you take delivery next week. We don't envisage it changing the operational capacity at all on the surface. In truth the newer design of the Egress collar, separating the payload area from the cabin, was slightly wider and thus heavier than originally planned."

Dan had touched the floor of the dry dock and from the ground, the engineering enormity of the sub was over-whelming. Dan had only registered a few of the words spoken from Marion, he was having trouble concentrating on what he was saying. His hand gently brushed the keel as he walked, mesmerised, following Marion to the rear. In a trance-like state he only managed to reply parrot fashion. "Egress collar?"

"Yes." Marion continued undeterred. He had witnessed many reactions to the full prototype, mainly men, or kids at heart, in awe.

"The slightly wider payload meant we had to adjust the size of the Egress collar to match." Marion knelt beneath the sub and pointed into the base of the hull. Dan crouched down; the hull towards the back of the craft had two doors which were hanging open. They hung down like bomb bay doors on an aeroplane's fuselage; a pair of legs protruding from the doors stood on a small step ladder. Dan crawled underneath so he could see up into the cockpit of the sub. The man was adjusting a hatch, which Dan assumed was the egress collar, leading into the secondary cabin, totally separated from the front cockpit.

"Dan, this is George, one of my talented engineers." They shook hands, George jumped down for Dan to get a closer look. "The egress collar is the secondary chamber, which is completely air and water tight. Once the hull doors are open, it allows access to enter or exit the sub. Originally the cabin was designed as a diving bell so didn't necessarily need the width of access; it's been adjusted for your proposed payload to be carried."

Dan climbed up the small step ladder and could see into the cabin through an acrylic separating panel. The cockpit's instrumentation panel was adorned with a wide array of gauges, a steering wheel and throttles along with what looked like GPS monitors, radar and countless other instruments Dan did not recognise. The position gave a great view to drive the sub. Was 'drive' the correct term, navigate maybe?

Marion continued to list the improvements to the hull and running gear to incorporate the extra sizing on the egress collar. Dan was taken aback by the size of this machine and the technical details began to wash over him as Marion enthused about the design specification and feature improvements compared to Hyper 1. As Dan descended back down the steps, he was a little surprised by the structure attached to the inside of the cabin above the egress collar. It was a piece of equipment which looked very familiar, the only part of the sub that did!

It was the lowering track used in the hydro pod back at the lab. Dan reached out and touched the tracks, they looked exactly the same but these were perfectly manufactured in stainless steel, fashioned to fit within the egress collar. Marion's head appeared below him looking up, smiling enormously.

"If you're wondering about the tolerance between the uprights, it is exactly as specified in the diagrams your Uncle delivered a couple of months ago."

Dan realising his mouth was open, tried to gain a sense of control. "I am sure it is, like everything, it looks superb." He was a little unsure what else to say but, taking the lead, Marion kindly filled the void with other structural details about the sub and improvements to navigation, plus the addition of auto pilot.

The rest of the tour was far more technical, the size of the new engine comparing power to weight ratio, increasing the speed to the plane to eight seconds and how much further the range would be on the same fuel load, above and below the water.

Marion explained intricate dynamic changes to the hull affecting stability and manoeuvrability. How the navigation system worked, piloting the sub for underwater navigation. Not a single detail was left unanswered which was good because Dan was still in a state of shock from his initial view over the railing down into the dry dock. He simply could not think of any questions to ask.

As a child he dreamed of a vehicle that would allow him to effectively explore underwater, like the movies and here it was, in actual reality. Plus, he owned it.

25

Marion retreated back to the design office where they had initially entered. Stacked up against the wall, either side of the double doors, were acrylic sheets about an inch thick. Dan stopped, they looked familiar. He had not spotted them on the way into the workshop. Each sheet was approximately three metres in length and recessed along one edge, forming a clear tongue and groove slot. Inserted into each channel was a small beading of rubber, acting like a rubber seal. Dan ran his finger down the edge of the rubber seal; it was primarily the same design as the water proof doors in the lab's hydro pod at home.

Marion poked his head back through the doors; Dan was looking at the sheets and turned to Marion. He could see the quizzical look on Dan's face and Marion knew the answer before he heard the question.

"Yes, the sheets are the same design as the doors engineered for your Grandfather's lab." Dan looked incredulously at Marion who smiled. "James and your Grandfather came to us to design some water tight doors for an experiment they were conducting many years ago."

"I thought they looked familiar but these are slightly taller."

"That's because these are for a different project. They're also thinner. We realised the unique seals could be used effectively to erect bolt and build underwater structures, underwater habitats. They are reinforced via stainless inserts acting as walkways and attached to the sea bed. It is basically an upside down acrylic box which is then pumped full of air to force out the water. It's like a twentieth century diving bell but this box is designed to be in less than twenty two feet. That's how deep people can go without having to worry about decompressing and they can stay at that depth indefinitely without having to worry about nitrogen poisoning their system or bother with decompression chambers. The Hyper Sub can ascend, docking in the centre of the box to let the occupants out. We don't talk about it much but we had the idea it could be used for film crews to shoot underwater sequences in comfort."

Dan liked the idea, it was very simple in its design. "You say you adapted the designs from the lab doors?"

Marion headed back through the doors. "Well not the first set. They were pretty simple as they were smaller and only three pieces. The second set was a bit more of a challenge because of their size, they were made up of several adjoining acrylic sheets. It was while we were designing them that we struck on the idea. The seals' strength came from the steel inserts. We realised, with careful planning, we could build a much larger and grander water tight structure."

Dan followed dumbfounded by what he just heard, a second set of doors? Why were there a second set of doors and why did they need to be bigger and stronger? Dan wandered into the design office in a state of shock; he wished everything would make sense.

He thought he knew his family really well but what had they been up to? Why had there been a second set of doors commissioned? The lab was complete, it was finished, it was beneath the house, all of it, including the acrylic hydro pod.

Maybe the second set of acrylic doors were for the secondary lab used by Aunt Pat and just never installed? There were so many details he did not understand and so many questions he needed to ask his family but could not.

Resentment brooded in him, there were so many questions he would never be able to ask. Lost in his own thoughts, trying to process the details he had discovered over the last couple of days, he idly thumbed through a set of technical drawings attached to a giant white board. Hand-written notes were scrawled down the right hand side of the board listing the remaining jobs which needed addressing to finish the egress collar. Underlined in red was the due date of delivery, which was a week Friday.

Dan lifted the sheets of the finalised design for the enlarged egress collar and marvelled at its gradual intricate redesign, incorporating the hydro pod track. He turned each sheet, like a flip chart, reading the hand scrawled ideas and material choices, a kind of flicker book reverse engineering of the initial concept. Stopping on the last sheet; it was a copy of the original final design proof of the track for the hydro pod, listing all internal and external measurements.

"When did Uncle Mike bring you the plans for the track to be incorporated into the redesign of the egress collar?"

Marion was carrying two mugs of coffee back to the white board; each mug had the Marion Hyper Sub with a futuristic concept image of the sub emblazoned across it. Marion looked at the diagram.

"I suppose that was given to us about three months ago when we realised Hyper 1 couldn't be adjusted to take the payload. It was simply not possible to reconfigure and remove the rear three passenger seats making the cockpit water tight to incorporate the diving bell. The hull and Hyper 1 would have to have been completely stripped, which is why Hyper 2 was commandeered by your Uncle because it was almost ready. I think she'll look pretty spectacular in the boat house! Of course if you are worried, legal entitlement and delivery of the hyper sub comes to you at the end of next week."

Dan was in shock, two hyper subs?

"Obviously there will be a snagging list of requirements which will need to be ironed out with the sea trials, which is part of our contractual agreement with you. The non-disclosure agreement is in place obviously, against your continued funding of our research or until the day when the Marion Hyper Sub truly comes of age and is ultimately released to the market. You are in effect leasing the sub for your personal use. We still own its intellectual property at the end of the day, although we don't envisage ever taking it back, unless you want to sell it on of course."

Two hyper subs? Dan wanted to say something but felt as though he was going to incriminate himself as an imposter. He could fully understand the family interest and continual investment, or the legacy Uncle Mike and Aunt Susan had felt obliged to maintain, but taking delivery of a submarine itself was something he had not envisaged at all, considering he never even knew they had bought a first. Dan tried to change tact slightly for fear of misunderstanding what Marion had said.

"I am a little hazy with the agreement Uncle Mike has left in place over the sub?"

"Oh of course. Mike had arranged to take delivery out at the family house in Santa Rosa towards the end of next week, after his initial inspection. I assume with your inspection today I trust you are happy with the delivery to go ahead?"

Dan still in shock and did not really know what else to say other than yes so nodded in agreement.

"Good." Marion continued. "A sealed container will be delivered to you with the sub next Friday. Myself and the team will follow to launch it and do some initial testing in the sea before you take complete ownership. Then it will be the usual suck-it-and-see with the equipment on board and general day to day running but I don't envisage any problems. I was hoping next week when Mike turned up the sub would be back in the water which would have allowed Mike to learn the controls. It's pretty simple, I know it looks complicated but trust me, it really is very simple. Shouldn't take you more than a couple of hours to get the hang of it and then its just practice."

Dan smiled weakly realising towards the end of next week he would be the proud owner of a giant personal submarine, which was unique but he kind of thought he would prefer a Ferrari or something less unique sitting in the driveway. Rallying his thoughts quickly and trying to look okay with what he had just discovered, Dan turned back to the plans. "Do you have a copy of the plan Uncle Mike delivered?"

"Actually that is already a copy; we keep all originals in the cabinet over there." He motioned towards the side wall where an A1 cabinet similar in size to the one in the lab stood.

"Do you think I could take this for my records? I can't find any at home." Dan pulled the sheet out from under the bulldog clips and started to roll it up.

Marion headed over to the cabinet and pulled out one of the drawers and rifled through, "Yeah absolutely no problem, we already have a copy and the original in here."

The rest of the meeting with Marion was left to small talk and continued condolences from Marion about Mike and Susan, ending when Marion was called back to the warehouse to oversee something on the sub. Making his excuses he returned to the dry dock and Dan left Marion Reynolds, the building, the sub and the extraordinary meeting behind him in the car.

He expected exciting new technology but nothing as advanced as what he had just witnessed. Maybe an initial concept but certainly not a full-fledged personal submarine and not something the family allegedly already owned. Where the hell would they keep a personal submarine and where is it?

Why had Uncle Mike continued with the company on such a personal level? Was it a sense of completion and duty he felt towards his own father? Dan could not decide but it puzzled him for the rest of the journey back to Santa Rosa, along with the ultimate conundrum, where would he find the original submarine, Hyper 1?

26

Fortunately for McAdams, Charlie and Dan had not ventured down into the lab the previous evening. When the panel slid open, revealing the stairwell to Charlie, he truly believed he was going to be eliminating both Daniel Morris and Charlie Price; the mission would have been over, permanently.

He stood listening to them discussing the CCTV footage from behind the closed panel. He knew at least he could not be recognised in the footage, that he was certain of. Morris fortunately had not recognised him. Unfortunately he now only had a 24 hour window to commandeer the secondary drives from Charlie Price's office, having inadvertently created a timescale, driven by Charlie forcing Dan to go to the police with the footage.

Once the drives were given to the police the whole investigation would change direction because the likelihood of law enforcement keeping the incident localised would be impossible.

McAdams was in his van, overlooking the exterior of the Marion Reynolds' building. He had hidden tracking devices on the family's cars; after Dan took the classic from the garage he had taken the step to place one on every vehicle the Morris family had, which was plenty. Global positioning information from the Range Rover, relayed back, allowed him to remain a fair distance behind.

He had been stationary for nearly an hour watching the building; no one had left or entered since Dan's arrival. He hated flying blind, however the situation needed constant monitoring, he had to track Dan at all times as he was running out of time.

McAdams did not fully understand exactly what he was looking for. The science was way beyond his intellect. Plus it was so unique, he was unsure he would even be able to take it; however taking the technology was not his mission. Locating and downloading all of the data connected with the technology was.

The original notes from the early experiments were difficult to understand. William Morris had written in indecipherable shorthand, the alleged experts had been unable to recreate his final positive tests. With technological advancements, the Government and Military had always assumed confidently they would be able to finish his work. It had been in excess of fifty years ago and no one was near to understanding his research or how to recreate his results.

William Morris had taken leave after the success of his first full presentation to the Navy and Government indoctrinate. What they never expected was him to leave permanently taking his data and final transcribed research notes with him, he simply vanished. They were able to track him leaving Britain via Dover and entering France. From there he must have driven on to Switzerland because his car was discovered abandoned a few months after his disappearance. The family's extensive fortune had been deposited to an account in Switzerland, protected by Swiss law, the trail had gone cold.

The lab under the house had been clean, irritatingly clean. There was no sign of the data or any equipment associated but the lengths the family had gone to build the underground facility was far too elaborate to simply have been constructed for fun. The lab gave a tantalising glimpse that the work had indeed been continued for many years and quite recently.

The family had been one step ahead of the government ever since they left Britain. Back in the fifties it was far easier to disappear. Hopping across a couple of borders could leave a trail completely cold, especially when you had money to bribe a few officials to misplace important paperwork. The scientific research however was far too valuable to forget, not only to the Military but also the British government, which was ultimately why an open case file was lodged with his department and for fifty years it remained open. The longest on record.

Underground, it had taken a while to figure out how Morris had escaped from the lab. At first glance the only exit was back up the stairwell and through the Panic Room. As the security lighting faded he had sat with his back to the wall, facing the entrance, just in case Dan and Charlie decided to come down.

Two shots was all it would have taken if they had. However as he lowered himself into position he realised there was a very slight salty breeze from the door of the open acrylic cubicle. He crawled through the tunnel finding his way into the boat house, where he waited, escaping under the cover of darkness.

McAdams sat in his van concentrating on Marion Reynolds. The green algae had long since dried on his clothes forming a cracked seaside cement. The algae had stained his hands a dark green as he had crawled through the tunnel, seeping under and accentuating his nails, which dug deeply into the steering wheel of the van.

Overnight he worried Morris would disappear, taking with him any chance of finding him again. He had not left his position, not even to get a quick shower or change of clothing. He had not slept for over 30 hours now and figured he would only have another 18 at most until Charlie made Daniel go to the police with the footage.

The entrance to the expansive building opened and Daniel Morris, followed by an unknown man, stepped into the sunshine. Morris carried a large piece of rolled up paper, which he threw on the back seat of the Range Rover. They shook hands and the man headed back inside the building, Morris climbed in and drove off.

Waiting a few moments McAdams started to get out of his van. He was just about to slam the door and head for the building when an alarm went off in the back to the surveillance kit. Panicking he dashed round, hurling the doors open and lunging at the headphones thrown on the floor. Pushing them over his ears, he could hear the Range Rover cell phone ringing.

It was the first time he had known it to be used since he started his surveillance. He had bugged the phone at the time of putting the tracking device on the car and had since assumed it was disconnected because it was never used.

Daniel could be heard impatiently. "Come on Lizzie, pick up, where are you?" Two more rings and then silence, the phone went to voicemail.

"Hi, this is Lizzie, I'm sorry I can't take your call right now, I'm either in a meeting or fetching coffee! Leave a message and I'll get back to you; eventually." There was silence; you could tell Dan was a little put out by the answer phone as he grappled for the words he needed.

"Hey Liz its Dan, um, where are you? You'll never guess where I presently am." Without pausing he answered his own question. "I'm out at Kingsley Lake! That's right and there's not a slave in sight! Very long story but I really, really need to talk to you. Um, it's just after one now, it'll probably take me six hours or so to drive home, well, that's if the traffic's good. I wondered if you were free tonight, so I can take you out for that dinner I promised? I'll swing by your place to pick you up about eight and we'll head out to the Lighthouse Restaurant for supper. I think I can afford it these days and if it's fully booked I'll just buy the restaurant." He chuckled slightly at his own joke and then added. "If it's not a problem don't worry about calling me back I'll just see you at eight. See ya later." He hung up.

McAdams sat in the van lost in thought at what he just heard. If he stayed to check out Marion Reynolds then he may miss what was so important between Daniel and Lizzie. Of course it could just be a date, but what if it was not?

Reynolds would have to wait, especially as there were still people in the building. Reluctantly he climbed back in to the driver seat from the back of the van, slammed the driver door shut and headed back towards Santa Rosa, the direction Daniel Morris had headed five minutes earlier.

27

Dan fortunately had a good run achieving the drive from Kingsley Lake in record time, less than five hours; although he was driving on fumes and his legs had been crossed for the last hundred miles. He was genuinely looking forward to the evening ahead. It was the first sense of excitement and normality since he arrived home, he also strangely felt slightly nervous.

The station was going through its twilight transition, from gas station to night spot. The younger kids were drifting home for their dinner, yet the diner still looked full through the windows. The high school kids were clustered in to individual booths, segregating their cliques even further with physical barriers between them.

Pulling in to fill the Range Rover with diesel, he checked the odometer. He was shocked at how many miles he had clocked up during the course of the day. It was the first time in many years he had driven any kind of long distance. It had been a common occurrence when he lived here, nowadays he was lucky to even take a drive.

His car back in London was a vain folly, which cost him more to keep on the road than was sensible, especially when comparing pounds per mile. Having a car was more about perceived sense of freedom. When he looked out of his apartment window, even though it never moved from one week to the next, he had his own mode of transport and was reliant on no one. Except maybe the odd jump start from the highway emergency service, a dead battery had unfortunately befallen him on more than one occasion.

He filled the car's expansive fuel tank and headed into the foyer, pressing the button to announce his presence. The dull tring of the bell echoed in the bowels of the workshop. Without waiting he headed into the back of the shop, no one was about, so he continued on through the office and out on to the Marina dock.

On the side of the dock next to the boat lift, still resting in its cradle, stood Hydrous. Joel and Niles were standing back admiring their handiwork. It was not the same boat he had seen earlier, it was gleaming.

Every piece of chrome had been polished, the decks scrubbed and oiled and the hull had been painted. The pastel blue hull had been sanded and replaced with a defining gloss black. The shape of the hull had changed, the darkness hid its elegant slender and beauty. Dan felt a slight shame in the choice of colour. He knew he would get used to the change but it would take time, a lot like the rest of his life.

Joel saw him coming, giving him an enormous smile. "We were hoping to surprise you and get it in the water as soon as possible, then you could have some fun. We decided you needed some, after recent events."

Suddenly there was an explosion of noise, Dan jumped back shocked by the extraordinary rumble erupting from the hull of the boat. A plume of blue smoke engulfed Joel and Niles as the engine fired for the first time and expelled the burnt oil settled around the piston rings, deep within the cylinders.

The smoke cleared and the revs died away as the engine was extinguished. J.J. appeared at the stern of the ship. "Yep, it was a fuel blockage. Loads of shit in the fuel bowl, just blew it through, sounds as sweet as a nut to me." He spotted Dan. "Hi Dan, we thought we'd get the old gal back in the water for ya. It's only been remedial work and the hull was in perfect nick for a quick paint job."

"Well it looks as though Niles has finished to me, it looks so different." Dan screwed his face up.

Niles saw the look; he had seen it many times on a customer's face when a boat had the colour of its hull changed, somehow it always altered the feeling of the vessel. It was like a woman crash dieting, her whole personality literally changed overnight. "Honestly, don't worry Dan, it'll look fine tomorrow. It's only the initial shock of the change; the black is harsh because of its size, once she's in the water it'll look great because most of the hull will be submerged. I have booked a sign writer in a couple of days and he's gonna edge the hull with a thin red line. That'll transition the black into the white. It'll also pick out the warm red of the teak decking. Trust me she'll look amazing. He'll also repaint the name Hydrous back to match the old typeface. Dad took a picture on his cell so the old guy could match it correctly."

Joel looked especially pleased; Dan was not sure whether it was because he took the photo or the end result. "We've been on it all day; in fact we've really enjoyed doing it. It's much better than most of the patches and general repair work we get to do all the time. Plus the three of us don't get much time to work together these days."

Dan was a little overwhelmed by their generosity and for doing the work so quickly, although he knew it meant a great deal. "She looks better than new, I really don't know how to thank you all."

"Just use her, that'll be thanks enough, plus it's what your Granddad would have wanted. He loved her and so did James." Joel almost looked as though he was about to well up with tears at the mention of Uncle James. "It really only seems like yesterday since she was last in the water. I know time slips by but it has been a little sad seeing the old gal sat out back."

Dan had forgotten how close Joel had been to Uncle James. As a group they spent many a weekend out on the yacht; Uncle James, Matt, Joel, Niles and himself; the boys together. Joel gave Dan his first beer, much to Uncle James' disapproval. Matt and Niles were pretty good friends as they played on the football team together at school.

"I suppose you were the last one to see the yacht go out before it was found?" Dan asked casually.

"No actually, I think Niles was the last to see it officially?"

Niles had not thought about the scenario in years. "Yeah, I filled the fuel tanks and Matt picked up some fresh cylinders. I had a bit of a laugh with Matt and Ashley; we arranged to go water skiing the following weekend as Matt had bought one of those new aero chair things, which looked like fun. I'd not seen either of them for a while, so Ashley was going to ask Lizzie and we were going to make it a foursome."

Dan strangely felt quite jealous. Niles had never kept his feelings towards Lizzie much of a secret, although she had never shown him the slightest bit of interest. Even his invitation to their high school prom, she had declined in favour of escorting Dan, who did not have a date and was refusing to go. Matt went with Ashley and Lizzie with Dan, the four of them inseparable, even at the end of high school.

"Do you know where they were planning to spend the weekend? Did Uncle James say what site they were planning on diving?"

Niles looked thoughtful. "I didn't speak to James or Pat; in fact come to think of it I don't think I even saw them."

"What do you mean?"

"Well I just assumed they were in the cabin, but they never came out on deck, not while I was there. It was just Matt and Ashley who I spoke to." Niles shifted uncomfortable. "I'm sorry Dan, I was interviewed by the Sheriff after they found Hydrous adrift at sea and he reckoned I was possibly the last person to see any of them alive." Niles looked upset by this confession, but Dan nodded appreciatively.

Joel chipped in. "I do remember Matt was on about diving down to the Oriskany. It was a little while after it was sunk and after all the hard work his firm put in to the preparation for the sinking he wanted to see his handiwork."

This jogged Dan's own memory. "Actually the last time we were all together was when we went out as a family to watch the sinking. Even Aunt Susan was there, which was unheard of. I can't ever remember getting her on a boat, she hated the water. We all went out on the cruiser to watch."

Dan was smiling with a fondness as the memory surfaced. He had come home for the special occasion, press ganged by Aunt Susan and Lizzie, they all had got very drunk. "Actually, speaking of the cruiser, it's not at home in the boat house. I don't suppose any of you guys would know where it was being kept? I didn't see it out back yesterday."

Niles and Joel shrugged, J.J. poked his head up again through the engine hatch. "I know where it is!"

All three of them looked up towards J.J. on the yacht, squinting into the sun. "I saw it down at Matt's old firm; it was moored up by the jetty the other week." He looked towards his father as if for confirmation.

"You remember, I took old Mr Hanson's wreck of a fishing boat down to get some welding done on the transom. Simon did it as a favour because it was stainless steel and I always seem to warp stainless. I'm crap at welding that stuff. I just assumed your Uncle Mike had taken it there for some remedial work like I had, didn't really think anything of it."

"I wonder why it was down there?" Dan looked at his watch, there was plenty of time to get to Matt's old engineering firm and check it out before his date with Lizzie. Date, that was funny, as technically, it probably was their first proper date. He had chosen the Lighthouse as it was the most expensive and exclusive restaurant in Santa Rosa and possibly the area and the fact they would not bump into anyone they knew, so they could talk openly. He had a lot to say.

"Right, thanks guys. I've just filled up Aunt Susan's Range Rover. Do you want me to write it on the account on the way out? Plus add the cost of the work for today on the bill and I'll settle it all up together."

Joel stepped forward. "Nonsense, the boat's on us. We wanted to do it and been talking about it for months. We decided it would be nice to get her back in the water and you just happened to give us the incentive to get on with it."

Dan could tell Joel wanted to do this, you could never argue with him when he made up his mind, his heart was pure gold.

"Okay, but I owe you all a beer … or three."

"Better than that, when you go out, we'll all go and take her for a proper spin and have several beers." They all laughed.

"Deal, that'd be great, not sure I could pilot Hydrous on my own these days anyway, it's been an absolute age since I last sailed her. See you guys later. Thanks."

28

Matt had been so excited after graduation. He was gifted in many things. Like his father and mother, he had been fortunate enough to inherit the analytical and academic mind of the Morris family. However, he also had another side to his personality to balance. Sitting in a lab or analysing data had not really sat well with Matt's passion for sport or his outgoing nature. He had wanted to combine his love of the sea with his engineering degree.

For a few years he had been employed as a saturation diver, working underwater for off sea oil rigs all round the world. Matt had spent weeks at a time in compression chambers acclimatising to the depth they were working at. Compression chambers are no bigger than a rounded garden shed, which meant the crew became incredibly close while watching one another's back. This bred a bond within the group, rarely seen outside the military.

The part Matt had loved about his job was the downtime this type of working arrangement had given him, one month on and one month off. The problem was that he had been too good, spending a large percentage of his time away from home. If he had not been crammed into a compression chamber, he was topside overseeing the secondary crew. The thrill of this working arrangement did not take long to wear off. Management had wanted him to put down the tools and run the crews permanently, so with a heavy heart he left to start his own business.

A lot of the work Matt's company undertook was reclamation of equipment from the sea bed, which could cost a lot to replace for the companies that lost them. He became extremely specialised within the business and gained many contracts across the military and the oil companies. The one person Matt had trusted implicitly, not only with his life but everything and eventually becoming his best friend, was

Simon Millor. In their line of work trust went further than simply knowing they were there to pick up the slack.

The pair met on their first tour together, becoming extremely close as you do spending weeks at a time together. They bickered like an old married couple and with Matt's backing they decided to set up and go it alone. The equipment for this kind of work was expensive but Matt, seemingly with the help of Morris funding and some personal investment, started the business.

Dan liked Simon; he was good fun, a ginger more compact version of Matt, rugged, slim and muscular. He had an intelligent articulation and demeanour that hid his rigger background. His father had always worked on the oil rigs but paid privately for Simon's university education in engineering. He was somewhat disappointed and very vocal about his choice of career following his father's path to work on the oil rigs after his degree.

When Matt and Simon struck out together with the business, he was ecstatic. Although deep salvage still had the same relative risks as the oil industry, it had a much higher return. It is strange how a parent still wants for their own child to be successful; happiness with what they do is not always a factor in their chosen ideal.

The firm was not too far out of town, from the outside it had not changed at all. The land had been derelict when they found it, an old ship yard down from the main port. The firm specialised in retrieval but also worked fabrication and engineering projects on all scales for marine projects, which was where both their engineering degrees were pivotal in the success and survival of the firm. It was their professional, friendly and flexible approach to problems which made them so employable.

For instance, Granddad had invented the concept for the valve controlling the water to the pit in the lab. It had been Matt who had physically realised the idea to working prototype. Matt had also been the one who built and designed it to tilt for inspection for easier cleaning, removal or replacement. It was this kind of inventiveness that had driven Matt, keeping him fresh and interested. Simon was the same except a little more grounded with how a business should be run, between the pair of them, it had become a runaway success.

The receptionist had gone through into the work shop. She was new, not knowing who Dan was. It had been a while since they last emailed each other, both bogged down with life but mainly not having Matt as the bond between them anymore. Simon literally exploded into reception.

"When the hell did you get into town?" Simon raced across the room hugging Dan like a long lost brother, although Simon's affection had always made Dan slightly uncomfortable. He loved Simon, he was great to be around but there was always a niggling doubt in Dan's mind because of something Matt had once said.

He had told him Simon had confessed, on one of their many underwater stints, he thought Dan was the fittest man on Earth and if he could turn anyone, it would be him. Matt loved this piece of information and relentlessly mocked Dan about Simon's confession.

Dan smiled broadly stepping back; it was still great to see him. "Earlier in the week. I thought I'd come over as I didn't know whether you heard but Uncle Mike and Aunt Susan had an accident."

"Oh my god, no I hadn't. Are they okay? I only spoke to Mike about a month ago."

"Well actually, I'm sorry to tell you this but they both died."

Simon looked like he was going to break down on the spot. The colour physically drained from his face, it was amazing to see someone so bronzed, look immediately like he had never stepped outside in the Florida sun.

"My God Dan, are you okay? Do you need anything? You know if you want or need anything you only have to ask. I'm so, so sorry." Dan was overwhelmed by Simon's sincerity. His heart was a bottomless pit, the family had surrounded themselves with truly selfless people over the years. Dan had witnessed firsthand what the loss of Matt had done to him. At the time Dan had pondered the idea Simon's confession was to actually mask his true feelings for Matt.

"Come on through to the office, I think I need to sit down."

Dan followed Simon through the small functional reception into the office. The last time he was here, it was a bit of a mess but now everything had been cleaned and finely decorated. It was very comfortable and extremely fashionable. Many of the old cabinets had been replaced with new modern Swedish versions; the place looked as though it had been taken from the front cover of a prestige furniture catalogue.

"What do you think?" Simon gestured round the office in a salute. "I gave the old office a good going over last year. It could only stay in its preserved state in memory of Matt for so long."

The office had been a monument to the forties. The décor had been tired and dysfunctional, totally inadequate for their needs but Matt loved it from their very first viewing. Although it suited Matt's style, organised chaos, it was completely different to Simon's slick and chiselled look, it was amazing it lasted as long as it did. Matt had had the habit of working like a one man mini tornado and the office, even on a good day, would look like an explosion had struck. Bizarrely though in all the mess, he had always known where everything was.

Dan settled in one of the comfortable tub chairs, placing the design tube he carried by his feet. Simon poured a coffee from the adjoining kitchenette. "Do you want one?"

"Yeah I won't say no, you always had great taste in coffee, not to mention interior design." Simon smiled with the compliment.

"I know Matt loved the old look, but I felt it was time the office and I moved on." He over emphasised the reference to himself and Dan nodded knowingly.

"I only really popped by to make sure you knew the news, I'm sorry to be the bearer. I was also here to make sure the cruiser was not an inconvenience, J.J told me it was here, I didn't know."

"Yeah Mike dropped it down a few weeks ago actually. He said they were trying to make room for a new boat. I gave him a lift back home, as he brought it round the peninsula to the Marina. I towed the trailer back for it to sit on. It was nice to see your Aunt Susan as well. I do hate English tea though." He screwed his face up.

Dan laughed. "I hope you never said that."

"Christ I know better than that. I chucked it down the sink while she wasn't looking, although it almost earned me another cup."

Aunt Susan could easily drip feed you tea, a constant never-ending supply. She was the type of person who thought it was rude not to entertain all that entered her home. Dan had always assumed it was a British thing but quickly discovered, while living in London, it was just an eccentric much loved Aunt Susan quirk.

"It's sat round the side actually, no harm where it is, plenty of room."

"Thanks, that's all I really wanted to know. I didn't want anything to be a nuisance."

"Like it ever would be. It's fine. If we do need to move it, which I doubt, I'll let you know but it's not like we don't have lots of space." Dan was kind of glad he had found the cruiser; it would have bugged him if he could not. It was another part of the family, another root to his past.

"What's with the design tube?" Simon prodded at the plastic tube by his feet.

Dan looked down having almost forgotten the other more important reason why he was there. "I wanted you to take a look at something. I've been clearing out some stuff and I found a load of Matt's engineering sketches. They seemed incomplete and I wondered if you'd know what they were of?"

Simon picked up the tube unscrewing the top, with a practised hand he slipped the transparencies out. Flicking through the individual sheets each showed a cross section of a technical sketch. His tongue poked out the corner of his mouth as he concentrated, studying the designs. He got up from the tub chair and crossed over to an A1 tilted drawing table. Rolling the sheets flat, using board clips round the edges, keeping them flat. Better than the odd stapler on each corner Dan thought as he crossed the room to join Simon.

Being transparencies, they faintly showed each drawing beneath. Simon flicked a switch and the drawing table hummed and stammered into life. The translucent smooth acrylic work surface illuminated, the board was also a light box. The images' lines stood out but judging from the detail and mismatched imagery, not a single sheet related to one another.

Simon studied them carefully. "It's odd really. They are numbered in order but only the even numbers are in the sequence. There are design sheets missing, is this all you had?"

"Yeah they were in one of the drawers. I thought you might remember them?" Dan had spent long enough trying to decipher them; if anyone knew what they were, it was going to be Simon.

29

Simon stood for several minutes looking at each individual transparency, tracing lines and examining cross sections throughout the pages. Dan had studied the drawings intensely discerning little from them. Any dimensions were omitted and they assumed considerable background knowledge for anyone to decipher them successfully. Simon studied the drawings occasionally nodding as though he completely understood what they were.

Dan was the first to break the silence. "Do you know what they are, or do you think they are just some test designs he never got finished?"

· "Matt never left a design unfinished, well not on paper anyway. There were loads of projects he designed which were never commissioned, or never got the financial backing, firmly remaining in concept form. They were mainly design sketches though, these are something else entirely and something I've never seen before. When I cleared the office I put dozens of Matt's designs in tubes out the back. I've just not had the heart to throw them away."

Simon leant in closer to the transparencies. "The odd thing about all of these designs is that other than our logo and the overlay naming convention, they have no details. All they have is these markers in each of the corners, which I assume are the coordinating points to whatever they overlay?" As Simon said the words coordinating something clicked.

"I wonder …?"

"What?" Dan was a getting little impatient, he had expected Simon to know exactly what they were.

"Well, whenever we worked on any form of technical diagrams, we used a specific naming convention and structure I put in place. I was adamant he used it so I could trace his sketches. It was always printed on each design tube cap; it was set up for ease of filing so we could find the relevant drawing in the cabinets out back. For example, if it was one of my projects it would use the letters SM, for Simon Millor and then the first numbers would be the year, so 07 would be 2007, then the company name and so on."

Dan was a little unsure what that meant relating to the transparencies, so Matt had not labelled them, so what?

"The point is, when I was cataloguing all the technical drawings of Matt's and entering the details into the database, there were very few that didn't have any company details, like these!"

Dan was still not following. "So that means what exactly?"

"Well it means Matt was either inventing an idea, which therefore had no billable hours to a company, or it was just a personal project or something."

Dan was catching on. "You said you didn't get rid of any of Matt's stuff, do you still have the ones that weren't labelled?"

"Yeah, as I said I put all projects and past jobs in the design cabinets out the back for future reference and those which I couldn't link to a client and couldn't be entered on the database, I rolled up and put in the loft above the office." Simon pointed in the direction of the roof space.

In the ceiling was a retractable staircase which Simon pulled down. The stairs were counter balanced on weights; gently lowering to the floor. Simon promptly disappeared into the void. His head and shoulders then reappeared a few seconds later, several tubes rained down through the open hatch bouncing across the office. He disappeared to retrieve some more while Dan stacked them on a table. After several short sharp bursts of missiles, firing through the hatch like several unexploded incendiary shells, Simon reversed back down into the carnage and the stairs effortlessly disappeared back into the ceiling.

Simon helped Dan load the last of the tubes on to the table; it was obvious Matt had been either a busy, or a very bored man.

"I never really took much notice of this stuff. Lots of it was unfinished or generally indecipherable to me, as it was a first draft or a sketch. Some of them though, I seem to remember looked pretty finished."

Dan and Simon started unscrewing the caps on the tubes and sliding out sheets of paper, dozens of the sheets were instantly discarded as they contained nothing more than a few indecipherable lines. Some were just battered and had all sorts of stains and coffee rings on them, plus a plethora of telephone numbers scrawled on the sheets, Matt's very own careful filing system.

However several started to reveal interesting design ideas and concepts for equipment to help with salvage. A new design of an inflatable bag for lifting machinery from the seabed, a hydraulic lift to attach to the submersible and the one that instantly caught Dan's eye.

He recognised it because it was the original design sketch by his Granddad of the two way valve for the service tunnel to the lab. Simon also discovered the final design concepts Matt had drawn with the tilting collar and removable plate. These went on a separate pile.

However the rubbish continued to mount up and the discarded tubes started to form their own obscure crystalline structure. Simon finally unrolled several sheets, packed tightly together, several plain in between a few transparencies, exactly like the ones they had fixed to the light box a few minutes earlier. Simon looked it over, trying to unroll the edges to get a better look, the size unmanageable like a broad sheet newspaper.

"Look here in the corner, it's the same coordinating points as on the transparencies." Simon pulled out the individual sheets, flicking through them he found the one he was looking for. "Okay, I've got sheet three of four, version A."

Simon cleared the light box and placed transparency two down first, followed by the recently discovered three and then four aligning the coordinating points. Suddenly all the disparate lines from the sheets started to make sense, even to Dan. Sheet three had all of the dimensions to the individual structure; it also included a few of the lines which gave the orthographic elevations of the final design.

Simon cooed. "This is incredible, it's an amazing design idea, how the individual diagrams fit together is impressive but why Matt would have split the design into all of these separate parts is beyond me."

Dan was puzzled by the whole structure. "Could Matt have split the diagrams in to sections so that anyone looking without all the information wouldn't know what it was supposed to be, or what they were looking at?"

It made sense to split them up if you were trying to hide the final blueprint, but even with this extra sheet it was not complete.

"So this box here." Dan pointed to the lower right hand corner which had basic labelling; the writing was on transparency three. "MM, is for Matt Morris, yeah? So what does CVA-34 stand for? A company?"

Simon looked at the naming convention puzzled and looked at Dan, his mind whirring. Without warning Simon spun round and headed through to the back room leaving Dan bewildered in his wake. He reappeared clutching several design tubes, throwing them down on the ground around Dan's feet and sorting them into a specific order.

Picking the first one up he showed the end cap in Dan's face who read it aloud "U.S.S Oriskany? What's that got to do with anything?"

"Well it could be nothing as these plans are the blueprint of the whole ship, but Matt as you know was obsessed with the Oriskany, especially when we were involved with its eventual scuppering. Interestingly though, the military classification of the Oriskany was CV-34 but better than that, the ship was later reclassified to CVA-34!"

Simon looked triumphant in his assumption; Dan could now see where he was heading with this line of thought. Simon picked the second design tube off the floor and showed him the end cap, USS Oriskany CVA-34. He unscrewed the cap gently slipping out the contents; the roll of paper was a single A1 sheet. Simon removed the transparencies from the board replacing them on the lightbox with the single A1 sheet.

The sheet was a carefully blown up section of the ship, recreated with full dimensional details. The information in the bottom right hand corner finally disclosed the engineering detail the transparencies lacked, including importantly scale, title and ultimately 1 of 4, version A. Simon placed over the top of the sheet the first transparency, 2 of 4 Version A lining up the markers which matched perfectly.

"We assumed the labelling was a particular order and it is but if you look at the rest of the tubes, each has been labelled alphabetically. The next set of technical drawings is CVB-34, CVC and so on. Clever Matt, very clever." He smiled like a lover remembering fondly a forgotten quirk about their partner.

Simon and Dan, using two other hastily erected light boxes, recreated two more of the complete drawings, CVB and CVC. Each had several transparencies that built up the detail within each overall diagram. Without the even numbered transparencies and base sheets from the individual design tubes, it would have been impossible to reconstruct each complete technical drawing. Dan could see why they had been separated, but as of yet could not fully comprehend why. They both stared at the three distinct boards with their individual schematic.

Simon broke the silence. "Did you know when we were involved with the Oriskany before its eventual demise, we were completely overwhelmed with work? I was working with the guys over in the North Sea on a salvage project, while Matt stayed here. We employed a freelance crew to oversee the environmental remediation work on the

Oriskany."

"I thought you guys never used freelance?"

"Well it was an exception really as we didn't need the expertise because Matt could oversee that, plus financially it made better sense hiring a few grunts to do the heavy work, leaving me to oversee the North Sea job. It was basically just contracted metal workers who could complete the removal of the hatches, ladders and any heavy machinery before its sinking."

This was news to Dan, Matt always worked with people he knew on everything, why would he have hired unknowns for a project?

"I think your Uncle James even got involved as he was looking forward to diving the ship after the sinking." Dan had remembered Uncle James talking about getting to know the layout of the ship before the sinking so he could explore it properly; it was a rare opportunity, too good to miss.

"Certain internal structures had to be reinforced, like a few corridors and some areas were sealed or removed completely, such as water tight doors. It would have been dangerous for diving in and around with potential hazards like that to catch a regulator or something on. Some of the corridors were just too narrow to dive with dual cylinders; it was Matt's expertise they were using for this part of the project."

Simon removed a few more sheets from the first bundle they had found in the loft spreading them across the floor. One of the sheets was a slightly different colour and paper to the rest; it was a blueprint of the ship. Within the bowels of the ship an area was highlighted.

The area was a part of the expansive hold, housing the internal hangars below decks for the aeroplanes. The main section was split into three individual compartments, each separately labelled CVA, CVB and finally CVC.

30

Dan was stunned collapsing in to the comfort of a tub chair. "Surely this is all hypothetical right? You're telling me Matt designed and possibly built three separate compartments which fitted inside the superstructure of a military warship, for what purpose? Let's face it, the bloody thing was sunk, we were all there to witness it. The Oriskany now resides at the bottom of the sea, off the coast of Florida. It's not like we can pop down and have a quick look, is it?"

"Look Dan, I'm only going by what I can ascertain from the technical diagrams. The way these diagrams read, the compartments are three separate reinforced rooms, interlinked via two walkways. CVB is in the middle, connecting to the two outer rooms, CVA and CVC. What is interesting though is that it looks as though this entire bulkhead would have to be moved across the hangar deck to fit in the proposed compartments."

Simon traced the bulkhead wall with his finger on the blueprint; its original positioning was shown by broken lines, moving it by several metres. Dan walked over and stood by the drawing board looking at the blueprint again.

"Okay, so explain to me why the three compartments are in effect floating above the hangar floor. They're not connected to the walls or supported in any way. All the other walls intersect or attach to part of the super structure, these appear to be floating. Except for this round circle situated beneath each box, what the hell does that indicate?" Dan's voice rose in exasperation.

Simon knew exactly what the circle was, he had seen it before. He was grasping to figure out what the true meanings of these designs were. He had an idea but needed to vocalise his ideas, fleshing them out.

"Right ... imagine you were in a saturation chamber at thirty metres below the water surface, yeah? They work perfectly fine when the chamber doesn't need to move. However what happens if it does? Matt designed a device, which we termed as gimbal control, allowing the chamber to attach to a surface that could be constantly shifting, such as a wreck that would move in the current; or worse shift under turbulent seas."

Dan was trying to comprehend the logic and what that meant. Simon pulled another design tube from the office shelves labelled 'Gimbal', unrolling it for Dan to see. The design depicted a set of large concentric rings, with orthogonal mounted pivot axis interconnecting them.

"You see, the three rings keep the chamber perfectly level at all times. Submarines use a much more sophisticated computer controlled device called a stable table. Matt modelled the idea on a navigation compass but enlarged it to accommodate the shape and volume of a saturation chamber."

"So let me get this straight, what you're saying is that CVA, CVB and CVC are effectively individual saturation chambers?"

"No, I'm not. I believe Matt designed a set of chambers, yep that's true, but these are much bigger than anything I know of that presently exists. That's why I don't believe they can be saturation chambers. To vent and control something that large would take an astronomical amount of maintenance and heliox mixture. Simply they would be too expensive and not viable to run. Plus, the proposed structure is heavily strengthened, far heavier than is needed. I'd have to run the numbers to work out its integrity within the structure. I think these designs are a theoretical idea for an underwater habitat, housed or hidden in the USS Oriskany. Maybe it was just a set of plans he had to hand ... he could test his idea out on, just to see whether it would be feasible on such a large scale. Or possibly whether the engineering concept for the gimbal would actually work scaled up beyond his initial design."

Dan's mouth gaped open; he was for lost for words.

"I'm only theorising Dan. From the detail we have in front of us, it's pure guesswork. Just think, the Oriskany was an unknown. It was sunk becoming the largest artificial reef overnight. One of the many stipulations placed on the sinking was that it remained upright. No one could have possibly predicted exactly how the vessel would hit the sea bed and in what position. Literally over night the Oriskany became one of the most exclusive dive sites in the world."

"The great carrier reef." Dan mused to himself.

Simon was trying to make the designs tangible in his head. He knew these plans would have taken copious man hours to complete, especially the way Matt had broken the individual separations of the transparencies.

If it was a design concept, or a product idea, then he definitely would not have wanted anyone to know but he would never have designed such detail on a mere whim.

"Maybe James and Matt were working on the idea of the first fully submersed diving station? Somewhere divers could rest staying submerged for longer periods, thus spending longer exploring the site."

Dan felt impressed by the idea, it made sense. It certainly played on James' love of diving.

"I'm buying your theory. It's certainly something that'd interest both Matt and Uncle James but I still don't fully understand the function of the gimbal you're on about?"

"It's simple enough; imagine my hand is the wreck." Simon held his hand out parallel to the floor, palm facing up. "Then you physically attach a chamber to it, like this." He picked up his empty coffee cup, turned it upside down and placed it on the palm of his hand. "All the time the wreck is level, your chamber also remains level. However if the wreck shifts …" He tilted his hand and the cup shifted with it. "… now imagine the chamber is connected via a complex system of pivotal rings. Matt's proposed gimbal, the chamber itself, is no longer directly attached to the wreck." Simon suspended the cup about an inch above his palm, tilting his hand on an angle, the cup remaining parallel to the floor. "Basically when the wreck moves, the chamber remains level at all times."

"So you're saying the gimbal Matt designed would keep the chamber and its occupant's horizontal, no matter what the angle it was attached to varied?"

"Exactly … within reason. There would be a limit where the angle would be too much for the gimbal itself and the chamber would start to tilt.

"Well how much would that be?"

"I don't know. I'd have to translate the measurements to the proposed arc of the gimbal against its size. I can work it out if you want?"

Dan suddenly remembered the time looking at his watch. "Shit! I'm gonna be late for Lizzie, she'll kill me. If you could do that for me and gimme a call later, I'd appreciate it."

"Sure that'll be fine. I'll have to cross reference the original concept drawings of the gimbal and compare them against the proposed chamber width; I'll get on with it."

Dan turned and headed out the front of the building, closely followed by Simon. He jumped in the Range Rover and started the engine. As the engine roared into life he lowered the passenger window to say goodbye and Simon leant in to speak.

"We'll have to go out for a drink. You can fill me in on how you're doing in the UK. It's been a while you know." Simon glanced down to the passenger seat of the Range Rover, where the copy of the plans for the hydro pod track rested. "Is that yet more plans to help piece the puzzle together?"

"No not really, I got them from one of the firms the family invested in. It was something Uncle Mike designed and had manufactured. I was down there this afternoon checking it out."

"Are you sure they're Mike's plans?"

"Well yeah, it's what I was given; they're a copy of the original Uncle Mike gave them a few months ago?"

"That makes sense then?"

Dan looked sceptically from Simon to the plans and back again. "What does?"

"It's just the info reads MM and after looking at the plans in the office, from here it looks like Matt's handwriting. I assumed it was but the MM must stand for Mike Morris, not Matt Morris, like father like son I guess! Their handwriting is bloody similar though, don't you think?"

Dan looked at Simon with the realisation something major had just occurred. He wanted to blurt out what had just dawned on him, the thought seemed ludicrous.

"Call me later to let me know what you find out about the gimbal and we'll definitely have that beer later in the week. Thanks Simon, you're a star."

Simon stuck his hand in the window and they shook. "Great to see you Dan, I'll call you later. See ya."

Dan struck the car into drive and slowly moved forward. Simon removed himself from the window smiling, waved, turned and walked back into the building. Dan watched him in his rear mirror disappear from view as he drove out towards the freeway.

Slamming on the brakes, he snatched the plans from the seat, spun them round so they were the right way up staring at the writing in the lower corner.

Dan had sat next to Matt at school for nearly ten years. It was unmistakeable and Simon was right; not only was the text Matt's handwriting it was also written according to Simon's imposed naming convention, or in this case written purely out of habit. Matt must have drawn these plans.

31

It was nearly half past eight by the time Dan tried to knock on the door to Lizzie's apartment. The door wildly flung open before his knuckles even hit the wood.

"You're late!"

"You're stunning."

"You're forgiven." Lizzie dissolved into a fit of giggles, he had an overwhelming urge to kiss her, she did indeed look stunning. "You know there's a sort of greatness to your lateness."

"Thanks, it's not achieved without undue suffering." Dan smiled; he had not used those quotes in years. Lizzie was a real film fan as they grew up, mainly the slushy romantic kind and for some reason she quoted certain extracts endlessly. She was just happy he remembered them. He was happy Lizzie never changed. "Are you ready?"

"I've been ready since about twenty past, I knew you'd be late, Dad and I had a bet."

"Who won?"

"He did. I'm not that much of an optimist when it comes to your punctuality."

"Harsh."

"But fair!" Lizzie flounced past with an air of righteousness, pulling the door closed, Dan followed.

The Lighthouse had a chequered history. Over its long life span, it had survived artillery bombardment, a couple of lightning strikes, an earthquake and countless hurricanes. During the time of its occupancy, eleven individuals had served as head keepers, nine of which had to be removed for reasons ranging from intoxication to dereliction of duty. The longest serving keeper manned the lamp for thirty-one years until full automation in the mid sixties.

The keeper's duplex eventually became derelict as no one ever ventured inside or maintained it. The whole site was decommissioned in the eighties as it was deemed obsolete. A dedicated local bought the site for a dollar from the coast guard and gradually restored the landmark back to its former glory, although unfortunately not back to its original use as a lighthouse, as so many people believed it should be. Much of its internal architecture, such as the lens and intricate machinery, had been removed leaving an empty unloved carcass.

The owner had installed a 1920s elevator, taken from an old building during demolition. Its art deco wrought ironworks matching identically to the ornate iron stairwell which sleekly spiralled upwards linking the separate levels. The ground floor rotunda housed a walnut deco inspired bar, arcing seamlessly behind the elevator which was the focal point of the ground floor entrance. The old keeper's dwelling to the left had been transformed into the main dining room, joining the rooms seamlessly via an intricate black and white marble floor.

The maître d' stood patiently between the rotunda and dining area. As Dan and Lizzie approached he made a slight bow in their direction. Lizzie could hardly contain her excitement, the Lighthouse was the most talked of restaurants in the whole of Florida, its reputation; quality of food and sheer beauty drew an extremely elite crowd. The whole interior was modelled in an Art Deco style with no expense spared in its luxuriousness, plus the pricing unapologetically reflected this.

Dan approached and spoke. "Good evening, I have a reservation for Daniel Morris."

The maître d' raised an eyebrow, the main restaurant was now full. Taking the guest list from under his armpit which was attached to what looked like a marble clipboard he scanned the list of names. Finally locating Mr Morris at the very bottom; it must have been a late booking. His demeanour instantly warmed.

"Ah good evening Mr Morris and Mizz ..." Over accentuating the miss, he turned to Lizzie, who started to colour slightly.

"Mizz, err Price, Miss Price."

"Enchanté Mademoiselle." The maître d' bowed lowering his head and eyes pointed directly at the floor, offering his hand. "May I take your coat?"

"Yes thank you." The maître d' gently removed the light summer jacket as Lizzie spun herself out of it, revealing a delicate and refined halter neck dress.

"This way if you purlease." The maître d' pointed in the direction of the elevator, after he had hung the coat in a hidden closet between the rotunda and dining room. Lizzie was a little bewildered. She had expected to enter the beautifully decorated restaurant before her but followed the maître d' as instructed. He pulled back the ornate security scissor action doors and ushered the pair of them in, stepping in behind. He closed the gates, checking they were sealed and then operated a small wooden handle, turning it in a clockwise motion by approximately ninety degrees.

The elevator gave a small tremor and creaked as the wheels above their heads turned the connecting cables, slowly moving the elevator upwards. As the first floor gradually emerged, looking through the ornate iron workings, it was filled with people quietly talking, dressed in their finery, each holding a luminescent cocktail of unknown alcoholic content. They were all patiently waiting for a spare table below to be vacated.

The Lighthouse operated a single sitting, only taking reservations for supper, strictly at eight and last orders were at eleven. Therefore if the diners continued to enjoy themselves, which they so often did, the table would only have one sitting of an evening. The restaurant itself only had a forty head arrangement, pre-booked months in advance.

It was the main rule of the house, if the original occupants remained seated, the table would never become available and the unfortunate people waiting on the first floor would not get a table. The staff referred to the would-be diners as the damned, or the room itself as the waiting room. The tips were disproportionately large in the waiting room because the overly enthusiastic damned believed tipping would elevate their position in the queue; none of the staff discouraged it.

Lizzie had the horrible sinking feeling they would also be joining the reluctant folly waiting for a table. The conversation in the room quietly halted as the elevators occupants came into view, all eyes looked expectantly as two more unfortunate souls would step into the waiting room to join the throng. The eyes of the people looked incredulous as the elevator in fact did not stop, it continued upwards. Lizzie looked at Dan who smiled triumphantly.

The elevator continued to the second floor where the maître d' slowly turned the handle back to the starting position and the elevator gently came to a halt. The maître d' looked down at the floor and visually admonished himself at not having correctly levelled the correlating floors. "Mind the step madam." He pulled back the security gate and motioned for the pair of them to exit, Lizzie exited followed by Dan. The security gate slid shut and without another word the maître d' returned back downstairs to the rotunda.

The second floor had a large walnut curved bar directly in front of the elevator, a single bartender waited patiently for them to emerge, bowing slightly.

"Sir, madam, I took the privilege of preparing you a number of starter cocktails to better endeavour to understand your palette."

Along the bar surface arranged in a neat line were a number of glasses, each containing an unknown liquid.

"For madam, on the right hand side I have taken the unusual act of preparing a number of gin based cocktails under sir's suggestion using Hendricks Gin. From right to left we have a Parisian, a Berliner, a Blackberry Bramble, a Bennett and a Park Avenue."

Lizzie looked over her shoulder at Dan with a wry smile and a wink. "Hmm … Hendricks eh, you trying to get me drunk Mr Morris?" The bartender continued without dropping his line of thought.

"For sir, from left to right we have a High Ball, a Red Snapper, a Rusty Nail, a Scotch Sour and a Highland Fling." His eyes leapt from the drinks bouncing between the two. "Or would you prefer me to make a recommendation?"

Lizzie loved cocktails but never really knew what she liked or disliked, she did however know they were too easy to drink. "Can you recommend one for me please?" Lizzie attempted to adopt a more formal tone in her voice but was already quietly in awe by their treatment.

"Yes madam, I'd suggest the Park Avenue. It is extremely elegant like yourself and for sir I would suggest the High Ball, a very sophisticated drink." The bartender pushed the glass holding each individual drink towards them as he mentioned the cocktails' names. He then quickly whisked away the remaining glasses leaving just the two. Dan and Lizzie picked up their drinks and sipped at them.

"Ooh that's lovely." Lizzie cooed.

"Mine's very good too, do you mind if I ask what ginger you use with the whiskey?"

The bar tender beamed an enormous satisfied smile. "You are too kind sir. It is in fact my family's traditionally brewed ginger beer recipe which gives it the heated kick. I am truly grateful sir likes it."

From behind a voice interrupted the overflowing gratitude of the bartender. "Would Miss Price care to follow me?"

Lizzie spun round to face two waiters, each holding a silver platter; the girl whom had spoken to Lizzie held hers out in front. Lizzie placed her half consumed cocktail on the platter; the girl turned and started to ascend the staircase to the right of the elevator shaft.

As Lizzie followed the waitress, Dan watched in awe, she looked stunning. The dress Lizzie wore looked elegant and refined from the front. As she moved to take the stairs, Dan marvelled that the rear of the dress plunged magnificently to below the small of her back, any further would have been indecent.

Not that Dan would have complained if it was. Her entire body had been bronzed, her long legs looked stunning and the look was finished with a matching clutch bag and high heeled shoes. Lizzie could tell she was being watched, she flicked her cascading hair with the back of her hand, turning, locking eyes with him. He had never seen her look so beautiful.

The second waiter coughed gently breaking the spell between them. Nodding his approval he lifted his platter towards Dan. "Would Mr Morris care to follow me as well?"

Dan gently placed his glass on the platter, his eyes still following Lizzie. The waiter spun on his heels and started to ascend the staircase to the left of the elevator. Both of them spiralled upwards on separate sides of the lighthouse to the third and final floor, the two staircases meeting together at the top. Dan and Lizzie stood smiling at each other while the waiters moved off, placing their individual cocktail glasses on an immaculately presented table, dressed for two in the middle.

Dan and Lizzie surveyed the room looking through the spotless glass towards the horizon. A three hundred and sixty degree uninterrupted view from the lantern room, it was magnificent. Each waiter held an individual balloon backed chair waiting patiently; they were used to the reaction from diners. In awe of the view it took both Dan and Lizzie a while to regain their senses and tear themselves away from the vista. They looked at each other and crossed to the table, enabling the waiters to tuck their chairs beneath them.

They both then bowed, the male waiter spoke. "Thank you, sir, madam; tonight's menu is printed on each parchment placed in front of you." He gestured to the scroll neatly tied with an orange ribbon. "When you are ready to order either food or drink, or would indeed require any other service, please pull the servants' bell and we shall endeavour to grant your every whim. As you are probably fully aware, there is no rush. Have a good evening." Both waiters reversed away towards the stairs slightly bowing, as if addressing royalty.

"Sir, Madam."

Then both turned to leave and Lizzie looked around the room, she could not see a bell of any kind? "Excuse me."

"Yes madam." Both waiters stopped, abruptly turning as if etiquette had been broken facing Lizzie, only the male waiter spoke.

"Umm, a bell?" She shrugged looking a little sheepish, swivelling and pointing around the room with her shoulders.

"Yes Madam." Smiling, he crossed to the area between the two adjoining stairs, against the glass hung a black wrought iron pole with a wooden handle attached. "Simply pull one of the four situated conveniently around the circular room." He tugged on the handle and below them a bell sounded quietly but distinctly.

"Like so madam … enjoy your evening." The pair promptly bowed again, divided and the male waiter took the stairs Dan had come up and the female waitress descended via the stairwell Lizzie came up. The pair of them sat looking at each other suddenly alone, stunned by their surroundings.

32

The lamp house at the top of the building had an enviable three hundred and sixty degree view of the surrounding panorama. Each individual sheet of glass was slightly curved to follow the slick lines of the metal window frames, the imperfections rippling and gently distorting the view.

Modern plain flat glass with its precision manufacture fails to imbue the same charm and beauty of the old float glass process. Every irregular pane and metal surround framed a singular view, which in its own right held its own idyllic picture.

The lighthouse was of course famed for its location. The sheer beauty of its interior, the staff and food created the ambience it was renowned for. However very few diners were fortunate enough to experience the exclusivity of the lamp house at the very top of the lighthouse.

The lamp house was reserved for proposals, honeymooners or exclusive business guests with extremely important deals to clinch. It was exclusive because it was rarely available. Bookings were taken months in advance and the staff who served the lamp house were the cream of the lighthouse crew. Each individual diner was treated with their own steward who looked after their every whim.

Dan and Lizzie were alone, an individual ornate round table just for the pair of them centred in the middle of the glass rotunda. If they had taken more notice they would have realised the dining arrangement was slightly lower than normal so when seated the metal window surrounds did not impinge the view. It was not a fortunate accident, it had been designed specifically that way.

They stared out across the expansive horizon. Dusk was beginning to settle over Pensacola and the sky was turning a lustrous flaming orange, magnified by the still cool ocean. The warmth streamed in through the glass and Lizzie's bronzed skin glowed in its radiance.

She absently picked up her scroll, slipping the ribbon from the paper, so luxurious it screamed decadence. The select menu was written in blood red ink, immaculately presented, a work of art in its own right. Many of the dishes were foreign, Lizzie having no idea what they were. Looking up from her scroll to Dan, who was staring intently off into the distance, smiling.

"Well I hope you bought your charge card?"

"Why's that?"

"Not a single thing has a price by the side of it, which either means it's free, or if you have to ask the price, you can't afford it." Lizzie looked around the circular glass room, overlooking Pensacola, a good hundred feet above the ground. "And you know what; I don't think their washing up gloves are gonna remotely match the colour of this dress!"

"I can afford it, plus I said I'd treat you, so here we are." Dan looked rather pleased with himself at her reaction. In truth he needed Lizzie to help form his thoughts about the last couple of days and what he had discovered. She had always been able to read him, searching his soul for the right words, although he was completely unsure how to broach the subject he wanted to discuss. With her help, by the end of the evening, he may even just about understand his suspicions.

"Lizzie, I'd like to ask you something."

She looked up from her scroll, putting it down, the ends rolling inwards. "You look serious, what is it?"

Dan took a deep breath, he had to start somewhere and this was a cue of sorts. He exhaled deeply, starting from a slanted perspective about someone only Lizzie would know. "It's difficult to ask. I was wondering, leading up to when Matt and Ashley disappeared on the yacht, what was Ashley like?"

"She was okay … what do you mean?" Lizzie drained the last of her cocktail and left her seat. "I need to try something." A mischievous grin spread across her face, crossing to one of the bell pulls directly behind her chair, she tugged on the handle. Within seconds the bar steward stood at the top of the stairs looking expectantly. Lizzie looked smug and as giddy as a school kid.

"Yes Madam?"

"Can I have another cocktail please?"

"What would you like?"

"Surprise me."

The bar steward bowed and swivelled on his heels towards Dan.

146

"And for sir?"

Dan stared into the bottom of his glass, frowning. "Actually, could I have a Guinness?" He half expected the bar steward to say Guinness was not on the bar list, instead he reversed and promptly disappeared down stairs. Lizzie was now staring at Dan expectantly, who cleared his throat.

"Well what I mean is, before Ashley disappeared did she say anything to you, or act strangely at all?" Dan wanted to blurt it out but felt like he was still trying to get the exterior straight edged pieces of a jigsaw puzzle together, before he could fill in the full picture.

"What, stranger than normal?" Lizzie screwed her face up and then laughed. To be fair Ash was never what you'd call normal, in the traditional girly sense. She had always been more interested in geeky subjects than basic growing up pursuits. When the girls were chasing boys, she was chasing a high grade point average. When the boys turned to men, she looked at learning another language or toward gaining her placement at Harvard.

In fact the preconceived normal pattern of growing up never worked for Ashley, she was just far too serious and studious. It was only when the four of them were together you could actually see Ash act her age, or even remotely like a rebellious teenager. Lizzie had had a way of getting Ash to lighten up.

Dan had always assumed it was down to Lizzie's tomboy fun and boisterous nature; however they just complemented each others' polar opposites. Between the pair of them they had the perfect balance of femininity, elegance, beauty and intelligence.

"I was just wondering if Ash mentioned anything to you. Did you think she was acting different at all?"

Lizzie had never really analysed much, most things washed over her but she had always treasured their last night together. "Well, I've never really thought about it before but now you mention it, the night before they all disappeared she just turned up at my place!"

"So?"

"Well that's the point. Ash never did anything like that. Think about it ... she'd plan every occasion, right down to the underwear she'd be wearing. It was me who'd spontaneously decide we were gonna drive to the lake, or just randomly turn up at University to take her out because she would be stressing about some exam. I was the one who made Ash do things, I was the spontaneous one."

"But she was back from Uni?"

"Yeah, she was only visiting though. The semester didn't finish for another three weeks after that and I know for a fact she had three more exams because she told me when we were chatting on the phone a couple of days before."

The bar steward quietly walked across to the table carrying a silver tray. On it was a balloon shaped cocktail glass filled with a cranberry based sweet smelling concoction. The pair, realising they were not alone, stopped their conversation, instinctively leaning back. The steward placed the cocktail in front of Lizzie, and looking very pleased with himself, placed an original Guinness glass in front of Dan, the gold harp purposely faced towards him. The thick head on the inky liquid had an almost perfect four leaf clover carved into the cream.

Dan was impressed, he could not even remember if the Toucan in Soho, a purely Guinness and Irish Bar, had ever served him such a perfect looking pint.

The steward retreated below stairs. Lizzie sucked greedily through the straw on her cocktail. Dan took a mouthful of the stout, it tasted as good as it looked. He concluded it was a myth Guinness did not travel, that or the bar steward was simply a genius. Lizzie laughed, leaning closer, she wiped the creamy moustache from his top lip with her thumb, rather too seductively. Suddenly feeling awkward, she lowered her gaze from his.

He shrugged. "Well, for once in her life, maybe Ash just needed some time off?"

"No Dan, she never worked like that and you know it. She would've just kept plugging away at her books until the last possible second." Lizzie took another sip. "This is good you know, wanna mouthful?"

"No thanks, I can smell how sweet it is from here."

"Oh live a little will ya, one sip ain't gonna wreck that perfect specimen of a body! We're in the lamp house, at the Lighthouse no less; it just doesn't get any better than this!" Lizzie pushed the glass across the table; Dan took a suck through the straw.

"That's not bad actually, smells sweeter than it tastes."

Lizzie smiled triumphant continuing the story of their last night together. "We went to the station, as you do; she just seemed like she had the whole world on her shoulders wanting to talk."

"Yeah but she was always like that, our Ash was far too intense."

"Well this night she got a little drunk and a few of the things she said made no sense. At the time I put it down to the alcohol."

Dan started to have a feeling that what Lizzie was saying had a bearing on what he had discovered today. "Like what?"

"In hindsight, it was as if she knew it was going to be her last night. Although again in hindsight, I could just be reading too much into it?"

Dan was leaning in desperately trying to work out if it was another piece of the puzzle.

"She was jabbering on about your Granddad's and her Dad's research, but as with everything to do with science, I tuned out, it simply went over my head. I remember she reckoned it would revolutionise the way we; that's us as a species, would live. The technology would be cleaner, more efficient and more importantly, free! Everything was slightly confusing and contradictory, like she was speaking in riddles and half truths ... hiding something? It felt like she wanted to confess something big but was scared and couldn't, or wouldn't. I'd never known her ever talk like that. It was then she started to say how the legacy had consumed most of the family but she made me promise never to tell you." Lizzie faltered taking a long sip from her cocktail, her mouth had gone dry. The secret she had struggled internally with for these last few years was about to be told. She never fully understood its implications, although with Ash gone maybe Dan would?

"Ash said the family secret protected you at its core. You knew nothing and it should stay that way. She asked me to look after you like a brother; in fact she asked more than that of me but that's something I just don't feel I can ... quite disclose yet." Lizzie lowered her eyes, as if she had perpetrated a cardinal sin and was deeply ashamed. Dan knew she had reluctantly told a secret; instinctively he cradled her hand in his across the table.

They both sat in silence; it was not what Dan had been expecting to hear. Why had Ash started to open up to Lizzie and ultimately, why did she believe he was at the core of the family? What did that mean?

33

The silence between them lasted for an age. They had always been comfortable like this together, although Lizzie was getting hungry and the evening was progressing. Lizzie was notoriously grumpy when hungry, deciding to order her food.

"Do you want a starter?"

"I've not really even looked yet. You can order though, I'll make up my mind as the waiter arrives."

"Well I'm going to go for a main and a dessert; you always gotta leave room for pudding."

Lizzie crossed back to the servant's bell and pulled on the handle. Before she had even returned to her seat a waiter arrived, followed by the bar steward who hovered behind. Lizzie scanned the hand written menu, there were so many dishes she simply had no idea what they were.

"Could you tell me please, what a Turducken is?"

"Certainly madam, a Turducken is a specially boned and rolled selection of birds, although not served as per tradition. The lighthouse chefs have created a house styled alternative, which consists of chicken rolled inside a duck which in turn is rolled inside a turkey. Tur, from the turkey, duck as in the duck and the en from the chicken, Tur-duck-en.

Traditionally the turkey was a full turkey; however for a single meal a whole turkey may be a little too much for a single diner, such as yourself. All the meat has been de-boned and rolled after being marinated in a special orange brandy sauce."

"Wow that sounds lovely, I'll have that." The waiter turned to Dan who was desperately looking through the indecipherable list, all of which he had never heard of before."

"Has sir made a decision?"

"The haunch of venison." It was the only dish Dan could recognise a single part of the ingredients. "I wondered what comes with it?"

"A most primal choice sir." He beamed. "The most succulent wild venison is cooked to your delectation and served with potato dauphinoise. The blood from the meat is added to a Beaujolais and reduced to add depth and character. How would you like the venison cooked?

"Oh, um, rare please."

The waiter smiled warmly, suggesting Dan had chosen wisely. He bowed and reversed. The position was instantly filled from behind by the hovering bar steward.

"Forgive my intrusion but having over heard your choice of dishes this evening, can I make a suggestion for a 1961 Bordeaux to accompany your meal? 1961 is regarded by many as simply the best vintage of the 20th Century; we only have a couple of bottles left in the cellar."

Dan looked at Lizzie who shrugged; Dan was certainly not a wine connoisseur but had often wondered what a truly expensive bottle would taste like, so what the hell. He decided this evening would be a no holds barred expense. Tapping his top pocket containing his yet unused black Amex card for comfort.

"That sounds lovely."

Lizzie leant forward quietly whispering, so the bar steward could not hear. "Yeah and expensive." They both grinned.

Outside, the sun was beginning to dip beneath the horizon and the lustrous glow was starting to fade. Dan had his back to the sunset, his face was set in shadow, his features had the pallid look of death. Lizzie knew him better than anyone else in the world; she could see something was troubling him.

"So, what's wrong, other than the obvious?" She meant the death of his Aunt and Uncle. "You have something heavy playing on your mind?"

"Well, er, yes, but I'm not entirely sure where to start. Have you spoken to your Dad today?"

Lizzie was in a bit of a mood with him. He had been elusive to say the least and ignoring his phone. He had turned up late, promptly disappearing again and had missed important client meetings, which she had to hastily rearrange, making plausible excuses as she always did. They were accepted graciously but she was less than amused with him. Dan's phone call for their long overdue dinner actually salvaged what had been, up until that point, a particularly crap day.

"No, he was late this morning; he swanned in, locked something in the safe and promptly buggered off, leaving me to handle irate clients."

"So he never mentioned last night to you?"

"No. He's been about as communicative and grumpy as a teenager. Why?"

Dan shifted uncomfortably, Charlie was a man of his word and tomorrow morning, the drives would have to be released to the police. After that deadline, all of the information would have to be disclosed.

"Did you know he came to the house last night?"

"Yeah, he left the office and said he was coming over to drop some paper work off to the house. Why? Did you two have a fight?"

Dan looked surprised at the idea. "What would've given you that idea?"

"He just had the look! The way he does when I've had an argument with him and he's stewing over something. He can be like that with me for days; I was beginning to think I'd done something. Glad it's you this time and not me. You do realise he looks at you like a son?"

Dan was floored by the comment but slightly warmed by it. "We never argued last night." He paused, unsure how to continue, the ideas he had swimming round his head were strange but when spoken out loud would give a different perspective or reinforcement to them.

"I showed your Dad something last night which upset him."

Lizzie stopped drinking her cocktail looking at him. "I've not seen him in that kind of mood for a long time, what on earth did you show him?"

"You remember the two keys that Aunt Susan left in the package for me? I told a little bit of a white lie, I said the USB key opened the Panic Room, well it opens more than that."

"What does it open then and why did your Aunt give it to Dad to look after?"

"The keys are actually mine." He sighed. "I gave them to Aunt Susan when I left for London. It made absolutely no sense to take them with me as they are useless, the USB data can only be operated by me. The main key opens a safe behind the family portrait."

Lizzie looked relieved. "Yeah I've seen it, your Aunt Susan put something in it once when I was there, she showed me a couple of rings that were family heirlooms."

"That's right but in the back of the safe is a security device to open the Panic Room, an iris scanner." Dan paused to see a reaction from Lizzie, there was none, so he continued. "The USB key holds the scan data of my eye and cross references it against a real time scan of my retina. Without it the Panic Room remains shut. We all had them, Uncle

James, Aunt Pat, Matt, Ash and me; of course I assume theirs disappeared along with them. I haven't been able to find Uncle Mike's and Susan's keys." Dan took another gulp of his Guinness. "The USB key opens the Panic Room, which in turn houses a far more elaborate internal closed circuit system I installed throughout the house."

"What, other than the basic cameras outside, you mean there are more? Does that mean they captured what happened to your Aunt and Uncle?" The penny dropped. "You mean you've got evidence?"

Dan lowered his head and nodded. "I've seen the footage Lizzie. I've seen the man who killed Uncle Mike and Aunt Susan. I showed it to your Dad last night."

Lizzie looked shocked, Dan could see it in her eyes. "The man came to the house as an alleged CCTV repairman, I say alleged as I believe he'd already disabled the cameras and landline. I found some form of tape stuck to the bottom of each camera. It disrupted the wireless feeds somehow. He came to the house using the deception of fixing the cameras, but ultimately he was looking for something else!"

Lizzie gulped, a tear sliding down her right cheek and asked matter of fact. "Did they suffer?"

Dan wanted to protect her, he wanted to scoop her up in his arms and hold her. Aunt Susan had been like a mother to them all, she had protected them for so long including Lizzie, probably her more so because of her own mother's death.

He resisted telling her how brutal the killings had been, instead he dodged the question and bowed his head. Lizzie knew what it meant, the tears streamed down her face. Dan absently wiped them away, but they continued to stream.

"He found the Panic Room, they tried to stop him and they paid with their lives. They did however protect the secret the Panic Room was hiding." Lizzie tried to stop crying and sniffed into the back of her hand.

"He found the surveillance monitors taking the hard drives they were recording to. He thought he was clever but I, for once in my life, was even more so. I had the drives mirrored, so could reconstruct them including the original footage, which is what I watched along with your Dad last night."

"So we know what the bastard looks like?"

"That's it, we don't." Lizzie's face fell.

"He wore a cap and managed to avoid looking at the cameras, whether he knew, or whether it was just coincidence I don't know. He didn't know he was being recorded until he got into the room, I assume that's why he took the primary drives."

Lizzie pondered the last few details. "You said he didn't find what he was looking for though?"

"Well the safe was full of many heirlooms, as you can witness, along with countless untraceable bearer bonds, he never took any of it. The Panic Room hides another more important secret though, a second door."

"A second door! To where?"

As Dan had started to talk it felt easier and quite natural, like an elaborate plotline unveiled, the detail having been concocted in his head, none of which had seemed real but had now started to make sense.

"When the original house burned down the family constructed a lab under the house so it could house Granddad's research and life work, continued by James after his death."

"So why would the murderer be looking for that?"

"I don't know; I've never understood what the research was about but if Ash talked to you saying it would revolutionise the world as we know it, then maybe it was industrial espionage? Maybe finding the Panic Room was an accident and not part of the plan?"

"But does killing your Aunt and Uncle help the plan? Why have you not taken the recording straight to the police?" Lizzie suddenly looked concerned and a little angry.

"I discovered a few more clues which Aunt Susan obviously wanted only me to find and the conversation with your Dad unearthed a few leads which I needed to follow up. Once the drives are released, it'll become a federal investigation and I won't be able to talk to anyone involved.

It also looks like I've withheld vital information towards the investigation, especially as I was the only one who knew about the hidden surveillance and CCTV set up. Ultimately though, I have no idea how to even begin to disclose the lab."

"What the hell were your family up to Dan?"

"That's just it, I don't know and I don't see what difference it would make to the investigation but withholding the information looks bad on my part. I can see that. But there's something else, something which can't possibly have been left by Aunt Susan!"

Dan looked at Lizzie holding her confused gaze. Reaching into his pocket he retrieved the black onyx handled pen knife, like his own, placing it in front of Lizzie. Dan opened the large blade like he had done the previous day in Charlie's office, the blade read Διόνυσος.

"I found it in the service tunnel leading off the lab. Like both of us, Matt and Ash always carried their knives with them." He looked at Lizzie; he could see she shared the same glimmer of hope in her eyes that thankfully confirmed his own belief. Finally whispering the words aloud he found so difficult.

"I think Matt's alive Liz."

34

Lizzie was silent, her eyes moved from the blade to Dan and back again. Her mouth opened and closed several times as if to say something, each time failing to find the words.

Instead she reached for her clutch bag, opening the side pocket on the inside pulling out her own pen knife attached to her silver chain, she opened the blade, it read Εστία – Hestia. Dan followed suit with his own pen knife.

"I didn't really think my knife would go with my dress, but I never go anywhere without it." Lizzie fumbled again in her bag, retrieving a second identical knife; she placed it alongside the three others. Two black onyx handled knives alongside two smaller tortoiseshell versions. Dan stared at it, then to Lizzie for an explanation.

"The night Ash and I were at the station she gave it to me. Like I said, she was acting strange, she wanted me to look after it for her. I've kept it safe ever since, part of me always hoped I'd be able to give it back to her some day. Go on, open it."

Dan's hand visibly shook as he reached over and pulled open the blade, it read Αθηνά - Athena, the knife was definitely Ash's.

"Now, turn it over, look at the reverse side of the knife?" Dan did as he was told, along the opposite side of the knife it had several numbers engraved in the stainless steel blade, the numbers looked familiar, a cell phone number perhaps? The numbers read 3, 0, 0, 2, 6, 8, 7, 0, 0, 4.

Dan looked at Lizzie confused. "Is it Ash's cell? What do they mean?"

"It took me ages to figure it out, look at the blade closer; the numbers are separated by very small marks which I originally thought were just marks on the blade."

Dan looked really closely realising Lizzie was right, each number was separated by a colon or a full stop. The numbers now read 30:02.6 & 87:00.4.

"I still don't understand, are they dates? What are they?"

"I only know because I wrote them down once. I scribbled them on a map for Matt when we took Hydrous out diving. It was the last time the three of us were together; we celebrated your birthday, even though you couldn't make it home."

Dan had been caught up on an investigation and all leave was cancelled. The four of them had planned to celebrate by taking Hydrous away for the weekend diving.

"Matt shouted them through to me from the cockpit and I wrote them on the chart. I couldn't find the china graph pencil so wrote the numbers down."

The pair of them finished Lizzie's sentence in unison. "In red marker pen."

"You know?"

"I spotted the chart when I was on Hydrous; I have it back at the house."

"I didn't recognise them at first because it had been a good few months when I wrote them and I honestly didn't pay any attention at the time. In fact it wasn't until I was watching the news about a diver who died and they gave the coordinates on the news bulletin of where he was found. It dawned on me they were in fact GPS coordinates."

"Matt would have programmed the GPS coordinates into the navigational GPS; it would pretty much self navigate the boat to that spot every time you brought up the protocol. Where were you diving, do you remember?"

"Of course I do, it was where the guy on the news died that spurred the memory. The coordinates are to the Oriskany, the position where she was sunk!"

"You're kidding me right?" Dan was a little shocked to hear about the Oriskany again today.

"No, after the ship was given the all clear, we used to dive there quite a lot. I don't have the same experience as Matt so he used to head a lot deeper than me and Ash. I only really ever went as deep as the island. I climbed the smoke stack and I did venture into the bridge with Ash one day, which was great."

Dan was alarmed by this latest revelation. Matt had dived on the Oriskany alone. He was an experienced diver but surely even he would never have been foolhardy enough to separate from an inexperienced group. Unless of course he had motive to do something he did not want Lizzie to see.

If Matt had actually built an underwater habitat on the Oriskany then it would have to be well located and within reach. Or maybe that was the point; it was not easy to reach and not meant to be found?

"Dan, I've always felt that in my heart Ash gave me her knife for a reason, like a momento. She knew she was gonna disappear; it's the only logical explanation. She would never have given me her knife, like ours, it meant more than anything. Your Granddad gave them to us, it was like a family heirloom and we all promised to keep them, always."

"Something bothers me a little though Lizzie, why didn't you tell me you had Ashley's knife." For some reason this tiny piece of news annoyed Dan, he knew they were close but after Ash's death, disappearance or whatever it was, why had she never told him?

"Ash made me promise not to." Lizzie held her head in shame, she felt like a child being told off.

"I'm sorry, the longer I never told you the harder it was. You became so distant after your Grandparents' deaths and when your Aunt and Uncle, Matt and Ash were never discovered, you simply stopped communicating with me. It never really seemed relevant; it was the first time I truly felt alone."

"I'm sorry too, you've always been here for me and I shut you out. I shut everyone out. When Aunt Susan was over in the UK she made me promise to come home more, she said I needed to learn to live again. Part of that was learning to live with the past, letting go of the loss and anger. She also told me you missed me more than you would ever admit."

Lizzie started to flush red, she had once confessed to Aunt Susan, after far too much Hendricks, she always looked at Dan as her soul mate. She had been slightly embarrassed and always somewhat worried Aunt Susan would tell. Although secretly hoped maybe one day she would. She could handle her love for him, knowing he was happy living his life but he was not. Unrequited love was a bitter pill to swallow, especially when it seemed neither party had what they wanted.

Lizzie glowed in the soft warm light, her hair shone as it fell across her face and she felt uneasy in his company, like a teenager with a high school crush. Dan also felt slightly embarrassed; he suddenly understood what Aunt Susan had inferred when she spoke to him on vacation.

Lizzie stared into his eyes, the confused feeling he had, the feeling he would cross a line and never be able to return evaporated. Lizzie was no longer the eight year old girl who had also lost her mother, just like he had. Her visage evaporated, Lizzie's tomboy and sisterly embodiment melted to reveal a woman, the woman Dan had somehow overlooked all his life because of their childhood bond.

Dan lifted his hand from the table and pushed Lizzie's hair from her face tucking it behind her ear as they stared into each others' eyes. For the first time they both understood that the chemistry between them was more than the memories they shared. Dan had tried to run away from everything because he was scared of losing anyone else, he had pushed everyone away in fear, suddenly he realised Lizzie was the one person he truly had left in the world.

Lizzie on the other hand was feeling coy for the first time in her life. She felt electric as his hand gently touched her forehead and brushed back her hair. The way Dan was looking at her was as if he saw her as a woman for the first time. 'It's the dress ...' she thought; '... maybe I should have worn something more feminine years ago.'

Dan leant forward to kiss her and she closed her eyes as his lips touched hers. Unlike most men she had kissed, his lips were soft and gentle. There was no immediacy to their embrace, it was a perfectly natural progression, with none of the awkwardness she had always worried about between them.

"Ahem, excuse me." The pair of them jolted back to earth by a lone male voice. They parted quickly, slightly flustered, turned to see their original waiter standing before them with his hands patiently held behind his back. He waited for them to part. Smiling broadly, he whisked away the outer cutlery, which included the unwanted salad fork and soup spoons, on the place setting in front of them.

He stepped aside to reveal their waitress who carried two beautifully crystal clear dinner plates; they were obviously hot as she was wearing pristine white gloves. The Turducken was placed in front of Lizzie and Dan's venison in front of him. The plates were both immaculately presented and the vegetables colour graded to coordinate.

The waitress retreated and the bar steward fell abruptly into her position, whisking the cocktails away and replacing them with delicate crystal clear wine glasses. The only splash of colour was a thin red liquid spiral of glass running through the stem, which flowed into the red wine as it gently filled from the 1961 Bordeaux.

Dan and Lizzie once more watched the spectacle before them, impatiently waiting for the steward to leave. They stared into each others' eyes wantonly across the table, both a little out of breath, suddenly not really bothered by the outside view or the amazing food in front of them. Dan outstretched his hand entwining his fingers into Lizzie's, rubbing his thumb along the side of her wrist.

The bar steward finished filling the glasses, placing a smaller glass alongside each and filled with iced water. He bowed and reversed towards the stairs.

35

Dan raised the nearest wine glass and drank, a little uncomfortable from being caught by strangers.

"Where were we?"

"I think, Mr Morris, you were kissing me." Lizzie smiled with the whole of her face as Dan put his glass down; she pulled him towards her with his shirt.

"Oh yeah!" Dan grinned as he was gently pulled towards Lizzie. Their eyes closed as their lips met again, across the table.

Dan's cell started to ring. If looks could kill, Dan would have been ready for burial in the family plot. Lizzie was unimpressed, not hiding her feelings well and visibly deflating. He looked at his phone apologetically, the display read Simon. He glanced at Lizzie and she glowered back as he answered it.

"Hi Simon!"

"Are you otherwise engaged?" Dan looked at Lizzie, he could tell from her demeanour and pout she was hardly enamoured by yet another interruption.

"No you're fine." He lied. "Did you manage to work out the drawings?"

"Yes, they're really interesting; I also managed to go through the rest of the design sheets and piece them together. As a whole Matt must have spent a long time designing the structure, cylindrical walkways isolate the individual chambers via hydraulic water tight doors. In effect, what you are looking at are three large connected water tight boxes." He paused gathering his thoughts. "Do you know what a hydro pod is?"

Dan froze, Lizzie could see him squirm physically knowing instantly something was wrong. "Umm, yeah, it was something my Grandfather worked on." Hearing his Granddad mentioned she mellowed slightly leaning forward, trying to listen in on the conversation. He cocked the cell phone for her to hear, their foreheads touched.

"Oh okay, well section CVB seems to be designed as an underwater lab!" Simon continued like a giddy school child relaying the most important news.

"Sorry, did you say underwater lab?"

"Yep, it's amazing. The individual section CVB is compartmentalised into an office, laboratory and a smaller wet area designated as the hydro pod, which is connected by some kind of smaller venting tunnel into section CVC as well as the walkway. CVC is basically the access compartment to the entire structure and operational control for the chambers. The drawings for that though are a little sketchy; CVC just doesn't have the detail the others do, although it looks as though half the area is a large moon pool or lock out chamber. Finally, CVA is basically the living area comprised of kitchen, bathroom and bedrooms ... it's all here on the diagrams. It's an ingenious design. I've scanned all of the individual transparencies and superimposed them into single images. I've emailed them to you. I assume you have internet access at the house?"

"Yeah I'll login and take a look when I get home later."

"I've sent you a copy of all the individual chambers' dimensions and sizing, plus a number of extra sheets I found which I think will explain how the whole design fits together."

"Simon, do you reckon it would be possible to actually construct the habitat?"

Simon exhaled deeply, pondering the question. "I've worked out the math on the structure, such as the pressure loads and reinforcement needed to build the chambers. Like I said, the size of them is restrictive because of their individual mass, but what I've discovered is they are what you would call, over engineered."

"So you're saying they could act as compression chambers?"

"No."

At this Dan felt slightly disappointed but he could hear the excitement in Simon's voice.

"What I'm saying is the entire load bearing structure of the inner chambers are strong enough to support standard atmospheric pressure. Putting it simply, if you compare the chambers against the blueprint of the Oriskany plans and where the hangar deck now lies, which is at a depth of roughly around 150 feet, you could easily dive down to the chambers in a wetsuit or sub and you wouldn't have to compress because the internal pressure would be the same as on the surface."

Lizzie was looking at Dan with absolute bewilderment, her jaw open. Dan held up his finger to her mouth to keep her silent. Hearing about a sub was not something he had expected to hear, possibly just coincidence but nothing seemed coincidental today.

"The external pressures and internal cross bracing are built to withstand a lot more. I also compared the positioning towards the stern of the hangar deck against the blast holes and where the hull was strategically cut. Its exact size allows water to flood the internal decks. The positioning gives the maximum distance from the explosive charges, which were set to sink the ship. Its positioning was certainly not an accident, given its maximum possible distance from the blast radius."

"I don't understand what difference would that make to the chambers?" Without a blueprint in front of him Dan was having trouble visualising the ship, part of him wished he had internet access here to view the design sheets. Lizzie was having trouble understanding any of the conversation, so kept quiet.

Simon continued as if he had thoroughly researched all the scenarios before making the call. "You have to remember a lot of the ship's internal layout will have changed dramatically, and the deck plans are no longer reliable! The rushing water and concussion from the explosives will have caused severe damage to the original lightweight aluminium bulkheads. They made up a large portion of the internal structure of the ship. Remember I told you we removed a lot of the internal hardware like door hatches, ladders, decks, and bulkheads prior to the sinking? Well it looks like Matt strengthened and moved individual sections as well, to isolate and by the looks of it, hide the chambers. I found a diagram detailing part of the redesign of the outer bulkhead, which was in steel. I sent that to you as well."

"Why would he move the bulkheads? Surely that would be a lot of work and not worth the hassle?"

"I think there are probably many reasons to consider but to me the biggest concern would be for protection against the force of the initial explosions. If left unchecked the explosions would have ripped through the weaker areas and as a result buckle the original RSJs. By moving the bulkheads and changing their build strength, including some of the materials, it would effectively form a protective shield around the chambers during the sinking. The reinforcement would withstand the blast and stem the oncoming water as it sunk, allowing the water to fill more slowly in the area around the chambers, thus protecting it."

Lizzie was nestling her head further against the ear piece of the phone, straining to hear the full conversation as the significance of what she was hearing sunk in.

"You remember the gimbal structures the chambers are attached too?"

"Your floating mug demonstration."

"Crude I know, well I think the chambers would have been fixed for the initial sinking as I reckon the forces exerted during the sinking would stress the chambers too much if allowed to simply be free. Once the ship had settled, the chambers would be released so they could self level. I believe the size of the gimbal would determine how much movement the internal chambers would have. I made crude calculations, cross referencing the size of the hangar against the internal chambers and I believe the chambers would not have much more than eighteen degrees of movement before the edges of the chambers would touch the floor of the hangar. I also went online and discovered after the sinking, the ship pretty much lay upright. After Hurricane Gustav hit the structure, it sunk a further ten feet into the ocean floor and listed by approximately eight degrees to port which would not be noticeable on the ship itself, but for the inner chambers it would be an immense angle, especially for the occupants and interiors."

Dan took a deep breath. "Let me get this straight. According to the drawings and technical data you've calculated, you reckon it would be possible to build three individual underwater chambers. To, in effect, survive explosive charges and the complete structural submergence to a depth in excess of 150 feet and these inter connecting chambers would form a theoretical fully submersed habitat?"

"Well I'm not sure I'd even say theoretical after my research."

"Why not?"

"Well, I managed to get hold of some of the freelancers we used. You remember some of the design sheets had telephone numbers scrawled on them? Well I rang a few and they were the numbers to some of the guys who worked on the Oriskany. Several of them worked at various stages of the project and I reckon between them they built the three individual chambers. They referred to them as cubes and they moved the bulkheads as per the drawings. Each one of them refused to speak about the engineering project having signed an NDA."

Lizzie interrupted. "NDA?" Simon was on a roll in his world of design and his own pure excitement was getting the better of him, he did not even realise it was a woman who interrupted, answering nonchalantly.

"Non-disclosure agreement. Until I could confirm certain aspects of the project; such as our company and Matt as the gaffer, they wouldn't talk. It was only when I mentioned other future projects they started to become slightly less tight-lipped. They were paid a fortune Dan and guess who paid them?"

Dan was stumped to where the funding for an obviously rather large and expensive project would come from. Although it was not inconceivable Matt had the money, he was not in the mood to hazard a guess but Simon did not wait for one. It had been more a casual comment than question.

"James Morris! Dan, your uncle funded the entire project, or so it would seem. He paid all the guys I spoke to privately under the table and extremely lucratively too. This would explain why James was far more involved on the project than I first thought. It would also explain why myself and the team ended up working on a project on the other side of the world. Keeping it completely secret!"

There was silence, neither party spoke as if trying to comprehend the complexity of what Simon had discovered. It seemed the evidence he proposed and with the fact there was a fully manned submarine being delivered next week, the Morris family had bettered the underground lab, designing and building an entire underwater lab. At least Dan now had a pretty good idea where the other submarine was possibly hiding.

"Dan … are you still there?"

"Yeah, we're still here, trying to comprehend it all but we're here." There was further silence until Simon quietly spoke, almost in a whisper.

"Dan, do you think Matt is still alive?"

"To be honest I'm becoming more and more convinced of it Simon, hour by hour and I'm sure as hell gonna find out! Can you do me a big favour though? Keep this quiet until we can prove it."

"Of course and you know where I am if you need my help."

"Thanks Simon, will do … you've done more than enough. Good night." Dan hung up.

36

Dan placed the cell between the pair of them. Lizzie stared unblinking across the table at it, a look of bewilderment spread her face. She stared at Dan, the look of a crossed lover.

"I think it's about time you told me what's really going on."

Dan shifted in his seat, he knew he'd have to fill Lizzie in eventually with his ideas but until now they have been just that, ideas, he had never spoken any of them aloud. Once spoken it would be like setting them in stone. Where to start? The package Aunt Susan left was probably the best place, Dan sighed taking a deep breath.

"After I left you and your Dad at the office with the keys, I went home, opened the safe and finally got into the Panic Room. I reconstructed the hard drives and looked at the footage, which I later showed your Dad. From the footage, you can see the killer's a pro. He was looking for something and he had the proper equipment to do it. He had a thermal imaging camera for picking up heat signatures, which was how he found the Panic Room; the camera's not your everyday piece of kit."

"Wasn't the Panic Room what he was looking for though?"

"No, finding the room was purely an accident but I do think he believed he had found what he was looking for. For him though, it was a dead end but I can only assume he thought he was close and at that point Uncle Mike and Aunt Susan became expendable."

Dan swallowed hard and took another drink. "However inside the Panic Room he was not expecting the surveillance monitors, it threw him off the scent as it were. He removed the drives retreating with them, taking their keys, closed the Panic Room door and left. He probably looked around the rest of the house and garden without finding anything. I'm only guessing because once he removed the hard drives the cameras stopped recording. The backup drives were purely

166

mirrors of the originals, without them in place the imagery had nowhere to be stored. As you know the bodies were discovered about 48 hours after their murder, by Aunt Susan's friend Mary, who was coming round for their weekly chat. She let herself in after there was no answer. The door as usual was open and she discovered their bodies in the study."

"I only spoke to Mary briefly at the funeral and I think she was still in shock. It must have been awful for her to find them like that." Lizzie shook her head sadly.

"It would have been pretty gruesome, especially after the time they were left exposed in the heat. As I said earlier the Panic Room is the entrance to the family's true lab. I would assume the surveillance set up confused the murderer and he didn't investigate the room any further. If he had he'd probably have found the door as it's only held shut by an electro magnet, a good shove and it would easily open. When I ventured downstairs everything was turned off, he wouldn't have got any readings at all with his camera. The only lighting is fed via an emergency feed from the house electrics. The lab supply comes in through the garage but you'd assume looking at the junction boxes it was for Granddad's workshop machinery."

"Back up a bit, I don't understand why there's a hidden lab?" Lizzie voiced the main concern of Dan's; he had never questioned it before but now he was questioning everything and for the first time he voiced his ideas.

"In truth I don't really understand it either. Basically the lab was built to hide Granddad's and James' work. I remember it was some time after James' PHD research was published in the academic world. I remember it vividly because government officials began turning up to the house, it was all a little heated but I was kept well away from them. I can only assume now, whatever James was researching was a continuance of Granddad's original government work which roused some suspicion."

Dan had started to remember details long forgotten. His memory began to fill in some of the blanks he had been puzzling over as he fleshed out his ideas.

"You remember the original house fire?" Lizzie nodded. "The cause was an electrical fault arcing the old water heater's circuitry. It destroyed pretty much the whole basement. I can remember it was around the time when there was Government interference in James' work. I can only believe it was at that point they decided to build two labs, one to be visible and the other to hide the more important research. The restructure and rebuild of the house would have hidden the underground remedial work without suspicion."

Dan strained with the next part; it was something he had never spoken about because it had always been a family matter. However Lizzie was now his only family and he finally felt it was time she knew the main reason he left.

"You remember when Granddad and Gran died?"

"How could I forget, it was when I lost you." Lizzie could feel herself welling up to cry at what she had just said but knew he needed her to be strong right now. So, with a great effort, stopped herself.

"Do you remember the reports of how they died?" Lizzie shook her head, she genuinely could not, it seemed such a long time ago. At the time she was more worried about Dan, how he reacted to their deaths and how he withdrew, becoming more and more insular.

"The local news reports said it was a gas explosion. I knew subconsciously there was a problem with this explanation because the outside lab never had any gas in it, or supplied to it! There was no way Granddad or anyone could have caused an explosion of that magnitude when the external lab was nothing more than a glorified office!"

Lizzie was looking curiously at him, not sure whether she should say anything, instead she nodded as he continued, he was pale.

"I tried talking to the rest of the family about it but they simply refused to talk. At first I thought it was because they were mourning our loss but after a while I realised it was far deeper than that. They were hiding something, the more I think about it now, looking back, I believe they were possibly murdered too." As he said it, the words stung like a fresh wound. In his heart he had wrestled with this idea ever since the alleged accident. None of the family would discuss it, the closeness of the family he had felt since his arrival evaporated in those few short weeks following their deaths.

At first he thought it was the stress of the investigation, the complete loss they all felt and then because his Grandparents' bodies would not be released by the authorities countless autopsies. In the beginning he never thought it was through intention, just a bizarre correlation of red tape and the family protecting him for some unknown reason. Now though he believed it was far more sinister.

The subsequent weeks after their death, he pieced together mismatched clues; there could never have been an explosion in the lab. There were no gas services for starters and the other thing that always puzzled him was neither of his Grandparents ever ventured in the lab, so would never have been in there in the first place. Aunt Pat used it as an office and studio space, it was more of a dumping ground for the families' junk.

Dan could see from Lizzie's expression she was trying to absorb his last few words, so he continued, trying to cover the awkward silence between them caused by this idea.

"Aunt Susan's package contained my keys to the safe and the underground lab; it also contained the house plans. Aunt Susan knew I would go down and get them from the drawers, as it showed the whole renovation of the underground lab. I assumed the house plans would indicate something she wanted me to see but I believe it was her way of directing me to the drawers themselves. The lab is completely empty now except for the cabinets. It was never like that and I don't believe for an instant Uncle Mike and Aunt Susan would have disposed of all the equipment, neither would they have destroyed the valuable research of Granddad and James' life's work. However in the drawers along with the plans, were schematics. One set was something Matt had been working on which I took to Simon before coming to you, that was who we spoke to a few minutes ago, and the other was a set of detailed plans to a submarine."

"A submarine?"

"Yep, a submarine! To be fair, with Granddad's background I wasn't concerned about the plans, they didn't seem out of place, at first. It was only when I spoke to your Dad about the business investments which he'd compiled that we realised Marion Reynolds Hyper Sub was heavily invested in, including a huge cash injection in the last few months! I drove to Kingsland Lake today to meet with Marion Reynolds, the genius who designed and built the Hyper Sub."

"So that was why you were out by the lake ... I thought you might be just reminiscing about our childhood when you left the message."

"It was a bit like that at first, the drive down there on your own allows some reflection to think about things." He reached out and gripped Lizzie's hand in his own, she smiled and he smiled back momentarily lost by the shine of her eyes.

"So what did he say?"

"Well a lot of things, some of which didn't make sense until Simon's call just then. For starters Uncle Mike has purchased a personal submarine! That was the cash injection. I take collection of it at the back end of next week."

Lizzie looked at Dan as if he was winding her up. "You're telling me Mike bought a submarine?" She would have laughed, had she not realised he was serious.

"Yep! But not just one, it looks like the family bought Reynolds' original prototype. According to the business records your Dad compiled, there was a massive cash injection to Marion Reynolds only a few months before Uncle James, Aunt Pat, Ash and Matt disappeared."

If Lizzie ever gambled, her poker face was second to none. She gave nothing away as she deciphered what he was saying. It was hard to tell how she was computing the information, either she was humouring him or trying to make sense of the facts as he presented them. He could not see any emotion, so continued.

"When I got back from Kingsland, I popped in the station to fill up the car. The guys have painted Hydrous and gotten her in pristine condition. While I was talking to them, I'm not sure how it came into conversation but basically Niles was the last person to see Matt and Ash alive."

Lizzie was obviously following what Dan was saying and was ahead of him. "What about Uncle James and Aunt Pat?" It was funny how Lizzie always called them Aunt and Uncle, she even called his grandfather Granddad.

"That's the point; no one ever saw Uncle James and Aunt Pat!" He paused letting the words sink in. "I don't believe they were on board at all. When I looked at Hydrous in dry dock she was empty, completely. There was nothing to indicate they were spending even the weekend away on her."

"What do you mean?"

"Well, think about it … when we took Hydrous out what basics did we always take? Clothes, books, DVDs, copious amounts of drink. It was empty, nothing was on board. Even the coffee caddy was empty, except a few items and even one of those was an old jacket of mine."

Both reached for their glasses and took a deep drink simultaneously. Dan continued as their glasses returned to the table.

"What I believe is that Uncle James and Aunt Pat took delivery of the original Marion Sub and rendezvoused with Matt and Ash above the Oriskany. The coordinates were engraved on the blade of Ash's knife and written by you on the sea chart. They then transferred all of their stuff into the submarine abandoning the yacht, setting it adrift to be found later by the coast guard. They used the submarine to dive down to the habitat Matt designed and secretly built, financed by Uncle James, hidden somewhere within the Oriskany itself."

37

Simon pressed the hands-free button on the telephone to hang up and for the first time in a long time he felt as though a huge part of his life made sense. Ever since Matt's disappearance it had been hard to put on a brave face continuing life as if unfazed. He had always had trouble believing Matt could have done something to have put, not only himself, but the life of his family at risk.

The more he researched, the more he had broken down the plans and math behind an underwater habitat, the intricate detail and the mysterious circumstances of the Morris family disappearance.

Add the fact that none of their bodies were ever discovered, it bizarrely somehow made the whole scenario seem much more plausible. The sea always left a sign, a body would have washed up at some point, or they would have found some indication of their demise, but there was nothing. All this time, he simply could not believe Matt would have taken a risk to harm his family, he was never that careless.

Simon had seen Matt save many lives over the years, including his own; it was probably why Simon had fallen so deeply for him. At first it had scared him, how he felt but as they grew closer, the love Simon felt was reciprocated. His family never knew about Matt's sexuality, he was bisexual. It had taken Simon a while to fully understand, and ultimately accept.

Being openly gay himself he had always felt Matt was in denial of his true feelings. There had been many lovers for Matt before they became an item, albeit closeted and hidden from their family and colleagues but Simon was so in love he had allowed Matt to lead this double life with him. He did not mind Matt playing away with women; in his mind he had never seen this side of Matt's sexual nature as cheating. He always came home to him and had never slept with another man since telling Simon he loved him. It was a strange ideal but it was something that drove their relationship and made it strong.

Coming out, Matt had truly believed, was a personal choice. It was something a gay man never did just the once, it was something he did every single day. Therefore he preferred to keep it a secret from his family, not because he thought they would be hurt but because before Simon he truly believed one day he would meet a woman, who he would fall in love and settle down with. However he fell in love with a man, the longer he had led his lifestyle the harder it seemed to finally tell the truth and the lie surrounding them both, continued to grow and evolve.

Simon loved Matt for who he was and accepted this side to him, like a lover with a strange fetish. He believed sleeping with women was Matt's fetish, a lot like rubber clothing was his. Matt had always loved the fact when they dived together Simon was inherently turned on by the smell or feeling of the tight neoprene rubber dive suits. When they were alone they often made love, half wearing the rubber.

Matt however was full of secrets; coming out to his family was one he believed they need not know. Not that Simon reckoned the Morris family would have worried. They were the complete polar opposite of his own father. If he ever knew of his attraction to the same sex Simon believed he would have been disowned in an instant. So their relationship suited them both because Matt's dalliances with the opposite sex created a smokescreen, which Simon tolerated purely because it had kept them and their families together.

With so many secrets surrounding them, the underwater habitat seemed an easy project to achieve and ultimately hide. Living with secrets bred a certain amount of containment lies, and lying became easier with practice. Matt had always found it hard to lie to Simon though and he wondered if that was why Matt packed him off on another job, so he did not have to lie to the man he loved. He knew there were other secrets in Matt's life. He had truly believed whatever the secrets were, Matt kept them to himself because he was protecting him and loved him.

As he put the phone down to Dan, his love for Matt was welling inside of him. The emptiness he had felt for so long seemed to be replaced with hope. His one true love was alive, believing it in his heart. The time for secrets and dishonesty was over. If Matt was truly alive, they both needed to sit down and be honest with their families about their sexuality and who they were, so they could finally live a life together in the open.

He picked up the phone and dialled his father, he knew the time difference would be late but he was hoping he would catch him in a good mood. It was time to come clean about his own sexuality; a decision had been made, the time was right and he would not let any more secrets rule his life, especially around his own family.

The phone rang but his father did not pick up, either he was asleep or he had not returned home. The phone rang and rang; Simon was disappointed he was not going to answer as he was ready to have the hardest conversation in his life. It continued to ring, it did not pick up and neither did the answer machine. The adrenalin surged through his body, disappointed but instead he spoke to get the words out in the open.

"Hi Dad, please don't speak I just need you to know I love you. I always have and always will. I know you raised me as a single father and you've provided and given me your undivided support, drive, understanding and more than enough love, more than any son could ever wish for. Please believe me when I say it is in no way an indication of you or the upbringing I've had without a mother. It's simple fate or pre-programming ... I'm gay. There, I said it. I knew from an early age about my sexuality. Please don't feel in any way you have let me or yourself down because you're the best father anyone could ever have wished or hoped for. Night Dad, I love you."

He hung up the still ringing phone, without the ceremony or massive build-up; it was cathartic to have just said those words out loud after all these years. It felt like the right thing to do for all concerned, especially as he wanted the time he had lost with Matt to be made up. Living a secret life would have stopped that. He felt like a weight had been lifted, he was going to call first thing and talk to his father for real. He spoke out loud to affirm his feelings.

"Matt when you get home we are going to start to live our life properly, together. I love you so much sweetheart, wherever you are."

Simon only momentarily registered the cold metal of the silencer as it touched the back of his skull. He never felt any pain, just a fuzzy warmth envelop his brain, like the heady rush from a deep sniff of a freshly opened bottle of poppers. His eyes rolled as he fell forward on to the desk. He was dead.

38

For the first time in their lives, ever since they had known each other, an awkward silence fell between them. They both sat, pushing the food round their plates, it looked and smelt fantastic but neither felt particularly hungry. After sitting in silence for an age, with a need to ask questions and fully understand what Dan was saying, Lizzie finally broke the lull. She had known him too long to joke about something as serious as this but she needed details and right now, more than that, she wanted proof.

"So what research was your family involved in that'd attract the attention of the Government?"

"I don't know. All I do know is that it whatever it was, used to be beneath the house, hidden down in the lab inside the hydro pod."

"Hydro pod? Simon mentioned that on the phone, what is it? You looked surprised when he used the name."

As their conversation started to return to normal, the atmosphere evaporated and they started to eat their food, relaxing again. The one sided conversation became more fluid as questions were batted back and forth.

"Of the two sets of plans I retrieved from the lab, one was of the sub and the other was what seemed like an unconnected set of blueprints. There were no dimensions or detail on any of them. However I visited Simon because J.J had mentioned the cruiser was at the yard and I wanted to make sure it was fine to leave it there, although I actually now believe Uncle Mike had taken it there to make room for the delivery of the new sub in the boat house. The other reason was to get Simon to check out the design blueprints which were printed on A1 transparencies, kind of like tracing paper. Simon recognised certain design details linking them together and fortunately, because Simon is so anal with how everything is named, he managed to find the missing sheets he had archived. Ultimately I don't think they were ever truly missing. I believe Matt had intentionally separated them so no one could piece together what they are. It was only Simon's knowledge and knowing Matt so well, that he was able to do it."

"Simon pieced together the blueprint. So you're saying that multiple sheets made up a single design, which Simon has compiled and emailed? So where does the hydro pod fit in and what is it used for?"

"I don't actually know what it is exactly, only that it was very important to the family research. The hydro pod housed some really elaborate experimental equipment enclosed in a persistent wet environment, it was how it worked. I can show you the pod at home, its empty now but what I can tell you, like the Hyper Sub, there are two of them."

"How do you know that?"

"At Marion Reynolds there were some acrylic sheets stacked against the wall, they looked exactly like the hydro pod doors in the lab at home. These were much bigger and more elaborate than those. Marion said they built a second set of water tight doors. I can only assume it was another hydro pod for the chamber Matt designed for the Oriskany and that's why Simon will have seen it on the plan in one of the underwater chambers."

"Do you really believe the plans were just an idea or actually built?"

"I'm beginning to think they were built and so does Simon. I reckon someone was getting too close to the research at home and they decided to disappear completely."

"You actually think your family faked their own deaths?"

"Well I'm not so sure of that part yet. I wonder if that was just a coincidence, possibly the coast guard finding the yacht adrift provided a convenient smokescreen, one to which Aunt Susan and Uncle Mike just collaborated and let run its course."

"Why would they do that though, surely that made no sense?"

"Well maybe not but after Gran and Granddad's death I never ventured home. I hated being here so it was probably easier to pretend they were dead and continue the charade, plus with their deaths, any ongoing interference would disappear. It would hide everything and the people who were harassing the family wouldn't be interested. Or maybe it was to protect me? The less I knew the less at risk I was, or am. Do you remember how Aunt Susan signed off the DVD at the office?"

Lizzie shook her head while consuming the last of her meal. Dan recited verbatim, the last words on the DVD which had puzzled him.

"'Remember Daniel, we all love you very, very much and we are all really proud of you.' I think she meant everyone, otherwise she'd have said I or referred to just her and Uncle Mike."

"I see your point but I think you're beginning to over analyse and see things that aren't there Dan. You're concocting an elaborate conspiracy theory, conveniently filling gaps with fiction."

Dan was a little hurt by the accusation although he could see many holes in his theories, he needed concrete proof.

"The sub's not fiction it's fact, I've seen it and it's been fitted with the same internal lowering track that's in the hydro pod at home! Neither is the lab a figment of my imagination, or the fact four of my family disappeared without trace and no bodies were ever found. The plans are not fiction either; Simon pieced them together without any prompt from me deciphering the naming convention. He was the one who worked out how the chambers fitted inside the Oriskany and contacted some of the men who built the structures."

"We don't know that for definite, we have no definitive proof. All we have, by your admittance, is the underground lab at the house and hearsay from a few random people. Finally the pièce de résistance, an alleged underwater habitat built inside the superstructure of a Government aircraft carrier now conveniently residing underwater off the coast of Florida. To be honest Dan these pie in the sky pieces fit together but anyone can shoehorn half assed ideas into a conspiracy theory which almost crosses the T's and dots the I's. To put it bluntly you sound like a mental person!"

Dan glowered at Lizzie, throwing his cutlery down on his empty plate in exasperation pushing it away. They stared at each other, Dan felt a huge rush of resentment, feeling let down, as though he should never have opened up.

Lizzie realised she had been a little harsh, even so, someone had to keep him grounded but at least he was talking again, she just had to keep him talking. When Dan clammed up about anything it was useless getting him to talk about it again. All the time he was in the UK he was alone, now he was here, she needed him to be honest about his feelings and also know what was going on in that skull of his. She especially needed him after the kiss she had just received; she had waited her whole life for it.

"Actually you may be right about a few things and although there are no hard facts, one bizarre incident springs to my mind which although doesn't add any more weight to your idea, it does add some strength to your story. You remember when the Oriskany was sunk?"

"It's hard to forget, it was a great day out, it was in fact the last time we were all together."

"You hit the nail on the head; we were all there, including Aunt Susan!" Lizzie felt unbelievable guilt using her to reel him back in. "The only person I know, who had a massive phobia of boats and the water! Yet she was there to watch the sinking of the Oriskany along with all of us. Now I think about it; that does seem rather odd to me, unless of course she knew more than she was letting on. If I had a child who was planning to disappear and live indefinitely underwater, then I'd want to know it was all going to be okay. I'd want to know where he was going to be and ultimately he'd be safe."

Dan smiled, she had him, the confidence was back and his eyes looked deep in thought, shaping a new piece of information to the puzzle. "You're right, I'd never thought about it like that. No matter what we said or did as kids she'd never come out on the boat, even getting her in the sea up to her ankles was impossible. Yet that day, which was one of the only times I was home, she literally ran on board. She was clutching a large bottle of gin admittedly."

"You do realise the only way we are going to find out the truth is to take a look at the Oriskany?"

Lizzie was right, to discover the truth they would have to dive the wreck, it was the only way they could get real proof.

More than three hours had passed since they had made it to the restaurant; Dan had kissed Lizzie and opened up some of his deepest personal thoughts to her. They had discussed his suspicions about the murder of his Grandparents and the growing possibility the rest of the Morris family were still alive.

However there was still one thing he needed to talk about but felt the time was not right. Lizzie need not know just yet he had been suspended from work and the information he had learned about his mother in Washington could certainly wait until tomorrow, or at least until after they had definitive proof.

39

The waiter appeared at the top of the stairs, it had been one of the longest courses ever at the restaurant and he was concerned there was a problem. The waiter approached cautiously, both Lizzie and Dan were glad of the disruption and turned but neither smiled. The conversation had been far more than a light hearted chat by a couple on the brink of happiness, or so it seemed.

"I presume everything was satisfactory for Sir and Madam?" He was rather worried the meal was not up to par. What every customer was unaware of was one of the Lighthouse's strict policies. If there was a legitimate complaint in the lamp house, if a meal was cold, uncooked or was a complete disaster, then the customer would not have to pay for anything across the entire table. They also were given a night for free.

It seemed a rather simple rule of the house, however when a single bottle of wine could cost thousands of dollars there was quite a substantial loss to be made. It did however keep the staff on their toes, not taking the position entrusted to them over casually. The rule however seemed redundant because in all the years since it's opening, there had only ever been one complaint and that was due to fog descending over the Lighthouse, obstructing the beautiful view.

It was still a complaint nonetheless and the owners had indeed given them a free evening. However it was only in the ground floor restaurant, good enough for an event outside of the Lighthouse's control, considering what the building was actually built for, it was a rather moot subject.

"Yes thank you, mine was gorgeous, thank you for the recommendation." The waiter seemed pleased with the response and turned to Dan, who was lost in thought.

The waiter was not used to silence at the end of a meal and it had thrown him. He was somewhat irked by this customer's lacklustre response.

Breaking etiquette, he asked. "How was Sir's venison?"

Dan broke from his train of thought and looked up forcing a smile. "Yes it was fine, thank you."

The waiter almost fainted on the spot … fine? Pizza was fine. The Lighthouse was splendid; gorgeous; magnificent; sumptuous; in fact in all his years he had never heard a masterpiece at the Lighthouse described as inadequately as "fine". That was as non-descript as thanking a waffle chef at the local diner. The waiter's visibly shaking hands cleared the plates and cutlery then retreated, allowing the female waitress to come to the fore, taking over from the somewhat rattled head waiter.

"Tonight our Italian master sweet chef is catering to your needs and has prepared a number of special treats including several homemade ice creams, from his own Mama's recipes, Vanilla, Chocolate and Pistachio or if you would prefer a cleaner palette; a few sorbets, such as Mango, Pineapple or Raspberry. There is also Tiramasu, Limoncello Cheesecake and Panacotta Chambord. However I personally would highly recommend Fabrizzio's speciality of Zabaglione."

The waitress turned to Dan first who was still lost in thought; Lizzie kicked him in the shin under the table. Dan looked up and smiled as if he had been listening intently.

"Er, they all sound lovely." Completely unconvincing. "Could I try the ice cream, I'll just have Chocolate and Pistachio please, I'm not a lover of Vanilla." The waitress turned to Lizzie who smiled and who also knew exactly what she wanted.

"Can I have the Zabaglione please?" She looked really excited. The waitress bowed and reversed for the stairs.

She enthused to Dan. "Zabaglione is like an Italian custard, they make it for you to order, it's gorgeous."

Downstairs a whirring noise started to reverberate up the stairwell, it started off quietly, gradually increasing, whatever the noise it was heading up the stairs. After what seemed like an age, a small wooden workbench inched its way into view from the left stairwell coming to a stop directly between the two spiral staircases.

The ornate handrails cleverly hid part of the Lighthouse's internal working structure. Attached to the bottom of the spiral staircase; what at first glance would look like nothing more than two tubes ornately spiralling upwards, were in fact simple runners for a stair lift. This clever addition to the metal stairwell was how all the heavy lifting was done throughout the levels.

Earlier in the day, after Dan's initial call, the stair lift removed the individual sections of the grand table from the centre of the lamp house. It then proceeded to bring up a more intimate table for a couple, positioned in the centre and the surroundings changed to a more delicate and informal tone compared to the business meeting that had been hosted several nights previous.

Strangely, the allure of the Lighthouse had once again captured their imaginations, the awkward conversation was momentarily forgotten. Following the wooden bench was a stout swarthy-looking man with a wispy moustache that concluded in spirals. He unhooked the bench, pressed a button and the stair lift continued, slowly inching across the landing disappearing from view down the right hand side staircase.

The chef wheeled the bench forward to their table. He was dressed in immaculately pressed chef whites, not a single stain or blemish interrupted his crisp white uniform. His dark features protruded from his double breasted jacket, topped with a tall rippled hat called a Dodin Bouffant. 101 ripples flowed around the outside, which was the traditional number, reputedly representing the number of ways a chef could prepare eggs. Tonight however he would show them only one and without a word, he bowed commencing his performance.

On the bench was a small gas burner which he lit with a match, on which he placed a metal saucepan filled with water, it gently steamed. He took three eggs, separated the yolks using the shells, placing them in a gleaming round-bottomed copper pan and discarding the shells in a small port hole within the workbench. He splashed a generous dash of Marsala wine in the bowl, adding three heaped tablespoons of sugar and whisking the ingredients together using an old antique wire balloon whisk. From the look it had probably been passed through generations purely for this job alone.

The round-bottomed copper bowl was placed over the simmering water and whisked vigorously for several minutes. His audience was rapt by his skills, the look of the dessert forming before their very eyes. Lizzie was grinning from ear to ear. She had seen it on the cooking programs she loved to watch but had never seen it up close. This was a very special moment for her and she was sharing the moment with the man she loved.

Their attention had been focused on the Zabaglione gradually thickening, increasing in volume before their very eyes, over the heat. They had not noticed the stair lift return with another cabinet.

On top was a small freezer which held the freshly prepared Gelato and Sorbet in its individual portions, alongside a number of other desserts their Chef, who was busy at work, had prepared earlier. Three smaller refined looking wine bottles were also included, a selection of rare ice wines the bar steward had obviously taken the initiative to pick for them.

The bar steward unhooked the cabinet, wheeling it towards their table. He whisked away their individual glasses, placing them in the lower portion of the cabinet. He replaced them with six fresh large wine glasses, three each and a large long stemmed glass in the middle. Each of the three wine glasses in front of them was filled with a generous helping of a German, Canadian and an Italian version of ice wine to compliment their dessert.

Whether it was coincidence or carefully rehearsed, as the bar steward reversed to leave, the chef removed the copper bowl from the steaming water. The bar steward whisked the workbench away, dousing the flames, attaching it to the stair lift, he promptly returned below as the lift quietly trundled dutifully behind him.

The chef continued to whisk, then with a flick of the wrist and final flourish, emptied the contents directly into the tall stemmed glass. He placed the utensils in the lower portion of the cupboard and after retrieving a flat plate placed the warm Zabaglione on top along with three lighthouse shaped sponge fingers and a piece of Belgian white chocolate on each, finally sliding the pudding across to Lizzie. Her face had the look of a five year old with a birthday cake. She grinned grasping a spoon in her hand upwards to the sky.

The chef took a clean bowl from the top shelf and motioned to the selection of freshly prepared ice creams in their individual stainless oblong bowls for Dan to choose. Gelato is frozen more quickly in much smaller batches.

High-quality artisan Gelato holds its intense peak flavour and texture for only a few days, because finer more delicate ice crystals form during the quicker freezing process. Even when stored carefully at the proper temperature, it has a short shelf life, which is why Gelaterias typically make their own Gelato on the premises each day.

Below each tray was a tiny headed stainless steel ice scoop for each flavour, Dan looked at the tiny portions and back towards the massive glass Lizzie was clutching, like her life depended on it.

"Can I just have the Pistachio and Chocolate please." The chef balled two scoops of each, from each tray and placed in the bowl and sprinkled a combination of crushed pistachio nuts and dark Belgian chocolate across the top. He placed the bowl in front of Dan and gave him a Gelato spoon, which was a little smaller than a teaspoon having a flat edge like a tiny spade.

He took a large knife from the cabinet and cut two small square sections from the Tiramisu and Limoncello cheesecake placing them on individual plates down the middle of the table, plus the two individual Panacotta's. A single spoon was placed alongside each extra portion and he too retreated, wheeling the cabinet back to the top of the stairs where the stair lift had returned, hooked it on and the pair descended back down stairs.

"Wow." Lizzie erupted, slamming her spoon down in the contents of her glass. Although Dan was impressed with the spectacle and showmanship he felt slightly aggrieved at the tiny portion mocking him from the bowl in front of him.

He picked up the delicate spoon taking a miniature shovel full of the chocolate ice cream and sucked on it. The flavour was intense and his mouth instantly salivated, all his senses were hit with the potent creation of this Italian master's ice cream. Suddenly he realised why the portions were so much smaller than any other ice cream he had ever experienced in his life, it was sublime.

Lizzie was also enjoying hers, as it was nearly all gone; she slurped in between each mouth devouring every little drop. "Wow." She said again, rattling and scraping her spoon around the inside of the glass bowl until it was empty. She used the sponge fingers to mop up the remnants.

When she had finished the three glasses of wine stood before her, she sipped the contents from one. "I've never tasted ice wine before, it's very fruity, lovely."

"I've never tasted Zabaglione, oh, and it looks like I'm not going to either."

Lizzie stared sheepishly into her empty bowl. "Oh sorry, I wasn't thinking, what's the ice cream like?" Without a prompt Dan spooned a combination of both flavours onto the spoon and fed her across the table seductively. Her eyes closed as she savoured the combination exhilarating her taste buds as it melted she was amazed by the intense flavour, far superior to any other ice cream, she had ever tasted.

Between the pair of them they finished all the desserts the chef had left, the ice wine eventually ran dry and the evening returned to the natural ease of a date, the previous conversation momentarily forgotten. The bar steward returned to collect the empty wine glasses and received more praise over his choice of wines.

The waitress returned with tea, a special request of Dan's. It was unusual because it was a loose leaf and, more importantly, Dan had asked for Aunt Susan's favourite blend, Yorkshire.

Where the Lighthouse had managed to get some at such short notice was a complete mystery but he did not care, it had been a great night and Lizzie was amazing. He had realised how much he missed her, of course things were different but for the first time he felt home, Lizzie was his home.

40

As the evening drew to a close, Lizzie noticed the lighting had gradually lowered throughout lamp house to a far more seductive and intimate level. Was it on purpose? She could only hazard a guess. Except for the intense conversation earlier, she had enjoyed their time alone, although she knew the coming weeks; even months would change both their lives.

The waiters busied themselves removing the last of their table adornments. Finally the maître d' reappeared. Smiling intensely, he wafted across the room to their table leaving a silver platter covered in a white cloth. He retreated back downstairs bowing as he went.

Impatiently Lizzie pulled the platter towards her expecting it to be the bill. Whipping the cloth aside she was slightly disappointed to discover a small solid silver credit card holder placed in the middle. The case was engraved with the Lighthouse logo and the lamp house was embossed with beams of light emanating from each side. She flicked open the top to discover it contained a number of beautifully designed business cards for each member of staff. Lizzie spread them out across the platter.

The bottom card was a thank you note, written in the same exquisite hand as the original writing of their menu, in blood red ink. *Please accept our humblest gratitude you chose the Lighthouse to serve you this evening, accept this small gift as a token of our appreciation. The case has a unique monogram across the front, which can be used for every future booking for an even more personalised service. We very much look forward to serving you again, please don't be a stranger.*

Lizzie looked at Dan disappointed. "Where's the bill? I wanted to know how much you spent on me."

Dan shook his head knowingly, personally he would like to know how much the bottle of wine cost. "You don't get a bill at the Lighthouse, it's considered vulgar! You either get invoiced or it simply goes through on a very specific set of credit cards only. I have no idea what it'll cost until I see the statement."

"So you gonna tell me what it costs then?"

"Nope." Dan grinned getting up before Lizzie could protest, stretching, they had been at the Lighthouse for four hours.

Out in the distance a few ships were traversing the horizon. He wondered to himself whether his family were indeed out there, or whether the idea was only a fanciful piece of fiction as Lizzie had suggested.

Lizzie came up behind him and wrapped her arms around his stomach, pressing herself against his back and squeezing him tightly, kissing his neck; he smelt amazing. She knew what he was thinking though and she also knew they had to prove conclusively either way what happened to his family, his sanity relied on it after recent events.

They walked hand in hand down the stairs Lizzie had first used to get up to the lamp house. As they reached the lower level, every member of staff had gathered to wish them well, they felt like royalty.

The walnut bar had been pushed back flush against the curving wall, hiding all of the bottles and glasses, plus the stair lift was hidden behind its sleek exterior. A crisp diamond white table cloth sat on top with an arrangement of flowers placed neatly in the middle.

Each member of the team lined the way to the open elevator where the maître d' patiently waited to take them back downstairs. The levels between the floors this time were immaculate. Lizzie and Dan thanked each of them in turn as they passed, to which they only nodded. However Lizzie could not help but thanking Fabrizzio for the Zabaglione. "Thank you for my dessert." She enthused. "It was beautiful."

The waitress who had served them for the entire evening stepped forward clutching a bouquet of blood red roses. The crimson of the petal seemed to radiate against the crisp whiteness of her starched shirt.

"Fabrizzio only speaks Italian but I am sure he fully understands and would thank you in return." She held out the bouquet towards Lizzie who took it and read the note, again in the same blood red ink – 'Thank you.'

As they passed the waiting room, the throng had evaporated leaving the bar immaculate, ready for tomorrow. On the ground floor only a few tables still had patrons enjoying the last moments of their evening, savouring the deep roast of a last coffee before the trip home.

The maître d' crossed the entrance retrieving Lizzie's jacket, holding it aloft for Lizzie to slip back into. On the coast, as they were, a cold breeze would blow in from the ocean. The maître d' opened the door saying their final farewell and the door gently closed behind them.

Aunt Susan's Range Rover was parked by the entrance, another member of staff from the valet team stood patiently with the back door open. Lizzie did not question the intention hopping up onto the rear leather seat. The valet closed the door trotting round and opened the rear door on the opposite side for Dan. Lizzie looked at him as if questioning but said nothing as Dan slid onto the seat next to her, entwining his fingers in hers. The valet closed the door, opened the driver's door and eased himself behind the wheel.

Dan realised what Lizzie was questioning in her mind. "Well you didn't expect me to drive home after the amount of alcohol we've consumed did you?"

"Actually I honestly hadn't thought about it but now you mention it, I suspect we've probably consumed quite a lot, especially with the cocktails."

The valet drove them back and it was not until they pulled into the gates Lizzie suddenly realised she was not heading home. She remained quiet; she had not expected this turn of events but had quietly hoped for it, especially after their stolen kiss earlier in the evening. The driver parked in front of the house opening the doors for them in turn.

He opened the rear of the Range Rover, retrieving a small bag, within seconds the contraption which was removed, gradually metamorphosed into a small motorbike. The valet handed the keys to Dan, bowing slightly. He donned a helmet, swung his leg over the seat and with a quick kick on the starter pedal, the bike roared into a frenzy. The valet pulled back the throttle rocketing off back down the driveway, leaving Lizzie and Dan in a plume of fumes, smoke and what smelt like unburnt fuel.

"Well I must say I was not expecting that!" Dan laughed as he stuffed the keys to the Range Rover in his pocket. He turned and held out his arm. "Madam."

"Why sir … " Lizzie grinned, she linked her arms through his and they headed inside the house.

41

Lizzie stood in the dark, not moving, slightly scared by what she had seen. So much of what Dan had said earlier in the evening seemed to be making sense now. She had known the Morris family her entire life, yet she never knew anything about the lab. In her heart she was slightly aggrieved by the secret but she also felt that maybe it was for the best.

She shouted towards the direction of the only source of light. "You know, when the car drew up to the house, I was expecting to see the upstairs a little more closely and intimate if you catch my drift? Rather than being stuck down here in a cold underground bunker that smells bad, really bad." She held her nose.

Dan had shown her the Panic Room; she had seen the surveillance system and then descended the stairs via torchlight to the lab. The emergency lighting, having been left on since Dan's last visit, had long since run the batteries flat. Dan turned the emergency lighting off to recharge the batteries from the mains supply above; a few minutes should give them long enough for Lizzie to see it completely. For now though it was viewed by torchlight only, the beam gave the dull concrete a surreal feeling. Its closeness was oppressive, the quicker the emergency lighting recharged the better.

On the island in the middle of the lab, Dan had laid out prints of the plans Simon had emailed. The family had an A3 printer in the study but even that was too small for the detail they really needed. From the post apocalyptic stash in the corner Dan retrieved a second torch, handing the first to Lizzie. He unscrewed the top and inserted some batteries so they each had a light.

Swinging the torch across the room, he let the beam rest on the architectural drawers. "That's where I found the house plans and the rest of the designs Simon put together into these." He motioned at the sheets on the cabinet. "Plus the original submarine plans you saw upstairs in the study." He randomly picked up a printout tossing it across the table.

Lizzie was leaning on her elbows, her torch directed at the blown up section of Oriskany's hangar. Inside were three compartments, linked via small walkways. They looked small but she was resigned to the fact they probably would be much bigger in reality, that's if they truly existed.

Seeing these detailed drawings alongside each other though and confirmation of this room's existence certainly gave more credence to Dan's wild-eyed theory. Matt would never have put so much effort in to an idea that would not have come to fruition; that was one thing she was certain of. Matt had never done anything unless he had truly believed in it.

Dan was pouring over the plans to the section titled 'CVC'. Simon had mentioned the details were sketchy on that particular plan but to Dan they made perfect sense. The compartment was separated into two distinct areas. One was further split into four rooms, comprising of a workshop, computer room, operations and a small room labelled compression which Dan believed to be some form of decompression chamber; an essential piece of kit for emergencies.

However what was more interesting was the second room, labelled 'Moon Pool', the room was divided in half by a broken line. If he had not seen the submarine earlier he would not have taken any notice of this feature. To him though it looked a lot like the bomb bay doors he had seen on the new Hyper Sub. More importantly comparing the dimensions of the original Hyper Sub plans he could judge by the internal measurements, the Moon Pool in CVC was designed to fit the sub exactly.

Looking at the complete plans, he concluded this was the way in to the habitat. According to the drawing, it was also the only area to be internally protected by hydraulic doors suggesting a submersible wet room; the other chambers only had them on the connecting walkways.

The Moon Pool must open, flooding the compartment for access, then sealed and emptied. The occupants of the Hyper Sub could enter the habitat easily and hide the sub within. An underwater submarine permanently parked alongside the Oriskany would draw some unwelcome attention.

Dan glanced from the plans to see Lizzie with an extreme look of concentration on her face. The last time he had seen it was when they had a midterm maths exam together. She caught his eye as he stared at her fondly and smiled.

"Okay, so I admit." She deflated dropping her shoulders. "There's a lot of evidence that backs up your wild theory. The only thing I can't see from all of this is how you gain access to the habitat."

Dan was a little perplexed by this as well, he was hoping the Oriskany plans would give an idea how to enter but he could see nothing to indicate an opening or space they could use. As if reading his mind Lizzie asked another relevant question.

"If they are actually inside the ship, why has no one found it? There must be literally hundreds of dives performed around the site every day. How can it be that well hidden?"

"I don't know, from this point on we're pretty much flying blind. I'd assume the only ones who would have known the secret of access would have been Uncle Mike and Aunt Susan but we can't ask them. The other thing, the depth of the habitat is below most recreational divers' depth, so there would be far fewer down at those levels. I would also assume they would be down there for comparatively short time spans."

Dan pulled the Oriskany plan between the pair of them, pointing at the moved bulkhead on the drawing. "I would say the most obvious place would be with the internal wall they moved. If anywhere, that would be my initial place to start. It has to be more than just strengthening and protection, it has to be the way in, why else would you move it?"

Lizzie wandered away from the table over to the acrylic glass of the hydro pod, shining her torch down into the pit. Dan went back to the light switches and flicked the emergency lighting back on, the dim greenish lights buzzed to life and they both turned off their torches. Grateful of proper lighting Lizzie spun round taking in the lab in its entirety. "It's a lot bigger than I was expecting."

Dan walked to the far wall and paced the length of the lab to the hydro pod where Lizzie was stood; he then did the same again across the width. Grabbing the plans to section CVB, he compared the measurements. "Well according to my quick measurement, the lab and the size of the compartment CVB titled 'underwater lab' are pretty much similar, if you include the hydro pod." He glanced up and looked through the glass. "What do you reckon, about three metres inside the pod?"

Lizzie opened the door and held her arms aloft like Da Vinci's Vitruvian man. "Well it's gotta be well over two metres because I can't touch the sides at all!" She pushed open the watertight door and peered down into the pit. It was dark so she turned on her torch to see the bottom, Dan followed and looked over her shoulder.

"You see the metal tracks either side of the concrete pit?" As Dan spoke, Lizzie trained the beam on them; the once shining metal seemed dull with the residue of salt erosion and decay. "That was the lowering track used by Granddad's technology. The new sub at Marion Reynolds has exactly the same tracks newly installed, you have to question why?"

"So what was the pit for then?" Lizzie was curious.

"The pit was full of sea water, which somehow fed the machine; which was lowered down into the water on the track. When they needed to work on or adjust it, the system was brought out of the water, up to the level we are stood now. I don't remember much about it; all I can remember was that it used to glow and change colour under the surface. Most of the time it was a cobalt blue but when they were testing, it would change into a deep purple colour, sometimes almost red. It was quite mesmerising and surreal at the same time."

Dan lowered Lizzie's arm pointing the torch beam into the bottom of the pit. "I found Matt's pen knife just there, disappearing into the tunnel." Lizzie pointed the torch at the bottom of the pit. "Move the torch back and forth."

"What?"

"Well when I found the knife, it was under a water bottle but I can't see it."

Dan climbed down into the pit, he was right it was not there. He ducked and shone his torch up the service tunnel, the bottle was a few feet from the entrance. Could the wind have picked up enough to transport it along the tunnel? He crawled in to pick it up and see how light it was. It was full, there was no way the wind could have carried it.

He swung his torch along the tunnel stretching away in front of him and stopped. The algae pools he had crawled through, they were different. There were now two clearly divisible marks in the green sludge. It was obvious, two people had crawled through the tunnel, one of them was him but who was the second?

"Dan, are you alright?" Lizzie could not see him from where she stood and was starting to feel slightly nervous, it could be heard in her voice. The emergency lighting was beginning to fail and was getting dimmer by the second; soon she'd be back in total darkness, alone with her torch.

"Dan!"

Dan's head reappeared from the tunnel and looked up. Blinded by her beam, he held his hand up to his eyes. "Someone's been down here."

Lizzie moved it from his eyes. "What do you mean?"

"I crawled down the service tunnel before and it was obvious no one had been down it, except for a few old marks on the steps in the boat house. However the sludge through the tunnel has a second path dredged through it." He stared into Lizzie's eyes as if to reiterate the seriousness of what he was about to say. "Someone else has crawled through the tunnel Lizzie recently, someone else knows about the lab, someone other than you, me or your father."

42

The boat house had always been Lizzie's favourite building within the Morris grounds. It was just the whole beauty of the setting; the picturesque setting, its décor and the veranda looking out across the sea all contributed to the allure.

Tonight was exceptionally beautiful, nearing full moon, the light danced across the open sea, bouncing from the veranda windows, reminding her the evening still had some romance to it. The way the evening had progressed they would soon be watching the sunrise and not because they had been up all night talking or making love.

Although Lizzie had protested, after his discovery a second person had been through the service tunnel, Dan wanted to check out the boat house. It was getting very late, or early depending on your view, and in truth the fantasies of being tucked up in bed wrapped together had long since evaporated. She sighed as she realised she was resigned to her own bed, as opposed to Dan's which she thought was looking good earlier.

This was not how she expected the night to have panned out. She had long since sobered and was now feeling slightly cross and irritable, tiredness was setting in. She was a little dismayed at herself. Her mind had wandered to the earlier part of the evening when they kissed. She felt a little guilty caring more about sleeping with Dan than the underground lab or his outlandish ideas, however she had waited so long for him to kiss her maybe she had earned the right to be selfish?

It was quite cold in the boat house, a breeze blew in through the door off the sea, she stood with her arms folded, clutching her bag. The deck in the boat house had been lifted and she could see down into the service tunnel. She was amazed after all these years she had never had the slightest inkling of the lab or the tunnel. One of the boats would have always covered the sluice gate, which flooded the tunnel, but even so it was still quite surprising.

Dan had disappeared for what seemed like an age but was now coming back up, his torch light bouncing around as he crawled back through the tunnel and into the opening, looking up at Lizzie.

"Yep, whoever found the tunnel, they've definitely crawled right through it."

"Do you think it could have been the murderer?"

"Well its highly likely. Whoever he is, he must be watching my every move, but how the hell he got in the house and into the Panic Room again, I have no idea. The coded keys would have been useless to him. Unless he watched me inside the house, then saw me exiting from the boat house. It wouldn't have taken a genius to work out there was another entrance; he could have easily found the lab." Dan was angry with his complacency towards the gravitas of the situation. "I've fuckin' well led him straight to it!"

Lizzie was unsure what to say or do to make him feel better, she was not sure if anything would. She knew their romantic evening had slipped from her grasp. Somehow their evening had turned from a date into an expedition. She did not know what else to do to get it back on track.

She made the unusual decision to take the bull by the horns. Placing her clutch bag on the window ledge, she kicked her heels off and stood before him. Seductively sliding her arms around his waist she looked into his gleaming eyes. He sighed with the warmth of her touch, feeling her against his body.

"I'm sorry; I've kind of ruined our date haven't I?"

"Well yes, you've been a little distracted to say the least but you can still make it up to me." She raised her eyebrows, smiling, tugging at his shirt, loosening it from his trousers. She unbuttoned it, slipping the fitted shirt from his shoulders and it fell to the floor revealing his unblemished skin. This was certainly better than the DVD she had seen of him in the flesh. As they kissed passionately, she ran the tips of her fingers down his chest and across his washboard abs.

The skin on his chest and arms goose pimpled under her delicate touch. They settled on the button of his ruined dress pants, smiling while holding his gaze she deftly unhooked them; they slid down around his ankles. He kicked off his shoes and stepped out of them. Surprisingly, apart from his dress socks, he was now completely naked. Lizzie smiled giving a look of appreciation of him in all his glory.

"What no underwear?"

"I prefer to wear a jock for support after my hernia but it always looks and feels a little odd under a dress suit."

"I much prefer the commando look myself." With a mischievous glint in her eyes she reached round and pinched his arse, then clutching both cheeks, pulled him towards her, kissing tenderly.

Dan unzipped the back of Lizzie's dress; it fell away into a heap of flowing cloth round her ankles. Lizzie also stood there totally naked. Dan smiled appreciatively. "Looks like you do."

"VPL looks terrible in a dress that close fitting!" She smiled touching his cheek. Dan ran his hand down the outside of her ribcage, delicately brushing her breast. Her breathing deepened with his touch, she pushed her skin against the warmth of his, her erect nipples pressing into his skin. He was stunned at how toned her body was, she was perfect, exactly the right combination of muscularity and femininity he adored. Too many women starved themselves, dieting without training, attaining an unhealthy emaciated and malnourished look. Lizzie was perfect, in every sense.

A phone rang, piercing the silence. They broke apart, Lizzie looking around confused. Dan had the look Lizzie had given him earlier when Simon rang his cell.

He shrugged. "Don't look at me; I left my cell in the study!"

"Shit." Lizzie swore and grabbed for her clutch bag on the ledge. Dan reluctantly let her body slip from his arms but still clutched at her left hand, gently spinning her back towards him, imploring.

"Just leave it."

Her eyes longing, she looked at him lovingly. This moment had been in her dreams most of her adult life, here it was and her cell seemed more important.

"It'll be Dad, he may have had one of his turns. He never rings unless there's a problem." She wriggled free and slipped her cell from the bag, answering it instantly seeing the display did indeed read Dad. As she did, Dan pulled her back towards him wrapping his muscular arms around her body, gently squeezing her and lifting her feet from the deck.

"Dad what's wrong?"

"I'm sorry sweetheart, did I wake you?" Charlie sounded distant; he was not his usual self, she could tell. He had not just been woken either, he was wide awake and there was a sense of urgency in his voice.

"Err no, I was um, just getting undressed!" She screwed her face up as if rumbled looking at Dan sheepishly, she started to turn red from embarrassment.

"Can you get to the office please? I'm with the police here, the silent alarm was tripped and we've had a break in. I need you to come in for an inventory check. I can't tell what's been stolen yet."

Lizzie deflated, wriggling free from Dan again, who heard and realised it was serious. He picked up Lizzie's dress and shoes, looking at her face as she frowned concentrating on what Charlie was saying.

"Okay, I'll be there in a few minutes." She hung up and looked desperately at Dan, wanting to stay; torn between the two men in her life. Dan could see the distressed look on her face.

"It's all right, if you need to head off I understand, your Dad is important too. We can continue what we started later; we have the rest of our lives together."

The smile reappeared back on Lizzie's face. "Did you just say what I think you said?"

"What?"

"You know, that we have the rest of our lives together?"

"Well yeah, if you want me?"

Lizzie suddenly launched herself at him like a mad woman. Grinning from ear to ear, both feet left the wooden deck and her arms flung round his neck. Her onslaught was unexpected, Dan lost his balance during the attack. Stepping backwards, the pair of them plunged into the warm water of the boat house. They floated back to the surface spluttering and coughing, Lizzie clung around his neck, still smiling feeling like her world was on fire. They kissed passionately bobbing up and down in the water, all senses alive as the water enveloped their bodies.

"Shit, I dropped my cell."

"Don't worry I'll get it later although I suspect it'll probably be a bit knackered."

Lizzie swam back to the edge of the deck, hauling herself out of the water onto the balls of her feet in one swift movement. Dan was in awe of her body, Lizzie was stunning, not only that, she was his. Lizzie looked around the floor, Dan had fallen in with her dress and shoes and they were floating on the surface, just out of her reach.

"Do you think you'll have some pants and a top I can borrow up at the house? I don't think I can turn up looking as though I've just walked through a rain storm!"

They walked back up the slope naked, hand in hand, back into the house and through to the kitchen, leaving wet footprints in their wake through the hallway. At the back of the kitchen was the laundry room,

Lizzie rummaged around in Dan's pile of washing, pulling out a pair of sweat pants and a vest top. For some unknown reason she held them up smelling the material, he had worn them; she could smell his scent.

Instead of putting them aside she slipped them on, something perverse in her knowing they had been worn by the man she loved. The vest top accentuated her breasts but she did not care, it was nearly four in the morning.

She wandered back through to the study; Dan was in the Panic Room. He was running his hands round the room, covering all the surfaces.

"What are you doing now?"

"Well the man knew the Panic Room existed, however he did not know the lab did, only after I'd been in and down to the lab did he discover the tunnel or the entrance. He must have bugged the room somehow. After finding the plastic strips on the external cameras, it's obviously not outside the realms of this guy's capability." Dan glanced sideways at Lizzie in his gym gear. "Nice threads, you look better in them than I do!"

Lizzie laughed. "This old thing, I just threw it on, you know I didn't want to overdo it on a first date! Do you actually know what you're looking for?"

"Not really but I'm sure I'll know when I find it." He stopped, his hand brushed down the inner edge of the left monitor on the surveillance system. He pulled the monitor forward, swinging it to the left looking at the side. He turned to Lizzie, putting his fingers to his lips and pointing to the device, he motioned Lizzie over. Hardly noticeable, taped to the outer edge was a small black thin looking matchstick. He pushed the monitor so it was aimed against the wall and motioned to leave, shutting the Panic Room door behind them.

"What was that?"

"It's a camera. I just don't know whether it would be transmitting sound and images. Whoever has been watching has been patiently waiting for me to gain access to the Panic Room. When I did, I'd assume he would have seen me and when the hidden panel slid open, he would have seen the stairwell. He probably saw me exiting the boat house, knowing he couldn't get back in directly through the Panic Room. He'd have tried from the boat house. Shit."

"How do you know it's a camera?"

"I've seen them before through work. It's a long story and I'll explain later, in the meantime you'd better get to your Dad's office. Use the

Range Rover, the keys are on the desk." Dan crossed the room and grabbed the keys which were resting on the hyper sub plans. He turned and tossed them to Lizzie, who caught them in her left hand and she headed out the door.

He shouted down the corridor after her. "You look fabulous by the way."

Lizzie grinned over her shoulder. "So do you gorgeous, but if that is a camera, he's just seen you in all your natural beauty and that my love is for my eyes only from now on!" With that Lizzie was gone. He could hear her chuckling as she headed out of the house.

Dan flopped down into the seat looking at the plans of the hyper sub. It was late and he was starting to feel tired but his mind was on overdrive. He needed to go back down to the boat house and dive down to get Lizzie's cell, not that it was truly worth saving.

When he was in the water earlier, the empty boat house had given him an idea. He folded the plans, grabbed a tape measure from the drawers of the desk and strode naked from the house into the emerging dawn. Time to check one more detail before he finally got some sleep.

43

Dan woke with a jump, his body felt as though he had only just fallen asleep. He rolled over and looked at the bedside clock. It had only been three hours since he finally crawled to bed. The clocks luminescent face read just past nine am. His excursions had been time consuming but illuminating. He finally felt like he had worked out the last piece of the puzzle. Before he slept he tried to call Lizzie to find out what happened at the office. Her cell ruined, he tried the office phone however it was transferring directly to voicemail.

The front door sounded like it was going to explode off its hinges with the constant hammering. He threw back the sheets and stumbled out of bed, grabbing his workout shorts from the bottom of the bed pulling them on. He sluggishly descended the stairs to the front door.

"Hang on, I'm coming." He unlocked it, opening the door. Stood before him were two of the Sheriff's deputies from the local Police Station. "Good morning, can I help you?"

The deputies blocked the doorway; their extremely wide shoulders prevented the early morning sun illuminating the darkened hallway, looking grave and intimidating. Both had their hands on their utility belts, clasping the grip of their guns in their holsters, in the vain hope of releasing the clip to pump off a few rounds.

He stood there practically naked, except for his extremely tight fitting compression shorts. The deputies passed less than impressed acidic glances up and down his near naked body before the officer on the left, who looked more angry for having to come way out of town, spoke gruffly and more formally than Dan expected.

"Daniel Morris?"

"Yes."

"Would you care to get dressed and come with us please?"

"Why, what's happened?" He immediately thought of Lizzie leaving earlier. "Is Lizzie okay? What about Charlie?"

"I'm not at liberty to say sir, but could you accompany us to the station. The Sheriff would like to have a word. Please get dressed and come with us."

Dan had flopped into bed earlier after his swim in the sea, he could smell the salt water that had dried on his skin, he felt dirty. "Do I have time for a quick shower?"

"No!"

Surprised, Dan stepped back letting the officers through in to the hallway. They scanned the room as Dan quickly went back upstairs and got dressed. Throwing on an old pair of jeans and a T shirt, he slipped into his sandals, expecting this to be a relatively short trip and headed back down the stairs.

"Do you want me to follow in my car?"

"No sir you're fine, you can ride in the squad car with us."

Dan picked up his keys heading out the door, closely followed by the deputies. Dan noted throughout their conversation, they stayed alert, watchful of him and their surroundings. They had obviously cased the kitchen and study while he was upstairs, he felt relieved he had closed the Panic Room door.

What he noted and concerned him somewhat was the fact their hands never left their sidearms, it was rather unorthodox considering the situation. Outside, two squad cars had been sent to collect him; there was something more sinister happening than just a quick chat with the Sheriff.

"I could have driven myself in if you had called, it's not a problem."

The deputy who had not spoken opened the back door of the squad car. "It's okay sir, the Sheriff wanted you brought down asap. He much prefers the personal touch. Mind your head." He guided Dan's head in under the door frame as he slid onto the back seat.

A musky smell hung in the air, a heady combination of sweat, bleach and vomit. An air freshener freshly opened, cloyed at the back of his throat. The vanilla scent failing to cover the stench of copious drunks who had been taken home or to the cells to sleep off their binge, but not before they had emptied their stomachs or bowels across the black vinyl seating.

Separating him and the front seats was a grill, which would stop anyone choking the officers from behind. The window openers and interior door handles had been removed. The only way out of the car was if someone opened it from the outside. It was oppressive and extremely claustrophobic, not to mention hot in the early morning Florida sun.

He knew he was not heading into town for a routine chat, alarm bells were ringing but what could have happened? Something in their demeanour was hard, almost uncaring.

The last few days had been entirely different to this, he knew how the police operated, he worked with them day in, day out. He also knew they would talk down to him if they felt superior; this was the impression he felt through their treatment. It certainly was not the way the Sheriff had talked to him the other day; the whole scenario was far more custodial, what had changed?

44

Dan had been led to a room and left for well over an hour waiting. He knew how these things worked, they left you to sweat. The only problem was he had no idea what he was sweating for, or why. They had dragged him in, as far as he knew, without any kind of motive.

In the back of his mind he started to wonder whether they had found his Aunt and Uncle's murderer, however he concluded the murderer was far too clever for the local law enforcement to ever comprehend, let alone catch. He had seen this kind of work; he had led good officers with irrefutable data to apprehend them and still failed, so why was he here?

The coffee in front of him was stale; it had been sitting on the hot plate for hours. It tasted bitter and slightly burnt, however it was better than nothing to occupy his hands. His mind had been going over the previous night, simply talking his ideas and worries through with Lizzie had formed a conclusion that in itself seemed irrefutable.

When he first arrived in the UK, he took time to explore the County's rich history. He had driven down to the New Forest in the south of England. Visiting a tiny village called Minstead, where his childhood hero was buried, Sir Arthur Conan Doyle.

His Grandfather introduced him to the detective shortly after he first came to live at the house. Granddad had loved the fact the detective's creator was Scottish, born in Edinburgh.

It was his love of detective stories growing up that guided his career path; his attraction came from sifting extraneous data connecting unrelated information to prove a theory, or as in a Sherlock Holmes case or his work, connect a crime.

In his cube at work, pinned to the wall hung an old copper engraving he found at a local table sale while touring, it depicted one of Holmes' most renowned phrases;

"When you have eliminated the impossible, whatever remains,
however improbable, must be the truth?"

His truth, he mused, seemed to be difficult to comprehend. Any sane person would question his ideas, it seemed impossible. Could his family truly be living at the bottom of the ocean in a purposely scuppered aircraft carrier?

It did seem improbable but so many of the facts pointed to the Oriskany. Lizzie was right though, the only way to uncover the truth was to dive down to the wreck and take a proper look.

The interview room was small, a far cry from what he was used to. He was also surprised at how backward it seemed in comparison to the state of the art interrogation rooms at New Scotland Yard where he worked. He was spoilt, he had the best of everything to do his job and had access to secret intelligence. He could access any database, almost having the highest level of clearance in the country. He often was scared by the freedom he was allowed by the Official Secrets Act.

The door to the interview room opened and Charlie was escorted in by the Sheriff. Dan got up through instinct; Charlie motioned at him to sit down and held his finger to his lips as he passed. The movement was not what Dan had expected but he flopped down into his seat as told.

The Sheriff eyeballed the pair of them, looking between the two. "You have fifteen minutes Mr Price, then we shall be coming in to interview your client." Charlie just nodded; the Sheriff turned and left the room.

Charlie visibly deflated upon his exit, dropping himself down in the chair in front, throwing a folder onto the table. He was drawn and tired, looking very pale. "Dan we're in trouble!"

Dan looked at him; suddenly realising why he was there. The break in had not been an accident.

"The drives are gone, aren't they?" Charlie did not need to confirm the worst, Charlie looked sick.

"I've been here all night Dan, I had to disclose the drives. They were the only things taken from the office safe and in doing so, I had to disclose what was stored on them. The Sheriff's talking about throwing the book at me, client privilege seems not to be a part of law he understands." Charlie removed his oval spectacles and rubbed the bridge of his nose.

"I've actually given a statement of what I saw on the drives, I had to, to corroborate your version of events. I really shouldn't be in here because they believe I will be coaching you, however because I gave them a statement, which I needn't have done, they have given us some leeway. How long it'll last is anyone's guess?"

Somehow Dan was not surprised the drives were gone, he was however surprised at the speed this man was capable of acting. The house really needed a specialist squad to sweep for bugs and other cameras. Charlie on the other hand seemed visibly shaken by the turn of events.

"The Sheriff is pissed because we didn't trust him with the truth about the Panic Room or give him the drives as soon as we gained access. However, at present, he does understand you were acting in good faith because you believed you were protecting the family's research. Although I'm not sure he'll believe any of it once he gets in the lab, seeing it's empty, and also if he starts digging into your family background?"

"Have you spoken with Lizzie?"

"She's told me bits about your evening together and in truth I am slightly disappointed you used your money to woo my little girl. I couldn't believe it when she turned up this morning at the office not only wearing your bloody clothes but driving your Aunt's Range Rover. She looked as guilty as hell!"

Dan bowed his head guiltily so Charlie grinned giving a knowing wink.

"Did she tell you what we discussed last night?"

"No. To be honest the Sheriff sent her home and hauled me in here, we never had chance to really discuss anything. Why?"

The door opened, the Sheriff re-entered holding three fresh cups of Java's. He held them aloft like a peace offering. Charlie was a little incensed by the intrusion.

"I thought you said I had fifteen minutes?"

"Well I did but I thought maybe it'd be better if we had a chat properly, just the three of us." He pulled the brown plastic chair in the corner of the room over to the interview table and sat down, sipping at his coffee as though the situation was just a few of the guys getting together to shoot the breeze. He sat turning to face Dan.

"Now tell me Dan, why didn't you mention the Panic Room and the alleged internal surveillance system when I was with you a few days ago?"

Charlie was obviously going to interrupt but the Sheriff held his hand up, his palm facing Charlie, stopping him in his tracks. Dan knew the time would come when he would have to talk openly about the lab. He was not sure what details he would need to leave out but there was no recording device present and he doubted they had the equipment to record covertly, so he knew the interview was informal. Charlie was also present which gave a vague sense of confidence. It was like being in the headmaster's office at school with a parent.

Dan leant forward. "It's all right Charlie. It'll have to come out eventually." He looked at the Sheriff. "The Panic Room was built after the house caught fire several years ago. During the remodelling my Grandfather and Uncle James decided to build a lab to continue their research in secret. At the time it was drawing unwanted attention from external forces and government officials. "

"What was this research, for the government to become involved?"

"I honestly don't know, it was far beyond what I understood or cared about, I was too young. Plus it was just a part of family life that existed, I never questioned it, I never felt the need to, it just was. They designed and rebuilt the existing house on top of what became the underground lab and garage. From the outside it looked like an extensive basement and then the house was built on top. I don't think the contractors would've understood what they were building. The internal structure for the lab was fitted and installed long after the building work was completed; then the equipment was installed, bit by bit. I know some of the computers and testing equipment are very expensive and I'd assume would draw attention if supplied and installed at a family home. Having seen the business accounts I believe many acquisitions were purchased through Morris Holdings." Dan looked at Charlie, who nodded in confirmation of his assumption.

"The Panic Room was installed, hiding the entire operation from view. Only the family had access. A second external lab was built on the grounds to give the impression from the outside nothing was happening."

"My deputies said there was no such room, they had a look when you went to change."

"It's well hidden. The only access is opened through the safe behind the family portrait. The only people to ever get inside were the family, not even Charlie knew of its existence. I only got my keys back when Charlie gave me a package left by Aunt Susan. Inside were my safe and data keys. Each key can only be worked by the owner, as it correlates the individual's iris scan to the opening of the Panic Room door."

The Sheriff nodded towards Charlie, so far everything Charlie had told them earlier was corroborating to the explanation, Dan knew this as well so continued.

"The man who broke in to the house and then consequently the Panic Room forcibly used my Uncle, after he killed him, to open the door. However he did not find what he was looking for."

"Which was?"

"Well I can only guess at the lab. I believe he thought he'd come to a dead end only discovering the internal surveillance system. He removed the hard drives but didn't realise they were mirrored. I recreated the system and witnessed the brutal killing of Uncle Mike and Aunt Susan, which I showed Charlie. I removed the ghost hard drives of the surveillance footage giving them to Charlie."

The Sheriff scowled and looked between the pair of them as though the story was making sense but he hated to admit it.

"And now conveniently the evidence on the drives has been stolen from Mr Price's safe."

Charlie interjected. "I was planning to give you the drives."

"Please be quiet Mr Price, I've heard your version of events. I want to hear Mr Morris'."

Dan looked at Charlie who shrugged. "In Charlie's defence he wanted to give you the drives straight away, it was me who wanted to wait until after I'd been to see Marion Reynolds over at Kingsland Lake. I knew not being open and telling you about the surveillance system and lab would look bad."

"That it does Mr Morris; that it does. So what is down in the lab?"

"That's just it, the lab is pretty much empty. The only things down there of interest are supplies, a copy of the house plans and some other design sheets, which is what directed me to Marion Reynolds."

The Sheriff took out a notepad from the top pocket of his shirt, this was a new piece of information and he wrote the name down. "Marion Reynolds you say? What does he do?"

"He is a specialist design engineer and he's been building a design prototype for a personal submarine over at Kingsland Lake." The Sheriff raised an eyebrow but did not interrupt. "The family had invested in the project and had given a rather large cash injection to the firm, just before Uncle Mike and Aunt Susan's death. I wanted to see why, especially as the plans were the only thing in the lab. It seemed important."

The Sheriff pressed a button on the underneath of the interview desk and one of the deputies immediately entered. He ripped off the top note he had just written, 'Marion Reynolds, Kingsland Lake.' Sliding it across the table, the deputy retrieved it and left the room.

"So you saw Marion Reynolds, is that the name of a man or the company?"

"Both."

"What did you ask him?"

"Well it's not really what I asked him as to what I saw at the facility. The payment to Reynolds was for the family to take delivery of a new prototype personal submarine."

The Sheriff's face did not even crack a smile or even question the existence of a personal submarine, as if it was a run of the mill everyday occurrence. However Charlie nearly fell off his chair with the news, choking on his Java's coffee.

"I know Kingsland Lake, most of us do, how long did it take you to get there?"

Dan suddenly realised he was having his movements tracked, so ventured into bullet point mode, leaving out what he considered important details. He needed to talk to Charlie before he gave up all the relevant information.

"Umm, I left home around 5.30am, it took about 6 hours to drive there. I stayed for just over an hour, maybe an hour and a half and then headed back to Santa Rosa. The drive back was a bit quicker and I got into town at about 6, filling up at the station. I had a quick chat with Joel, Niles and J.J as they're putting the family yacht back in the water for me."

The Sheriff scribbled another note down, pressed the button and the deputy reappeared taking the note and left. Dan continued, knowing full well he was in an informal interview but for what, he had no idea.

"J.J. mentioned the family cruiser was down at Matt's old engineering business. So I nipped in to see Simon Millor. Simon is his old business partner. I wanted to make sure it was okay to leave the cruiser there. J.J informed me where it was, Uncle Mike had dropped it down there a few weeks ago and we started reminiscing about life and history."

"As you do." The Sheriff cut him off in a rather condescending manner but Dan chose to ignore the comment.

"I left him just after eight. I was running late, went home, changed, picked Lizzie up around 8.30 and headed to the Lighthouse where we had a fantastic evening and dinner together. We left around 12.30, maybe even 1am. The valet scooter service drove us back to the house."

"So you and Miss Price ate and then headed back to the house for sexual intercourse."

Charlie sat bolt upright at this point and interjected. "I don't think that has any relevance on last night's events and I don't see how something so personal is, at this time, any of your business."

The Sheriff glowered at Charlie. "I'll decide what is relevant and what is not Mr Price. I am in charge here, not you." The Sheriff rose from his seat heading to the door to leave. "Thank you Mr Morris, this chat has been most enlightening."

45

"I need a drink and I mean a proper one, a large one, none of your short measures, maybe the bottle!" Charlie was dumbfounded, a look of complete surprise across his face, his brain in meltdown trying in vain to compute what he had just heard. His pallid features looked as though they had withdrawn further during the course of Dan's lengthy detailed explanation.

The facts as Dan had laid them before him were hard to process. There were too many subtle events to connect, the video footage he had seen of the murder, the Panic Room, the underground lab, even the small insignificant detail that Ash had given her knife to Lizzie the night before she disappeared with the coordinates engraved on the back of the blade indicating the position of the Oriskany.

The submarine blueprints, along with the new designs by Matt, updating the latest submarine prototype with the addition of the same lowering track installed in the pit of the hydro pod.

Until fifteen minutes ago, he was completely unaware a personal submarine even existed, let alone two. Many of these small facts seemed coincidental on their own, however interwoven together so intricately as Dan had, gave the premise huge credibility.

Niles' confession that he never saw James and Pat on board Hydrous when they left dock, only Matt and Ash ... was this enough evidence to prove they were not on board? As a lawyer he would say no, every scrap presented so far was circumstantial, an elaborate piece of fiction or spin presented by the defence to arouse doubt, casting suspicion away from the accused. However no one was accused of anything, this was not a trial.

The biggest concern for Charlie was their only evidence had been stolen last night, only Dan and Charlie knew of its existence. Lizzie was completely unaware because she had not seen it. So the small camera

Dan found in the Panic Room must be watching and directing the perpetrator, which would explain how he was able to find the underground service tunnel.

The facts seemed trivial taken individually but all together the argument was quite compelling. Dan accumulated indiscriminate information professionally as an analyst and then pieced them together.

As a lawyer he knew many scenarios fitted, whether they were correct, who would know? In his heart he had never wanted to believe his best friend was gone, like Dan and Lizzie, Charlie was hopeful they were alive, maybe it was false hope but at least it was hope and that gave a slightly warm feeling.

The hardest part for Charlie to digest was Simon's piecing together of Matt's blueprints against other design sheets at Matt's old office. He would have to take a look at the compiled sheets to see the relevance. Simon also needed to be made aware of the possible dangers of the information he possessed, two lives having already been lost so far.

Charlie for once agreed with his daughter, the only way to ascertain fact from fiction was to dive down to the wreck to check it out for themselves to see whether an underwater habitat truly existed. This seemed the only logical way forward. How they achieved this with the knowledge their every move was being watched was going to be the hard part.

Dan felt physically drained. Whenever he pieced together data for a crime or investigation, it always put a severe mental drain on him, leaving his body wasted. The only way he usually worked around it was to hit the gym which somehow always reinvigorated his senses. However there was one piece of the puzzle he had not vocalised to anyone yet and Charlie was now that sounding block to form his final ideas.

"After Lizzie left this morning I checked one more thing before finally going to bed. When I first ventured in to the boat house the other day, the day you dropped by with the business portfolio."

"What, when you were covered in the green shit?"

"Well yeah, but that was algae after crawling through the service tunnel. I thought there were a couple of strange things when I was first entered the boat house. One was obviously the boats were missing, but the other did not sink in until last night. On the boat house overhead doors, there was a dry tidemark about three feet higher than the water line. When I lifted the door, the bottom was only submerged by about a foot in the water. It used to sit in the water where the higher tidemark now is, four feet used to be submerged."

"I don't see the relevance? The door may have jammed and they simply adjusted it to sit higher?"

"I thought so too but last night I realised when I was actually in the water, low tide was below the bottom of the garage door. Anyone could look directly into the boat house from the sea. I went back down after Lizzie had gone and took a tape measure with me, along with the blueprint to the hyper sub. By the time I got down there, the tide had dropped even further. I measured the gap between the bottom of the door to the floor of the boat house."

Charlie looked confused and was screwing up his face. "I don't understand, what difference would that make?"

"Well I believe the higher level of the door would allow clearance for the hyper sub to enter. According to the original plans, at high tide there'd be enough clearance between the back spoiler and the keel to enter underwater! No one would ever have seen the submarine enter or leave the boat house!"

Charlie's face started to enlighten and he finally dawned on the relevance of what Dan was saying. "So the sub could enter the boat house unseen and then whoever was driving could enter the house through the service tunnel?"

"Exactly, they also removed the intricate equipment from the lab and transported it to the Oriskany in the sub. No one would have ever seen them or suspected what was going on, plus the convenience of their alleged deaths, which I reckon just became another part of the charade. The original deep scrape marks on the steps exiting from the tunnel to the boat house happened when the heavy equipment was hauled up. Also the supplies in the lab were there so anyone visiting could just take what they needed. When I first went down into the lab I assumed the shopping list was in Aunt Susan's and Uncle Mike's writing but it wasn't until Simon pointed out the similarity between Mike and Matt's handwriting it twigged. Yes it was Aunt Susan's but I compared the other writing against Matt's on the hydro pod track plans from Reynolds and it was the same. Simon was right, Uncle Mike and Matt had very similar handwriting. He must add stuff to the list as and when they needed it, or were running low."

"Bloody hell Dan."

"The other thing is the diesel bill from the station. The bill was huge and without the cruiser or speed boat about, who, or more importantly what, was using the fuel?"

"You reckon the sub was filled up when it docked at the boat house?" Charlie was getting in the swing of it; he was beginning to see how all the little pieces fitted together.

"Yep and the final thing I realised after I dived in to do the measuring, on the bottom of the dock is a cradle, the same type of cradle I saw yesterday at Marion Reynolds with Hyper 2 resting on it. I reckon at low tide the water must be too low for the depth of the submarine. Its keel is deeper than the cruiser, so it rests in the cradle during this time. Which begs one more question, why had no one ever seen it from the sea?"

Charlie had not seen the sub but surmised. "Well would it not just look like a normal boat from a distance, so not raising suspicion?"

"Actually that's true and I hadn't thought of that, however I realised the boat house door has two settings programmed into the lowering mechanism. You press once and it goes to the higher level for the sub to enter. If you hold it, the door returns to its old original position. Simple really, it was just set at the higher level when I went in and I only pressed the button once to close it."

There was silence between them as they both mulled over the conversation. "I take delivery at the house next week of the second hyper sub. It can't be coincidence the boat house is already fully equipped to take delivery of the new one."

46

The clock in the interview room crept slowly. It was boring to watch as the second hand slowly swung around the dial. A continuous sweeping movement used to be the sign of an expensive clock but electronic devices have made sweeping second hands much more common.

It somehow seemed slower and possibly more mesmerising watching a continual movement, instead of the snap jerk of a mechanical second hand which has the feeling it dictates the passing of time. The pair of them felt like they had been in the hot stuffy room for hours, the silence between them was starting to grate.

Dan finally decided to ask the most obvious question. "Why are we here Charlie?"

"You know I was beginning to wonder the same thing. Something is going on other than the theft of the drives but I don't know what."

At that moment, the door to the interview room opened. The Sheriff strode back in to the room with purpose and sat down. This time a second officer was stationed by the door and the Sheriff had an A4 pad with countless hand scrawled notes and crossings out. He sat directly opposite Dan, clasping his hands together.

"Tell me Daniel, other than yourself, who would benefit most from the deaths of your Aunt and Uncle?"

Charlie was concerned at this turn of events. He could suddenly see the dangerous angle from which the Sheriff was fishing. He tried to interject. "I don't understand the relevance."

The Sheriff's easy demeanour was souring. "Mr Price, unless you are instructing your client not to answer my questions, I kindly suggest you remain quiet." He glared at Charlie who contentiously glared back.

Dan could see the logic of the question; he was actually surprised he had not been asked earlier. "Well considering I am the last heir in the family lineage, then all the assets and family money comes directly to me."

"Which is a considerably large sum, is it not?" The Sheriff smiled as if he already knew the net worth of the man sat across the table from him.

Charlie interjected. "So what are you accusing my client of Sheriff?"

"I'm not accusing Mr Morris of anything. Yet. I believe I'm merely suggesting, if it's not clear through my line of questioning so far. As you're both intelligent gentlemen and for the record Mr Morris deals with these kinds of incidences every day, I believe that Daniel Morris is connected, if not ultimately responsible, for the deaths of his Aunt and Uncle. I believe the motive is money."

Charlie raged from behind the Sheriff, who casually looked over his shoulder at him. "That's absurd. My client has no need for the family fortune. He's already an extremely wealthy man through birth right. His trust fund alone, left by his mother after her death and consequently inherited on his 18th birthday, was in excess of $8 million dollars. That was without access to the expansive family money pot, which he has been entitled to since he reached 21."

The Sheriff scowled in the direction of Charlie. "Then tell me Mr Price, why is the only evidence, by yours and Mr Morris' admission, been stolen from the protective custody of your safe? Mr Morris was the only one, other than you, who knew of its existence."

Daniel interjected. "That's not true actually, Lizzie knew. I made her aware of the recordings last night over dinner."

"Yes we know. Miss Price has been kind enough to have filled us in on the details of your evening. She is presently sat next door in the other interview room."

Charlie exploded out of his seat, his face instantly turning red with fury. Dan was shocked; he had never seen Charlie ever raise his voice before. "That's outrageous, how dare you interview my daughter without me being present. What gives you the right?"

"Sit down Mr Price before I have my deputy restrain you. I'm the law round here and the right is given to me by the state of Florida. Miss Price is not under arrest, she came under her own volition and if I feel the need to interview Miss Price to corroborate both your stories then that's what I'll damn well do. It is in fact why both of you have been left in here. Now I'll ask you again politely one more time, sit down Mr Price." He turned back to face Dan.

"Okay Mr Morris, I'll make this perfectly clear. Most of your account of the events over the last few days correlate with Mr and Miss Price. Some however, you seem to have missed out, or how shall I say delicately, excluded completely. However I'd like to give you this opportunity to fill in the blanks, as it were?"

Dan looked from the Sheriff to Charlie for support, who could only shrug. He was unsure what the Sheriff was angling at, he could not be sure what Lizzie had told him, he was feeling a little stuck as to what to say.

The Sheriff felt the need to push a little. "Mr Price here … " Indicating towards Charlie over his shoulder with his pen. "… informed us, you showed him the footage of the murder of your Aunt and Uncle. He also indicated it was clear from the murderer's action he was fully aware of the cameras in the house as there was not a single shot where the perpetrator revealed his face. Now, don't you find that slightly odd Mr Morris? He easily disabled the external cameras, which you so eagerly showed me when I visited. Yet he hid his face from the internal ones, which no one knew about, except you and the immediate family. Don't you find that strange? What does that suggest to you Mr Morris?"

Dan looked at him, he could see where the Sheriff was heading. He was trying to pin his Aunt and Uncle's murders on him. He was trying to trip him up or get him to confess. Much to Charlie's relief, Daniel remained silent.

The Sheriff continued to fill in the blanks as he saw them, due to a lack of response from either party present. "Well to me it suggests someone who has an intimate knowledge of the workings to the interior of your family home. Or someone who has been coached where the cameras are and how to hide from them. What I would like to know is, who would have that knowledge?" He paused for effect with his assumption. "For your benefit Mr Morris that is purely a rhetorical question, as you are the only one, who's alive I may add, who does."

"Please tell me where you believe you're heading with this." Dan said with a hardened poker face.

"I'm not heading anywhere Mr Morris. I'm making assumptions, forming a hypothesis if you may, on what actually happened at your family home a few weeks ago."

"No, what you are ultimately saying is you're clueless who murdered my family having no leads whatsoever. So the next best thing is to rattle a few doors and blame the closest living relative who inherits everything – the catalyst being money of course. It seems very convenient Sheriff and may I be so bold as to say rather Agatha Christie-esque!"

The Sheriff started to turn red with anger and bellowed across the table. "Look young man, you're in a whole heap of shit, it'll only help your case if you start cooperating with this investigation and start telling us the truth."

Dan looked at him blankly. "The truth, the truth? You'd not fucking recognise the truth if it was hand delivered personally by the President of the U. S fucking A. You're just clutching at straws because you don't know who else to pin this on. It's out of your fucking league and you know it. Any fucker'll do to hang out to dry, because I suspect you're getting your superiors pressuring you for results to close this case."

Charlie had never heard Dan ever speak like it in his whole life; he could not even remember a time where he had heard him swear. Part of him still looked at him as a kid and he was quite shocked by Dan's bravado but also immensely proud, although the lawyer in him felt he should at least calm the situation. "Dan please, there is no need, just remain quiet." He turned to the Sheriff. "What proof do you have that Dan was in any way involved in the murders of his Aunt and Uncle?"

Charlie and Dan both peered at the Sheriff, who suddenly looked deflated. He had made a call to try and bluff a confession but neither was biting. Maybe he just needed to bait the hook further, he exhaled deeply. "Why did you go and see Simon Millor?"

Dan began to think Lizzie must have told him about the plans and how Simon pieced them together. "I told you earlier, the family cruiser was down at the yard and I wanted to know whether it was okay to leave it there until I sorted a few things out. I was thinking of selling it."

"So you two didn't have an argument or anything?"

"We had nothing of the sort. Simon and I have always gotten along really well."

"How well?" The Sheriff leaned in to see if there was a reaction.

"Look Sheriff, if you're trying to insinuate Simon and I are lovers you certainly have your wires crossed. Yes he's gay, I'm straight, and he's a friend, nothing more. You should ask him."

"I can't."

"Why not?"

"He's dead!" The sheriff said it so matter of fact, so forthright, the words hung like stale air in the room. Dan at first was stunned, then the pessimistic side of him tried to gauge whether this was a trick, but as the Sheriff stared intently at him trying to assess a reaction, he realised the Sheriff was telling the truth.

He stammered. "When? I only left him last night and I spoke to him on the phone with Lizzie during dinner."

"Yes we know; we have Simon's phone records which correlate both your stories and pinpoint the time of the call at 10.48pm, lasting approximately ten minutes. You didn't leave the Lighthouse until just after 1am according to the maître d' and waiters. The valet parking attendant said he dropped you to the house just after 1.30am. Miss Price confirmed that she saw the Panic Room and ventured down in the lab, after which you both went for a dip in the sea. Simon's body was discovered this morning by his unfortunate receptionist at 8am. He had been dead approximately eight hours according to the coroner." The Sheriff looked through his list, which he'd traced with his finger to see if he left anything out, he hadn't so he looked directly at Dan.

Dan sighed on the inside; Lizzie had obviously not mentioned the plans or anything else. "How did he die?"

"He was shot in the back of the head at point blank range. We believe it was as he put the phone down to his father, which was the last number dialled according to the redial."

Knowing Simon had been murdered shed even more serious implications on their situation. The murderer was following them closely and seemed to be tying up loose ends.

"What was the murderer looking for?"

"Well there are a number of plans missing, the office was ransacked and it looks as though Simon's laptop has been taken. So until we can trace his internet provider, we're unable to find out when his last emails were sent and to whom.

Dan decided to confess now that he would probably be the last email, he knew in his line of work it would only be a matter of time before they found the details and discovered the email trail. "Simon's phone call was to tell me he had emailed some plans to me. They were of a design Matt, my cousin, and Simon's business partner had been working on prior to his death. I found some plans I thought would interest Simon and dropped them over, he compiled them and sent me a copy to take a look."

"The office has been cleared out completely, so I assume whoever was there was looking for these plans and promptly took his laptop as well for the electronic versions. Can I have a copy of them?"

Charlie stepped in at this point. "I think my client has cooperated enough with your investigation, he will release the plans to me and I shall get you a copy."

The Sheriff was beginning to hate this lawyer more and more, every fibre in his body screamed Daniel Morris was guilty. He had killed his Aunt and Uncle; he also believed Simon Millor was his accomplice who he now had eliminated.

There was meaning and motive behind his actions, it may or may not have been money but the situation stunk. At present though he could prove nothing. His gut instinct was to throw the book at him but without evidence, he was flailing.

There was a knock on the door and a female deputy walked in with a note, which she handed to the Sheriff. He looked at it and nodded at the deputy whose eyes accusingly cursed a glance over Dan. She turned and left. The Sheriff seemed to be gaining momentum; too many events were falling into place, connecting them however was proving difficult.

"It appears Mr Morris that Marion Reynolds also saw some nocturnal activities last night. It seems strange to me and maybe far more coincidental, that everyone you've been connected to has either been burgled." He motioned in the direction of Charlie. "Like Mr Price here, or in fact Marion Reynolds, who also seems to have had an unwelcome visitation early this morning but was disturbed and fled at around 6.30am this morning! Or in fact the poor soul, who ends up with a bullet lodged in the brain for their inconvenience."

Dan was dumbfounded. Over the course of one evening Simon had been killed, Charlie's office had been broken into and Marion Reynolds had a break in. It could have been coincidence but at the minute coincidences were more ammunition for the Sheriff.

"I'll lay my cards on the table Mr Morris, as you're a very intelligent man. My initial reaction was that you and Mr Price were in this together. However with the additional timescale of Mr Millor's death at approx 11pm, Mr Price's burglary around midnight and having been with my officers all night, then the break in at Mr Reynolds' facility this morning at approximately 6.30am, which I believe on a good drive would take roughly five hours commute at that time of the morning, I can't in all truth place the perpetrator as any of you, especially as all your alibis remain solid, at present." The Sheriff looked a little annoyed at his own summation.

Charlie interjected. "So we're free to go then?" He got up to leave.

"Yes, but as I say your alibis are circumstantial at best." The Sheriff was feeling a bit sick, his gut was screaming Morris was his man but there was no way he could have been at any of the crime scenes because of the witness' statements corroborating his movements all evening. He could never have been at Mr Millor's or Mr Price's break in, as he was placed at the Lighthouse and he would certainly never have been able to drive to Kingsland Lake in less than two hours. Either Daniel Morris had a partner or all three of them were in this together. He did not like any of it, no finger prints, no forced entry, no clues; it was like a ghost had made a fool of him. It was exactly like the scene of the murders of Mr and Mrs Morris. He hated the unknown.

The door opened to the interview room and the female Deputy entered again, this time silently whispering in the Sheriff's ear, his face cracked an enormous grin. She left and he turned to look at Dan in the eyes, this was going to be good.

"Tell me Mr Morris, we have just gotten off the phone with an Inspector Harnell of New Scotland Yard. A most informative chap who says you were suspended a little over three weeks ago for an incident that happened during an interview with a suspect. He says you are officially relieved of duty until further notice, pending investigation. He also said you were unavailable as you'd gone home to the United States for vacation."

The Sheriff smiled as though pressing the point. "So please tell me, Daniel, how come you've been in the United States for just over two weeks? You entered via Washington Dulles Airport sixteen day ago, is that correct? Where have you been and what have you been up to?"

Washington DC

Dan's security clearance was revoked by the end of the following day; he had been suspended forthwith and told to go home. Officially he was on garden leave with pay until further notice. In effect his career at the Yard was over, he knew that.

Once they started delving deeper, it would not take long before his family's past would come to light. His reputation was being dissected and his professional life lay in tatters. Even worse they could not charge the murder of Sophie Stephens on Jon Doe. After the shambolic interview, his testimony would never have stood up in court and he was released in less than 24 hours by order of some high profile government official. As he surmised Doe conveniently and promptly disappeared.

The Yard had tried to follow him placing agents on his tail but he was far too good for that and he had disappeared without trace within a few shorts hours of leaving New Scotland Yard. The chances of ever finding him again were slim. Daniel Morris was now the unwitting patsy for the whole unfortunate saga. MP Stephens was out for blood and Dan was in the firing line.

His suspension was swift but not as fast as he could work. As soon as he calmed down after being dragged from the interview room, he headed back to his cube. No one was in the office as it was late and his colleagues had headed out to the pub, as was the norm.

He quickly commandeered several search engines and computers throughout the offices' individual cubicles, each examining selected areas of the comprehensive network of secret data. At first he found nothing, a complete blank, there was no information relating to his Grandfather whatsoever.

This in itself was strange because he knew his Grandfather was of serious military and government interest. William Morris, according to the files, simply did not exist. This spoke volumes in itself. Such a highly prolific scientist on the cutting edge of state security and research, the files were suspicious in their absence. However he knew many files never returned a hit unless an individual's security clearance covered them.

In his line of work for New Scotland Yard, his clearance level usually provided many, if not all of the answers. He had never questioned anything higher before because he had never needed to, he had always gotten the information he required and would have never known anything was missing. During his tenure in Special Operations he had always found the information he was looking for and provided the relevant information to the correct investigation. He knew files were missing because his Grandfather had to be in the system somewhere.

A few of his colleagues hinted of higher clearance levels throughout the unit. However he made the most positive hits within the department, so he had always just assumed their boasts were simple bravado trying to garner greater respect within the team. The fastest search engine was using SO's super computer, it had direct access to the databases of the top intelligence agencies within the UK; such as MI6, the Government Communications Headquarters, MI5 and the National Criminal Intelligence Service. However its clearance level was only dictated by an individual's own login, Dan only ever used the computational power as a quicker search tool when he was pressed for time, it spread its net faster, wider and much quicker and this was a time when he needed the speed.

What he attempted shocked even him. He had initially entered the vault only to perform a search solely on his mother, however he realised his operations manager was searching the database overnight. He had committed the ultimate cardinal sin, which normally was a dismissible offence but Dan was quite grateful for his manager's irresponsibility because he had not only left the super computer running but basically open, giving him the highest level of clearance using his manager's login.

He set off two cross streams to search, maximising the systems performance, one for his Grandfather, William Morris and the other on his mother, Deborah Morris. He had surpassed his own search skills; he cross referenced the data to highlight similarities between blocks of text within files, which normally would have taken hours to cross match and reference.

Within milliseconds of hitting enter, the system started to retrieve files dating back to the early fifties, mainly consisting of files from the

M.O.D. archives. Experiments; classified warship tests, submarine deployment tests, nuclear reactor tests, the list was extensive right up until 1954 when it abruptly stopped.

Dan opened the last MOD file on William Morris reading the carefully transcribed passages. He could tell it was not an original document as there was reference to the original archive it was taken from and where to find it in storage, however the files were not coded in the usual MOD sequence.

Instead they were coded above that of the Official Secrets Act, meaning the contents would never see the light of day to the general public, or for that matter his level of security clearance. He scanned through the blocks of text all written in capitals. According to the text his Grandfather had taken leave after an extremely successful presentation to the MOD, Royal Navy and many governing officials in attendance, including Winston Churchill who at that time was Prime Minister, his second term in office.

There were countless technical files all relating to this particular experiment, again all marked above the Official Secrets Act. Dan was shocked to discover such files. William Morris was cited as the lead researcher, but his own research notes and technical documentation in connection was missing. He could only assume this was when his Grandfather left the UK, taking his research with him. Back then it would have been hand written without multiple backups until the research was proven, the data verified, hand typed or scribed and then transferred to microfiche.

Further data was taken from MI6, this detailed the search for William Morris after the MOD realised he had skipped the country. He was classed a high security risk and had been tracked leaving the country via Dover along with one Mary Austin, his Grandmother. Their car, a blue 1953 Jaguar XK140 was found abandoned at the Zürich Airport, Switzerland.

There were many documents related to alleged sightings in the Soviet Union, he had been blacklisted as a political target having become a communist and defected. After the documents from the fifties there was a considerable gap before the search retrieved anymore data referencing Morris, importantly they were more recent and far more detailed. They were not however what Dan expected.

They mainly referenced James Morris. The data started with his original published research papers, linked in turn to a myriad of MI6 operational files directing the research back to his Grandfather, William

Morris. It was at this juncture the data started to cross reference each other. William and James became one, countless intelligence agencies, including the Americans started flagging files with their details. The Morris family were back on the radar in a very big way. No wonder Dan had never been able to access any of these files; they had the highest security clearance level he had ever come across, especially those referencing the technology.

It would take months to sift through all of the data of which he did not have the time so he copied the data to several external USB drives. Highly encrypted for the system but he knew how to break the encryption at a later date.

However it was the final few files in his search that completely floored Dan. It was direct government interaction with his mother. It seemed she had been under surveillance for many years, even by the FBI whom she worked for. There were literally hundreds of intercepted surveillance scripts backing up communication. It was not just UK intelligence agencies making a play, they continued to watch from a distance. Other agencies were making noises about the high profile nature of the target.

William Morris was garnering attention, especially from the Americans; James' research had woken the government and stirred action. It was obvious these other intelligence agencies knew about the technology as they referred to it by code name, the Americans used HUDOR. Dan recognised the word because of Ash's Greek obsession; Hudor meant water, now normally represented by the prefix hydro.

The UK government had taken the opposite stance, although closely watched, they concluded leaving the Morris family alone would eventually yield results. One of many files Dan skimmed through had been internal communication between MOD departments. It suggested that as and when the proprietary source, Dan could only assume they meant the family research, was operational, they would take control and eliminate all bystanders.

In other terms, they would delete the family once the project yielded results. He was beginning to see why there had been such secrecy forced upon him while he was growing up.

The last file which he read involved his mother, discussing how she had gone rogue and was touting the research on the national stage to the highest bidder. The transcript suggested she was in talks with Russian and American Intelligence agencies. The outcome was unsure, proceed with caution, terminate if necessary.

He only managed to scratch the surface on the massive amounts of data he had retrieved, but it seemed clear on the surface Jon Doe had been telling the truth. His mother had been killed, ultimately though it seemed it was for selling the family's research.

His world imploded in those few short hours before his suspension, he wandered dazed. The data he had methodically retrieved now saved on disks gnawed at his soul. The happy childhood he remembered with such fondness covered an immense lie as well as protecting him. How deep it went, how much the family withheld through kindness or some other truth he was unsure but he needed to know why.

Dan left London with the intention of returning home to confront the last remaining family he had, his Aunt and Uncle. He believed the family had been warned his mother's death was not an accident and he wanted to know why.

Had they been warned if they ran again, they would also be terminated? The missing piece of the puzzle that Dan could not find was how or why his Grandparents had been killed. In his heart it made sense their deaths were no accident, he had always felt it. Obviously now he knew, neither was his mother's, which was why he was here for the first time in two decades, in Washington.

The Pentagon

It was the first time Dan had been inside the Pentagon since he was eight years old, shortly before his mother's death. It carried a strange homely feeling, the expansive marbled floors covered the foyer from reception to the security booths and then into the building itself.

He vaguely remembered the last time he was here, sitting on the exact same wooden bench opposite security. Although back then, while seated, he swung his sneakered feet wildly as they did not reach the floor. He waited patiently for his mother to pick up some documents from her office before they could go home.

The only visible difference he could see between then and now, was the security seemed considerably tighter, he assumed it was probably reinforced after 9/11 in particularly after the attack on the Pentagon. The first screening booth looked like a conventional metal detector which you would see in any airport worldwide. However the second X-Ray technology employed performed full-body scans in order to detect hidden weapons, tools, liquids, narcotics, currency, and other high security devices.

Several people huddled around monitors as each person walked through the device; occasionally people were stopped and searched as well. Dan considered the professionalism needed to man one of these devices as he watched. Imagine being able to literally look beneath clothing at what a person is wearing, or for that matter what someone is concealing, believing it to be private.

It could be quite good fun, if a little embarrassing. He remembered a guy at the gym who was infamous for his love of chastity devices. His partner either never trusted him, or it was a form of dominance or role play but he allegedly always had his manhood locked and sealed. Dan was always puzzled how he was able to live like that and more importantly why he was never embarrassed or hid the assortment of penis contraptions he was locked into from fellow gym goers. Maybe he was proud to show them off?

Dan had entered the Pentagon from the Metro entrance as he had done those many years ago. His elementary school had been situated in Crystal City, which was just across the Potomac from down town Washington, a few stops along the line from the Pentagon. Elementary school was where he first met Terry. It seemed like a lifetime ago, in fact it seemed so much longer.

Cameras viewed him from every angle, he knew a visual 3D print would be instantly flashing through databases. His features would be scrutinised by facial recognition software and by now the receptionists would already have a detailed breakdown of his life on their individual screens as he approached.

Behind the desk sat two hardnosed receptionists, evaluating potential threats before the first security sweep. The sour faced old boot sitting smugly behind thick bullet proof plexiglass strained a smile at Dan, her nicotine stained teeth momentarily flashed into view. She spoke in a deep gravelled smoker's voice, each word drawn out as if it was her last. The speaker system further deepened the carefully rehearsed script to unnerve any visitor.

"Good afternoon, if you'd be so kind as to write your name on the screen and the person you're wishing to contact today."

Dan scribbled the name of his contact using a plastic wand on a touch pad, Terrence West, plus his own name in capitals and then his signature. He wondered if software was busy analysing his own handwritten signature against a database. He was becoming increasingly paranoid, the events leading to his departure from London had been excruciatingly quick and the information he had in his possession scared him.

In truth no one would ever be able to decipher the information unless they knew what to look for, but it still scared him. If he was stopped and scanned, the information he possessed would put him away, probably for life. New Scotland Yard had begun an extensive investigation into his background and he was no longer a hero for capturing the suspect. He was already deemed an enemy of the state. Before his departure he had been hauled before the Yard's disciplinary board for 'conduct unbecoming.' They also interrogated him about the suspect's story and the validity of Doe's claims surrounding his family.

"Thank you Mr Morris, we have you down for a meeting with Agent West. Can I ask where you are from and your business today?" The receptionist asked nonchalantly.

Dan was suddenly concerned his meeting was being watched. He could say he was with New Scotland Yard's Special Operations but if they checked and discovered his dismissal, he would be thrown in jail as a security risk. Instead he decided to play it safe, putting on his widest grin he smiled as innocently as he could muster.

"I'm a very old school friend of Terry's; we go way, way back. We were at school together and I'm in town for a few days on vacation from England and decided to catch up for a natter and a good old chinwag before heading home to Florida."

The woman looked at him through the plexiglass, a blank look across her face. "A chinwag?" She mouthed, copying his turn of phrase.

"Sorry, it means a chat, been in London far too long, starting to become native."

"Not too native I hope?" She said with the most deadpan expression. "Head through security, take a seat and Agent West will be with you shortly, he's been notified you're in the building. Please display your visitors badge at all times. In case of an emergency please head back to this exit to be checked out, it's a maze in there sir."

She popped a freshly printed visitors' card into a badge sliding it through the tiny gap beneath the plexiglass. It had his name printed on it and Agent West's. Dan proceeded through security without incident. They looked through his paperwork, fortunately they did not look too closely at the pages of printouts. The documents looked official enough but non-threatening and they gave only a casual glance to the USB drives.

His laptop was only given a cursory inspection after the X-Ray. They asked him to boot it up quickly just to make sure it worked. He assumed there would be tighter security getting into the offices. They would probably look at the laptop in more detail and the USB drives. For now he was okay but to email them would have been suicide.

It seemed ironic a school friend from his early days living in Washington, had ended up working the same field as him, although on opposite sides of the pond. They had worked surreptitiously together for a few months on a collaborative exchange of secret data. His colleague's name had been bugging him since their initial introduction via email.

In the back of his mind he recognised the name and after receiving some sensitive coded data, Dan rang him for a chat. After the initial conversation about the data, Dan asked him where he was from. On further exploration they discovered they both went to the same school in Crystal City before he was shipped off to Florida.

Terry even remembered him, it turned out most of the kids at school did. He was infamous because his mother died, all sorts of rumours circulated about her death and it was mainly because he was from a single parent family. At the time it was rather frowned upon within the community, which probably fuelled the conspiracy theories. They had been emailing each other for a couple of years now and originally he had laughed about the rumours but now he wondered how much of it was true.

Dan had never so much as taken a flight from Washington since he left at the age of eight, so they had not seen each other for nearly twenty years. It dawned on him he had no idea what Terry even looked like. At the end of the corridor was a group of seats around the perimeter of the room, facing three elevators. Stood between them were two security guards, both thick set and armed.

The elevators were operated by key passes; depending on your security clearance you would only be able to enter that specific floor. The middle elevator promptly opened and a man stepped out scanning the foyer, as Dan was the only one there it was obvious who he was. Terry approached; beaming an immaculate smile holding his hand out to shake firmly, Dan managed to relax for the first time since he left London.

Terry was physically huge and Dan was impressed, which was unusual, his wide shoulders and expansive chest gave away the physique of a bodybuilder, hidden beneath his immaculately tailored white shirt. Maybe their lonely pursuit searching data bred an affinity with the gym and an individual obsession with the iron. Dan warmed to him even more.

He had remembered Terry as a sickly child, he had suffered from all sorts of ailments culminating in an operation to remove part of his stomach. He suffered from Crohn's Disease but to see the size of this man mountain towering before him, you would have thought he had remembered the wrong kid. He may have packed on a huge amount of muscle, however the same kind features shone through. The bright smile and caring look seemed to resemble the bright uncaring eight year old Dan remembered.

As Terry approached he inadvertently gave the same cursory glance over Dan's physique, which obviously met with the same resolute admiration on his condition and muscularity. They shook hands warmly but Terry did something unexpected, he pulled Dan into a heart stopping bear hug. At first Dan was unnerved and then relaxed as the two men warmly slapped each other on the back, holding each other, it was a great feeling. A moment Dan actually needed, maybe Terry knew about the situation in London? Theirs was a small group, it could happen to any of them in their line of work but the warmth and physical heartfelt gesture was most welcome.

Terry broke first holding Dan by the shoulders; he looked at him, square in the eye. "Well look at you." He eyeballed him up and down. "And I was expecting a slob, like so many in this business, especially as you were based in the UK." Terry had warmth and charisma with the way he spoke, you instantly felt at ease, plus it was genuine and not forced. In those few isolated seconds Dan felt like a true friendship had been re-forged.

"Come on, I was running late this morning and didn't have time to prep my food before the gym and I'm a bit sick of protein bars. You being here is a good excuse for a cheat meal of epic proportions."

Terry purposefully strode away from the elevators; Dan picked up his bag and paperwork from the chair following in his eminent wake.

Terrence West

The Pentagon, contrary to popular belief, is not actually located in Washington. It resides just inside Arlington County, Virginia, across the Potomac River. It is the world's largest office building by floor area alone, of which only half is designated as office space.

Approximately 25,000 military and civilian personnel work in the building day to day. It has five sides; five floors above ground and two basement levels, plus five ring corridors per floor which is where its name derives from. The Pentagon also includes a five-acre central plaza, informally known as ground zero, a nickname originating during the Cold War where it was assumed the Russians would target.

The centre courtyard café was a recent addition for the otherwise overindulged personnel at the Pentagon. The Navy Exchange operate many fast food services and retail outlets throughout the Pentagon building, including many popular franchises such as Subway, Starbucks, McDonalds, Taco Belle and Dunkin Donuts, to name a few. The employees can shop, bank and in general never feel the need to leave their offices for weeks on end, just another ploy for an employer to keep you at your desk.

Terry was finishing his third quarter pounder, between the pair of them they had consumed a large portion of their protein and calorie intake for the entire day, both tried to ignore the general fat and salt content.

Bad news it seemed had travelled fast. His suspension had been doing the rounds amongst the data researchers, however not simply because of idle gossip. New Scotland Yard was verifying Dan's background with Terry's department.

Terry had listened like a friend throughout as he told him the events leading up to the capture of the suspect known informally as Jon Doe, never once interrupting throughout his explanation of the interview and the admission about his family's past. He also listened rapt as he discussed the secret data he discovered using the departments supercomputer using his manager's account.

When Dan had finished Terry looked at him. "Okay Dan I have to confess something, presently you are highlighted in my data requisition."

Dan was stunned, that meant Terry was the point of contact for New Scotland Yard over his investigation. Dan felt as though he had just been slapped in the face, he got up to leave.

Terry's hand shot out grabbing his wrist. "Sit down! I'm verifying the data. I don't necessarily believe it, or for that matter trust all the sources. I'm more inclined to believe someone who I've known." Terry nodded at the vacant seat and Dan reluctantly sat back down. "Plus ultimately you travelled here to try and gather answers for yourself. That's not the actions of a man who already knows the truth. If you ran and disappeared, then personally I'd expect you're hiding something but you're here, that says a whole lot more to me than the data. You came to me for help, just like I'd come to you if the roles were reversed and I'm here for you. You can trust me, honestly."

Dan slumped back in the chair, he had nowhere else to go, he was right. Terry smiled.

"Look Dan, I know you've come here looking for answers and I know what you've come here to ask." He paused. "You want me to look into your mother's death."

"Yes." He stuttered. "How did you know that?"

"I read the transcript of that bastard's interview. For the record Dan, you never did anything wrong. Sure you lost it but fuckin' hell, who wouldn't? Suddenly learning after all these years that your mother was murdered, it's gotta mess with your head. You never should have been put in that position in the first place, that'd shock anyone to react out of character. The thing is Dan, they're not interested in you directly, what he's done is refuel interest in your Grandfather's technology, that's what it boils down to."

Dan relaxed slightly although he was unsure how to continue. Terry could see his unease and wished he had been less blunt about the situation however he felt obliged, as a friend, all angles should be out in the open.

"I can't lie to you and say that what I'm researching will not be forwarded to London because if I don't do it, a colleague will. Either way they'll get the information they requested, you know that." Dan knew he was right, but knowing it was about him made it a bitter pill to swallow.

"In truth from what I can see there is not much to tell, you probably inadvertently know most of it. Your Grandparents came to the states in 1955. They entered via Washington, travelling from Switzerland. They toured the length and breadth of the States, marrying in a small Las Vegas wedding at the end of that year. A few months later, in the spring of 56, James Morris was born in a private clinic in Miami.

That same year your Grandfather applied for a green card under the name Frederick William Morris. Something we are unsure about at present is whether it was given in 56 when a Green Card Amnesty was declared. I can only assume Frederick is in fact your Grandfather's real name. I think somewhere along the way it was dropped day to day, which was probably why you couldn't find any more info.

Without confirmation from the UK Records Office of Births, Marriages and Deaths I can't be sure and there would also be confirmation of the application in the UK if that is the case. However as the files are inconclusive I assume it was given through the 1956 Amnesty or Dream Act as it's known. During these times many details were simply never recorded. It would also indicate why the application fell under the British authority's radar, because your family would not have been flagged, they'd have simply to all intents and purposes vanished into the system.

So there are two lines of research to follow, whether your Grandparents received citizenship through an Amnesty or under your Grandfather's original name Frederick. The American lawyer overseeing the paperwork was a Charles Price."

Dan sucked in a deep breath at the mention of Charlie's name.

"I take it you know who this Charles Price is?"

"Yeah he's the family's lawyer and a good friend. I went to school with his daughter Lizzie after I left Washington. He oversaw everything for my family, including all of the family's business dealings."

"Well I'd bet Charlie knows more than your average lawyer, he would be a good first point of contact."

Terry was right, he knew most of the family history, whether he knew about his Grandfather's research he did not know, or at least he never let on that he did. However Dan was unaware his Grandfather's name was actually Frederick, or for that matter his Grandparents married in a cheap tacky Las Vegas wedding. Part of him was quite impressed at his Grandparents' forwardness for their age, basically eloping and also that his Uncle James must have been conceived out of wedlock.

"I'm wondering if Uncle James' conception was what started the process of staying in America? If they were travelling around trying to stay under the radar and Gran fell pregnant, it would make sense they would just find a place to raise a child. It may also have been the catalyst as to why they did not return to Britain. They just happened to discover Santa Rosa, Florida while travelling; their arrival would have stirred little or no interest within the community."

"Precisely, and your Grandparent's money would have greased the wheels, so to speak."

Dan could see what Terry was saying, his research would not affect the events; there was no real detailed information that could adversely change anything. He was relieved but also worried about what might be found in the future.

Dan had to ask. "It begs the question, why I'm here in Washington." Terry looked at Dan expectantly, he knew what he was asking for but he needed Dan to say it. "What happened to my Mom Terry, have you found anything?"

Terry bowed his head, he remembered Dan's mother. She had been stunning, you could see where Dan had acquired his good looks. After they had first made contact through work, he went through some of the pictures from elementary school to remember who he was. The one that stood out was a group shot of his class mates on sports day, behind each of their class stood their parents. What was blindingly obvious was that Dan's father was absent but the pair of them seemed oblivious and extraordinarily happy in the shot. Terry had brought the picture with him to the office; he passed it across the table to Dan.

Dan studied the picture; he smiled and looked at Terry. He remembered the day but like so many things surrounding his childhood it was fogged in memory. His mother stood with both hands on his shoulders, they were both smiling broadly for the camera. It was a sad shot really because less than a month after the picture was taken, she was dead.

Dan slid it back across the table. "Thanks, I don't have many pictures with my mother."

Without thinking Terry slid it back across the table to Dan. "Keep it, it's yours." Dan smiled, for a moment the smile he wore on the day of the sports day resurfaced and he was eight again.

Terry cleared his throat. "Dan, I have looked into the details surrounding your mother's death, and it all seems rather vague considering the background and circumstances, which to me suggests a burial of some sorts."

Dan nodded; Terry meant, in data terms, that she had been buried.

"Your mother by all accounts was a dedicated single parent. Your birth certificate has no entry for your father, so she either didn't want anyone to know who he was or she didn't know who he was."

There was a pause as he studied Dan for a reaction, there was none. Dan's mother had never spoken about him and until her death he was happy and never felt the need to ask, plus growing up he never really felt as though he lacked a father figure.

"I'd suggest she took the identity of your father to the grave and maybe this caused the friction with your Grandparents because she was unmarried. I wonder whether it was an old fashioned streak in your Grandparents that fuelled the rift?"

"Surely that makes no sense though, especially if Gran was pregnant with Uncle James before they were married."

"Ah yes, but if you think about it, your Grandparents married quickly, probably straight after they discovered the pregnancy giving them, at least in their own minds, respectability. Even so they may still have frowned on your mother's infidelity, indirectly causing a family rift.

Maybe they expected her to be more careful, maybe they never approved of who your father was? It's something we'll never know or find out."

"Not unless Uncle Mike and Aunt Susan know?"

"Well that might be something to discuss with them further? Whatever fuelled the rift ultimately pushed your mother into making a big mistake. It seems she was approached by the CIA for information. Details are sketchy but they convinced her to take your Grandfather's research data.

However for reasons known to your mother and family she made a play and was trying to sell it within the intelligence community. She used her job at the Pentagon to approach a few government officials, which remain top secret as to who they were. To put it bluntly, she simply pissed off the wrong people."

Terry could see this was not news. "It's well documented within the files of what she was up to. She was under surveillance by the British Government and the CIA; that we know of. Other parties may certainly have been involved but we have no confirmation of this. From what I can tell she was never deemed a threat, just more of a nuisance."

Dan sat and listened to this last part with interest, like so many data sources between countries they conflicted. Dan pushed the printout of the file he had retrieved about his Mother towards Terry; he quickly scanned through the text looking up at Dan shocked.

"According to your data, your Mother was caught selling the research? Terminate if necessary! Where did you find this? If this is correct then our data is inaccurate and your Mother was indeed murdered as Doe said in the interview!"

"I know; I've been trying to get my head around it ever since my chat with the little prick. It makes no sense, especially if you're saying she's deemed not a risk. The other thing I've been pondering, Doe killed Sophie Stephens by using, in his own words, a methodology chosen because of my family's background. More importantly he knew she was killed and how she was killed. This was what dictated his methodology of killing Sophie. How did he know?"

Terry read the passages before him a few times trying to take it all in; his mind was fresh to the details, unlike Dan who had been going over the alleged written facts for hours.

"It has been often spoken within our circles, that licensed agents have their own specialised data. They use it to keep track of past hits and to intimidate targets; maybe that is what he was referring to?"

Dan looked at Terry with a quizzical look. "Licensed?"

"Licensed to kill! Do you have any idea what killed Sophie in the end?"

"Yes, the killing agent was potassium chloride, it's in the report, basically administered under the armpit through the hair follicles using a small insulin needle. It takes skill and patience because performed incorrectly the marks would be seen but done well they could easily be overlooked under a normal autopsy. The end result looks like a natural heart attack. It would be difficult for the coroner to realise it was murder rather than a natural heart attack, as in the case of Sophie, over exertion in the gym. If so they'd probably never perform further toxicology tests under normal circumstances, except I caught him red handed with the syringe."

Terry looked at Dan with dead pan eyes, his heart was heavy and he knew he was the bearer of news that Dan did not want to hear.

"Deborah Morris was given a verdict of death by natural causes, heart failure. According to the pathology notes, no other tests were called for or carried out. To all intents and purposes your Mother died of natural causes, a massive heart attack."

47

Charlie and Lizzie had never questioned why Dan had flown in from Washington; they had both assumed he had caught the earliest flight from London when he finally heard the news. The flight happened to land in Washington and then Dan simply grabbed a connecting flight down to Florida for the funeral.

They also never questioned why they had been unable to get hold of him in London, assuming he was working as he so often was. It had taken two days for him to return their urgent messages left on voicemail, the ones left at work were never listened to because he was not there. Once he was home, it was academic and they never enquired and never felt the need to. The time had come to tell the truth; they looked at him with an air of concern and disillusionment on their faces.

Dan felt like he had betrayed them. It was not his intention but his problems in the UK seemed far removed from the concerns that faced him, when he first arrived in Florida. Both Charlie and Lizzie were in the interview room, sitting directly in front of him by his invitation. The Sheriff was triumphant having backed his prey into a corner, to make his statement.

Little did Dan know he had also taken the opportunity to organise several officers to take him away after his confession. More importantly he had made a few phone calls to the local press hinting at an imminent arrest. The local press were starting to swarm like bees outside the Santa Rosa Police Department waiting for the story to break.

Charlie looked painfully ill at ease with the situation, wanting time to talk to Dan alone. Dan had waived this right and he feared the worst, he pleaded with him. "Dan we can take a fifteen minute break and you can fill me in on what you are about to say? I'm speaking as your lawyer, not your friend."

Dan wanted to hug Charlie for his concern, however there was a lot he was hiding and he needed to get it out in the open.

"It'll be all right Charlie, I'm fine but I want you and Lizzie to be here, you'll understand why." He looked at the Sheriff. "You ready?"

The officers who had been part of the initial investigation lined the perimeter of the small cubicle; all eyes boring into Dan. The female officer that looked at him accusingly earlier also now looked very smug. The room held the promise of a confessional; except lacking the presence of a priest to read him his last rights.

Lizzie edged forward on her seat sitting on her hands, rocking backwards and forwards, looking as though she was going to cry, he smiled at her. Under her shirt he could make out his vest top she had worn in the early hours of the morning. Dan wanted to hold her, explaining the events before he arrived in Santa Rosa but this was the right time and although he would prefer time alone to form a plan of attack, once again he was flying blind.

He knew he had all the data he needed, he also knew how to form the correct arguments, and of course certain parts were irrelevant and would be left out. Those details Charlie and Lizzie already knew and would understand why he held them close to his chest like a poker player, they hopefully would also be able to add gravitas to his so-called confession.

The Sheriff pushed a piece of 21st century equipment across the table towards Dan, a digital voice recorder, it seemed totally alien within the walls. To counter balance this new-fangled technology the receptionist, staring over the top of half mooned glasses, was also present, armed only with a pencil and pad. She would be taking shorthand notes of the forthcoming conversation.

Daniel looked at all of them all, sitting expectantly in front of him waiting for some kind of bombshell to drop. Instead he reached into the left hand pocket of his jeans pulling out what looked like a thin black matchstick, without a word he placed it on the table in front of them. The Sheriff leant forward, picked it up and held it up to take a better look.

"What the hell is this thing?"

"It's a wireless camera."

The Sheriff looked at Dan as if he was on drugs. "It's tiny! How the hell can it be a camera? It has no wires."

"Trust me it is. It's tech you'll never have seen before, except maybe at the movies and hopefully, never will again in your lifetime. Not unless you've done something pretty bad or pissed off someone with high government links! Its state of the art covert operations equipment, exactly like the tape I found attached to the outside cameras at home."

This opening gambit had the desired effect, all eyes were no longer on Dan. All eyes had shifted, transfixed on the tiny black matchstick held between the Sheriff's sausage fingers. He placed it back on the table. Dan rummaged around in the right hand pocket of his jeans pulling out a second black camera placing it alongside the first, they were identical.

"This one was taken from the apartment of my friend and neighbour in London, Sophie Stephens, daughter to a prominent British MP, Edward Stephens."

Dan pushed the second camera forward on the table for effect. "A little under three weeks ago I tragically discovered the naked body of Sophie in her apartment, when I popped by to see if she wanted to hit the gym, as we so often did." Lizzie flashed a look of anger in her eyes, he knew what she was thinking but the time to tell her about Sophie's sexuality was not now. He continued but avoided eye contact with her.

"The family had been targeted politically and threats had been made several days prior to her murder. Along with the body, I inadvertently discovered the murderer still at the scene of the crime and after a violent and brutal struggle, I managed to subdue and consequently arrested him."

The room looked sullen. The Sheriff deflated, this was not the confession any of them expected but no one spoke, all eyes though still focused on the tiny cameras.

"The reason I know they are cameras is I took another, also taken from Sophie's apartment, to an agent at the Pentagon in Washington. If you'd like to check Sheriff, his name is Agent Terrence West. This was the sole reason I was in Washington."

The Sheriff's shoulders sagged, he gestured to one of the officers in the room who ducked out to enquire as to whether he was truly at the Pentagon. He picked up one of the tiny cameras again and looked more closely at it; in one end was a tiny glass lens no bigger than the head of a pin. Dan could see the curiosity was beginning to show, he continued.

"The camera you're holding was found in the early hours of this morning, at home, hidden against the side of one of the monitors in the Panic Room. Lizzie was present when I found it."

The Sheriff turned to Lizzie. "Is this true Miss Price?"

Lizzie still looked angry with Dan over Sophie but she hid it well. "Yes." She glared at Dan; this fact was obviously overlooked during her statement earlier. "But you said it may still be transmitting?"

"Yes it was, however I disabled it when you left. You simply snap it in half and it breaks the delicate transmitter inside. Terry showed me how to do it while I was at the Pentagon."

The Sheriff bent the camera between his fingers, it flexed and he could feel that it was indeed snapped in the middle. "Okay I'm curious about the cameras but what the hell has any of this got to do with you murdering your Aunt and Uncle?"

Charlie exploded at the accusation. "My client is here through his own volition, he waived his right to consultation with me before this interview. I suggest you tread carefully before accusing my client of the murder of his own flesh and blood!"

Charlie was bright red from the outburst. Lizzie grabbed his arm, gently tugging him back into his seat. Charlie reluctantly dropped back down, he had shocked himself with his outburst but the adrenalin felt good pulsing through his system.

Dan looked at the Sheriff. "I'm glad you asked, but for the record, as you have accused me, I did not murder Uncle Mike and Aunt Susan but I do know who did."

There was an audible gasp throughout the room. The Sheriff was beginning to get nervous; his bright idea of letting the press know about an imminent arrest was going to blow up in his face.

"The man I captured for the murder of Sophie Stephens, we called him Jon Doe because we never discovered his true identity, is the man behind the murders of my Aunt and Uncle and more than likely Simon Millor too."

Puzzled looks were exchanged around the room; the Sheriff asked the most obvious question. "If you captured this man … this murderer, then how the hell is he over here from London continuing his crime spree and why your family?"

Dan looked to the floor with guilt; he was ashamed of what he had been coaxed into doing during the interview. Looking back, it was exactly what the bastard had been angling for.

"Because I fucked up and he was consequently released." He paused gathering his thoughts as to how best explain what happened, he could not think of an easy way. "I strangled the bastard during an interview, not unlike this!"

There was a second audible gasp throughout the room, mainly from Lizzie. Dan bowed his head. Further ashamed by his own admission. As he looked at Lizzie, she could see the pain in his eyes and Sophie was temporarily forgotten. She wanted to hold him.

"Jon Doe's a professional, he's a spook."

The Sheriff laughed. "A professional what?"

"Killer." Dan said it so bluntly, looking at the Sheriff, the word sounded evil in its own right. "He's licensed to kill. He's a spook, an agent, a spy, call him what you will but somebody hired him to scare the politician Edward Stephens into silence over some political information he had in his possession."

The room was suddenly different, the accusatory looks had disappeared, the expressions had changed, realising this was bigger than a simple local murder.

"Originally Stephens was threatened with disclosure to the press that his daughter, Sophie Stephens, was a lesbian." Lizzie exhaled deeply at this revelation, she tried not to, but she smiled, he was instantly forgiven.

"Although Sophie was secretive she knew hiding her sexuality in the long run would damage her father's career. Instead of taking cover, they made a statement to the press about the blackmail and about the information in his possession. Instead of shutting Stephens up, Jon Doe made a martyr of him. If anything happened to him after that, questions would be raised politically. He was suddenly pretty much untouchable."

Dan looked at Lizzie and she nodded in his direction. He was relieved, at least she knew now he was not having sex with her.

"Instead he went after Sophie to silence him. The idea that an outed daughter committed suicide, the press would lap it up. His pedestal would be destroyed and privately he would be informed she was murdered. Knowing that, the information in his possession would be buried for good. His job done."

Dan knew the hypothesis he had given was exactly as Jon Doe had wanted the operation to unfold. Unfortunately for him he never expected Dan to casually pop by to go to the gym.

The Sheriff seemed to be taking everything in and finally spoke. "So what exactly has Jon Doe got to do with your Aunt and Uncle's murder?"

This was the delicate part, how much to tell, how much to retain? "When Jon Doe was arrested he refused to speak to anyone, except me. I'd never been in an interview situation but the case was too high profile to ignore. My boss, Inspector Andrew Harnell didn't want me to go in but we could not see any other way forward. The suspect had no finger prints, no identity and refused to cooperate. Anything, any information would have been useful."

Charlie spoke. "What do you mean no finger prints?"

"Well usually anyone working in elimination will have their finger prints removed, sometimes surgically but that's quite drastic and they never grow back. It can also look quite unsightly. However Jon Doe's finger prints were as smooth as glass. It frightened the boys at work; it takes days, weeks maybe, of gradual and gentle sanding of the skin until its smooth. Thus you'll never find a finger print at a professional hit."

He spoke slowly so they understood exactly where he was heading. "Which is why you never found any up at the house." The Sheriff was finally listening intently; his story and where he was headed with it was beginning to make sense.

"As someone who was watching Sophie Stephens, Jon Doe researched me because I was in contact with her. He would have researched everyone around her, especially the people in our apartment block. However I was of interest in more ways than one, which is what I found out in the interview room, in fact he took great delight in goading me. Jon Doe baited me into a confrontation, which was part of his intention. He murdered Sophie with a drug, potassium chloride, to all intents and purposes it looked like a natural death. However he was caught red handed by me, with the syringe in his hand. The correct toxicology tests revealed the drug used caused a massive heart attack. What he suggested in the interview was that his methodology used for killing Sophie was mirrored from a file in his possession, involving my family, in particular the death of one Deborah Morris."

48

Charlie squirmed in his seat and Lizzie was obviously concerned at the mention of Dan's mother. The Sheriff was equally confused by this turn of events, staring blankly as his mind desperately tried to process the last few minutes. "Who's Deborah Morris?"

Charlie stood up pulling his chair to the table. All eyes left Dan focusing on Charlie, including Lizzie. He needed to clear the air and also hopefully his conscience. "Deborah Morris is, or was, Dan's mother."

He pushed the chair next to Dan's and sat down alongside, squeezing Dan's wrist which rested on the table. "Deborah died when Dan was eight after which he came to live with his Grandparents in Santa Rosa." He looked at Lizzie and then towards Dan, visibly slumped in his chair.

"Shortly after you came to live at your Grandparents, I had a visit. I was the one who implemented your Grandparents' green card application, under his true name of Frederick William Morris. The American Government approached me, not because of his application as I thought, they knew all about your Grandfather's background including his research for the British Government. They waived the Green Card through without so much as a single background check. I knew this was odd but I spoke to William, he explained the situation about his past. Your Grandfather never lied to me about past. However he truly believed, to protect everyone surrounding the family, including Lizzie and myself, it was better that we never knew all the details."

Charlie looked at Lizzie smiling. "I trusted William implicitly. He protected us all for many years. He concluded his citizenship was granted because the American Government believed he was going to continue the research out of sight of the British. It was within their own interests for him to become an American citizen. We can only assume however that the British, who he tried so desperately to escape, ultimately felt he had defected and betrayed his country. They continued to monitor him over the years and demonstrated Big Brother was always watching."

Charlie reached forward grabbing a bottle of water from the table. The room was listening; the only noise in the room was from the feint hum of the air conditioning unit as it worked overtime compensating for the extra body heat in the room.

"The original house fire was a warning to your Grandfather not to fuck with them, or they would hurt him. I begged him to stop for the sake of the family but he promised me the work was bigger than him, or surprisingly, even his family. Mary supported him, she had total unerring faith which naively gave me mine. I never truly understood the implications of his work but I did understand the need for secrecy. I helped put him and James in contact with the people who designed and built, what I now know to be, the underground lab.

Over the years I've drawn up many non-disclosure agreements so no one would talk about the work carried out on the property or the many business ventures the family undertook. I believed in what your Grandfather and James was pursuing. I never understood what but it was their tenacity and the determination that it would benefit everyone, it was infectious. However I genuinely never knew what it was."

Charlie looked at Dan; tears were streaming down his face. "I never expected the misery that followed. Your family were more than my friends, in fact they were, are, my family." Dan reached out squeezing his shoulder. Charlie placed his own hand over Dan's; Lizzie wanted to hug them both. Charlie shrugged him away, a weight still hung round his shoulders along with shame.

"I think you probably know by now, especially if you've been to see your connections in Washington, your Mother's death was far more sinister than you were ever led to believe and I'm so sorry you found out in this manner. Your Grandparents wanted to protect you from the truth; they never wanted you to know."

Charlie looked at Lizzie who seemed to understand why they protected him; she assumed it was what Ash had alleged to on their last night together. "Your Grandfather felt enormous guilt; he felt it was his fault and sheer bloody mindedness which led to the death of your mother. For reasons only your Mother understood, she stole part of the new research. Whether she was approached by government or external forces, we have no idea, but she talked to the wrong people including the British Government. They wanted the research continued, they also wanted Deborah brought in line. They threatened your family but your Grandfather basically told them to fuck off, in no uncertain terms."

Charlie held his head in his hands; tears streamed down his face, scanning the faces round the room from Lizzie and then back to Dan.

"Your Mother was murdered to stop her releasing the research, ultimately forcing your Grandfather to continue his work, which he did, but a part of him died with your mother. His resolve and steely determination faltered but he continued albeit at a slower pace and with a heavy heart. We even investigated a way for your family to relocate and disappear again, hopefully this time without trace. It was pointless running from the government again, they could track anyone easily now and they knew where he was, constantly watching. Unfortunately at the same time your Uncle James published certain parts of the research, putting the data out in the public domain and they came down heavily on both William and James."

Dan looked at Charlie and held his gaze. "I know my Grandparents' deaths were not an accident Charlie, I worked it out years ago. I even told Lizzie my suspicions last night!" Charlie looked at Lizzie who nodded in agreement. "Not a single detail pointed to a gas explosion, and also the fact their bodies took weeks to be released for burial. But why?"

"I don't know why. They got impatient? Maybe they wanted results? Maybe they finally wanted the research and they pressured your Grandfather for it? We'll never know for sure. But your Grandparents died protecting the family and ultimately his life's work. However his death simply transferred the focus away from himself, making James the target. His research was more approachable, open and understandable by today's scientists and academics; by default your Grandfather became obsolete."

Some of the officers had gradually vacated the room. It was obvious the Sheriff was wrong. The alleged suspect was innocent and they had more important things to do. For starters they had to fend off the local press who were laying siege to the station baying for a story. The only story they could see at present was how much tragedy had befallen the Morris family.

The Sheriff had stopped the digital recorder ushering the last of the people from the room as he realised the interview had headed in an entirely unexpected direction. His immediate problem was damage control, this could look bad if the press found out he had made a massive mistake.

"Well I'm truly sorry Daniel. I hope you can understand my situation and why the evidence directed me towards you? So what you are suggesting is your perpetrator, Jon Doe, used the same methodology to kill and then coerce the intended victim to do what he wanted."

Dan had not actually thought about it like that. He had just assumed Jon Doe referred to the drug that killed his Mother and Sophie. Not the fact both daughters were used as a weapon against their intended victims. MP Stephens was forced into silence and his Grandfather was forced to continue his research. It made sense and he was alarmed he had not seen the connection himself but he was too fixated on his own Mother's death to see it clearly.

The Sheriff was still a little dubious. "I assume your story in the UK can be corroborated but you have to understand the whole tale is a little farfetched, being that he disappeared without trace."

Dan could see the lack of evidence was why he was being questioned; he did not hold any grudge against the Sheriff for doing his job.

"If you give Inspector Andrew Harnell another call, he'll email you a transcript of the interview with Jon Doe and myself, along with his arrest sheet. If you explain that it may be him who committed the murders here he'll forward all the relevant information. He wants the bastard behind bars as much as I do. After he was released he was followed but disappeared without trace, fingers are being rapt over the fuck up, unfortunately my head is the one for the chop. I'm under investigation within Scotland Yard, it's only a matter of time before my HR records are tainted with the Morris family history and my suspension becomes a permanent dismissal. My career is effectively over!"

"I'm sorry to hear that, although I was also alluding to evidence surrounding your Grandfather, William Morris. I assume as this was a while ago and the secrecy involved, nothing would exist?"

Charlie cleared his throat. "Actually there are a few pieces of evidence in my possession. At the time I was recording some of my client meetings, something I'm not proud of but one has to protect one's self. I was a little worried about the situation, especially after the initial brusque visit from the Government. I have a number of recordings dating back to certain events which should corroborate many details, plus some paper work William and Mary signed just in case something like this happened. I never kept it at the office, somehow I always knew I'd need it one day. It's held in a strong box at the bank."

"Well I'd appreciate if you could get me the recordings and documentation to have a look through." The Sheriff's face looked as though he had just heard the greatest piece of fiction since Big Foot. In his head he did not believe a single word he had just sat through but he had little choice but to let them go until it was verified or debunked.

"I still have one important question though." There was silence in the room; the air cons compressor finally halted. "You mentioned the family was investigating a possible disappearing act again? Was that before or after William and Mary died, and ultimately is the disappearance of James, Patricia, Ashley and Matthew Morris simply that; an elaborate act?" He stared challengingly at Charlie. "Are they alive Mr Price, considering no bodies were ever found during the air, sea reconnaissance effort that went into the search?"

Dan and Lizzie shifted uncomfortably in their seats looking at each other, Charlie remained calm and collected. "As far as we are aware Sheriff, the disappearance of James Morris, his wife, daughter and nephew was an accident and totally unconnected. We have no hard evidence to suggest otherwise."

"Thank you." He nodded at Charlie. "And please Daniel, accept my apologies for the manner in which we have proceeded today. I hope you understand why I felt the need to clear up the many inconsistencies over this unfortunate incidence. I am truly sorry for your loss and hope you can forgive me for my tactics."

He nodded at Dan as he got up heading to the door. "Thank you for your cooperation today, please if you can think of anything else we would truly appreciate it." He held it open motioning for the three of them they could leave. They got up and left the confines of the interview room heading to the front of the building.

As Dan and Lizzie strolled out through reception, they walked hand in hand. Not a single journalist or photographer, who waited patiently for a story, paid any attention to them. Charlie brought up the rear, trying to look casual and not bolt for the exit. Dan opened the door for Lizzie, she ducked under his arm smiling at him, as Charlie followed. Dan did not lower it, blocking his path.

"You lied through your teeth, like the lawyer." He grinned. "And friend you are."

"No, my dear boy I never lied, I simply manipulated the truth. We don't have any real hard evidence presently but when we dive down to that wreck, we will. We will."

49

McAdams waited patiently in the reception of the police station. He was quietly amused by the turn of events. He had spoken to one of the deputies posing as a journalist, she had been quite open the Sheriff believed Daniel Morris was the murderer and he was presently being interviewed, an arrest being imminent.

Morris' arrest would be fun, but it would come at the most inopportune time, especially when recent events were starting to make headway. The blueprints he retrieved from Simon Millors' office had shown detailed drawings of a secondary even more elaborate lab.

Although he had seen the depths the family had gone to hide the research in the underground lab beneath the home, he was sceptical about the possibility of an underwater lab. Even Governments never made such technological leaps of faith, it was pure science fiction but then everything surrounding the family had an air of incredulity.

However this morning, after watching Dan and Lizzie's naked encounter in the boathouse, realising it would be a long and lonely night, he had taken the drive back to Kingsland Lake and Marion Reynolds to check out the warehouse. The whole scenario of an underwater lab seemed absurd, there had to be another more plausible explanation. No matter how he ran the details through his mind it seemed impossible.

That was until the early hours of this morning, when he found himself in a dry dock standing before the Marion Reynolds prototype submarine. It was impressive and he had been privy to some amazing gadgets over the years. He had never seen engineering on such a small domestic scale.

The submarine was a thing of exquisite beauty. Sleek immersive lines of plastic and chrome concealing delicate internal organs making it extremely special and unique. He had been lost in its wonder, mesmerised by its design; however his reconnaissance mission had been cut short.

He was almost caught. He had been careless again. Everything surrounding the Morris family was astonishing, it surprised even him that they had been able to keep such intimate secrets, especially from the Government.

His inquisitive nature and interest in technology ruled his head and heart when he saw the submarine cradled in the dry dock. Having climbed down to get a better look, he was hardly expecting anyone at the warehouse that early in the morning and was taken unaware as the rear warehouse doors opened.

His instincts told him to get the hell out, he was at a disadvantage not knowing how many were milling around the building and who knew how many more through and beyond into the offices.

Huddled beneath the submarine, over hearing their conversation, they were going to flood the dry dock for testing. That was why they were early; it would take a couple of hours to fill completely, gently floating the submarine from its cradle. He had to get out fast; he had left his gun in the van expecting no one at this hour.

In his rush he was spotted climbing the ladder and the employees gave chase. He barely got away unscathed, they also saw his face but getting caught would have been a disaster after all he had worked for during the last few weeks.

McAdams watched intently, hidden by the throng of journalists as Morris left the police station, alongside the lawyer and his daughter, they seemed in high spirits. He would have been very surprised if he had been stupid enough to expose everything completely.

Morris knew how much information to disclose to get the job done. His instincts suggested Morris was playing the Sheriff, stalling tactics, but he was unaware of what was going on behind the reception desk and that made him nervous. He gently patted the gun tucked inside his jacket, his comfort blanket, one he would never leave behind again.

The Sheriff entered from behind the reception counter, shortly after Daniel Morris, Miss Price and Charlie Price exited the building. The journalists surged forward to the counter hoping to get a scoop. By the look on the Sheriff's face it had not quite gone as well as had been expected. He raised the palms of his hands towards the oncoming pack to settle them down.

"Ladies and gentlemen, thank you for waiting patiently, I trust you've been comfortable? I have a short statement to make to update you on our investigation in conjunction with the Morris family murders." A few camera flashes erupted around the room and several dictaphones thrust into the air.

"In the early part of yesterday evening, C. H. Price, a small lawyers firm in the centre of town, acting on behalf of the Morris family, were targeted. Their safe was forced open and a number of hard drives, containing important internal CCTV footage of the savage murder of Michael and Susan Morris were taken. Daniel Morris, the last surviving member of the Morris family has been helping with our enquiries. He had managed to reconstruct the footage and had given it to his lawyer who was going to submit it to us this morning."

McAdams felt a slight smugness at having acquired the drives last night; his hand shot up but did not wait before he asked a question. "Sheriff, how come it has taken so long after the initial murders for the footage to come to light?"

The Sheriff sighed as the dictaphones were forced a little closer towards him. He could hear mutterings of agreement from the rest of the journalists, scribbling as they made illegible notes. He could see this was going to be a torturous few moments; he turned to face his questioner, using the most disarming smile he could muster.

"Inside the family home was a Panic Room. From within there was a CCTV console which monitored the inside of the house. We believe the perpetrator was after money as the Morris family is very wealthy."

McAdams liked this game. "So how come you were unaware of the Panic Room and the CCTV footage before now?" All the dictaphones in the room swung round in McAdams' direction, then promptly swung back towards the Sheriff in unison. Mutterings to the question chattered round the small reception.

"Daniel Morris, has lived in London, England for many years. It was only upon his return for the funeral that a package, which was left in the care of the family lawyer, was given to Mr Morris containing keys to gain access. We were unaware of the footage until last night."

"Initial reports suggested the CCTV cameras at the house had been tampered with?" McAdams was on a roll.

The Sheriff shifted uncomfortably, someone had been a little open mouthed within the department and he looked at his deputies disapprovingly. Unfortunately it was a small community and these things did slip.

"Again Mr Morris helped us uncover how the external cameras were technically disabled and we are still investigating this line further." He looked at McAdams expecting another question but he remained silent at this revelation, so he continued in the direction of the rest of the journalists. "Due to fresh evidence we believe the murderer, also wanted in connection with the recent killing of a senior politician's daughter in England, is our chief suspect for the Morris murders."

McAdams smile instantly disappeared. If they had evidence connecting him to the murders it would not be long before his profile would surface and the fact his face had been seen during his retreat from Marion Reynolds was cause for concern.

"Do you have a name or a photo of the suspect Sheriff?" One of the other journalists shouted from the back of the room.

The Sheriff looked in the direction of the voice. "Presently we don't have a name we can issue to the public, however we're working in conjunction with New Scotland Yard in England and we should have a picture of our assailant very soon for release. We will send everyone a copy as soon as we receive ours. Further to our investigation, I have the unhappy news to announce that Simon Millor, of the firm Millor and Morris, was tragically shot and killed at around midnight last night. His family have been notified. The death is being treated in connection with the ongoing Morris family investigation; more details will be released in a further statement. Thank you for your time ladies and gentleman."

The throng of journalists milled about, swapping stories amongst themselves as McAdams quietly headed for the exit. If his photo was being released, he only had a relatively short timescale before he needed to disappear and this time for good. He had seriously underestimated Morris again. Maybe it was just time to eliminate him and head for the sun. He jumped in the truck and drove towards the station, the Morris Range Rover was parked outside according to the transmitter.

The Sheriff returned to his office, slumping in his chair. On the desk amongst the coffee mugs and fast food cartons was a printout of the transcript of Daniel Morris' interview with Jon Doe. He scanned through the details and was quietly surprised as to how much of what Morris had said linked to the interview. There was also Sophie Stephens' autopsy reports and a number of naked photos of how she was found. Even in death she was a beautiful young woman, such a tragedy and waste of life.

The Sheriff shuffled through the paper until he found what he was looking for, the arrest sheet. He marvelled at the first page. Ten black blobs printed and separated into ten boxes, five for the right hand labelled R. Thumb, R. Index, R. Middle, R. Ring and R. Little. Below, five for the left in reverse, L. Little, L. Ring, L. Middle, L. Index and L. Thumb. Not a single ink print revealed any part of a fingerprint, they were completely erased. Like Dan, he was intrigued as to how anyone would achieve such perfection.

He turned the sheet over containing the fingerprints, scanning the arrest sheet. It gave little away, nothing more than what he already discerned from his earlier conversation or from the transcript of the interview. He flicked to the last page and almost dropped it.

Staring back at him was a black and white image entitled 'Jon Doe'. The same man who not five minutes earlier had been asking him questions in his own police station.

"Deputy!" His scream carried throughout the length of the office as he burst back into reception through the double doors. The stragglers of journalists turned to see the Sheriff storm through, launching himself through the exit. The Sheriff stood there panting, scanning up and down the street, no one was in sight. One of the deputies came running out behind him, clutching his utility belt and weapon as he ran.

"What's wrong Sheriff?"

The Sheriff turned giving his deputy a dirty look. Storming back inside, he slapped the photo of John McAdams against the deputy's chest.

50

Hydrous looked resplendent moored in the Marina. She cut an elegant sweeping profile, alongside the many CAD uninspired plastic boats. Her stainless steel sparkled brightly in the early afternoon sun. Her teak deck, bleached white, looked as though it had been washed and thoroughly cleansed of the last few years of neglect. The Hazle family had transformed her in less than 24 hours from a sad shunned vessel, into a pristine and illustrious yacht.

After all these years she still managed to pull a crowd of boating enthusiasts who enviously admired her grace and beauty. A few hand-scrawled notes had been tucked in to the rigging by the locals who knew her, wishing her well on yet another rebirth. Some however had hastily scrawled cell numbers in the vain hope of buying her.

The sign writer had arrived the previous evening, after Dan had left to see Simon, and had worked into the evening. The beautiful text had been lovingly recreated on Hydrous' exterior. As Niles had promised, the red line running the full perimeter of the hull did indeed look stunning. It was only on closer inspection you could see the line was separated further by an intricate hand drawn line of gold.

The detail was astonishing and quite beautiful; this kind of creative free form art was dying out, like so many of the old trades which permeated through older boat yards. The gold also picked out the elaborate hand drawn loops in the text of Hydrous, in particular the low slung 'Y' that hung beneath her name ending in Poseidon's pitch fork.

The three of them stood side by side, Lizzie entwined her fingers in Dan's as they stared at the yacht in awe. Dan knew his Grandfather would have approved, Hydrous looked spectacular and he was extremely proud of Joel, Niles and J.J for all of their hard work.

Lizzie was the first to speak. "So Dan, did you choose the black in honour to match the handle on your penknife? If you did, it's very fitting and works beautifully."

During the ride from the Police Station back to the house, the three of them, after the grim discovery of yet another death related to the family and with the loss of the drives, decided there and then to dive to the Oriskany.

Dan was convinced Jon Doe would understand the plans. Simon had compiled them so intricately that they revealed every detail of the ship and how all the compartments fitted together. The man had now killed four people and whether or not the underwater lab truly existed, it was time for them to find out for certain, before he did.

They had stopped off at Charlie's, retrieving his wetsuit and spare clothes, then at Lizzie's who already had packed a bag in anticipation. She prepared after returning from the burgled office. Her mind was made up as to what the plan of action would be the instant she discovered the drives were missing. She finished packing her bags shortly before the Deputies arrived and took her to the Police Station for interview.

Back at the house Dan had thrown a number of supplies from the underground lab in the Range Rover, plus the compiled plans from Simon, the nautical charts of the Pensacola coastline originally taken from Hydrous a few days earlier and a number of tools from the garage, just in case. They then drove directly to the station. Dan was going to ask to borrow Joel's work boat, Hazletine, it was a shock and a welcome surprise to discover Hydrous waiting for them, like the poised elegant lady she was, already moored inside the marina.

Dan was happy because he was expecting the yacht to still be sat in her cradle on the quayside and wanted to be out of there as quickly as possible. Time was of the essence and launching a boat would take ages, especially when the crane was already in use. Doe always seemed to be one step behind them, no matter what they did. He was obviously watching Dan's each and every move.

Niles placed two full dive tanks down gently and stood next to the three of them. "In my wildest dreams I never thought she'd come out as beautiful as she has. You know she is the sparkling jewel of the Marina, always has been."

The three of them turned to Niles, Lizzie's hand entwined in Dan's even further and Dan subconsciously gripped her hand tighter. It did not go unnoticed by Niles but he always knew who her heart truly belonged to and he felt glad they had finally found each other, especially after all the tragedy which had befallen Dan. Quietly relieved she was off the market, Niles felt a chapter finally close, allowing him to also move on.

"Tell me Lizzie, I didn't think you'd ever done any penetrative diving before. I know Dan and Charlie are old hands but are you sure you don't want a couple of proper lessons first?"

Lizzie looked at Dan and Charlie for support, who shrugged. "It's all right Niles, I don't intend going deep. I'm going just to sunbathe more than anything, packed my cossie. These two'll be off exploring and I'll be supping a G&T on the deck of Hydrous after the first swim. It'll be like old times." She gave Niles her most disarming smile.

"Well next time, give us some warning and we'll all go. We're a bit bogged down here with work shit. Dad is being harassed to sell the Marina for development for housing, as per usual, the Marina sucks us dry. The Port Authority insists it should happen so have stopped funding the up keep of the public slipways and pontoons. Dad is personally trying to keep it afloat and save it from the developers."

J.J. shot Niles a look, he realised he had said too much but shrugged as if to say its only Dan and Lizzie, so instead changed tact. "We'd heard on the vine you'd all been arrested, what was that all about?"

Dan was surprised at the developer news and felt quite saddened, but not about his arrest. It was a small town and gossip was par for the course.

"The Sheriff is basically scratching at leads and I was taken in for enquiries, you know the score. They don't know who to blame, so they go for the family member who allegedly has most to gain. Oh and considering I'm the only one left, it was a simple deduction."

"Oh I hear ya, bloody Sheriff, the only thing he can do successfully round here is catch people leaving the station for a DUI. When something serious happens, he's no idea what to do."

J.J walked down the pontoon with a sack truck carrying four more dive tanks. "Right, all the tanks are full. Your dive gear is already stowed on board in the lockers. I've charged the batteries on Hydrous and the diesel tanks are full. I also changed the alternator which will keep the batteries topped up now. It was knackered; fortunately there was a spare in the shop. I hope you don't mind but I also took the initiative to restock the flares and I've put new life jackets in the lockers, along with a new up to date medical kit! Dad also suggested we installed a new 4 person life raft; it's in a canister in the front locker for easy access. Don't accidentally pull the handle!"

Dan was truly stunned but grateful. "Thanks J.J." Not knowing what to do and feeling emotional at their kindness, he gave him a hug, which was unexpected but reciprocated. Charlie had climbed on board and was now smiling at the pair. "Niles, pass me a tank and I'll stow it below."

"If you use the front locker at the bow, I've put some proper tank retainers in front of the life raft. You can just clip them in and they won't move around. The old ones were a little seized, so I took them out."

Charlie nodded, moving to the bow opening the front locker housed in front of the main berth. A trap hatch and a small section of the deck swung effortlessly up on hydraulic rams. The life raft canister looked tiny, for some reason though he felt happy to see it. He slipped the dive tank down into the bow securing it tightly. Right at the front of the locker was a small electronic device, looking not unlike a broadband WiFi box. The slick plastic cover looked totally out of place in context to the yacht, a red LED was lit, he could not recall the device in the yacht before.

"Guys, what's the little box of tricks installed at the front with the LED?"

J.J. looked at Charlie as he helped Lizzie into Hydrous, then at Dan for his approval. "Dad made me install it."

Charlie looked at the small box and then back at J.J. "What is it?"

"It's a new emergency transmitter, an E.P.I.R.B. – Emergency Position Indicating Radio Beacon. The emergency locator you had on board was broken, as well as completely inadequate for today's safety standards. The EPIRB is a category one version. If anything happens, God forbid, and the boat sinks or capsizes, it'll transmit a position signal along with an identifier, unique to the Hydrous. All new crafts are now being fitted with them and many older ones retrofitted. Category ones are automatic but it can be started manually by pressing the push button on top. Two clear LEDs will illuminate when manually started. I thought the best position would be by the life raft. There is also a remote button by the command console next to the satellite phone inside."

Lizzie walked to the front of Hydrous with another tank handing it to Charlie, they both looked down at the EPIRB, it was small but neat. The Hazle family were taking all the precautions to protect them. It seemed ironic, they were taking the same boat out because they believed the tragedy befalling the Morris family was engineered and not because of any of its previous safety failings.

The five of them formed a human chain handing the dive tanks down the length of Hydrous. As Charlie stowed the last of the tanks Joel appeared looking flustered but forced a smile at his friends.

"Everything okay?"

It was the first time Dan had ever seen Joel looking worried. "More than okay, you guys have surpassed yourself. Hydrous is stunning."

"It's all part of the service, hopefully one we can keep running as a family." He shot Niles and J.J. a glance, his disillusioned face said it all.

"Joel can I have a quick word?" Dan ushered him back down to the end of the pontoon out of earshot from the others, shouting over his shoulder to Lizzie and Charlie. "Be back in a minute. Get her ready for the off and we'll get going. J.J. can you show Charlie how to start the engines, I know there's a knack."

Joel and Dan walked to the end of the pontoon. "Look Joel, I don't mean to interfere or anything but you have been such a close family friend over the years and done so much for me, I want to return the favour. J.J. let it slip about the developers moving in for the kill."

Joel's massive shoulders slumped. He was a proud man but even Dan could see he was broken.

"The fucking developers have the Port Authority eating out of the palm of their hands. The Authority are trying to force a compulsory purchase of the station and the Marina. Everything we have worked for as a family is literally being forced out from under us by big business. I'm a small fish in a big pond Dan and I'm totally out of my depth. I have no idea how to fight them."

Dan had never seen Joel look so sad; it was his life, not only his but his whole families. The part that struck him most it was not just a family business they were disrupting, the Port Authority and developers were trying to destroy the very essence of Santa Rosa. Dan once again could see why his family had settled here. It was a community that had passion; he understood why his Grandparents had loved this place so much and why they originally settled here.

"Look Joel, I know you won't take charity but I hope to be staying. I think Lizzie and I may even get married, but that's between you and I for the moment. My career in London is pretty much finished but if you'll accept my offer of help, I would, if you'll let me, invest in the station and Marina. Let's keep it as it is. It's what my family would want, it's what they came here for and I'd love to be part of that."

Joel looked at him. "What are you suggesting?"

"Well if they want this place to develop then allow me to invest in what you want to do, keeping the station and the Marina as it is. The last thing I would ever want to see is this place torn down for sad looking generic architectural condo's that no self respecting local would be able to afford anyway. The family has a portfolio of investments which I wish to continue. I'll become a sleeping partner, it's not about profit Joel. It's about the future of this community and giving back to it."

Niles, J.J, Charlie and Lizzie jumped in fright when they heard an almighty roar from the end of the pontoon. Joel was screaming and shouting with Dan bouncing around like a rag doll in his arms. The four of them ran along the pontoon expecting some kind of fight from the commotion, but as they approached Dan and Joel were both laughing like a couple of school kids.

51

As Hydrous left the Marina's shelter, the Hazle family waved them off enthusiastically. Joel put his arms round his boys, talking animatedly. Both Niles and J.J. leapt in the air, jumping on their Dad, they turned hollering in the direction of Hydrous as she set out towards the open sea.

Over the roar of the diesel engines none of them could hear what they were saying, although Dan had a good idea. Charlie and Lizzie waved back enthusiastically, like when a cruise liner leaves port for a cruise.

"What the hell is that all about?" Charlie looked to Dan, who expertly piloted Hydrous out of the Marina. Dan felt enormous pride about what he had just proposed, and for the first time in many years he felt part of the Morris family and more importantly home.

"I've just expanded the family investment portfolio." Charlie gave Dan a sceptical look. "I've offered the Hazle family a lifeline. I'm going to become a sleeping partner in the Marina and you Charlie, are going to broker the whole thing. The Morris family is branching out to develop the Marina for the locals, keeping it in the community." Charlie looked bemused. "Okay, so it's not technology, but it's something my Grandparents would approve of and it will give me something to do, especially as I'm planning to stay." He looked longingly towards Lizzie, who smiled; she could see the promise to his commitment, finally having him home at last.

The ocean stretched before them, a shimmering calm. The weather was clear, the sun bright and the wind blew steadily from the south, filling the billowing sails; it was perfect sailing weather. Considering it had been years since Dan last sailed Hydrous, the controls came back to him as though it were yesterday.

Hydrous surged forward through the waves, the wind ballooned her expansive sail. The mainsail flapped, pushing the tiller away the sail filled completely becoming taught, straining the ropes against the cleats and Hydrous began to pick up speed. Dan relaxed at the helm as Hydrous settled leaning slightly to starboard as she powered to sea.

He had missed this heady sensation. At one with the elements, the salt and sea air, it was hard to believe he had shunned this lifestyle for the cold and damp climate of London.

The feeling was not unlike the sensation he got from the gym, maybe even a little more exhilarating. The thrill of the excitement at the helm was once again invigorated by a pure adrenaline rush. He had missed it immensely.

Lizzie and Charlie had gone below to store their gear. Dan looked up as he tightened the main sail adjusting course slightly, his jaw almost hitting the deck. Lizzie ascended from the cabins interior.

"Now that's the kind of response I was hoping for." She giggled and seductively waved her body in front of Dan's face. Lizzie stood before him in a two piece black swimsuit tied at the sides, the tiniest swimsuit Dan could ever remember seeing in the flesh, as it were.

"Jesus Lizzie, you can't wear that, your Dad's on board!"

"Can't wear what?" Charlie poked his head from the cabin peering around his near naked daughter and looked her up and down. "Oh it's all right, I've seen it all before. She's never been one to worry about covering up in front of me." He shrugged and disappeared back into the cabin.

Lizzie climbed down in the cockpit behind Dan putting her arms round his neck smiling and kissed him on the cheek. Dan whispered in her ear.

"I wasn't really worried about your Dad, its more me I'm worried about, that doesn't leave much to the imagination, well not mine anyway!"

Lizzie pulled his T shirt over his head, stroking his bare abs with her index finger. "Well I'm glad my body at least has your attention."

"You've always got my attention Liz, you know that?"

"Not when you're on a mission, I know you too well. So do you know where we're heading?"

"Not exactly, I need the coordinates for the GPS. Can you get the nautical chart from my bag, you wrote them down on it in red marker."

Lizzie untangled herself from Dan and shouted through into the cabin. "Dad, can you bring out the folded nautical chart I put on one of the single bunks. It has red marker pen written on it."

Charlie poked his head from the cabin again tossing the folded chart to Lizzie, who in turn passed it to Dan.

"Anyone want a coffee?" Charlie offered. "I have the kettle on; someone round here has to be domestic goddess, especially when we don't have Java's to rely on."

"Well you do have some uses."

"Cheeky mare, you're still not too old to put across my knee you know, even wearing next to nothing." He smiled and tried to whack Lizzie's butt with the back of his hand but she expertly ducked aside.

"I've put all the gear away and stowed yours and Dan's in the double at the front, I take it you two will be sharing?" The last part of the sentence was more of a statement than a question, however his eyebrow raised quizzically grinning, Lizzie turned red.

She shouted back through as he disappeared from view again chuckling. "Dad!" Whining like a petulant teenager but agreeing with his sentiment. Her mind however was in the gutter looking at Dan's torso. She decided making love for the first time with a thin sheet of plywood between them and her Dad was probably not one of her greatest ideas.

"There's instant coffee in a bag I threw in the galley cupboard, plus creamer, along with some ginger nut biscuits!" She turned to Dan. "Aunt Susan would be so proud of me." She gushed.

"That she would, that she would." Dan was smitten. Lizzie was so beautiful; her candour was so like Aunt Susan. It was amazing how much of his own families' traits were instilled in Lizzie. It was like she had managed to consume the most desirable traits from everyone and able to see the best in everyone. He jabbed the standby button on the GPS unit and unlike earlier in the week it sprung to life.

The old black and white display pictorially displayed in dots. A navigational compass appeared on screen, fortunately its direction exactly mirrored the old Sestrel Moore compass, one of only a few original sea fairing parts of Hydrous' cockpit. The GPS took it's time to load the Pensacola coastline and, after what seemed like forever, it eventually appeared on the small display giving their exact position.

Dan pressed the menu using the up and down arrows to scroll through the index until finding the last used GPS coordinates, hoping its internal memory would have retained the old data. Success was achieved as the first line of entry were the GPS coordinates N30:02.6, W87:00.4. He compared them against the chart, they were the same.

"Look, the last GPS coordinates match exactly what you wrote down on the chart." Lizzie peered over his shoulder squinting at the tiny display, rubbing her near naked body against his back. Scrolling through the coordinates he could see Hydrous, according to the stored date stamps, had been taken out on many occasions to the exact same GPS position.

He logged the coordinates as the point of interest and a little cross appeared in the bottom left hand corner of the screen. Along the top of the screen their exact position was displayed and below the position of their programmed destination; the Oriskany. You could alternate the display showing the two positions and the distance in nautical miles, 22.4 miles.

Charlie appeared shakily from the cabin carrying three tin mugs expertly looped through one finger on his left hand, desperately trying not to spill them as the boat rolled and dipped over the waves. In his right, he carried the printouts from Simon's emails and a packet of ginger nut biscuits under his armpit.

As Hydrous headed out to sea, the ocean was getting slightly rougher. For the three of them, whose sea legs were a little shaky, it felt very rough. He handed a mug each to Lizzie and Dan as he half stumbled and fell into the comfort of the cockpit.

"I could see on the monitor in the cabin you know where we're going. What's the plan when we get there?"

"Well I think, being as though Lizzie has never dived as deep as we need to go, you and I'll go down to scout the exterior first. We'll probably need to penetrate quite a distance into the hold before getting to the hangar deck. It could be tough, I'm pretty sure it won't be as simple as swimming up and knocking on the front door."

Charlie spread the sheets on the floor of the cockpit. Now the GPS system was synced and working properly, Dan switched Hydrous over to the autohelm. The tiller went slightly lax in his hand as an electronic controller took over. He knelt next to Charlie and Lizzie who were examining the plans.

"What puzzles me is if there really is an underwater lab, why has no one found it before now? Surely someone must have gone deep enough into the wreck to have seen something? Anything."

"Dad has a point Dan, there must be countless dives and recreational diving every day considering the Oriskany is now one of the top dive sites in the world, someone surely would have seen something?"

Dan looked at the plans and traced his finger down a side corridor that ran below the hangar deck, stopping with a dead end.

"Would they though? If you think about it, a huge percentage of recreational divers would only dive as far as Lizzie has. Down onto the bridge and mainly around the island because it is where most of the interesting bits of the wreck are. There would only be a small minority of divers who penetrate deeper, over the course of a day, realistically how far would they get? Whatever my family did to the interior of the ship, they did with the express idea of hiding everything. They wouldn't go to all this trouble without hiding it from view, that'd be madness!" Charlie and Lizzie for once nodded in agreement.

"Look at the underground lab at home, or the Panic Room; it was designed as an anti-chamber, hiding its true identity. It concealed itself in the study behind an antique bookcase and hidden within was another room. It doesn't take too much of a stretch of the imagination to consider that something similar will be waiting for us down there."

Hydrous, invigorated by her fresh paint and woken from her deep hibernation, seemed to love the freedom she had been given again on the open sea. Her hull exuded a whimsical grace, slicing through the water as she effortlessly headed towards the wreck of the Oriskany.

Sitting on the edge of the deck, Lizzie watched as the water raced by, catching the odd glimpse of fish as they darted underwater as the hulk of Hydrous drifted over. Their change of direction mirrored the rays of light bouncing through the lapis clear water signalling a silver blur, then they were gone.

"How long do you reckon it'll be till we reach the dive site Dan?"

Dan checked the cockpit's speedo, compared to the rest of the modern technology squeezed in, it looked so antiquated. The chrome surround was pitted and the glass had a cruel weathered look courtesy of the salt, it was difficult to read.

The tiny little impeller beneath Hydrous was old and worn, he knew it was never exceedingly accurate but at these speeds it was close enough. The GPS unit could also be used to gather information such as speed, but it was slow updating because Hydrous was not a fast craft.

"Hydrous is skipping along at about 4 knots, I don't think I've ever had much more out of her without the spinnaker up and I'm not sure I want to get that involved considering none of us have sailed her in such a long time. I reckon if we can keep this pace up, then we should get to the wreck in about five hours, which should give us plenty of daylight to get sorted and at least take a first reccy."

52

Hydrous was de-rigged and floated a couple of hundred meters from the wreck. Her anchor deployed, she floated listlessly, tugging against the bond to the sea bed, her bow heading into the current. They were lucky, not a single vessel was around the dive site as recreational divers would have long since headed back to shore.

They would have set out very early to dive during the best light. Diving at this time of the evening posed its own problems. It was going to be more difficult because the sun was low and the light penetration was going to make the wreck a lot darker, especially at lower depths. As they penetrated the wreck itself, very little, if indeed any natural light would reach the interiors. They would rely solely on underwater torches to navigate.

During the five hour trip to the site, the three of them had poured relentlessly over the multitude of plans from Simon's email. It seemed clear a massive rear section of the hangar had been moved, rebuilt and strengthened. Not only was it moved to shield the interior compartments but strengthened so the bulk head would survive the explosive shock waves through the detonation process when it was sunk and also to stem the force of the incoming rush of water.

Each plan they carefully examined did not show a single entry point to the enclosed compartments. Dan knew the way in would be hidden but was uncertain what they would be looking for. A trap door of some description was one of his suspicions, something much more elaborate even than the Panic Room at home, he was positive they would know when they saw it.

They had decided to concentrate the search around the rear section of the hangar, where Simon had superimposed the internal compartments and where almost all of the reinforced structural modifications had taken place. There were a number of passageways heading nowhere, leading to dead ends, which was odd but they considered these junctures to be their first attack points.

There was a bang, followed by a jolting thud and Hydrous listed lazily to the side. A low moan emanated from the cabin. Lizzie and Dan tore themselves from the plans, looking anxiously towards each other and then lunged for the cabin. Sprawled across the floor was Charlie. His legs doubled backwards where he had fallen from the seating area.

Looking extremely uncomfortably, a considerable portion of his body was stuffed inside a wetsuit, however by the amount of excess flab pushed up around his mid section, the suit looked about three sizes too small. He gasped for breath, moaning helplessly from the floor, his face molded to the angular construct of the corner of the galley where it was pushed. He glimpsed the pair of them out of the corner of his eyes.

"Don't just stand there smirking, help an old fool up!"

Reaching down, grabbing the back of the wetsuit's neoprene, Dan pulled Charlie to his feet in one swift movement. He tried not to make eye contact stifling a laugh into a cough, as if trying to clear his throat.

"Oh yeah, that's it, laugh. My bloody wetsuits shrunk!"

Lizzie patronisingly patted him on the back. "Yeah Dad, that'll be it. Not the fact you've been stuffing your face with anything you can devour behind my back."

"That's an outrage, how dare you suggest such a slanderous defamation of my good character. A lesser man would take the appropriate action."

"What? Like diet?" Lizzie burst out laughing; Dan tried hard to contain himself but also started to laugh.

"All laugh at the fat person. You know, the trouble with you two perfect gorgeous specimens of humanity, you're fattest."

"No I think you'll find you're the fattest." Dan said extremely dead pan. Lizzie fell about laughing, Charlie scowled.

"Oh shut up and one of you zip me up." Dan stepped forward and Charlie turned his back to him.

"Breathe in then."

"I am."

"Oh right."

They were all grateful for the moment of stupidity, the last few hours had been serious and the pressure was mounting on the three of them. The zip gradually moved upwards, it was stiff from dried salt and lack of use but gradually pulled the neoprene ever more tightly around Charlie.

"Look at that, I'm almost thin again." He looked down shrugging despondently. "I think I need a new wetsuit?"

"No Dad, you need to lose some weight."

Dan gave Lizzie a withered look, a quiet suggestion to drop it.

"It'll be fine once in the water, it'll loosen up; it's only where it's not been used for a while."

Dan had checked the tanks and regulators, everything was in working order. He was grateful to Niles and J.J. as they truly knew their stuff. Part of him had actually wondered whether to tell them what they were planning but decided against it. He was concerned about putting anyone else's life in danger.

Right now he was more concerned about whether there were enough tanks on board to do what they needed, would they have enough? It could be like searching for a needle in a haystack once underwater. The ship was massive and he simply had no idea how long they would need to be down there.

He was also frightened about leaving Lizzie on her own. She was capable enough but what worried him was whether or not they were being watched. He could not see another vessel on the horizon and he had closely watched the GPS monitor for day craft, all of which were heading back to their individual ports, he felt relieved. Unbeknown to Charlie and Lizzie he also had scouted the cabin for bugs. He had found nothing which had quashed his fears for now.

One of the biggest problems surrounding Hydrous was she was never rigged for diving. She was designed as a majestic sailing yacht and as such served her purpose well, but it was difficult to suit up and get in the water from the deck. Both Dan and Charlie jumped over board and then swam back to the side.

Clinging to the ladder, Lizzie lowered their individual flippers, then tanks and respirators over the side one at a time and they helped each other to get the equipment on, one slip and it would sink to the ocean floor. Dan always thought a platform at the back would make such a difference, however it would change the whole aesthetic of Hydrous.

With their checks done, Lizzie leant way over board holding herself from the deck. It took enormous upper body strength to achieve such a manoeuvre, kissing them both on the tops of their heads. She regretted not kissing Dan properly before but had not thought about it until they were in the water. She passed them a white board each. Dan looked at it quizzically?

"What's that for?"

"I thought it might be difficult to communicate to each other down there, so I've rigged an underwater board for each of you."

Charlie smiled. "Thanks sweetheart, good idea."

"Be careful, please don't take any risks!"

They both donned their masks and breathers, Dan gave her the thumbs up as they both gently disappeared beneath the waves. She watched as the water gradually erased them from view while they descended. Lingering a while, staring at the spot, waiting for a last glimpse, but they were gone.

Heading back into the cabin Lizzie poured another tepid coffee, rummaged through her bag pulling out her iPod, grabbed a blanket and returned to the deck. Wrapping it round her shoulders she sat cross legged, absently dialling through a myriad of tunes and looking out across the expanse of ocean. The sun was getting low, a breeze was stirring and she shivered, pulling the blanket ever closer to her skin. There were only a few hours before the sun would finally set.

Lizzie had spent many happy hours, if not days, in this very position on Hydrous over the years. She loved the sea, it had been part of her for so long, but it had also been so cruel. For the first time in her life she found herself praying.

Praying they were not chasing a folly; chasing a dream; because none of them could truly accept the tragic loss they all felt, especially Dan. She longingly stared at the water, where moments before her father and the man she loved had been; she was alone.

53

The U.S.S. Oriskany's keel was laid down on May 1, 1944 at the New York naval shipyard. During her commission the Oriskany mainly operated in the Pacific Ocean, earning two battle stars during the Korean War and five for service in Vietnam. Her exemplary military record acquired the endearing nickname "the Mighty O". Her pedigree was second to none but somehow it seemed rather strange, after such an illustrious career, she now rested in the Gulf of Mexico.

She was decommissioned in 1976; her rusty hulks demise had a painfully slow and turbulent death, like so many behemoths before her. Finally selling for scrap after 19 years in 1995, she was then repossessed in 1997 due to lack of progress and towed to Pensacola, Florida. Exactly 30 years after leaving service, she was scuttled using 500lbs of C4.

37 minutes after the charges detonated; she slipped gently beneath the waves, 24 miles south of Pensacola lying upright in approximately 212 feet of water. As she hit the bottom, ownership of the ship passed from the Navy to the state of Florida, becoming the world's largest artificial reef.

Charlie and Dan had witnessed the ship sink, the whole family had been there and it was the last time they were all together. It had been the event to witness because the entire local community was behind the adventurous project. It was believed it would bring in a much needed influx of tourist trade to the area and within weeks of the Oriskany slipping beneath the waves the warship became a world renowned tourist attraction.

The Times, a daily national newspaper published in the United Kingdom, declared the Oriskany as one of the top ten wreck diving sites on the planet, a very lofty accolade, something the community was still immensely proud of.

Charlie had dived here on many occasions but somehow for the first time the Mighty O seemed foreboding as they descended towards her dark silhouette. The island which housed the bridge cut a lonely sight. Charlie had explored inside on several dives, working his way up the many internal corridors and flights of stairs to the bridge, which gave a great view out across the flight deck.

Even getting to the bridge took some manoeuvring. There were so many different ways through the maze; even this was relatively difficult to do. Charlie knew that heading deeper inside was going to test both of their dive skills. Dan may be a lot younger, faster and fitter but down here those attributes counted for little, experience was a far greater asset.

As they slowly descended side by side through the gloom on the island, an American flag lazily drifted in the underwater current. Usually the bright stripes stood out against the luminescent water, but in the murky gloom they looked subdued and washed out.

They touched down on the flight deck which stretched off into the distance in either direction. The Oriskany was 888 feet long but today she seemed to go on forever as she disappeared out of sight. Dan gave the okay sign to Charlie who returned it, although he felt far from it. He was apprehensive and extremely nervous, something he never felt while diving.

The excitement he usually felt had disappeared, leaving him with a dark sense of foreboding; this dive had far too many repercussions either way. Dan dropped over the port side of the ship, gradually descending deeper into the gloom, Charlie watched as he headed down.

They were looking for a particular entry point cut from the ship towards the stern. It was specifically removed to allow the ship to flood evenly during the sinking. Simon had charted the cut outs over the ship and they had concluded this one would give the easiest access route to the identified corridors, and hopefully the hidden compartments within.

Charlie had never been this deep, he had not let his nerves show on the surface but he was worried. Having penetrated the island on many occasions, he was concerned about what they would find. Would the concussion from the explosives have ruptured parts of the internal structure? Snagging a line or gauge was easily done and could be deadly at these depths.

The wreck, having been submerged for a few years was now teeming with marine life. Prickly sea urchins and crusty barnacles clung to the rusting metal. Giant barracuda prowled the tower's empty windows and the man-made wreck attracted many species of fish making it their home, plus more deadly animals including mako sharks. Their aggressiveness, speed and power meant the mako were among the most dangerous sharks alive. Charlie had seen them in the distance on previous dives, but going deeper, he was fully aware they were heading into their territory and did not fancy meeting one up close and personal.

Dan stopped several feet in front of him, his hand casually brushing the side of the hull. Charlie had been taking in the magnificent scenery, scanning for external movement and not paying much attention to the ship.

Fortunately Dan had been concentrating on the number of sections which had been removed. His descent from the flight deck had been carefully calculated from the plans on the surface. He had dropped off the edge by a set of steps, from this point he had counted the number of sections specifically removed along the hull towards the stern for the sinking. However he was confused by the shape, size and precision of the cut out he now floated in front of. Was this what they were looking for?

The precision of the opening compared to the rest was astonishing, it was almost too perfect. To look at casually, anyone would assume it was a part of the original hull and part of the Oriskany's original structure. In fact, unless an Oriskany expert, you would probably not have even given it a second look.

Every other removed cut out along the length of the hull looked as though it had been rushed with a very clumsy hand-held cutting tool, no care or attention had been paid to the shape or evenness of the cuts. The edges were not straight; they were dangerously jagged where the cutting torches had melted the thick metal and as the weight tore the section away, the metal caused stress fractures where the metal had ripped itself apart.

This opening was not on any plan he had looked at or was aware of, he was sure of it. It was higher than a full grown man and several arm widths across in diameter. He looked at Charlie who now floated alongside staring into the gloom. Dan lifted his torch and turned it on, barely penetrating twenty feet inside, but what struck him was how clean the area directly in front was.

Either side of the massive opening led discarded twisted metal stairs. Pipe work, like entwined spaghetti, snaked around the outside, but through the middle was a clear gangway leading directly into the interior of the wreck, even the marine life was less prominent shrouding the metal.

As they swam inside the ship, Charlie was also struck at how big and wide this section was. He had spoken to a few divers in the past who had penetrated the O. Many had said there were very few pathways clear of debris leading to the hangar. They had also inferred the hangar was difficult to get to, especially from the lower depths and for less experienced divers. However there was such competitiveness between divers, you could never be sure if it was simple bravado to dissuade others from attempting what they achieved.

The pair of them swam along the corridor, their torches barely illuminating the gloom. Once past the initial opening, which was wider and shaped like a T, the corridor narrowed somewhat, although the width and height closely matched the size of the opening. Either side the corridor was lined with many doors. Dan wondered whether he had missed it on the plans, could the opening have been used as the ships loading area? All of the ships' food rations and supplies could have been carried on to the ship through the opening, it was large enough. Would the corridor lead directly to the hangar bay?

Dan tried the first of the doors on the right hand side but it would not budge. Looking closely, moving the beam of his torch over the rusted door, he realized it had been spot welded around the edge to secure it. Charlie, taking precedent from Dan's lead, tried the doors along the opposite side of the corridor but all were welded shut.

After the third door on each side, a stair well headed up. Charlie swam over to Dan and indicated they go up the stairs on his side. At the top was a small landing with a single door in front. Dan shone his light around the outside of the door gap. There were no welds so he grabbed the wheel to open the door. Charlie suddenly had a bad feeling and put his hand on his, stopping him. He unclipped his slate from his dive belt and wrote on it quickly turning it round to show Dan.

What if the room is not flooded?

Dan suddenly understood why he had stopped him, he was right; they were completely unaware what was on the other side. Dan took out his penknife which he had tucked inside his dive belt, placing his ear against the door, he tapped the folded blades metal against metal.

There was no hollow ringing like there would be if there was air on the other side, only a resounding hollow thunk. Dan gave the okay sign to Charlie and twisted the wheel. He pushed the door inwards, the water pressure against the door resisted at first and then slowly it swung open. The pair of them stood in the doorway, shining their torches through the void.

Suddenly a silver-grey blur emerged from the darkness, moving incredibly fast. Before they could even register what was happening, a snout rammed between them, pushing both sideways and backwards with its momentum.

Charlie's mouthpiece shot from his mouth as he slammed backwards against the wall, the great fish's tail whipped wildly powering itself between the pair of them, swatting Dan full in the chest, winding him. Wide eyed he dropped his dive light, clasping his chest, gasping for breath. He whacked his head against the metal wall as he surged backwards in the slipstream of the fish's wake.

Charlie groped behind for his regulator tube, which would lead to his mouthpiece but could not find it, starting to panic with the primal need for air.

Regaining his senses somewhat, his breath returning in short gasps Dan realized Charlie was in serious trouble. He reached out finding his mouthpiece forcing it into Charlie's mouth. Charlie, still panicking, forgot to exhale first and sucked greedily for air, he started to choke until finally the mouthpiece cleared and he inhaled a painful first breath.

The pair of them stood in the doorway not moving, physically shaking. Both scared in case it came back, the adrenalin surged through the pair of them. Charlie retrieved his slate and wrote.

I think that was a mako shark.

Dan looked in the direction it had headed and wrote on his slate.

Fuck, it happened so fast, are there anymore?

He showed it to Charlie who shrugged the best he could underwater with the dive cylinders on his back. They both tentatively turned, knowing they had a lucky escape, heading into the room. Charlie was beginning to control his breathing but the thought of how insane this all was, meant his heart continued to race.

Inside the room, the shark had obviously entered via a cut out in the side of the hull. The long room was totally empty. They had learnt a very valuable lesson, to take more care.

The second room across the corridor was tentatively opened and, much to their relief, it was found to be empty. The far end had a corridor that led nowhere, which in Dan's mind was a good sign as it was what they were looking for, corridors that had no purpose.

Past the two stairwells there were several more doors, which were all welded shut. It dawned on Dan as they progressed down the corridor that unlike the two doors at the top of the stairs, the doors either side did not have secure closing mechanisms. This was probably why they had been welded shut. Towards the end of the corridor, it ballooned out either side into a large square, there was a single door leading straight ahead.

This door was also not welded and had the locking mechanism like the other two doors; Dan looked at Charlie who gave the okay sign. Dan tapped on the metal with his penknife, to a dull thunk, he turned the wheel pushing the door inwards.

The room was pitch black, an interior room, there were no outside hatches or external light sources, it remained still and dark. Their dive lights penetrated the room bouncing off the walls, causing shadows and lighting the room with an eerie dilated light. Whether intentional or a mistake, the room had not been stripped at all. It was a stark reminder of life on board for the officers and men who served their military career upon the Oriskany.

Around the perimeter of the room remained built in booths, the dark wood had swelled in the salt water but retained their original circular shape. The oxblood vinyl covers strained against the foam inserts which had expanded against the material and stitching. The aluminium and sixties formica inlaid tables remained secured to the floor in the middle of each, bolted so they did not move during rough seas.

Along the far wall, the bar, which had served many cold beers during its use, gracefully curved the corner of the room, lined with antiquated fonts for Budweiser and Coors. All the taps were open as if on a never ending pour.

The mirror behind the bar reflected the beams of their torches, bouncing around the room as they swam the length of the bar. An old Budweiser neon was fixed next to the optics, long since absent of spirits. To the left, at the end of the seating an old billiard table, the purple baize cloth floated gently, several inches above the slate and on the far wall, three pool cues stood upright in the rack ready to play.

To complete the look of any bar in the world, fixed to the wall to their right stood an old 70s Wurlitzer Jukebox, Dan swam over and looked inside. Many seven inch vinyl records were scattered around the inside of the glass, including ABBA's SOS which seemed highly appropriate. He absently pressed the numerical pad, expecting the deck to start revolving and the internal speakers around the room to start playing.

Charlie was sat on one of the tall chrome bar stools looking over the bar at him, as if expecting service. It was a surreal moment, yet a real treasure trove. He was shocked no one had ever reported this gem, or at least he had never heard whisperings. Sometimes things like this are kept secret by divers to stop treasure hunters from raiding it for the spoils.

On the wall between the Jukebox and the bar was a notice board. Dan stopped to look, casually wiping the glass with his hand. Inside were many photos, starting to decay under the salty conditions, depicting times of merriment on board, Christmas' and New Years past, spent many miles away from loved ones.

Dan stopped dead in his tracks; at the bottom of the notice board was a silver plaque. The engraving was familiar, it depicted a coat of arms, one he had been familiar with his whole life, it was unmistakable.

The engraving was exactly the same as on the family portrait at home. He almost screamed, looking for Charlie, who was swimming round the edge of the billiard table, half hidden by the billowing purple baize which undulated in his wake. Dan flashed his dive light on and off, capturing his attention. Charlie swam over and Dan motioned to the silver plaque.

They both looked, Charlie took a moment to recognize what he was seeing - a shield with a lion rearing on its hind legs, above the shield was a Knight's helmet and around the edge were flourishes of acacia leaves. He grabbed Dan. Through his mask he could see his eyes were wide open.

Dan reached out to touch the silver plaque. Beneath the solid wooden frame of the notice board he groped for the familiarity of a hidden latch which he found instantly sliding it to the left, exactly the same as the family portrait at the house. Dan immediately pressed the silver engraving but nothing seemed to happen, they both waited. The notice board gently swung away from the wall, to reveal what was hidden beneath.

54

They both surfaced screaming at the top of their lungs. At first Lizzie assumed something had gone terribly wrong and panicked, diving from the deck of Hydrous in to the water to help.

They were as giddy as school kids on a field trip. By the time she managed to haul them on board calming them down, they began to recount their dive, the corridor, the mako shark and finally about finding the underwater bar.

If Lizzie did not know better she would have said they had been drinking but in the last twenty four hours she was beginning to believe many odd things.

"So let me get this straight. Inside Oriskany there's a bar and on a wall, there's a notice board with an engraving similar to that of the coat of arms in the study at home?"

Dan was excited but still a bit daunted, they had found a massive clue but he was not sure if his idea of how to proceed would work.

"Not similar Lizzie, I'm telling you it's exactly the same! It also has the same locking mechanism as the family portrait."

Despite the three having finally dried off, Dan was desperate to dive back down, however Lizzie was making them rehydrate first. She was enforcing a surface interval break, of which she was unsure how long, but the longer the better as far as she was concerned.

They had been down deep and come up quicker than they probably should have. She was fearful of a nitrogen build up causing the bends. Charlie, exhilarated by what the pair of them had seen, with fresh vigour had grabbed three fresh dive tanks from the locker and was already preparing to dive again.

"It's true Lizzie, I was shocked. It's a clue and only someone connected to the immediate family would have known how to open it."

Lizzie was intrigued but was also trying to be pragmatic. "So what's on the inside of the notice board? What is it covering?"

Dan had been waiting for this question. "Inside there is a second silver engraved plaque but it would only mean something to Ash, Matt, me or you!"

"Me! Why would it mean anything to me? I'm not family. What is it?"

Charlie was also confused by the plaque. He did not understand it one bit but could see its relevance from the coat of arms. It all seemed very random making no sense to him whatsoever. Dan had been visibly excited underwater, so much that they swam straight out and headed for the surface.

"You remember the den when we were kids?" Lizzie nodded; of course she did, it was a huge part of her childhood which held so many happy memories for her. Charlie had never been allowed inside so had no idea what Dan was talking about. Granddad was the only adult who had ever made it in and that was only on one occasion, when he gave them their pen knives. "Do you remember the entry system that Matt put together?"

"Of course, but what does that have to do with anything, or me for that matter?"

Charlie was not following at all and talk of their childhood seemed irrelevant to the task ahead. "I don't understand what you two are talking about. What has your childhood den got to do with an engraved silver plaque with five names on it, hidden behind a notice board on a sunken ship?"

"Five names?" Lizzie frowned at Dan. Her jaw dropped open and he nodded, the penny had finally dropped as to what Dan had alluded to. Five names, their names, what they had always been as they grew up; Matt, Ash, Dan, herself and Bowie. She nipped into the cabin and returned with three penknives, hers, Ash's and Matt's. Dan gave her his, his keys were attached to the boat ignition so he removed Bowie's dog tag also handing that to Lizzie.

She sat down and pulled out the blades on each of the four knives in order – first Matt's knife, which had Διόνυσος engraved along the blade. Then Dan's knife, which was engraved Απόλλων. Ash's knife was engraved with Αθηνά, Lizzie's knife, Εστία and finally rotating the stainless steel tag on Bowie's dog tag to reveal the engraving Κέρβερος.

Lizzie sat them down on the teak deck one after the other. Charlie stared over her shoulder as she laid them top down underneath each other, staring at them in amazement, then at the pair as the realisation of what they had discovered earlier down on the Oriskany's underwater bar became blindingly obvious. The plaque was a clue left for either Dan or Lizzie to find because they would be the only two in the world who would ever understand what it was.

"Look, it's getting late, would we not be better off to get a good night's kip and heading back down to the wreck in the morning to work out this puzzle once and for all? We've hardly had any sleep in the last 24 hours and it's been a very long day today, what with one thing and another."

Dan looked at Charlie. "I understand your logic Charlie and I hate to say it, but we're running out of time. The recreational divers'll be back in the morning and the last thing we want is for them to see or follow us. Plus we have to work under the assumption that Uncle Mike and Aunt Susan's killer is watching us closely and will be here at some point soon. He could be out there right now!" He dramatically waved to the ocean. "Patiently waiting for us to make our move."

"Dan's right Dad, if there is something to be found, we need to do it as quickly as possible and get the hell outta here."

Charlie reluctantly agreed. Diving at night was not the most sensible thing to do, nor did he relish the idea of diving in the dark but he could see no other option. "Okay then, but let's have something decent to eat first and I could murder a decent cup of coffee, but what we have on board will have to do. We'll wait until after dark, then we'll dive. If we are being watched, at least he'll think we're not stupid enough to dive at night, which of course we are."

He rolled his eyes slightly. They agreed with him and set about looking as though they were settling on board for the night. Charlie stowed the tanks back in the locker and seated himself back in the cockpit next to Dan. It was difficult to make small talk, so no one really tried.

They all desperately wanted to get back down to the bar. The outlandish idea which seemed so farfetched had suddenly taken on a reality none of them could deny, even Charlie, forever the pessimist was convinced.

Lizzie went below deck to find something for them to eat; she connected her iPod through the external speakers taking piping hot coffee on deck for the boys while she cooked. They settled down to watch the sunset as she returned with pasta covered in a sun dried tomato sauce. It was going to be a long night but they were all finally resigned to it.

55

The three of them floated in front of the open notice board. The silver engraving sparkled under their dive lights, shimmering and refracting the individual light beams back into the room. Lizzie was shocked upon entering; the underwater bar was like an undiscovered time capsule. It did seem a very strange part of the ship to have left, but then maybe there were no toxic dangers from the bar interior itself and was deemed safe, so left for prosperity.

The silver plaque had started to oxidise under the harsh salt water conditions but the speckled patina gave more an antiquated charm, even though they all knew it was far from an antique. Lizzie held out her hand and traced the five names with her finger. She was astonished how something like this could be here. Dan however was right, no one other than the four of them would ever have any idea what the names meant or what they were connected to, even if someone accidentally discovered what was behind the notice board.

Lizzie carried in a net bag hanging from her weights belt, the four pen knives and Bowie's dog tag. She took it and pulled the slip knot, handing the first knife she retrieved in no particular order to Dan who opened the blade. It was his own knife; the blade read Απόλλων for Apollo.

Somehow the engraving and significance of the name seemed even more important, it was a gift from his Grandfather and like Lizzie he treasured it. The significance of finding Matt's knife and Ash giving hers to Lizzie was becoming crystal clear, it had not been an accident.

He wiped the silver plaque with his hand, removing a fine layer of sediment. The silver shone brighter under the concentration of their three dive lights. He traced the Greek name Apollo with his finger. To the right was what looked like a capital 'I' with a feint circle around the outside, anyone looking at it would assume it was simply a part of the

276

engraving, one next to each name on the plaque.

Dan and Lizzie would ordinarily have no idea what the symbol meant. However when they had built the den during one particularly long summer, Ash was reading all manner of books on Greek mythology and legend. Part of her many alternative studies were directed towards the Greek alphabet.

The three of them knew better than to mock her when she became obsessed with anything academic. For an entire summer all she recited were memorized texts about mythical creatures such as the Minotaur of Crete or Greek Gods which was where their individual names came from, until eventually obsessing and for some unknown reason learning the entire Greek alphabet.

When Matt built the den's crude entry system, Ash insisted that each of their names be spelt in Greek, so no one would understand the code. What actually looked like an 'I' in a round circle was in fact the Greek letter Phi – Φ. Dan had recognised it instantly on his first visit with Charlie.

He took the large blade, engraved with Απόλλων sliding it into the vertical slot in the Φ next to his childhood name. As the blade seated perfectly, to his shock, plus that of Lizzie and Charlie, the end of the black onyx handle illuminated red in the darkness. Underneath the thin onyx inlay was a small LED which radiated through, the three of them stared at it transfixed.

Dan was mesmerized, like watching a firefly in the darkness; he never had an inkling his knife would ever have had an LED in the handle. Lizzie as ever, was impatient and dug him in the ribs with the next knife retrieved from her bag. He opened the blade which read Εστία, he turned to Lizzie who nodded. He slid Lizzie's blade into the slot and marvelled as its tortoiseshell handle also illuminated red.

Their three faces bathed in a warm red glow emanating from the two pen knives. It seemed odd to both Lizzie and Dan that they had carried them around for all these years and truly never knew there was more to them than just a knife. The last two knives slotted into their individual slots and both glowed red, all four psychologically radiating warmth in the cold water.

Lizzie handed Bowie's dog tag to Dan, he looked and held it with such affection, he still missed Bowie. Even underwater Lizzie knew what he was thinking; she rubbed his back, the sympathy heartfelt. He twisted the tag open inserting it in into the final Phi on the silver plaque. As it seated itself, it too glowed red and then all five of the LEDs started flashing in unison.

Dan looked at Lizzie; he was not expecting the lights to flash, in truth he expected something more physical to happen. Lizzie looked at Dan, expecting him to continue but he did nothing further, what was he waiting for? Charlie wrote on his dive slate holding it up to the pair of them.

NOW WHAT?

Dan honestly did not know, he assumed the action alone of seating the knives would have set something in motion but nothing did, he was slightly confused.

Lizzie realized he did not know what to do and impatiently barged her way past him. She was surprised he had forgotten the next step, it was however forgivable considering it was so long ago. She reached in, grabbing hold of the top knife she twisted it clockwise, as she did the LED turned from red to green and they all stopped flashing, the remaining four were still red. Dan felt a little sheepish he had totally forgotten how the entry system worked.

His mind raced back to their childhood. He pictured the opening mechanism and then the inside of the den's door. Beside each Greek name was a keyhole, which was attached to a crude lever on the inside of the door. You inserted your knife and turned it through ninety degrees, the action simply swung a lever away from the door frame on the inside. Matt built it so that when all four knives and Bowie's dog tag were inserted, simply rotating each through ninety degrees the levers would clear the door frame to gain entry.

To be fair any implement thin enough would do. No end of times they used screwdrivers or hacksaw blades having temporarily misplaced their knives plus you could always rotate them individually. As kids they truly believed all had to be together to enter the den, except Bowie, who used to impatiently crawl underneath the door to flop down on his bed inside.

Lizzie gradually moved down, from top to bottom, twisting each knife clockwise. As she did each handle turned from red to green. She looked at her Dad, then Dan as she grabbed Bowie's dog tag, she turned it and it also turned green. They stared at the plaque for what seemed like an eternity before the green lights started to flash in uniform, the plaque smoothly slid to the left.

Charlie impatiently pushed his way forward to get a closer look, as he shone his torch inside he was crestfallen to see what was there.

Lizzie pushed him back with her backside and illuminated the inside with her own torch, so both she and Dan could see. On the inside was a numerical keypad. Beneath, was a display which had room for ten numbers. Lizzie reached in randomly pressing a few, as she pressed them they illuminated and filled the display from right to left, reading 5, 3, 6, 2, 1, 4, 7, 8, 9 & 4. The way they were separated on the display she instantly recognized the format; she had been inadvertently carrying it around with her for years.

She grabbed the knife from the middle Phi from the silver plaque and quickly looked at it; it read Αθηνά in the dim light. She flipped the knife over and frantically stabbed at the keypad, reading the engraved numbers from the blade, 3, 0, 0, 2, and 6.

The numbers rapidly appeared across the display as Lizzie's secretarial experience rattled through the number pad. Years of numerically entering the accounts data for her father finally paying off. Dan realized what she was doing, as she entered the last number, 4. The code entered read 30:02.6_87:00.4. It was the GPS coordinates for the Oriskany.

All three of them stared at the numbers she had entered. Nothing happened. The display lazily blinked at them. Lizzie looked at the blade to make sure she had entered the numbers correctly. They waited, still nothing happened.

Charlie reached to Lizzie's hand having watched over their shoulders throughout the entire exercise, not understanding but fascinated. He removed the pen knife from Lizzie and slid the blade back into the Phi slot from where it came, rotating it clockwise. The handles on the pen knives which had been red since she removed the knife, instantly turned green, the numerical display stopped pulsing, also turning green. They waited with baited breath for something to happen, anything.

Outside the bar in the corridor, there was a deep guttural sound. A reverberating groan, like the whirring of cogs and gears, they could feel its vibrations through the water. The three of them swam to the doorway of the bar, looking back down the corridor towards the open ocean, they could see nothing in the gloom. Their dive lights were useless in the thick darkness, giving very little penetration down the corridor. There was a grinding of metal which shook the doorway they were crammed in, the walls trembled and felt as though they were going to fall.

The large square of the corridor in front of them illuminated from the roof above, the unexpected brightness overpowering in the darkness.

All three of them looked up as the ceiling moved in one solid metal piece, sliding backwards into a recess above the ceiling of the bar where they stood. Around the edge of the ceiling, now visible as it slowly disappeared, were millions of white LEDs brightly indicating the perimeter of the square where the corridor ended and disappeared into the space above.

The three of them were blinded by this unnatural light after the darkness they had been blanketed in. They watched in awe as the riveted rusty slab slowly retracted above their heads. The grinding metal lurched to a halt leaving the entire roof of the square corridor open like a ragtop peeled back on a car.

The space above was huge, the expanse of darkness was broken by tiny LED lights spaced evenly, leading up the wall like a vertical runway strip pulsing along their individual lines like road works warning lights, disappearing out of sight into the cavernous space above.

56

McAdams had to lay low. His photo was circulating, the Sheriff's office had released it to the papers, plus it was being shown on the local news twice hourly in relation to the Morris murders and possibly in connection to the Simon Millor murder. The last thing he needed right now was to be recognised.

Whatever had happened in the Sheriff's office, Daniel Morris had really pulled a number. He was now locally, public enemy number one. Every part of his being screamed to get the hell out of town but his pigheaded nature rarely afforded him the luxury to quit, not when there were loose ends and especially when he felt the end game was in sight.

He hated Daniel Morris. He had never let his personal feelings get in the way of a job before, they could easily compromise a mission with knee jerk reactions but Morris had made this a personal vendetta by capturing him. He was going to pay, one way or another.

He had parked the van in his usual position along from the Morris house for most of the day. He assumed no one was going to bother come looking in this direction; there was nothing left to see. He waited, brooding, his mood dark, constantly watching the tracking monitor in the back of the van. He expected the Range Rover to leave the Station and head back to the house; however the car had not moved all day. All he could assume was they had already headed directly out to the Oriskany. This certainly would make life difficult; he had to be more careful with his actions.

As darkness fell he drove back to Simon Millor's engineering firm. While there terminating Millor, he had noted a few pieces of equipment in the engineering stores he knew he would need. He did not have time to acquire the materials through his usual covert channels and he was not even sure he would be able to considering, as far as his superiors were concerned, he was supposedly totally off the grid.

Any material acquisitions would be met with stern force. If they knew he was active, they would have his balls on a platter, he was already in trouble for the mess in London. If his superiors even sniffed he was operational he would be tagged as rogue and his career in effect would be over, along with his life.

In the back of his mind he was concerned his mug shot was circulating the local news, it would not be long before it would be picked up internationally. However it would not make any difference in the next twenty four hours, he should finish the job one way or another and be gone. If all went to plan, his superiors would not care what happened, they would have what they want and he would have his revenge.

If the mission went wrong he would be out of there and would pretend he was sitting on a beach in Indonesia all the time, recuperating after a little reconstructive surgery. When he left the UK, he purchased a ticket for Indonesia; his unregistered arrival could easily be explained by a simple clerical error as they never confirmed his entry properly through passport control.

He would make his way in the back way. It would cost a lot more but with his contacts, not impossible. His arrival in the States was under a pseudonym's passport, even his superiors could not track who he was and he had disguised himself through the airport.

The Marina had two entrances, one through the Marine Engineering workshop run by the Hazle family which was now secured for the night. He would never get through with his kit unnoticed. The second was a gated code entry system, leading down on to the floating pontoons; unfortunately this access was in full view of the car park and highly illuminated.

Many of the locals, mainly teenagers, knew the code and used it to sit on the dock for a few beers. Tonight though, it was devoid of activity and completely empty. Most however were from further afield who moored their boats on the Marina, only using them at the weekend, many never left their mooring from one month to the next, simply used as a floating gin palace, the most decadent waste of money and a pure luxury status symbol.

McAdams had parked next to the Morris Range Rover. He had been watching the Marina for the last hour. He needed to commandeer a boat that would not attract too much attention; he also needed to get his gear on board the vessel with minimal fuss. There was no easy way of doing it but he decided to time his walk to the gate, coinciding with someone who was exiting the Marina.

The coast was clear; all the teenage kids were inside the station sharing a milkshake and burger. He crawled through the back of the van and exited through the back doors, hidden from the view of the large windows. The open doors also hid him from anyone parking alongside. Removing a four wheeled trolley, he loaded on several dive tanks, a wetsuit and other equipment removed from Millor's workshop.

On top he piled the thermal imaging camera and other electronic items all sealed in water proof cases, plus a stack of clips, guns and anything he felt uncomfortable without, including several pounds of underwater explosives and detonators. He covered all of the items with a sleeping bag from the back and a large jacket. All that was visible were the diving tanks. Anyone being nosey would assume it was just a normal weekend away with the boat.

McAdams pulled on his cap, pulled up the collar of his jacket and pushed the trolley towards the gate. No one was in sight. Leaving the trolley by the gate he quickly walked back to the van, slamming and locking the doors shut. No one was paying any attention to him so he started to relax.

From the inside of his jacket, he pulled out a pack of cigarettes removing one. Standing down from the gate and casually leaning against the trolley, he lit it taking a long powerful drag, blowing it into the night sky. The smoke caught a slight breeze and drifted down the pontoon, illuminated by the powerful down lights before dissipating.

As he stood waiting for an opportunity, he could hear a group approaching from down below on the pontoon, they were chatting animatedly about their day's excursion. Great, they were German, the chances they would have seen or heard any news would be slim. They were heading to the station for a beer and something to eat, that much he could ascertain.

Taking a final drag on his cigarette, as they approached, he flicked the remains unceremoniously into the water through the railings. Grabbing the trolley and timing it perfectly he reached the gate just after they opened it. He grabbed the handle holding the gate open, ever the chivalrous gent, let them pass through. They nodded their appreciation as they passed him.

He heard one of them ask a friend what time the bar closed, he believed the accent was from The Black Forest region, without thinking he answered in perfect German.

"Die Küche schließt um elf, aber die Bar schließt um rund zwei." (The kitchen closes at eleven but the bar closes at around two). He was astounded by his own brazen stupidity.

The group stopped and turned; the one who had casually asked spoke to him with a broad smile in English.

"Finally someone who speaks German, we have been shocked at how few do, your accent is good but I assume you are English?"

McAdams could have kicked himself but he smiled casually, going with the flow. "Yes I'm English but I worked in Germany for many years."

"Well it's nice to meet you. Are you just off out? Surely it's a bit late to be heading out to dive?" He tapped the trolley with his foot.

"Yes and no, it is late I agree but I tend to dive extremely early as I'm an underwater photographer and the early morning light is better. I'm trying to get some shots of a particular bottle nosed dolphin school which has been seen. I'm making a start because by the time I get to the site and set up to dive with my equipment it will just be getting light." McAdams was shocked at how easy the lies flowed, it even sounded plausible to him.

"Wow, that sounds fantastic, where is the school, we'd all like to see that."

McAdams smiled. "Well I'd really love to oblige but I don't want them scared off, not until after I have the shots I need, I hope you understand?"

"Oh yeah that's fine, of course we understand. If you are back tomorrow during the day then please come for a drink. Our boat is the cruiser at the end of the dock called Fools Errand, we have some amazing beers on board and more importantly some decent Schnapps."

McAdams had found his boat, he smiled broadly. "That'll be great, although I don't understand why you'd be going to the bar to drink the American so-called beer?"

All four of the men laughed and agreed, the man who had been speaking perfect English answered. "Well, when in Rome." He shrugged as if in apology.

"Exactly, have a good evening, see you tomorrow then. I shall look forward to it."

The Germans excitedly moved off towards the bar having finally made a friend, they turned and waved as they reached the bar entrance then disappeared.

McAdams watched until they were inside and then hauled the trolley through the gate heading down the pontoon towards the end of the dock. Moored at the end conveniently pointing directly towards the marina entrance was the cruiser – Fools Errand.

He knocked on the hull and shouted through in German. "Hallo?" Nobody answered. Quickly he threw the contents of the trolley onboard jumping into the cockpit. The navigational control was extensive for such an expensive boat but it was easy enough to follow. The helm operated via a keyless ignition which posed a problem, however he had his laptop and they rarely utilized encryption to prevent theft, unlike car remote keyless systems.

Remote keyless systems operated by broadcasting radio waves on a particular frequency, North America worked on 315 MHz. His netbook had the relevant software and after quickly booting it, he located the range and the boat started with a quick push of the ignition button. The diesel tanks were full, obviously filled so the Germans could leave first thing in the morning. He felt slightly sorry for them, they seemed nice and the loss of the craft was going to cost them a small fortune, losing much, if not all of their deposit.

McAdams jumped down and unhooked the securing ropes from the pontoon; he gently gunned the twin diesel engines heading out of the Marina, making sure he did not break the speed limit as that would attract unwanted attention. Several yachties firmly ensconced aboard their gin palaces, already three sheets to the wind, waved energetically as he headed off into the night. He waved back smiling, mainly due to making such a clean and easy break.

57

The LEDs pulsed upwards, racing into the cavernous space above, way into the distance. The three of them apprehensively looked up into the enclosed darkness, not entirely sure what to do, or indeed exactly what they would find.

Dan kicked with his flippers and started to ascend into the space above. Lizzie looked at her father locking eyes through their goggles. Although they had pushed to venture down to investigate, now here, the impossibility of the situation was beginning to sink home.

They had initially believed Dan had to do this for his own sanity; Lizzie had been worried about his continuing mental state and obsession. Charlie had initially believed it was Dan's over active imagination, speculating an underwater lab could even exist, plus with recent events, he truly believed it had left his reality slightly warped.

On the surface the underwater lab sounded quite plausible; however the extremely elaborate conception, only malleable in Dan's mind, seemed quite surreal. Now looking up into the vault above, Charlie was beginning to fear this was not a piece of fiction, it was reality, Dan was completely right and they needed to finish what they started.

He swam upwards following the landing strip lights, Dan slightly ahead. Lizzie looked over her shoulder, part of her felt uncomfortably exposed. They needed to close the bar door and the entrance but she had no idea how to do it. What would happen if the corridor roof closed, how would they get out? She watched her father and Dan in the bluish haze of the lights, giving a last look up the corridor towards the exit she pushed off from the corridor floor to follow.

As she swam upwards to join them, what struck her instantly was the clarity change. The turbid nature of the water was entirely different to that of the corridor. There was no haziness caused by particulate matter floating around, continually being dispersed through tidal variations.

The LED lighting shimmered with the crystal clarity of a well kept swimming pool. Everything was clean and completely free of marine matter, even the interior walls were still clean. The other thing, which she shook off as paranoia, was the water temperature, which seemed to rise significantly as she passed from the corridor into the compartment. Not just a little variation, it felt like several degrees and compared to the open ocean, it felt uncomfortably warm.

Her father and Dan were only a short distance above but they had stopped. The landing lighting on the wall ended, replaced either side by a pair of alternating flashing lights. She looked at the flashing lights and then at Dan and her father, the pair of them had their backs to the lights and instead were looking into the cavernous space. She looked past them, in to the direction they were staring.

If she could have let her mouth drop in awe without the loss of her breathing apparatus, she would have, without hesitation. Directly before them, illuminated in the warm azure light were three individual boxes of incrementing size. They levitated above the floor of the vault, attached but each giving the illusion of floating in mid air. She could not tell what they were but she recognized the compartments from the design blueprints Simon had compiled. The designs were imprinted in her mind, in reality the sheer scale of them was awe inspiring.

Below them the lighting strip continued in the opposite direction from the opening where they had entered, across the centre of the retracted ceiling, across the floor, ending beneath the largest of the three compartments on the right.

The three of them swam along the direction of the lighting strip, side by side as if coming in for landing, heading towards the compartment indicated by the lights. The deck below was crisscrossed with parking bays, rubber and scuff marks, painted lines defining the position of each billion dollar plane. Their securing shackles were clearly visible in the floor; it must have been a hive of constant activity during its time at sea.

As they swam closer, Dan could see clearly from Simon's analogy with the cup, the ship was indeed listing by several degrees. The gimbal, designed by Matt, was keeping all of the compartments level; it was way beyond what he expected. The right hand side of each compartment was clearly closer to the deck and as you viewed through the sight line of all three, each looked as though it was at odds with the horizontal deck line.

The cylindrical walkways interconnecting the separate areas had the persona of the middle of a London bendy bus, collapsing together like a concertina, allowing for the differing levels. The structure was immense and the engineering feat was second to none.

Niggling in the back of his mind there was a considerable amount of apprehension. He had lived for the last few years believing the majority of his family was dead. For the last week, he believed he was the last remaining family member. What if this was just an installation that never got used; or even finished? What if they truly were dead continuing the folly and pipedream of his idiotic Grandfather?

The three of them swam beneath the largest end compartment, which was named CVC on the blueprint. The entire structure was brightly illuminated underneath from the runway strip lighting. Beneath they could see the complexity of the gimbal which was holding the entire structure above the surface of the hangar deck. The massive stainless steel concentric circles intricately linked and fitted together was astonishingly complex and quite breathtaking.

Suddenly behind them, there was a shudder and the creaking of gears. The three of them heard it long before they felt the water surge around them. Lizzie spun round terrified, her worst fear being realised, watching helplessly as the retracted roof of the corridor started to glide back to its original position.

Panicking she darted forward, kicking as hard as she could racing back along the runway lighting. The distance was far greater than she thought and as she neared the massive sheet of metal, the gap was narrowing. She hesitated, part of her wanted to escape and squeeze through but in her mind she visualized not making it and losing a limb, or worse. This small hesitation sealed the vault, she watched horrified as the corridor beneath, their only way out, disappeared from view.

She turned back towards the guys, panicked; a sense of foreboding fell upon her. They were sealed in. She looked at the two men in her life who she loved with all her being, they had not moved, they watched from a distance. The gearing system halted; the grating sound of metal against metal stopping abruptly as the metal slab seated back into position above the corridor. There was deathly silence, all she could hear was the blood rushing in her ears from the exertion of the quick sprint across the deck.

Suddenly and without warning the LEDs from around the opening extinguished. She watched helplessly as the LED strip also fell to darkness, running away from her in sequence back towards Dan and Charlie, one after the other until the last little light faded beneath their feet. The only lights left in the compartment were the three dive lights they held which they had completely forgotten about until total oblivion fell around them.

Lizzie swam back to Dan and Charlie, they waited for her to join them but she could tell from the way they held themselves they were both concerned. Dan picked up Lizzie's gauge and looked at her remaining air, she had over exerted herself. They were okay at present but if they could not find a way in, or out, they were going to be in trouble real soon.

As Dan let go of her gauge Lizzie grabbed at it and saw it was low, starting to control her breathing and breath shallow to try and conserve her air supply. She gave the okay sign to Dan and her father and they turned to look for a way into the compartment.

Dan shone his light up underneath the compartment. In the distance the light picked out the shiny concentric rings of the gimbal, giving the impression a snake was coiled around the base. The front section of the compartment had a V-shaped indent into the base. As Dan ran his hand across the lower point, he could feel the two pieces of metal joined via a big rubber seal. Shining his light along the edge, it stretched the entire width of the compartment. Dan concluded it was of a similar size to the boat house. It dawned on him that this was the entrance. The corridor inlet and the retractable roof guided the submarine into the bowels of the ship, the LED strip allowed for easy navigation with no natural light.

There had to be a manual override system on the outside to let them in. Everything else had always been so well hidden, would it be that easy?

Charlie had swum to the opposite end of the compartment and was sweeping the underneath looking for any kind of opening. There was a hole which disappeared into the compartment. He swam up the small tube, slightly bigger than a man, at the top was a hatch. Grabbing the wheel with his free hand he tried to turn it. It would not budge. He clipped his dive light onto his belt and tried with both hands; it was either jammed or locked from the inside. He banged on it with his light in the vain hope that someone, if there was anyone on the inside, would hear. His heart sunk as all he heard was the same hollow thunk he heard earlier when they ventured into the room where the mako shark was hiding. It was flooded above the hatch. They were trapped and their air was running out.

Lizzie was randomly swimming around the perimeter of the compartment. Dan was immediately to her right feeling his way along the V-shaped bottom edge and she watched her father cautiously disappear from view into a small opening.

A longing to be at home was running through her mind, to be home in bed with Dan, making love. She was never going to get that chance. She was going to die, she was going to drown in a secret compartment aboard the U.S.S Oriskany. No one would ever find their bodies, just like Dan's Uncle James, Aunt Pat, Matt and Ash. The authorities would find Hydrous abandoned, empty and lifeless. She would be towed back to the Marina once more hiding another deadly secret, yet this time it would be the last of the Morris and Price family lineage.

An enquiry would be held, but as there was no immediate family from either of the Morris or Price family, it would not be scrutinized all that thoroughly. Their deaths would pretty much go unnoticed, maybe lodged as death by misadventure diving the Oriskany. A tiny footnote in the local papers obituaries would commemorate their lives.

Lizzie felt a warm surge of water against her face, not just warm it was hot. She held her hand into the flow; it was definitely hot and fast moving. She traced her way back along to find it was surging through several large vents along the edge of the compartment. Through the vent she caught a glimpse of light, a warm orange glow. It pulsed vividly and then vanished; as the light faded so did the warmth of the water, gradually turning colder until the flow was no longer noticeable.

Lizzie pressed her hand down against the vents as the flow ebbed away; inadvertently she pushed the vents inwards, removing her hand, the vent swung opened. She realized they were secured with push release latches, like a door latch on a bathroom cupboard hidden behind a mirror. Beneath each vent were tubes leading into the exterior. Lizzie moved her way along opening them one by one, until she reached the last one at the corner of the compartment. It swung open like the rest but inside it housed an old style breaker switch, an electric knife switch. It looked like the kind that would be thrown in a horror movie to awaken Frankenstein.

Looking towards Dan she grabbed her air gauge, she did not have long before they would have to buddy up and then between the three of them, they only had at most five minutes of air before it would all be over. She felt a tinge of sadness for the last one alive having watched the others drown. Gripping the lever, Lizzie pulled it towards her with all her might.

Without warning her whole body shot upwards, slamming her breasts and chest against the vents. The outgoing flow she had felt previously had reversed, she could feel the suction envelop her as the water pulled inside. Her wetsuit was being pealed from her body blocking the vents, her skin chaffed as the neoprene squeezed tightly, hardly able to breathe through the pressure on her chest.

Dan saw her struggle, swimming across, desperate to reach her. As he neared, the surge of water pulled him faster; before he could react he too slammed into the vents, narrowly missing Lizzie.

Charlie had reversed out of the tube where the hatch was, he had given up trying to budge it. In the distance he could see Lizzie and Dan's dive light thrashing around, something was wrong.

He started to swim to where they were but as he got closer he could see they were desperately trying to push themselves from the edge. The water pulling him towards them increasing his speed, he tried to swim backwards against the flow but the drag was too strong. Realising he was going to crash into Lizzie and Dan, he stopped fighting, heading feet first, he landed heavily but upright against the vents.

The flow of water rushed around him, Charlie struggled against the immense surge, shuffling along by sliding one flippered foot at a time. He reached Dan first who was looking up wide eyed. Locking hands he tried to pull him away from the vents but the onslaught of water was far too strong.

Slowly he knelt taking hold of Dan's wetsuit pulling the excess material away from the vents. He could feel the water starting to dislodge his goggles, then with one swift movement he rolled Dan off the vent, away from the compartment. Crawling along he did the same to Lizzie before the pair of them, pulled Charlie to safety.

58

Charlie, Dan and Lizzie kept above the bottom edge of the compartment; the water surge was still quite powerful. If they dropped lower they could feel it pulling them but keeping between the compartments, they were able to stay out of the undercurrent.

A smaller diameter connection tube stretched between the two compartments, unlike the walkway at the opposite end, its structure was comparable and made from the same pliable concertina material. They found staying above this, the water tended to be less virulent.

Dan had grasped the plastic exterior when he was first released from the vents after Charlie's quick thinking. It vibrated to the touch, the resonance through the pipe had a familiarity but he could not place where he had felt it before. The water flow started to ebb and the three of them felt it stop.

Dan signalled with the palm of his hand stretched out in front, immediately followed by a thumbs down, which meant you stay and I am going down. Before either of them could object Dan dipped below the pipe disappearing beneath the edge of the compartment. The water had ceased its rapid flow; whatever the hell it was doing he had no idea. He tentatively looked into the vents, he could see nothing.

Charlie looked at Lizzie's gauge, her air was dangerously low. He clenched his fist at Lizzie to signal the fact, but she already knew she was low on air, she could feel the labouring drag through her regulator as she tried to take each individual breathe, it was becoming harder with every tiny lungful.

She signalled with both forefingers pointing upwards touching together, she would need to buddy up and soon. Charlie pointed to his own regulator to give it to her, she held up her hand against it. He tried to take it from his mouth but she held it firm, not yet.

Dan could hear a rumbling from the inside of the compartment, a gurgling noise, like the water running from a plug hole. He placed his head against the V-shaped underside of the compartment where several minutes earlier he had been running his hands. His body pressed against the metal concentrating and listening at the sound.

The V-section he was pressed against was opening. He was gently being pushed towards the flat surface of the compartment. The underside was folding back like the underbelly of an aircraft deploying missiles, he moved quickly before he was crushed against the side walls. Dan let himself drop away as the separate sections of the hull peeled apart, flattening themselves against the exterior of the compartment. The inside was flooded which made his heart sink.

From underneath he immediately recognized the intricate hull of the Hyper Sub, he would never forget the shape after looking at it from this angle before in the dry dock at Marion Reynolds. The submarine was secured to stop it from moving in a cradle, similar to the one in the boat house at home.

The interior of the compartment was rectangular and around the outside, with what would be the Hyper Sub's natural displacement level, was a galvanised steel walkway that extended round the perimeter of the room. The Hyper Sub took up less than a half of the space.

Dan swam up level with the sub, looking through the canopy. The interior was empty, it gave little clue whether it had been used recently. You could see small differences in the design compared to the newest prototype, Hyper 2. Minute profiling changes and dynamic details to the exterior, side by side he suspected there would be drastic changes. The interior had the luxurious quality of a Mercedes motor car, leather seats, chrome dials and beautiful components, the build quality looked fantastic.

Dan's attention left the submerged submarine, unlike Hyper 2 it was not accessible underneath so of little use. His attention turned to the room; he still needed a way into the inner structure, other than the open bomb bay doors for sub access. The only other exit was a single water tight hydraulic door on the walkway. He could not see a visible way of opening the door at all from this side. There were no internal latches or electronic pads, the door could only be sealed or opened from the other side, or maybe it was an automatic door, he had no idea.

He turned and swam out motioning for Charlie and Lizzie to follow. Lizzie had no regulator in her mouth, he rushed across and gave the buddy signal to Lizzie, she nodded. He extracted his mouth piece giving it to her; Lizzie hungrily dragged a breath, consumed like a first nicotine fix of the day. He pointed back towards the underside of the compartment and they followed. Charlie and Dan swam either side of Lizzie, alternating their mouth pieces for her to breathe.

As they entered underneath the chamber, there was a hiss from the vents. The three of them flinched from their previous experience, expecting to be sucked backwards against the grates. Inside the chamber, red flashing lights started pulsing in the water above the walkways. Lizzie could see the submarine in front of her but was having trouble concentrating; she was trying to hold her breath but was feeling lightheaded and dizzy.

They were just inside the doors when the vents expelled a huge blast of air and surge of water, the power blasted them into the chamber, like a tornado tossing a tree. Lizzie wanted to get out, her mind was hazy, she was unable to fight the flow and her energy was spent.

She flailed aimlessly as her body whipped around, resigned to take her final breath. The hard punishing liquidised breath that would be her last. How long would she survive? Would she be able to watch her father and Dan while she could no longer breathe? Would she drift in to unconsciousness as if asleep or would she feel every second of her painful last moments on Earth?

The doors closed beneath them, she vaguely registered the dull thud as they sealed shut. The water erupted into a frothy mass around her; curtains of bubbles distorted her vision and her body felt at peace within the warm bubbling torment. Lizzie no longer felt where her limbs ended, only a numb sensation as the bubbles caressed her, not registering which way was up. Was she dying, was this the end, was this actually what death was like?

Hands grasped under her armpits pulling her. She felt like a rag doll, limbs disjointed and loose as she rose. Breaking the surface of the water, she drew in a huge lungful, gasping deeply for air as she opened her eyes. Stood on the walkway waist deep in water, her father and Dan pulled her towards them.

The water continued receding in the room fast. They led her on the galvanised grate; the water disappeared past her ears settling about six inches beneath the walkway, still a writhing bubbling mass, instantly subsiding, reminding her of a Jacuzzi turning itself off. The only light in the room were the four rotating red lights, which moved a continuous crimson shroud across the entire room.

"Are you all right sweetheart?" Charlie was knelt above Lizzie, pushing the hair back from her face.

"Well if that's what a twister feels like!" Dan kissed her on the lips; she reached up and put her arms round his neck and smiled. "No, that's what a cyclone feels like." He smiled back at her.

"Are we alive or dead?"

"Well we seem to be alive for the moment, but for how long I don't know?"

Lizzie looked up and round the metal room. "I pulled a lever on the outside hidden under some vents, hot water was streaming from them. I think maybe that's what opened the doors?"

Dan looked at Charlie. "Thanks Charlie, I reckon if you hadn't arrived when you did we'd both have drowned. Against the suction it felt like I was being crushed." He rubbed his ribs, feeling the bruising.

Charlie just felt happy to be alive and looked round the room. "How the bloody hell are we going to get out of here now?"

"I don't know."

"I take it that's the missing sub you've been talking about, could we use it to get out? I found an inlet hatch on the far end but I couldn't undo it. I tapped on the metal too, it was flooded Dan, the whole fuckin' metal box is flooded." Charlie sounded panicked.

The red lights stopped flashing and turned green. There was a loud hiss as the room's pressure equalised. All three winced in pain as their ears popped. The hydraulic water tight door released, clicked and slid open. The lights in the moon pool illuminated as the door opened showering them in brilliant light, comparable to daylight. Through the door stood a lone figure, with a gun aimed directly at the three of them.

"Don't move or I'll seal the door again and let you all fuckin' drown." Charlie looked up from Lizzie towards the door, the voice was familiar but it had been so very long.

"James?"

59

James lowered the gun, stepping through the open door onto the walkway of the moon pool. "Charlie, is that you?"

The pair of them grabbed each other and hugged, parting they looked at each other with great affection. Charlie stepped aside as Dan was helping Lizzie to her feet. James lunged at Dan and held him tight.

Dan reacted badly, pushing him away and screaming; Charlie and Lizzie were shocked but not surprised, they had been waiting for this to happen, for him to crack.

"What the hell? We thought you were dead, we all thought you were dead!"

"I know son, we had important things to do, something we …." He faltered lowering his head, not knowing exactly what to say. He looked at Charlie, his best friend, for the words, to Lizzie and then back to Dan.

"They had threatened the family, they wanted Dad's …" He breathed deeply, changing tact. "Your Grandfather's research, they killed him and your Grandma for it. I live with their death on my conscience every day, but it was your Grandfather's wish that the technology never falls into Government hands, not just the British Government, any Government."

"Then why not just destroy it. Destroy it, like it's destroyed our family. Ripped us apart, it's been a curse on our family since the day Granddad fled Britain."

James looked at Dan; he could see the pain in his face. "You don't understand?"

"You're fuckin' right I don't understand, I never will. I only hope the sacrifice everyone has made with their lives is worth it."

James looked at Charlie, who happened to feel like Dan but not being blood did not know how to express his feelings as openly as Dan, or felt he even had the right. James was stubborn just like his father, William; they were driven by the same ideals and focus.

296

Whether it was passion or blind courageousness he never knew, but whatever it was Ashley, his daughter was driven by the same streak and it flowed throughout the entire Morris family, except Dan and in truth his Mother, Deborah.

James stood awkwardly, he knew he could never justify to Dan the madness, the obsessive nature of his and his father's work but demonstrating what they finally had achieved after all of their sacrifices would hopefully change his mind.

"Come on through, welcome to wet lab and our humble home."

Archetypes often overlap; a mad scientist may not necessarily be an evil genius, they may simply be a scientist having become obsessively involved with their research, developing tics way beyond what was considered normal.

Not just science, even a higher level of intellect breeds this higher level of eccentricity and quirkiness. A genius with a definitive goal could on one hand seem selfish or on the other quite endearing. A group all sharing the same ideal or common goal clearly become illusioned their individual or group path is the correct and only one, ignoring all others around them. James and his father before him, was like this.

Except with James, there was an unassuming quality to his intellect, a softness that somehow belittled the passion and brain function, making him someone you felt you could engage with about any subject and talk to about anything. This was what made James so likeable and friendly; he was interested in everything, no matter how small.

However his father's cause, through the passage of time and unerring commitment to the research, could cloud even the greatest of thinkers. James had been a slight misfit in his youth. Now though his mind was focused so intently on the job at hand, his own personal identity was second to the work, which in turn, became his identity.

He was the kind of man who only through necessity would dress. His socks would mismatch, nothing would be ironed, his clothing would be pure function and no excess thought would be applied to the way he looked. That was until he met Patricia, his wife. She realised these traits in him were endearing, not something to be scared of, like so many women before her. She moulded the exterior of the man to match his passion inside, something she shared.

Instead of dressing him every day, she chose clothes for him that meant none of his daily routine would be interrupted by excess thought patterns. Because of Pat, James looked quite exemplary in his own skin.

His clothing was the same every day, black pants, paired with a black

T shirt, black socks and functional underwear. This way he always looked familiar, he never even gave his clothing a second glance, it was pure function. To James, dressing down was simply wearing a pair of sneakers or going barefoot.

The rest of his look was total unadulterated stereotyped scientist; his hair, grey and receding, what little he had was mad, shooting off at jaunty angles, which never ever saw a comb and his large forehead over powered the top of his head.

Horn rimmed spectacles perched at the end of his long nose. He peered over the top of them with his deep entrancing blue eyes, which Dan had inherited, the only true Morris feature he had. James was extremely thin, looking somewhat gangly because of his excess height, which he managed to hide because of his rounded shoulders, lowering his bulk by several inches to an average height. A trick he learnt throughout his life which had not helped with his posture.

The three of them trudged behind James, suddenly aware they were all still in wetsuits. Both Dan and Charlie had removed their tanks before grabbing Lizzie from the water. All three discarded their flippers at the doorway as if entering someone's home for the first time, removing their shoes. James like the proverbial host proudly gave them the tour.

"Of course you've just entered through the moon pool; we mainly use it as a swimming pool to keep fit."

Lizzie grumbled in the background. "Yeah it was like a trip through Alice's bloody looking glass!" Charlie smirked and even Lizzie smiled at her own joke, under the circumstances.

James continued. "This is the operations module, to your right is the computer room with all of the data banks, backups and computer servers. The workshop is straight in front of you, including a compression chamber if needed. Not that we have used it as that. It's mainly used to get in and out to maintain the external superstructure."

The moon pool and connecting rooms within operations were of minimal design. A simple solid reinforced metal structure, bolted and seam welded together, crudely painted with the visible internal infrastructure showing.

James turned to his left walking down the connecting walkway. From the inside, the concertina effect was more like an armadillo's armour; the ornamental exteriors' bendy plastic covered an internal metal structure. They walked in single file as the walkway only allowed for one person at a time. Either side was a wooden handrail. The connecting walkway, which was slightly suspended above the outer armadillo structure, was a single solid piece of non slip metal, hinged at either end keeping the compartments an exact distance apart. The slight listing of the Oriskany could truly be seen and felt walking down the incline into the laboratory.

The laboratory was entirely different in its set up. Like a hospital clean room, the walls were clad in crisp white plastic PVC sheets stretching from floor to ceiling. The lab was illuminated by day light lamps, it was almost blinding after the relative gloom in operations. It was not as wide as the operations compartment but whereas that was split into smaller rooms, the lab was almost a single massive one, with a small office along one end.

All round the room Dan recognised some of the intricate equipment, much of which used to be in the underground lab at home along with countless other experimental machines, he had no idea of their use, but the X ray machine and especially the electron microscopes he had fond memories of when he was growing up.

However at the far end of the lab, stretching across the compartment like an imposing clear Plexiglas cupboard, from floor to ceiling, elevated above the water well, was the much larger hydro pod.

Lizzie walked towards it pressing her nose against the thick glass, staring into the well. Full of a crystal clear liquid, the intricate machine suspended in mid air, she turned and looked at James, seemingly unimpressed. "Is this what all the fuss is about?"

"Pay no attention to that, I'll explain everything later. We were just about to have dinner when the alarms went off, please, come and join us."

James headed through the second walkway disappearing. Charlie, Lizzie and Dan looked at each other and then followed, feeling as though they were simply guests on a tour of some tacky tourist attraction.

As they entered the final compartment, it was a world of difference to the previous two. The living quarters were luxurious, decorated like a penthouse suite, except for the lack of windows or a view; instead beautiful pictures covered the walls, a massive original film poster of '20 000 Leagues Under The Sea,' plus more importantly many family portraits.

Comfy couch's lined the walls, a coffee table with magazines and journals scattered across it sat in the middle. Along one wall was a projector screen, which was showing a DVD. The sound was low but Dan caught an unmistakable glimpse of a fedora. They could be in anyone's front room in the world, yet they were on board the U.S.S. Oriskany at the bottom of the ocean.

They could hear voices to their left, the three of them tentatively followed, leading down a small opening. Along one side was a galley kitchen, they stood there looking a little lost, still soaked in their wetsuits. James was at the far end grabbing extra cutlery and dishing up three more plates of hot food.

"So what the bloody hell were the sirens firing for this time?"

"We have guests." James said smiling as he motioned to the three of them standing awkwardly in the doorway.

Ash rotated on the stool by the breakfast bar, along the opposite wall to the kitchen units, she was piling Spaghetti Bolognese into her mouth as she did so. She screamed, sending meat sauce and pasta all over Matt who also had his back to them facing James.

She launched from her chair towards them, throwing her dinner to the counter, not sure who to hug first, instead simply flinging her arms round the neck of Dan and Lizzie together, squeezing them with all her might.

Aunt Pat opened the door to their right, which was the bathroom sticking her head out. "What's all the fuss about, why were the sirens ...?" She looked into the eyes of Charlie almost feinting on the spot falling into his arms, Charlie held her up smiling.

"Hello Pat, my lovely." She swept her arms around him pulling him into her ample bosom. "Oh my God, what the hell are you doing here?" She screamed excitedly.

When they untangled themselves from the hugging and kisses, they all turned to face Matt, standing with his arms crossed who looked unimpressed.

"Yeah, what the hell are you doing here?"

Ash pounced at Matt. "Don't be such a twat Matt!"

Dan looked up, staring at his family as if they were ghosts. It had been a long time since he stood at the family plot, witnessing four empty caskets being buried, yet it felt like yesterday. Watching Aunt Susan and Uncle Mike's caskets being added had been crippling. His mouth was dry but he seethed with an inconceivable anger towards all of them.

The past few days had stirred heavy emotions in him, death being his utmost enemy and lifelong shadow. He stared at each of them in turn with such venom, even Matt looked concerned. In all the years, he had never seen Dan look at anyone with such hatred.

"I could ask you lot the same fucking question. I've believed for so many years you were all dead." Aunt Pat tried to put her arms round him but he swiftly pushed her off. "I've been mourning your loss every single day, along with the rest of my family, and you all act like you've just returned from a fuckin' vacation."

Charlie knew the anger Dan felt deep inside, he felt as though he should stop Dan's outburst but the family had lied to him and Dan needed to vent this. They really needed to know how much pain they caused him. He had closed this hurt away for so long, shutting his life down and running away from everyone. Charlie put his hand on his shoulder and Lizzie grabbed his hand, both reassuring him he had every right to be angry.

Dan had spent most of his energy the last few weeks processing, in the only way he knew how, the murder of his mother, then Aunt Susan and Uncle Mike. He squeezed Lizzie's hand bowing his head, when he raised it, a tear rolled down his left cheek.

Remembering the CCTV footage from the Panic Room, he watched again as Uncle Mike was hit in the chest by the fatal bullet, the blood, and then Aunt Susan's continual scream. His own anger subsided; he suddenly realised why he was there. He was the bearer of the worst news anyone could carry. His had unceremoniously unfolded several thousand miles away, in an interview room in London from a total stranger.

He let go of Lizzie's hand walking forward to Matt, he lifted his arms putting them round Matt's shoulders. Matt did not know what to do, instinctively hugging him back. Dan gently whispered in his ear, although none of them in the room could hear exactly what was said, Charlie and Lizzie knew. Charlie put his arm round Lizzie and she buried her head in his shoulder. Matt burst into tears, it was all Dan could to do to hold him upright as his knees buckled.

The grief and sadness of losing a parent can be unbearable, Dan knew this only too well. His grief was still raw, uncovering the truth about his mother's death made it very real again, but somehow it felt like a distant memory. Matt's was fresh and cutting, he was the bearer of this news and somehow this burden quelled his own anger. He realised Matt was the reason they were all together.

They ultimately were all victims but he had only just lost his Mother and Father. Instinctively Uncle James, Aunt Pat and Ash surrounded the pair of them as Matt cried into Dan's chest. They were a family once more and they mourned as one.

60

Charlie, Lizzie and Dan spent a couple of hours filling them in on their adventures up to the point of entering the wet lab. Matt was particularly silent on discovering Simon was dead. Matt knew his feelings for Simon ran far deeper than just brotherly love but this was neither the time nor the place to discuss Matt's sexuality.

"So this guy you captured in London, you reckon he knew all about Deb's death?" Aunt Pat looked at Dan with a pained expression. She had the kind of demeanour to make you feel incredibly comfortable, even when your whole world felt like it was imploding.

Aunt Pat was a voluminous woman, yet she remained incredibly sexy and attractive. She dressed to flatter her curves, not to over accentuate or hide them. Her passion for life by default poured into everything she did, who she talked to and surrounded, she was infectious yet slightly mischievous in her nature.

Her rounded pale face was topped with dark almost ebony hair, immaculately straight and neatly tucked behind her ears on which perched a unique pair of half moon glasses. She would peer over the top at you with her kind crystalline hazel eyes.

Her voice had a soothing tenderness only motherly school teachers manage to accomplish over a lifetime of calming riotous children. Her accord endeared everyone to her, her loyalty, structured nature and technical skills made her incredibly organised. She was the complete antithesis of her husband, James, bright, bubbly and infectious.

"Yeah, I have no idea but I lost the plot in the interview room. I could've killed him. I wish I had, things may be different if I had." Dan looked at Matt concerned; in his heart he knew if he had kept his cool things would have been different. Uncle Mike and Aunt Susan would still be alive. "I've been suspended indefinitely, which in New Scotland Yard's terms means my career is effectively over."

Matt looked up. "So how would this guy have information on us anyway?"

"I don't know but I'd assume he would've researched the apartment block residents, thus I would have been flagged. If he is a spook for the British Government as I believe, he'll have access to all sorts of sensitive data, which would include stuff on me and ultimately lead to the family. When I first joined Special Operations I activated a search on myself, like a web search but it only flagged basic stuff. Looking back, the lack of data I found would have been sufficient to dig deeper. I just assumed, a little naively maybe, it was because I was from America. It wasn't until I used a higher clearance status I discovered how deeply the whole situation went."

Dan looked to Uncle James, who throughout the whole story had remained stoically silent. "Did you know my mother was killed?"

Aunt Pat looked at James, who shifted uncomfortably as everyone stared at him; he never did well under pressure. "Well bloody answer him James!"

James looked coy. "I had my suspicions, yeah, but Dad was so secretive when it came to many things. He saw it as his duty to protect us all; he never forgave himself for what happened to Debs. I think it's why you were so molly coddled while growing up and everyone tried to protect you."

"So why did Mom take Granddad's research?"

James looked at Pat for help, who shrugged her shoulders. "Dan's old enough James, he should know, he's no longer a child and he now knows her death was no accident. You can't hide the truth anymore sweetheart. He has a right to know."

James sighed. "When your mother was at University, Mom and Dad were so proud of her gaining a place at Harvard Law School, we all were! She was the top student in the whole year, she was gifted Dan. Your mother was extremely intelligent, she could have been anything she wanted. I reckon it's where you get your analytical skills from."

He smiled at him, as if trying to make the news seem less painful. "In her second year she somehow dropped in with a crowd of socialist activists. One in particular your mother deeply fell for, Debs was besotted by him and he brain washed her against everything, pretty much poisoning her life. She dropped out of her studies starting to live a rather bohemian lifestyle with the prick. However the extravagant lifestyle they had was funded primarily by Deb's trust fund. He started siphoning money away, financing Greenpeace trips and other such trite.

We're talking tens of thousands, if not hundreds. Mom and Dad tried to let her get on with it, making the decision if they interfered it would only make their bond stronger, believing eventually it would fizzle out so naturally they left her to it. However Debs came cap in hand to Mom and Dad when her money eventually run out."

Dan was confused. "If Mom had spent her trust fund at such an early age, what are we talking, nineteen, twenty? Then what the hell did I inherit when I turned eighteen?"

Charlie sat upright knowing the time would come. "I can answer that James." All eyes shifted from James to Charlie. "Your mother managed to spend her entire trust; well, at least her boyfriend did. It ran in to millions, he became rather dependent on her money and began to enjoy the lifestyle it afforded. When it ran out, which it did incredibly quickly, she came home asking for more. Your Grandfather refused and for the first time in her life he said no to his little girl, which didn't go down well at all. He wanted to know whether she would finish her education, she refused saying it was pointless. Why should she earn money when she already had it?"

Charlie looked round the room, he could tell from the concentration in everyone's faces this was news to all but James and Pat, who simply nodded in agreement. "Your Grandfather was angry; I've never ever seen him so angry, not like that, not with any of you. She decided as she was only months away from her 21st, she should have immediate access to the family money. Your Grandfather flipped and with the unusual blessing of your Grandmother they decided it was time she realised the value of life and how hard it can be so they cut her off!"

Charlie hung his head in shame. "I drew up all the legal paperwork. In effect she was pushed outside the family unit. What they truly hoped and believed was she would see sense, continue her education and support herself, thus learning a valuable lesson."

Dan jumped in. "I don't understand. So where did my trust fund come from then if she was cut off and spent all her own money?"

"I'm getting there! The situation completely backfired on your Grandparents. With no money, Deb's boyfriend left. You would have expected that to be enough to bring her back. However all it did was strengthen her resolve. She was as stubborn as William and you for that matter Dan, she hated your Grandparents. In her mind it was them that drove him away, it was never the money, and she never truly forgave them. It was a long time before they saw her again; in fact the first time was the day you were born."

"That still doesn't explain where my trust fund came from if Mom or her boyfriend spent it?"

James stepped in. "Your Grandfather put over $7 million in trust, legally sorted by Charlie and by the time you turned eighteen, it was nearer eight. It basically matched the amount in Matt and Ash's trusts. We all decided it was only fair the three of you all had the same start in life."

"Okay, so that explains the trust fund, thank you. I can understand why Gran and Granddad would do that. So the million dollar question or eight million dollar question is, who's my father?" Dan looked around the room from Charlie, to Pat, to James, then back to Charlie.

Pat stepped in, her usual calm and soothing overtones, which had settled so many family frictions over the years. "Sweetheart, nobody knows. The first we even knew Debs was pregnant was when you were born and we got a call from the hospital. Unfortunately for all the happiness you brought, you never truly healed the rift between Debs and your Grandparents. By the time you entered the world Debs had become totally self sufficient. She no longer needed, or for that matter, cared about the money. She landed a decent job at the Pentagon and we rarely saw her, or you. We always hoped somehow you would know who your father was but you didn't and for some reason she never trusted us enough to confide who he was. I'm so sorry Dan."

"So if Mom was never interested in money, why did she steal Granddad's research and try to sell it?"

James looked at Pat for help, who shrugged. "Revenge, that's our best guess."

"What?"

"The man your Mom loved, he turned up several years later dying of pancreatic cancer. He literally only had days to live but for some unknown reason, he crawled back to your Mother. Whatever happened between them in that short time, she blamed your Grandparents for ruining her chance of happiness. She genuinely believed they were the ones who drove him away, not her lack of money. The fact he returned proved he truly loved her; it was their fault he left. She believed they had stolen their happiness."

James butted in. "When he died, Debs came back to the house for a weekend, she brought you home for your 8th birthday, do you remember? While everyone was celebrating, she snuck into the lab and stole Dad's research, including mine. Plus she managed to grab unpublished material that tied our work together, which is what we'd been working on."

Pat took over from James as he was being harsh with his tone, shooting him a withered look. After all these years he was still very angry towards his sister. Only couples who have been together for such a long time know how to step in on each other's conversation.

"We don't truly know what happened after that Dan. The following week the Police turned up at the house to break the news of her death. Your Grandparents were asked to go and identify the body. You probably remember, that was the time when you came to live at the house. Your father was completely unknown so couldn't take responsibility for you as there was no name on your birth certificate, nor did we know. Your Grandparents would never have let you go into a foster home so they became your legal guardians."

James continued. "During the time you came to live with Mom and Dad, we suspected Dad had been threatened over his work. After you arrived he started to change, becoming very secretive. He was great with you kids but he started hiding his research, even from me."

Dan was saddened hearing the events leading to his mother's death but equally he had learned to deal with it over the last few days since he had spoken to Terry at the Pentagon. Her death was so far removed from his life now; the intense sadness and anger he felt was abating.

He finally knew his mother had not abandoned him, as he had believed throughout his childhood. The feelings he had felt most of his life were like looking into a shaken turbulent snow globe but as he understood the events leading up to her death the storm inside was subsiding. He was quite matter of fact about what he said next, it even shocked himself.

"I think Mom was murdered ..." The room sucked in an audible gasp. "... and although it was set up to look like an accident it was done to shut her up. Plus ultimately it was to give Granddad a shock, coercing him into continuing his work and to protect us all."

Everyone in the room looked as though they had been shot. Deborah's death had always been raw. Losing a sister, daughter or mother before their time is always hard, causing much heartache and pain. Even James' anger towards his younger sister dissolved in an instant.

James' analytical mind mused on this latest idea from Dan. "Dad was protecting us, but we never truly knew from what because he kept it hidden from us all. So he was scared. Scared of what else could happen to any one of us in this room, especially if he didn't continue the research. When the house caught fire due to one of his experiments backfiring, that was when we designed and built the underground lab, to hide the work and ultimately stop anyone from stealing it. With the lab out of sight, he began to relax again, probably because he felt safer having the work hidden."

Dan could see the logic. "Yes during that few years even as a kid I remember the mood changed, Granddad changed. I guess we were safe for a number of years, but they grew impatient."

Charlie looked up. "Who's 'they' Dan?"

"The British Government, maybe the American, who knows but eventually they lost patience with Granddad and they came knocking again, didn't they Uncle James?"

All eyes shot back across the room at James, who bowed his head. "Yes." He sighed. "They threatened Dad again over the research, although they tried a different tact. After my naivety in publishing some of my work they believed I had the knowledge to finish it and he was superfluous, threatening him. He told me shortly before he died that he'd told them to leave us alone and if they didn't, the technology would never be finished or ever see the light of day. The next thing Mom and Dad were dead." James bowed his head, the pain still vivid for all of them.

James continued, even though he was trying not to cry. He had carried the weight of the family on his shoulders for so long after his father's death, taking the reins, he could not look anyone in the eye.

"Dad left his final data analysis sealed away with Charlie which was released to me, upon his death. It was written in long hand, as he so often wrote his research. Pat and I transcribed the data and remodelled it extensively. He'd cracked the technology years previous but must have been scared of what would happen to any of us if it was released to the Government. The last thing he gave was written instructions never to let them have it, always protect the family, as they would never ever stop or leave us alone."

Pat chimed in. "Dan it was never our intention to hide anything from you but after your Grandparents death, you changed, you shrivelled into yourself and none of us, not even Lizzie, could get through to you. We never meant to lie but we felt if you were heading to London, as you did, the less you knew the better."

Matt looked up, he had been quiet listening, so much was new but it all made sense. "The wet lab was initially an idea of mine; it was something I was working on independently as a chamber for divers on the Oriskany. I thought there was a commercial idea here but Uncle James saw the plans. It was never intended to become what it has." Matt indicated their surroundings.

James chirped in. "We only planned to disappear but the sinking of the Oriskany gave us a platform to build on, hiding the lab and more importantly the research completely. However we didn't want to leave anyone exposed, especially you, so the staging of our deaths was primarily done to protect you, Mike and Susan."

James lowered his head crying again, whispering. "We failed."

61

Lizzie yawned. "What time is it? I feel like I've been up for days." Matt was aware of the time shift between them. "We've swapped our working schedule so our body clocks have been reversed."

"What do you mean?"

"Well because of the amount of traffic around the Oriskany during the day, we have to schedule everything so we work through the night when the wreck is empty. We sleep during the day and the wet lab transitions to silent mode; most of the automated venting is done slowly throughout the day."

Lizzie shrugged. "So why the hell has no one found this place? I'm shocked there haven't at least been rumours. Especially of the bar, someone must have found that. It's an underwater gem, not to mention absolutely bloody amazing; any diver worth their salt would want to see it!"

Ash smiled. "Well actually, no one other than you would be able to see it."

Lizzie laughed. "Well yes we kind of realised the significance of the trail left for us. I'm particularly in awe of the names on the plaque in Greek."

"Matt reckoned after all these years, neither of you would remember them, I knew you would. What I actually meant though, is that no one other than you or Dan would be able to get in the bar because of the way it's designed and implemented."

Dan had been talking with Aunt Pat, but over heard the conversation and he interrupted. "How is that possible, the bar opened, there was nothing to stop us at all."

"Matt, show them." Matt left the galley, returning several seconds later clutching a small dark mahogany wooden box. Placing it on the work surface, he lifted the lid and turned it round to face Dan and Lizzie.

They both stared, totally gob smacked by the contents. Dan looked at Lizzie, who in turn looked equally dumb founded.

Inside the wooden box was a grey foam insert, with die cut sections, five cutouts in total. The two top cutouts were filled with black onyx pen knives, the two below, tortoiseshell knives, slightly smaller and below that was a black onyx dog tag.

Lizzie ran her fingers down the knives and looked at the pair of them quizzically. "What? I don't understand? What are these?"

Dan removed the top black handled knife in the box from its foam bed. Examined it closely, it looked exactly like his knife. Opening the blade, even the script was the same, it read Διόνυσος, Dionysus in Greek, it was Matt's knife. Picking up the second knife, he opened the blade, which read Απόλλων, Apollo, exactly like his.

Lizzie picked the fourth knife down; she turned it over carefully studying it. "This can't be right?"

Ash looked at her patiently. "What can't?"

Lizzie ran her thumb nail through tiny grooves scratched in to the handle. "Years ago I dropped my knife into a small stream when we were on one of our walks. I accidentally scored three lines across the handle. This knife has the same identical marks and to be honest, looking closely, the similarity is pretty scary. I'd know my knife anywhere and if I didn't know better I'd say this was it."

"That's because it is!"

Lizzie looked at Ash bewildered, laughing nervously. "How? I mean, it's never left my side plus it's presently slotted into the plaque in the underwater bar!"

"Your original knife is in your hands, the one in the Greek plaque is the replica. You remember the night we went out shortly before we disappeared? I gave you mine to look after which of course was a replica with the additional engraved coordinates on it. When you were in the restroom I took imprints of the tortoiseshell shell exterior of yours, using a moulding rubber. Aunt Susan discretely swapped the knives for the ones you have both been carrying all this time."

She smiled, the replicas were obviously good as neither of them had realised they had been swapped. "Dan, yours and Bowie's was moulded when she was over in London for the first time on vacation. We employed a specialist forger to recreate both your knives and Bowie's dog tag, down to the minutest details, including the scratches on your handle Lizzie, but they were both slightly enhanced."

Dan studied the knives and looked at Matt and Ash. "You mean the

LEDs, the ones that lit up when we pushed them in the plaque, they were inserted inside them?"

Matt smiled. "No, not just the LEDs. Each knife was fitted with a tiny transmitter. Without it you would never have been able to enter the underwater bar. Every knife including Bowie's dog tag was fitted with the same unit. It activates in proximity of a transponder, which is inserted on the inside of the bar door. No one else, other than you, could open the door without one of the four knives or Bowie's dog tag; it simply would appear like the rest along the corridor, locked and sealed."

Lizzie suddenly panicked. "We left the knives in the notice board. When the ceiling opened, the last thing on my mind was closing the bar door, then the hatch closed trapping us inside."

Matt seemed unconcerned. "It's alright. I'll turn the motion detectors back on in a bit, then we'll know if anyone is snooping outside. They are disabled automatically when the hydro pod vents blow. The re-circulating water for some reason tends to set the sensors off as they are just a little too sensitive. The sensors are installed so anything moving up the corridor over a certain size will shut the doors automatically, just in case we have any uninvited visitors."

Dan was suddenly concerned by a small niggling detail; his analytical mind could see a flaw. "Hang on a minute, you say Ash gave Lizzie her replica knife and Aunt Susan secretly swapped mine and Lizzie's. I found yours, at least the replica, on the floor of the hydro pod when I was checking out the lab."

Lizzie looked at Dan. "Yeah that's right; Dan showed me where he found it on the floor down in the water pit. If you had planned the whole operation to such minute detail, why was the knife on the floor? It could have easily have been missed."

Ash looked concerned. "I thought your knife was left on the centre island in the lab?"

"It was but Dan did find it, so we never had to worry."

"Worry, why the hell was it in the pit of the hydro pod in the first place." Ash scorned.

"Well actually I can blame you for that one?"

Ash looked like she was going to punch Matt. "Why am I to blame, you're the only one who ever goes home to pick up the gear."

"Well that's just it, you remember the backup raid array; you know that bloody great lump of hardware you ordered?"

"You mean the new data storage you broke!"

"Yep, that'll be the one. Well the caddy came in the biggest fuckin' box you've ever seen in your life and I got it jammed down the service tunnel. Being as I'm the only idiot who's moved any of the lab equipment, I know anything that does not fit down the service tunnel through the two way valve, won't fit in the sub."

"Oh boo fuckin' hoo." Ash mimed a baby crying, Lizzie and Dan both laughed, they had really missed the familiarity of the banter between the four of them. It was also great to have some normality after such a long time.

Matt shot her an evil look, but smiled. "Well I got Dad to pass down something to cut the nylon packaging straps. He gave me the knife and I removed the exterior packaging and he cleared it all up. I can only assume he must have dropped the knife in the pit as he took all the cardboard and foam protection back out. Whether he realised or not I don't know, he met me in the boat house later as I was about to leave."

Ash was unrepentant. "So after all that you still managed to damage a couple of the drives?"

"Oh yeah blame me, they could have just been duds in the first place."

"Well it's just a good job I ordered spares isn't it?"

Dan cut in. "Okay you two, pack it in!"

"Christ Dan, you should see the amount of hardware we have in operations, it's shocking."

Lizzie suddenly realised that Uncle James, Aunt Pat and her Dad had disappeared off leaving the four of them to catch up, so they probably could as well. "Okay, so I'm intrigued, all I've heard about is family secret this, hidden technology that. I've seen it and it looks pretty uninspiring in the hydro pod or whatever the hell you call it. What does it do?"

Ash smiled at Matt. "Liz, I said it would change the world as we know it and it will, we've cracked it." She was like an excited school kid. "Come on let's go see. You go get the olds Matt. Come on Dan, you'll never believe how much everything has changed and improved."

62

Fools Errand had made good headway to the Oriskany dive site. The water was calm and a new moon danced on the crests as they moved gently across the surface. McAdams had waited silently, watching from a distance. His boat conveniently drifted in the current towards Hydrous, which was moored over the wreck.

There was no movement on board and the boat was in total darkness. Over the years he had witnessed many occupants, when trying to convince you they are home, leave the lights on. This behaviour never happens in reality, as when in residence and asleep, they will turn everything off. Total illumination is a sure sign of an empty dwelling. He was a little apprehensive of what he would find.

He left the cruiser drifting in the current while he checked and double checked his equipment; he had an idea of what he needed to do but not an exact plan. He was in uncharted territory and was in an uncomfortable position of going in totally blind. He did not have time to carry out his usual reconnaissance over the scene; time was definitely no longer on his side.

His only real source of intel were the maps and detailed drawings from Simon's laptop. However the data was not concrete. It was like basing an entire operation on a single informant's word. He had trouble believing it entirely. His only consolation was Hydrous was moored above the spot of the wreck, giving some relative comfort.

What did pose a problem with his mission ahead was the entrance, if it existed; unsurprisingly it was not on any of the drawings. Of course it could be a complete fraud, another white elephant covering their tracks, but having seen the length the family had gone to, the idea seemed more plausible every passing minute, especially studying the immense blueprints.

He was going to concentrate his search on the port side towards the stern of the ship. There seemed to be many corridors ending in dead ends, especially towards the hangar bay. He had been on enough military ships over the years to know that corridors were a luxury that rarely, if ever, ended in a dead end. If there was a hidden entrance, this area seemed the most likely spot.

McAdams checked the equipment; many of the items taken from Simon Millor's workshop would be extremely useful. They would allow him to take some extremely heavy equipment he may need down to the depths. Everything was working perfectly, the equipment was ready and it was time to move in.

He started the engine and turned the cruiser towards Hydrous. He was going to have to be quick to get on board. If not the noise of the engine, the sudden bump as he parked alongside and boards, will wake them. Glancing at his trusted gun he tucked it in the back of his pants, he was never going to leave it behind again.

Fools Errand unceremoniously crashed into the side of Hydrous, sending her listing perilously to starboard. McAdams killed the engine running across the top of the cruiser, leaping the rail, landing on the deck of Hydrous. He was at the bow of the boat. Pulling on the portal, it slid back. Grabbing the gun from his pants he aimed it into the cabin. The bed was empty. It had obviously not been slept in.

He jumped down and edged through the cabin, the twin births too were empty. On the stove was a kettle, he held the back of his hand against the side of the metal, it was cold. They had been absent a long time, longer than a dive tank would allow for.

McAdams jumped back aboard Fools Errand; starting the engine he turned the boat round reversing it towards the bow of Hydrous. Using the power trim, he tilted the propeller out of the water, gradually drifting the boat backwards, until the propeller was barely in the water. Revving the engine hard, with the last of the cruiser's momentum, a tumultuous cascade of water spun from the speeding propeller grinding itself into the hull of Hydrous. Scoring through the fresh black paint and tearing into the wooden hull before jamming. It was enough to have done the damage he was after.

The hull had split, the wood splintered, sending water spilling into the front compartment of the boat's hull. It was not a massive breach but enough to sink her slowly, buying him time if they surfaced. They would have nowhere to go except on the cruiser. He moved the boat away from the disabled Hydrous, who was sat forlornly, now lower in the water listing towards the bow. Deploying the cruiser's sea anchor,

McAdams disabled the engine by removing a wire to the ignition system, just in case anyone managed to get on board alive, trying to make a getaway.

Sun up was in less than three hours, many recreational divers would be arriving to dive the wreck and then whatever he found. This would be his only attempt, he would need to get out and lie low. His face would be all over the news and he would be forced to use the back routes out of state and then finally disappear.

However with the data and information his superiors had been after all these years in his possession; with a single phone call he would be airlifted and given the formidable protection of the state. It was worth the risk. His previous indiscretions in London would be forgotten, it would be the difference between active service or total obscurity. The latter scared him immensely, he knew nothing of real life, nor did he ever want to. He had little inclination to conform and join the rat race, forced to become anonymous, he loved the seedy underground world he knew.

McAdams threw a bright green air bag over board, like a parachute but with hooks attached to it. Underwater it had the look of a jelly fish with its tentacles splayed out beneath. A compressed cylinder fed air inside, controlled manually, allowing heavy objects to be lifted off the seabed. Or in this instance, to lower all the equipment he needed, which had been strapped onto a sled balanced on the edge of the diving platform at the back of the cruiser.

Suited in his dive gear he dropped off the back and into the water. He inflated the bag as much as he could. Tugging on the sled, he pulled it from the dive platform sliding it into the water. The air bag momentarily bobbed beneath the water and then resurfaced. Attaching a dive light to the straps, he gently turned the release valve; the bag started to dispel air and disappeared beneath the black water. McAdams put on his breathing apparatus, swept the horizon for any sign of lights or movement and disappeared beneath the surface after his apparatus.

63

The family had lost so much, struggling so defiantly against past and present governments to realise and create what stood before them. Was the suffering worth it? Were the deaths surrounding the family worth the sacrifice? Each and every heart in that underwater room knew it was not, but to have sacrificed and abandoned the research because of external pressures would simply have never suited the family's ethos, proportionally linked to William Morris' drive and passion.

The pod was silent in its watertight casing. Raised above the water line on its lifting rig, the strange technology looked like a huge egg timer cradled on its side. Around the central structure protruded two glass bulbs, interconnecting stainless steel pipes intricately wound round the small glass aperture converging around the centre.

Extruding into the centre of each individual hourglass was a metal rod, ending in a small mushroom like dome; each was expertly machined from a different material, solid silver on the left and solid gold on the right. Floating around the shaft of each metal rod was a set of arms consisting of three intricately designed hemispherical cups, looking similar to an anemometer from a wind monitor, but far larger and more robust.

The central pipe work and connecting tubes, precision welded, would not have looked out of place from the propulsion unit of a rocket destined for outer space. It housed the main technological infrastructure between the two hour glasses and was comparable in size to a large washing machine. The glass bulbs, which looked like huge bulbous test tubes, housed a clear liquid and were approximately two metres in length. Each metal rod was just over one and a half metres in length, with a diameter of around ten centimeters, the mushroom heads were the size of a child's football.

Dan, Charlie and Lizzie stood before the hydro pod looking at it, mesmerised by the familiarity and sheer futuristic look of the device inside. None of them dared even guess what it did. Dan had been around the technology his whole life but like so many things while growing up, never questioned anything inherent, as it was seen as the norm.

Everything seemed familiar but on a much bigger, much more industrial scale. Dan turned from the pod looking at his family who had retreated back behind banks of computer monitors. Ash looked up over hers smiling at Dan. "Hold on to your britches, this thing really rocks."

Lizzie turned to Ash. "You said it would change the world as we know it, what does it do?"

"All in good time Lizzie, lets crank it up first and then Dad can explain."

Charlie retreated behind James; the pair of them were already sipping an expensive whiskey from crystal tumblers, just like old times although Charlie rather missed their comfy wicker furniture while sitting on the veranda at the back of the house watching another glorious setting sun. For him the feeling of claustrophobia down here was a little overwhelming.

There was a low hum as the external valves opened and a surge of water refreshed the pit below the machine, bubbling and undulating. A high pitched audible sound emanated from behind the Plexiglas, which visibly vibrated. The internal anemometer on the right hand gold metal rod started to slowly rotate clockwise.

The clear liquid inside at first resisted the rotation until it gradually built up to the same momentum; the cups were barely visible as the speed of revolution increased. Inside the glass, the liquid separated into a beautiful crystal vortex, spiralling and tumbling, dancing within its glass construct.

The anemometer on the left hand side reluctantly kicked into life, starting to spin on the silver metal rod, this time anticlockwise. It was not long before both sides of the hour glass spun and rotated like two twin horizontal tornados, totally hypnotic, they defied gravity swirling in there captive glass tubes.

The lab lights were dimmed. Dan and Lizzie turned to see Matt turning the daylight lamps down in the lab. James looked over his monitor and raised his whiskey glass as if to raise a toast but was signalling for them to look at the hydro pod.

"Now watch?"

The gravity defying horizontal tornadoes spun in their separate glass tubes, the anemometers barely registered as they were spinning so fast, each rotating the liquid in the opposite direction. Hardly visible in the darkness, the mushroom-like domes at the end of each metal rod began to glow.

Subtly at first, a feint cyan encapsulating the metal and illuminating the liquid torrents within the glass. The glow deepened substantially as the mushroom domes erupted with purple lightning sparks, like a plasma ball. The sparks, caught in the spiralling of the current, were whisked away down the tornado's funnel towards the central pipe work.

Aunt Pat broke the silence and spoke with the composure of NASA mission control. "We have ignition, temperature running at base, three hundred and fifty degrees Celsius, maintaining core temperature."

Ash chimed in. "Lowering pod."

The pod descended on its lowering track into the pit, submerging itself beneath the water. The cyan glow deepened in the water and the whole pit began to steam, which gently rose forming condensation on the inside of the acrylic glass.

Lizzie turned round to face the family, who viewed her expectantly. "It's a fabulous light show but what the hell is it? What does it do?"

James had stepped out from behind his monitors, with his whiskey glass in tow. "That is the trillion dollar question Lizzie. I suppose the best way of answering it is to go back to Dad's original research and progress to what you see before you and ultimately answer the reasoning behind why Dad deserted the UK after such a prolific career for the Government and Military."

In the middle of the lab was a massive work surface holding many of the family's expansive testing machines and their own individual workstations. The worktop was designed in the shape of an H, the bottom left hand leg of the H doubled as a conference table for them to sit and discuss ideas. Impregnated in the middle of the surface was a large touch screen monitor on which they could develop ideas together, pushing the project forward.

They all gathered round the table as the screen booted into life. James controlled the imagery on the surface as he moved folders and images around. He tapped on a folder titled 'history'. Within the folder, lots of documents and images became available. He double tapped a small thumbnail and an old black and white grainy image filled the screen. A young man the spitting image of Dan, proudly wearing his military uniform.

"Your Grandfather." He pointed at the screen but the entire group instead stared at Dan, mesmerised by the likeness. "This was taken just before Dad deserted. He was instrumental in a new piece of hardware allowing submarines to stay underwater indefinitely. It was an efficient way of extracting breathable air from water, thus dive periods would be extended exponentially, plus pollutants and other such hazardous problems from air scrubbers could be removed from the internal workings of a submarine. He single handedly developed and designed a system that basically converted water to breathable gas, supporting an underwater habitat such as a submarine. But also they, the Government, wanted to use the technology covertly, inserting underwater operation centres closer to enemy shores."

Dan, along with everyone else, was still astonished by the picture on the screen but he managed to ask a question. "Did Granddad succeed in getting the system to work, or has what we've just seen only been possible since you joined in the research?"

James pressed the screen for the next image and a crude hour glass shaped device was shown on the screen. A sepia photo looking like a cheap elaborate prop used in a B horror movie. He sized it up to fill the screen and continued.

"Yes and no. Yes he succeeded but the consequence of his design was only fully discovered by himself and that was why he fled. Let's first off explain the initial submarine work and what you have just witnessed inside the hydro pod and then we'll discuss the byproduct of Granddad's invention, which is why we're here today."

James changed the screen to a basic diagram of what the internal structure of the pod itself looked like and how it connected together.

"To collect the oxygen from the water, the system essentially makes a whirlpool in the glass bulbs. The air migrates to the centre of the vortex. The dense water migrates to the outside and the relatively light air bubbles move to the centre where the metal prong collector removes the gas pumping it from the system, thus providing clean and enriched oxygen indefinitely."

Charlie was fiddling with the enormous screen zooming into the picture and moving it along. James impatiently swatted Charlie's hands from the screen like a misbehaving child.

"Originally Dad created a single glass chamber with the rotating anemometer to create the whirlpool. However it simply did not produce enough oxygen to sustain a submarine. So instead of sizing the glass bulb exponentially he added the second chamber, thus looking like a giant hourglass. He discovered purely by accident after fitting one of the anemometers round the wrong way, that if you reverse one of the two vortexes inside, so the turbulence is in effect fighting against each other causing more air to migrate, producing not twice the amount of oxygen as he calculated but more than ten times the amount, he had cracked the problem by making a simple error." James smiled, so many breakthroughs in science were caused by error and the mistake made by his father had made the project monumental. "However when Dad turned the power unit off it continued to operate, he pulled all the main feeds away from the unit but the system remained self-perpetuating!"

Lizzie looked at James. "What do you mean, self-perpetuating?"

Ash looked at Lizzie all excited. "The system fed itself; the unit somehow kept itself continually working. No intervention was needed once it was running."

Dan looked towards Ash and then back to James, with a look of confusion. "I thought perpetual motion was hypothetical. Nothing can maintain perpetual motion? I thought it went against the laws of Physics as we know it?"

James looked at Dan with a proud smile. Dan may have chosen a different path from science but he certainly had the keen analytical mind of his parentage. "That education paid off Dan, you're right and that was how your Grandfather tackled it. He removed the water from the bulbs and the engine stopped, as it were."

"What do you mean engine?" Dan looked confused now.

"Well an engine's a strange way of looking at it; let's try the word cell or generator instead? If you remove the central pipe work ..." He pointed to the diagram on the screen. "... inside the centre is a third round chamber where the glass tubes connect. This is what Dad and I have been working towards all these years. What he realised is that through his blunder and without getting extremely technical and vying to far into the world of quantum field theory, or specifically quantum electrodynamics, the space where the spinning vortexes meet produce a vacuum polarisation. That is the product of a background electromagnetic field, inadvertently producing enough current to back feed the system, thus producing perpetual motion and running the anemometers indefinitely."

Dan looked at the pod in disbelief concentrating on what he had just listened to, breaking the data down in his head. "So what you're saying is, from an initial concept of producing clean oxygen for a submarine,

Granddad managed to build a self sustaining electrical current? Is that right? Like a never ending battery?"

"Pretty much spot on Dan, although it's far more complicated. This pic on the screen ..." James moved the image back to the grainy sepia photo of his father's original design. "... this is the original concept that was shown to the military. It did what they wanted it to except it was not sustainable because of the way it worked, or at least that was the way Dad demonstrated it. They never knew about the secondary functionality of the technology. One of his colleagues questioned him about it afterwards and Dad told him that he could not reproduce what they had seen in the lab during the previous experiment. He lied. He could reproduce it but this Eureka moment was a turning point in energy production. It was a free commodity and if harnessed correctly, could save the planet."

Lizzie could finally see where this was heading. "So basically this machine produces not only clean oxygen from water, which is sustaining the habitat we're in, it also produces clean electricity?"

Matt loved Lizzie, even at school she could always sum up anything technical in five words or less making it sound far less dramatic or exciting. "Bingo."

Lizzie was shocked. "You mean there's absolutely no waste, or damaging radiation, or anything?"

James looked really smug. "Nope, just breathable oxygen, clear hot water, oh and a massive self perpetuating energy source!"

Ash also finally felt like wallowing in the glory. "Just think, a small unit could be used to power anything such as an electric car, purely from water. Or a unit as big as inside the hydro pod could, when fully utilised, replace the electrical output of an entire nuclear power station!"

Dan looked at her disbelieving this final statement. "You mean to say the power output of one of these things would be as big as a nuclear power station?"

"No Dan, it can be exponentially greater!" She gushed with excitement. "Lizzie, I told you the technology would change the world. It will be clean, more efficient and most importantly, free!"

They all stood there looking at the pod in awe. Suddenly they could see its perceived value to the world; any government controlling such monumental technology had the chance to change the course of history.

It would be the world's saviour because green house gas emissions would be virtually eliminated over night from coal fired power stations and other pollutants. Nuclear reactors could be decommissioned for the ultimate Holy Grail; clean sustainable energy.

64

McAdams had equalized the lifting bag to free float effortlessly; it drifted perfectly along the outer length of the hull, propelled by gently kicking his flippers. He was gradually advancing the port side towards the stern of the wreck. More by luck than judgement he discovered the opening Dan, Charlie and Lizzie had entered the lab through earlier in the evening.

He, unlike Dan who had spent hours sweating over the plans and blueprints, assumed it was just another part of the ship because of its perfect precision in the side of the hull leading to the corridor. The cut outs, which were savagely hacked and cut from the hull bore no resemblance to this inlet, therefore feeling like an original part of the ship. He paid little attention to its interior. He drifted his kit into the opening with the idea of continuing the search further towards the stern without its hindrance.

The sled holding his equipment led on the corridor floor; he deflated as much air out as possible from the lifting bag and removed it, so as not to disrupt him in the future. He uncovered the equipment and unpacked several items, laying them across the floor. Many of them were in waterproof hard cases, containing technical equipment. Other containers included explosives and magnetic timers which could be attached to metal surfaces, punching holes through metal walls if needed.

Time was of the essence and he could ill afford to waste it on gaining access. Ultimately the worst case scenario was to destroy everything, everyone in his way and access the technical data or equipment at a later date. A retrieval specialist team could be here and strip anything underwater in less than twelve hours; of course this was worst case scenario. He was hoping to get in covertly, retrieve the data and leave with minimal collateral damage.

After repacking what he considered the important items, he turned to head back out of the opening to continue his search along the ship, however as he did, a green glow illuminating the far end of the corridor caught his attention. It was very feint but looked surreal deep down in this environment. The colour reminded him of a diver's glow stick. He looked along the passageway ahead, swimming towards the light.

As he moved along the corridor and headed deeper into the ship, he realised he was unarmed again and had nothing to defend himself. It could be a trap? The glow became stronger, picking out the silhouette of an open doorway directly ahead. He waited, unsure as to whether to continue or return back to the sled and get a weapon. There was no sign of movement, just the feint demonic glow of green neon, an alien colour. As his eyes adjusted in the gloom he could pick out shapes through the doorway. Was he imagining things or could he see a bar?

Curiosity started to get the better; he swam on down the corridor switching off his own dive light, cautiously entering the room. It was empty, except as far as a wreck was concerned, it was not. He was shocked the room still had its entire contents left. He believed like everyone, the ship was supposed to have been fully stripped. It was amazing. He had dived many wrecks before but this was simply second to none. He was surprised he had never heard or read anything about this. As a dive site, it was something many would like to witness. This room alone would be infamous amongst wreck divers.

It suddenly dawned on him; no one spoke of this because it was not normally open to anyone. His heart leapt, this was the way in, somehow this was the access to the underwater habitat. Like the Panic Room, this room was built to act like smoke and mirrors.

A room designed for total deception, to hide its true motive in case someone managed to get this far. He instinctively knew he was in the right place. He had to find the hidden room behind the walls, it was essential. Swimming back up the corridor to the sled, he retrieved the piece of equipment he had originally used at the Morris house. It seemed so long ago, so much had happened since then, part of him wished he had never read Daniel Morris' file.

The thermal imaging camera was an expensive piece of kit and fortunately water proof; it was the one thing he knew of, or at least hoped, would find the entrance. He entered the bar. Turning the camera on, he pointed it at the walls, scanning for a heat signature. Much to his dismay, the coloured screen was awash with dark blue and green outlines as he rotated round the room.

Anything hotter than the surrounding area would show in warmer colours depending on temperature, such as red through to white, as the heat intensity increased. He impatiently crossed to the notice board where the room's neon glow was illuminating from. He stared at the plaque. He knew it was a clue but had little understanding of its significance. Instead he scanned across the plaque with the camera, the little LEDs individually glowed on the screen as they warmed within their blades' protective housing.

The numerical pad to the right needed a ten digit input so there could be around ten billion combinations. Using his laptop on the surface he could easily crack the code; however being underwater made these things far more difficult and he did not have the time to crack such an expansive code.

The thermal camera could pick nothing up behind the notice board, no heat signatures from bodies or other anomalies. He was beginning to get frustrated. Was this yet another dead end? Had the Morris family outsmarted him yet again? He spun round in the bar waving the thermal camera before him like a weapon, holding it in both hands like a gun.

As he aimed the camera randomly around the room. Inadvertently he pointed it towards the doorway, stopping and looking at the small screen intensely. The doorway was picked out, like an indelible mark against the dark blue of the interior walls. The exterior corridor in contrast, through the door aperture, was bright green. He pointed the camera back into the room. The water temperature in the room was far colder. He moved forward to the door, watching the screen intensely. The water temperature was far warmer in the corridor. It randomly moved across the LCD display reminiscent to a dynamic green Mandelbrot.

The top of his screen was warmer so he angled the camera to the roof of the corridor. The image on the screen showed plumes of clouds seeping around the edge of the corridor ceiling, looking like contrails you see free floating in the sky after a plane has passed overhead.

Excited, he removed his glove placing his hand in front of the sensor of the camera. A warm orange and red shape appeared on the screen, he moved it through the trails he could see on the camera screen. The difference in temperature was astounding as he passed through the cottonous clouds. Along the edge of the roof, where the ceiling met the walls, there were small outlets which were letting much warmer water seep into the corridor.

Checking the screen of the thermal camera, using a particular mode, he took a screen grab of the corridor's upright wall temperature. Storing it on an internal disk, he then moved the camera to look at the ceiling, taking another screen grab. Comparing the two, by wiping between the two images, there was a notable temperature difference between the ceiling and the walls.

McAdams placed his ungloved hand against the ceiling. It was warm to the touch, very warm. Gradually moving down the surface of the roof, towards where the corridor narrowed from the T junction, as his hand passed over a ridge, the steel instantly turned cold. He took a third screen grab of this area. On screen was a physical dividing line where the steel was obviously several degrees warmer compared to the corridor's ceiling where it narrowed.

McAdams swam back into the bar aiming the camera at the ceiling, tracing his way perpendicularly away from the entrance. As he moved towards the back wall of the bar, the ceiling changed temperature, graduating to an almost insipid yellow. The back ceiling of the bar was very warm, almost hot to the touch. There was something above the bar and somewhere there had to be an entrance.

He realised he had to get above the ceiling. Placing the camera on the bar, McAdams swam as fast as he could back down the corridor. Grabbing the lifting bag he reattached it to the sled, shortening the attaching hooks, so it could be transported along the corridor.

He was lost in his endeavours re-inflating the lifting bag and at first did not see a white light gradually creeping up the corridor towards him. There was a low rumble as he felt a warm rush of water rush past his body, the temperature in his wetsuit rose substantially. The corridor was illuminated in a bright white light almost blinding after the impenetrable darkness which enveloped him since the start of his dive. He watched dumbfounded as the light intensity increased spreading its reach along the corridor, like the rising sun slowly, creeping across the ground.

Suddenly from the ceiling of the corridor, a figure came into view and promptly disappeared into the bar. McAdams briskly pushed the sled down the corridor as quickly as he could. He left the lifting bag resting on the ceiling of the corridor, just before the edge of the opened ceiling. The corridor was illuminated by millions of LEDs and the water spilling down from the cavernous room above was crystal clear and extremely warm.

Peering into the bar room, the figure was at the notice board. He could see the figure was realigning the plaque, removing the items that were illuminated with the LEDs, as each was removed the LED extinguished. Finished, the figure closed the notice board.

The figure turned to leave but stopped, instead crossing to the bar top, picking up the thermal imaging camera McAdams had abandoned several minutes earlier. Fuck. McAdams panicked, he quickly swam back to the sled. Hauling himself through the straps, he pushed against the edge of the ceiling and the lifting bag rolled into the opening. McAdams looked over his shoulder to see the figure slowly heading towards the doorway with the camera in both hands, paying little heed to what was in front of him.

McAdams looked up, his view was obscured by the lifting bag, he was blind. He cranked the valve full open, the compressed canister exploded air inside the lifting bag which took off at speed as he clung to the sled in terror.

The ascent was too fast, he knew it was too quick, how far did it go? For the first time in his life he found himself praying to God, praying he would not get the bends.

The sled disappeared through the vault roof just as Matt came back into the corridor, paying little attention to the bubbles left in McAdams' wake. He pulled the door shut, waiting and listening as he pulled the proximity of the knives away from the door, reactivating the solenoids and locking the bar shut again, sealing it from the outer world.

Matt swam back into the space above the corridor. As he did, he pressed a handle towards the end of the runway strip. The retracted roof of the corridor started to glide back to its original position and he casually made his way back to the habitat, with the replica knives and newly acquired thermal imaging camera in tow.

If he had looked up, Matt would have seen a compressed air propelled sled spiralling out of control upwards with an impressive turn of speed heading towards the hangar roof. McAdams hung on for dear life.

65

Ashley had a smug look about her, exactly the same as when they were at school after an exam, knowing full well she was going to have full marks unlike Matt, Dan and Lizzie who would rather have gnawed their own hands off than sit through yet another test. Ashley however thrived on them.

Ashley was a difficult character to judge. She was withdrawn from all except those that were close, such as her family. She found it difficult to relate to strangers and strike up a conversation at random and even with friends and family she was not the sort to nonchalantly chat about the inclement weather. She was most at ease when working on something complicated and technical. In company she only relaxed when the four of them were together. Lizzie was the exception. They were best friends and Lizzie was as close to family as could be.

Ash was the spitting image of her mother, albeit on a somewhat thinner frame which was most likely inherited from her father's genes. She was incredibly thin, almost flat chested, with little or no hips. From behind she always looked like one of the guys. Especially as she always had short hair. However since being in the habitat, her hair had grown much longer. She had accrued the most beautiful ebony locks which cascaded and shone against her delicate white face. Her lips were ruby red, giving the impression of a prominent figure from a fairy tale.

Lizzie gushed. "You know Ash you look absolutely stunning. Your hair really suits you at that length, you look gorgeous."

Ash was never comfortable at taking personal compliments, her academia record yes but never about herself.

"Ya think?" She blushed, her white skin glowed against the stark environment of the lab. She quickly changed the subject. "I'm so glad you found us, although I'm not proud about the situation or events leading up to you being here."

Her voice cracked, her confidence slipped and the façade fell. "Oh Liz, I so wanted to tell you that last night we went out. I knew you'd be able to keep the secret but I was scared of putting you in danger." She bowed her head as a lone tear fell from her hazel eyes, also inherited from her mother.

Lizzie pulled a chair next to her putting her arm round her shoulder. "It's all right Ash, I understand."

"Do you? Do you really? I wrote so many letters explaining what we had done and why. I just never ever managed to send them." Ashley pulled out the bottom drawer of her desk retrieving a familiar leather writing set Lizzie had given her as a gift when she headed to University. She wrote once a month without fail, sometimes twice, detailing everyday humdrum life and exploits at University.

Lizzie loved to receive the letters, it was something they both enjoyed. It was a ritual they practised and the letter would be replied to usually within the week, so it was like a day to day diary of life and of what they had been up to. It was the kind of things they would talk about when together, some serious, many just silly but far too often they concerned family and life. It kept them in contact and close, for some reason the pair of them loved it because it was far more intimate than email.

After Ash's disappearance, Lizzie had reverted to writing in a journal not wanting to break the routine, spilling her innermost thoughts, general day to day emotions and feelings to paper. She always felt the words were somewhat empty considering no one else would probably ever read them, even though she still addressed them to Ash. Their conversational letters backwards and forwards always seemed to have purpose, questioning life and love and of course it was great to receive something in the post.

Ash opened the writer's set. Lizzie could see the monogrammed paper and envelopes were long since used up but there was a half written letter to Lizzie which was dated in the last week. Ash then retrieved a box and gave it to Lizzie, who lifted the lid. Inside were literally hundreds of envelopes, each one addressed to Hestia, her Greek God, it was how they titled them.

Lizzie was physically pained. They had lost so much time, but in this box was the day to day ramblings of their time apart. She could read them to find out exactly the emotions and fears her best friend had been through. She started to well up also but smiled with excitement, the time would never be lost because she could read all about it.

"When we get home I'll give you my journal. I started it after your funeral; it feels funny saying that now. Every page of it is written to Athena."

Ash looked at Lizzie in astonishment, the pair of them had tears streaming down their cheeks as they hugged, both smiling. Dan walked back into the lab from the operations habitat, Lizzie and Ash parted, hurriedly wiping their tears. Dan stopped as if embarrassed for walking in on an obvious intimate moment between the pair. Lizzie gave him a loving look so he knew he was okay to continue. Ash picked up on it, digging Lizzie in the ribs, like a couple of teenagers they giggled.

Lizzie looked around, expecting Matt to follow. "Where's Matt?"

"I just helped him suit up, he's gone out to reset the bar, retrieve the knives from the plaque and lock everything down."

Ash looked at the clock. "Actually yeah, we need to get the systems shut down and back into silent running mode. It'll be sun up soon and the wreck divers will be about."

Ash started to flick a few buttons on the control panel in front of her. The pod rose from the water pit, the vortexes inside the glass bulbs were spinning and undulating around the core and the glow diminished from inside.

Dan looked at the pod and then turned to Ash. "You said earlier the pod could replace a nuclear power station's power output. How can something so small produce so much power?"

Ash was back in her element, talking facts, the brief emotional reunion with Lizzie had passed. "Dad can explain the technicalities of it far better than I." Lizzie groaned rolling her eyes, knowing full well Ash could easily explain it and now probably would. Ash realised the technical theories and practices were probably way beyond Dan and Lizzie's comprehension and more than likely they would not care about them, just how it works. She felt deflated, it was like high school science class all over again, reluctantly dumbing down the answers for her classmates.

"Think of the energy in a battery, it is potential energy until the circuit is completed, and then, most probably it will become heat; unless part of it becomes light, or sound, or something else. If a nuclear generator is churning away, and no power is being drawn, it will have to work less and it will consume less energy. However they are highly inefficient as they are constantly at work. So, if the electricity is not used up as it is generated, then basically it is wasted because they have to keep generating the power, regardless of whether it is actually being used or not."

She looked at Lizzie and Dan to see if they were following. "Well basically as the pod system has more energy drawn, it generates exactly enough for what is attached, the pod is very efficient. The feedback status colour indicates what state it is running at, cyan means its barely making anything, just enough to self perpetuate. We finally managed to hone the system to output the equivalent of a nuclear reactor. It tends to be almost white at those outputs but we were concerned our internal systems would not take the power output. The pod works, we are now ready to take it topside and release it to the world."

"So is that why you have taken delivery of another submarine, to get it out of here?"

"Yes."

"Is it really ready?"

"The pod is as ready as it will ever be and needs to be used and tested to its maximum unknown output. We simply can't do anymore down here in this environment. Plus we're all going a bit crazy with cabin fever, it's time to leave."

Dan looked round the lab, peering through in to the computer room at the back. "Where are Uncle James, Aunt Pat and Charlie?"

Lizzie looked up from thumbing through her letters, she had phased out somewhere around battery. "Oh they're in the living room catching up properly." This in laymen's terms meant drinking. "I think Dad is already half cut."

"Yeah along with my Dad, he's hardly drunk since being down here; our fathers together are a bad influence on each other you know!" Ash laughed.

Matt stomped back in to the lab in his wetsuit, water running out onto the crisp white floor and dumped the thermal imaging camera on the worktop. "I think you left something expensive in the bar."

Dan picked it up looking at the camera. His face dropped, without a word clutching the camera he ran through to the living quarters to find Charlie. Matt, Ash and Lizzie looked at each other but said nothing.

"Matt, can you check the valve please while you have your wetsuit on? The water has been running a little warmer over the last few days and I wanted to know whether there might be a problem."

Matt scowled in Ash's direction, sometimes he just felt like the hired help round this place. Even though he designed the habitat and kept all the systems operational, it was still like he was an employee instead of one of the family. He went through the lock out chamber, ducking beneath the raised pod barely making a splash into the water pit, disappearing from view. Ash continued pressing a multiple of buttons across the operations desk and the pods mini vortexes began to slow down inside, until eventually they each collapsed in on themselves as the energy dissipated and the water became static.

Matt surfaced in a swift energetic movement, turned and seated himself on the edge of the pit. He held down a push button speaker system on the metal wall behind which could communicate to all parts of the habitat, he pushed the link between the soundproof hydro pod and the lab, his voice echoed round the lab walls.

"The valve seems to be only opening at roughly 95% efficiency; I suspect that'll be what is causing the water temperature to rise. I opened it manually and it seems to have overcome the sticking point, so next time you cycle up let me know the temperature. If it's still slightly high I'll send the ROV in via the moon pool to see what is happening while under pressure, I reckon that'll fix it though, just a bit sticky."

Without warning a claxon sounded deeply throughout the habitat, its deep reverberating voice echoed off the walls of the lab. The strobe lights flashed red on the outside of the cubical. The automated flushing procedure was in operation. Matt screamed into the mic. "What did you do?"

Ash grabbed the mic from her console shouting back. "Nothing, I've literally only lifted the gear and shut the hydro pod systems down." Matt looked at her in disbelief, thinking she must have done something wrong during shutdown to cause an automated vent.

Ash screamed into her microphone. "Well don't just sit there with your feet in the fuckin' water like you're on vacation, get out before the dump valve reverses the flow and you get locked in!"

Matt exited the hydro pod shutting the inner chamber door, just in time; there was a loud rush of air expelled from inside, the door automatically locked. The pressure valve released externally and a savage undulating torrent of water started to rise up the inside of the chamber, gradually filling the hydro pod from floor to ceiling.

He exited the lock out chamber back to the lab, cursing in Ash's direction. "What the fuck were you tryin' to do, kill me?"

Ash looked at him with a deadpan expression and back at the control panel as if looking for an explanation. "It wasn't me, honest; I only ran through the shutdown protocols." She glanced at her watch. "The hydro pod shouldn't flush for a few hours yet, so what the hell has caused it. None of the systems are reading any errors and there are no temperature anomalies or electromagnetic feedback."

The three of them stood and stared as the entire hydro pod filled from floor to ceiling with water. The claxon continued to sound throughout the habitat, the red lights flashed warning of the vent flush. It seemed to last forever and was deafening.

66

Dan hurried into the living habitat, through the connecting armadillo, down the incline from the lab and into the lounge area, where Aunt Pat, Uncle James and Charlie were laughing, having a great time. The expensive whiskey was flowing and it looked just like old times.

Dan stood there, feeling lost, like he did as a child, not sure whether to interrupt or wait until addressed. Charlie was laughing but he looked at Dan quizzically. "What's wrong Dan, you look like you've seen a ghost?"

"I have." He held out the thermal camera to Charlie, who put his whiskey tumbler down on the table in front of him taking the camera.

Aunt Pat rose from the couch crossing to the drinks cabinet. "Do you want a drink Dan, or do you still not drink."

"No I'm fine thanks."

"No you don't drink or not at the present time?"

"No thank you, I do drink I'm just not presently in the mood for anything."

"I can make you some tea; Aunt Susan sent down some loose tea. We still have some sophistication, even if we are several fathoms below."

Dan looked away from Charlie who was turning the camera around in his hands. "I'm fine thanks honest. Don't you recognise it?" He said impatiently, he needed confirmation.

Charlie knew by Dan's insistence that he should but he honestly did not recognise the camera at all. "I can't place it, why?" He handed it back.

Unlike Charlie, Dan had watched the CCTV footage of Uncle Mike's and Aunt Susan's murder several times, he knew it inside out.

"It's the camera from the internal CCTV footage."

"What CCTV footage?"

"The footage from the house, the stuff I showed you in the Panic Room, the internal cameras capturing ..." He looked up at Uncle James and Aunt Pat, who were listening intently. "... Their murder!" He said it through clenched teeth as if trying not to say the words.

Charlie suddenly registered what Dan was saying and looked at the camera in a whole new light, his mind stretched back to that day and the grisly viewing. "It can't be."

"It is, I'm telling you."

Uncle James sat up, he realised something monumental was happening, hating not knowing anything of importance. "What is it Dan?" He reached out with his hand and Dan passed the object to him.

"Oh it's a thermal imaging camera, where did that come from? We could do with one of these in the lab to check the heat signature of the pod."

The last part of the sentence hit Dan like a lightning bolt, he said quietly. "He's here, he's found us."

"Who is Dan?" Aunt Pat said in her usual charismatic way.

"Uncle Mike and Aunt Susan's killer!" He said it with such venom they felt a chill run through them.

Charlie looked at him concerned, now he realised what it was. His mind started to recall the horrific images he witnessed that day. "Where did you find the camera Dan?"

"Matt just brought it in, he went out to close the underwater bar and found it, he thought it was ours. He must have been out there; he must have followed us or found the corridor leading to the bar?"

Charlie sat up concerned. "Would he have been able to get in?"

"He could have followed Matt but there was obviously no one else in the chamber when he came back in the habitat. I think Matt would've noticed."

"Maybe the guy has realised there is more to the bar than just the fittings and has gone topside to get more equipment to open it or something?" Charlie was trying to rationalise the situation.

Uncle James sat forward turning the camera on, he skimmed through a few of the images, stopping on the most recent. They all crowded around the tiny LCD screen, looking over his shoulder.

He quickly scanned through the images stored on the camera, which were few. Aunt Pat did not understand? "What are they?"

Uncle James pointed at the screens image. "Well basically the camera measures heat in the area it is pointed at, the darker blue the colour, the colder the area. Whoever has been using this has been searching for heat signatures."

"What like a body?"

"No." In unison they all looked at Dan. "Yeah he could be looking for the heat signature of us but more than likely he's searching for the technology, the pod, that's gonna produce a massive heat signature."

"Are you definitely sure you've seen this camera before Dan?" James finally understood the seriousness of the implication.

Dan nodded slowly, definite in his head. "Yes, I managed to reconstruct the internal cameras footage at home. I mirrored the drives when I installed it, purely as a backup and the perpetrator only took the original drives. I showed them to Charlie, we both saw him using the camera in the study, before …" His voice trailed off trying not to relive the memory of his Aunt and Uncle's death again, although it would be visible for a very long time.

James knew it was hard, it was his brother but there were far more pressing matters at hand, so interrupted, saving his pain. "So this guy is definitely looking for the lab? Maybe he has more knowledge than we've given anyone credit for."

"Or is it just that he knows there is something technical but does not know what and used the camera as matter of coincidence?"

James nodded. "I don't really believe in coincidences." He scrolled through the images, looking at them trying to make sense of the swirling colours, finally giving up and listing the details and their individual date stamps. James looked at them stunned; everyone peering over his shoulder; also reading in disbelief the details on screen.

Alongside each thumb nail was the date stamp, more importantly the time. All four of them looked at each other slightly alarmed. Aunt Pat broke the silence, voicing what everyone else was thinking.

"Can that be correct James? The date stamp is today's date but within the last twenty minutes. Everyone was already inside the habitat by then!"

The room was deathly quiet, the four of them realising the danger was real and imminent. The threat seemed removed from the present, yet they knew they had to act, but how? Was he out there? Did he know how to get in and what does he hope to achieve?

The words from the government report he stole from the super computer in Special Ops reverberated through Dan's mind - when the proprietary source was operational, they would take control and eliminate all bystanders.

Suddenly the lights dimmed throughout the living space, a claxon shrieked into life within the quarters and red strobe lights flashed archaically. James was the first to jump. "Fuck!"

Dan glanced round the room, startled by the sound. "What's going on?"

"Someone is coming in through the moon pool, exactly the way you guys did!"

James ran through to the kitchen then back through carrying the shot gun he had aimed at Dan, Lizzie and Charlie several hours previous, at the same time trying to unsuccessfully load the barrels. Charlie and Dan dashed after him following as fast as they could. Aunt Pat hauled herself from the couch and trundled in their wake, twisting her ankle on a fallen shell, sending her gin and tonic hurtling to the ground.

Ash heard her father running through the tunnel, she turned to defend herself thinking she was in trouble, but only managed to stammer the words I don't know as James streaked past, closely followed by Dan hot on his heels, Charlie and then finally her mother looking worried and limping heavily.

She had spotted the gun in his hand and looked at Matt. "It wasn't me Matt; someone must be coming through the moon pool."

Matt ran after them. "Come on you two." All three of them dashed up the armadillo into operations, James was stood with the gun aimed at the hydraulic door. Impatiently he barked orders.

"Silence the fuckin' alarm, Matt!"

Matt pushed a cut off switch on the wall behind them outside the computer room. Although the sound stopped, the red strobes continued to flash either side of the door. They watched, waiting for the pumps to reverse and the water level fall on the opposite side of the hydraulic door. The only indication was an acrylic tube from floor to ceiling, with a small white plastic ball on the inside, looking like an over scaled version of a water indicator on a kettle.

All seven of them watched silently as the water was pumped from the moon pool. The ball descended, reaching the bottom it dropped into a U bend, disappearing from view through the solid metal wall. As it did the red strobes stopped flashing and turned green. The moon pool was at its correct level, the door could be opened.

Nothing happened. They waited, no one attempted to open the door from the inside. James was a little unsure, like the rest of them, how to continue.

"Matt, open the door and stand aside. We don't know who or what we are dealing with. The rest of you get back against the walls."

They all did as they were told, the women quicker than the men but all knew it was important. Matt looked to James, who nodded his head. Matt depressed the lock out switch. The water tight hydraulic door hissed slowly, sliding back into the wall to the left. James stepped forward, pushing the barrel through the widening slot of the doorway.

"Whoever you are, we know you're in there, come out with your hands up. We mean you no harm but be warned, I will shoot to kill if I have to."

67

"I'd lower your weapon if I were you. Unlike some, I don't make empty threats. I will not hesitate to kill any of you."

The voice came from behind; none of them expected it and spun round surprised to be looking into the barrel of a gun. The weapon protruded from the doorway of the workshop. The features of the man holding the gun were shadowed in darkness, the only illumination came from the operations room lighting in the door well.

Everyone instinctively held their hands in the air, except Dan who recognised the voice instantly. James still held the shot gun, more in shock than with the intent of using it.

"I will not ask again." The gun motioned to James to drop the weapon. James placed the gun on the ground pushing it away with his foot into the middle of the room. Jon Doe stepped into the light from the shadows of the workshop in his wetsuit.

Dan lunged forward, fists clenched and raised, face distorted with rage. "You murdering sack of shit!"

McAdams hardly flinched as he side stepped Dan's clumsy charge and expertly cracked the butt of his hand gun on the side of Dan's neck. He crumpled to a heap on the floor. Dan lay motionless. McAdams sent a wild savage kick into his ribcage. Bending down, grabbing a fistful of Dan's hair he lifted him several inches off the ground.

"Fucking hurts doesn't it!" He sneered into his face, covering him in spit. Dan was face to face with the empty callous black eyes of Jon Doe. He threw him back to the floor. Dan lay there winded, clutching his ribs and in excruciating pain.

James spoke, shakily; shocked by the sudden violence but more so by the absent smile on the tormentor's face as he inflicted pain, it was obvious he enjoyed it.

"Who are you and what do you want here?"

McAdams' polite mannerisms returned; the same as when Dan interviewed him back in London. He flashed the ladies a smile of alarming warmth and very theatrically bowed.

"Forgive me, how remiss, I should have introduced myself sooner, or I should have gotten an old acquaintance to introduce me instead. It's very bad form you know Daniel." His heel flashed backwards into Dan's rib cage one more time and Lizzie lunged forward to protect him.

McAdams cocked his head on an angle as if weighing up the girl. He looked in pity at her, motioning with his hand to attend Dan who still lay winded on the floor, as if the situation was all his fault, continuing as though nothing had happened.

"Yes Daniel and I are old friends we go way back. I'm sure he's mentioned me. We recently met up again in London, my name is John. However not Doe as Dan has referred to me in the past, my name is John McAdams. Like your good selves, I'm of Scottish decent, but still resolutely British." He saluted in mock fashion.

James scowled. "So what do you want Mr McAdams?"

"So formal, please, we're all friends here, call me John."

"I assure you sir, you're no friend of mine nor this family. I'll ask again, what do you want from us?"

McAdams shook his head, the smile faltered somewhat, his eyes darkened. "Such disappointing hospitality, I expected much more. However under such difficult circumstances, I guess pleasantries can be somewhat over rated although I would very much like to know who each of you are. Although James ..." He rather over emphasised James' name simply to provoke a reaction, and ultimately because he had not been given the informality of having that pleasure. "... The pictures in your file and your publicity photo on the jacket of your published books, I must say you seem far less, academic, in the flesh."

He turned to Charlie and then Lizzie in turn, who was still nursing Dan. "I know all about you two, so you can remain quiet for a few minutes while we all introduce ourselves. You." He pointed at Ash who was actually looking paler than normal, if that were possible. "You my dear, who are you?"

Ash swallowed hard and tried to speak which at first was difficult. "Ashley Morris."

"Ah, your daughter James, interesting, the same academic passion as the rest of the family. Brains as well as beauty, you must be very proud, a chip off the same Scotch block. A pleasure my dear." He took a few steps forward towards Pat who was stood to Ash's right. "You must be the long suffering wife of James, Patricia I assume?"

Pat nodded. "I would hardly call it long suffering and I prefer Pat, but you can call me Mrs Morris."

McAdams smiled looking at James. "Passion and loyalty hides a keen mind I can tell. You know they always say behind every great man ..." He let the words trail off, Dan was getting up from the floor helped by Lizzie. "I suggest you stand back against the wall, next to Matt. I assume its Matt isn't it? That would make you the fabulous four who disappeared, lost to sea, missing, presumed dead. You know it's amazing but then I guess with all the mishaps that have befallen the Morris family, which are tragic, very tragic, I guess no one would even second guess something as elaborate as this wonderful set up!"

He motioned around the habitat. "During my career, I have seen some astonishing sights and witnessed many wonderful things. However I have to say, what you have achieved here is simply amazing. The extraordinary lengths at which you have gone to, to disappear and hide the family's work. I am truly inspired, if only everyone was as passionate and proactive as you, then the world would be a far better place."

He darkened slightly; obviously his mind had wandered to the mission in hand. The pleasantness in his voice instantly disappeared, a coldness replacing the warmth. "I take it the technology has been perfected?"

McAdams scanned the faces in the room, as if trying to visualise each of their innermost thoughts. "I take it from your silence you have indeed managed to succeed in finishing your Grandfather's work."

Silence.

"Fabulous." He beamed at them in turn, a malicious grin spreading across his face. No one spoke. "Come now, no need to be shy. You must be very proud of what you have achieved? It has taken nearly half a century to perfect. You really should want to show off your hard work, think of this as a test run. I'm your first potential client; pretend you need to convince me it's working so I can give you the accolades you truly deserve for your dogged determination in beating the government system." He smiled menacingly and motioned with his gun that they all head into the lab.

They trudged in single file into the lab, like a school outing, Lizzie helping Dan and McAdams the teacher, bringing up the rear keeping them all in line with his jovial patter. McAdams stopped, looking round the lab, momentarily scanning inside the office at the opposite end to the hydro pod as he passed.

"Well, well, this is all very, very impressive. I take my hat off to you. Tell me Matt, the design for the underwater habitat was it all your own work or did the lovely Simon help you at all along the way?" He mocked the word lovely, camping it up, at the mention of Simon's name his wrist holding the gun fell limp in mid air.

Whether by instinct or simply by the nature of understanding people, McAdams swung his gun level with Matt's chest. He could see Matt was seething, ready to pounce as he took a step forward, McAdams willed him on. A feint flicker in his cold eyes showed something other than a dead soul. What everyone saw was excitement, this was a game.

McAdams wanted someone to die, he wanted to shock them. He wanted to give them a death, only then would he earn true respect like so many other times. The shock they had from seeing Dan beaten to the ground and kicked had somewhat receded. Someone please step out of line, let's spill some blood.

Matt held firm, he wanted to kill him, he knew from the moment he clapped eyes on the man as he ventured from the shadows, he wanted to slowly kill him. This thing who stood before him had murdered his parents plus his soul mate. He was not a man, he was an animal. Matt had kept Simon in the dark about the habitat to protect him, like so many others, but the family had let him down. He was dead because of them.

Dan grabbed Matt's shoulder instinctively knowing what he felt, pulling him back into the group. Lizzie grabbed his hand, he gripped it tightly, Ash entwined her fingers holding his other, cupping his hand with both of her own.

James stepped forward. "What are you planning to do?"

"My orders are to retrieve the data and designs to the technology. I'm assuming that everything I need is now in this room and the computer room's data banks. However I think being as though you're already officially dead, I have two options. Those who are closely linked to the proprietary hardware may survive, albeit a prisoner to Her Majesty's government. Or I can kill you all and have the entire habitat, including the hardware and computing software, removed in less than twenty four hours." He shrugged his shoulders as if to say it did not matter. "To be honest, I've not really had enough time to compile a full plan, I am, how shall we say, flying by the seat of my pants!"

"No." All eyes fell on Dan as he walked forward defiantly.

"No what? I don't understand Daniel. You are in no position to predict or even tell me the future."

"You may be right, but I do know a few things about your situation John, you don't mind if I call you John do you?"

McAdams shifted his stance, anger flashing in his eyes; he aimed the gun holding it with both hands into Dan's face. Dan stared down the barrel but did not flinch.

"John McAdams, if that is indeed truly your name. You were caught red handed. Your status has been compromised, you've been flagged and your face is now on record which means it will have gone live in every intelligence agencies' database and every search engine throughout the western world. I'm pretty confident to say your career, if you can call it that, is ruined, much like you ruined mine. You have no orders, I know as well as you do, you're flying by the seat of your pants to what end? Why are you doing this? Is it revenge because I caught you, or is it simpler than that? For reinstatement?"

As McAdams snarled, Dan shook his head and laughed, mocking him. "It'll never happen, you're on a mission without orders in direct conflict with protocol. You're a lone wolf operating without clearance from your superiors. Do you really think whatever you achieve down here will truly get you back in?" Dan shook his head in mock exasperation and laughed.

McAdams raised the gun and pressed it against his forehead stopping its movement. Everyone gasped. Dan did not flinch, he stopped laughing but smiled and staring in to the cold dead eyes once more of McAdams. He pushed his head harder against the barrel of the gun defiantly. This time though he had a name and did not feel at so much of a disadvantage compared to their first conversation back at Scotland Yard in London. He understood more than he cared about the psyche standing before him, he had profiled so many like him, he thought he was unique but he was not.

McAdams was cocky; he needed you to know why he did what he did. He thrived on it. It was what made him who he was, he needed to explain and until that point of final clarity Dan unconsciously knew they were safe.

"So tell me John, how did you know about my family? How did you know about the Morris history when New Scotland Yard had no idea and ultimately personally what I want to know is; how you knew my mother was murdered?"

68

McAdams remained silent; his mind was racing trying to work out a plan of attack. Morris was right he had never known an agent who acted outside of orders, or who had in essence gone rogue to be looked on favourably by the powers above. This was nothing more than a vendetta, it was revenge and he did not care in the slightest. In fact it gave him an enormous sense of closure. Morris had ended his illustrious career and in return he would end his life along with his entire family. That to him was fair and in his warped world, justice.

He lowered the gun. Dan breathed a sigh of relief, for a moment he thought he had read him wrong, half expecting him to pull the trigger. Walking around the lab facing the hydro pod, McAdams gazed at the technology behind the glass. All of the files he had read relating to the technology had not prepared him for such a bizarre looking machine; it was like nothing he had seen before.

The information had been vague. The only real detail was from the initial experiments back in the fifties, although the notes were second hand transcribed by other scientists and not from William Morris' research, so much of it did not make sense or at least was contradictory.

Nor could the Government make the technology work, no matter how many resources they dedicated to it. Much of the original data and research was devoted to extracting oxygen from sea water. Whatever the technology did, the fact a Government had hounded an individual or family for half a century biding their time for results, was monumental.

McAdams turned to face the group, who hovered silently behind Dan; they were scared which was understandable. He was in control; he knew that, there was plenty of time. He spoke in a completely different manner to the way he had addressed them earlier. This side of his nature was likeable and feigned interest, or at least he conveyed warmth to the question.

"Forgive my ignorance but tell me please, why exactly has so many consecutive Government agencies been watching your family, or at least tried to, for nigh on half a century? What does this do?" He motioned over his shoulder to the pod. "Why, is it so important to so many people and why have so many consequent Governments kept you and the technology secret for so long? Surely if it was of such prolific significance it would be far better to be in the public domain?"

James looked at everyone as he stepped forward to answer. "My father created a piece of technology purely by accident from one of his experiments for the MOD. The true significance of it has only become relevant in the last forty years, particularly as the world's economy hinges primarily on oil production. Recently statistical reviews of world energy demonstrate the world still has enough 'proven' oil reserves to provide 40 years of consumption at current rates. Once again the Governments and oil producers gallantly push back the estimate of when the world will run dry."

James was on a roll, he loved talking about this field. There were so many contradictory statistics and much Government spin on the subject. It was exceedingly difficult to tell reality from truth, unless you speak to the true scientists who are the real oil prospectors; they will give you a far more realistic evaluation on timescales.

"However, scientists led by the London-based Oil Depletion Analysis Centre, say that global production of oil is set to peak in the next four years before entering a steepening decline which will have massive consequences for the world economy and the way we live our lives from that point on. According to peak oil theory, our consumption of oil will catch and then outstrip our discovery of new reserves and we will begin to deplete known reserves. Thus the cost of a barrel will sky rocket and the world, as we know it, will simply grind to a halt because everything, including food, goods and services will become too expensive. The rich will prosper and the poor will starve."

McAdams nodded, following the economic plight of the western world's over-reliance on oil. "So what does that have to do with the technology behind me and what the Morris family have tried to hide from the British Government and hidden from the world for so long?"

James smiled, he was proud of what they had achieved. There had been enormous personal loss and upheaval, he knew the repercussions still had to be felt and dealt with emotionally but they had done it. He defiantly walked round the work surface standing next to McAdams staring absently into the hydro pod, like a proud father looking through the glass window of a hospital nursery at his child.

"The system in front of you will replace an entire nuclear power station; or existing power stations that burn fossil fuels such as coal, natural gas or diesel/petroleum, i.e. oil, to produce electricity. In the United States alone, in excess of 45% of their electrical output comes from coal. Imagine, if you will, the amount of oil that is consumed simply mining and transporting coal to a power station to keep the huge inefficient turbines working." He paused as if to let the gravitas of the situation sink in.

"What you have in the hydro pod is the future; an environmentally clean, self-perpetuating energy source. A monumental technology that has taken half a century to perfect. Overnight carbon emissions from fossil fuelled power stations could be eradicated as they could be permanently decommissioned, cutting down the need for the huge quantities of oil worldwide. Can you understand what that would do to many countries economies?"

He paused for effect. "They would crash; they are solely based on the production of oil. Millions of people worldwide are employed in the oil industry and it would no longer be the driving force behind economies. Scale the technology down and you have a power plant that would indefinitely run electric powered cars, or the entire needs of a small household. Whoever controls the technology basically could hold the world to ransom, which is why consequent Governments, including the British and the Americans are shitting themselves it could ever see the light of day."

McAdams stared at James, the look on his face was of shock. You could see it was a rare trait for him as his features were hardened.

"I can see why the British Government is so interested and frightened by it. If another country takes control of such superior technology, it certainly wouldn't be within our country's interest. I understand completely what has been resting on the shoulders of your family."

He now knew and fully understood the complexity behind the technology; he at least had a fundamental respect for what they had achieved and why they had gone to such extreme lengths to protect it. The Morris family had single handedly undertaken the unique responsibility to try and save the planet, many would have shied away from their position.

However he was not here to question their individual motives, he was here to do a job. He found himself smiling. He now realised this was a way back in. His superiors would be more than willing to forgive any of his previous misdemeanours when he delivered what so many had failed to do.

"Thank you James, very interesting, you are very passionate about what you have done here, I am indeed grateful. I now know at least I am in the right place and fortunately I have come at the right time. Please step back with your family."

Dan stepped forward. "Even knowing what the pod does, doesn't mean you have the understanding and knowledge to remove the data and relevant information and take it topside to make it work."

"Daniel, you have no idea what I am capable of. I assure you I've no need of your services anymore, you have led me to where I need to be. For that I thank you. It has been, how can I say, somewhat emotional."

He raised his gun and pointed it at Dan. Lizzie and Ash screamed, which made him hesitate. He needed the others to co-operate, maybe killing Morris would be a little irresponsible until he had all of the data needed. He had been somewhat premature killing Michael and Susan Morris.

"Move." He motioned with the gun towards the door into the living space. He levelled the gun at Matt as well. "You too." Matt and Dan shuffled sideways down the armadillo walkway.

Dan assumed he was going to be eliminated and decided he had nothing to lose. Matt was ahead on the walkway. He spun, facing his tormentor. McAdams was impressed with the man's bravado. He hated him, yet admired his voracious tenacity.

"Tell me John, in the interview room, how did you know about my Mother?"

"I'm surprised you are concerned with something that happened so long ago, especially under these circumstances?"

"You don't get it do you? This is my Mother, I loved her, this may be a difficult concept for you to grasp but you told me she was murdered. I want to know how you knew?"

McAdams sucked in a breath. "You're right. I don't get it, I'm an orphan. I never had a mother and I never had anyone to look out for me to give me the unconditional love you had."

He paused as if recalling memories and past moments. "I remember being very jealous of you. I had never seen a family so close before, you made me angry. You were so happy and carefree, your childhood was everything I wanted and never got. I guess it was what my mentor intended me to understand, through that experience, to make me jealous and hate what I did not have, or for that matter understand. I was taken by a man who taught me everything I know, or at least trained me in my profession. A profession I excel at and one in which I need no one." He seemed to remember his mentor with a fondness.

Whether it was a form of love or respect Dan could not tell but it was a memory McAdams treasured. He had never been close to anyone before, or since.

"I was twelve when I was taken to Washington for the first time. My mentor took me to an apartment which I learned to wire for the first time. We watched you come and go for several weeks. I never truly understood the details as to why we were there, however I did know who you were. I passed you every day on your way to and from school. I monitored your routine, I watched you closely, like a shadow. I learnt your habits and who you spoke to. It was clear you were a bit of a loner, a single mother can be terribly smothering, don't you think?"

Daniel wanted to know whether this was a lie but did not want to make him angry, instead he turned the question around. "I don't actually. Why would you think that?"

"You had to be in directly after school, homework finished by 6.30, dinner and then TV till bedtime." Dan was shocked, that was exactly his routine after school to a tee. He never saw it as restricting; he saw it as his life and a positive structure.

"Your mother was in contact with an American CIA agent, which was no threat; we were monitoring who she was speaking to. However she suddenly started to play the CIA against a few others, I forget who, Korean or Chinese maybe, it was so long ago I was young, the details escape me. She was deemed a threat and my mentor was given the order to remove her. Your mother was the first person I saw die." McAdams said the fact without inflexion, no malice was meant, he simply saw no wrong in the statement. "I was used to calm her and to show he was serious."

Dan was beginning to regret asking, now he was close to the truth he was not sure he actually wanted to know how his mother died. McAdams relayed the information like a basic story, without feeling or warmth, just the cold hard facts.

"Your mother had arranged to meet her contact the afternoon of her death. We broke into the apartment removed the wire taps from the phones and the hidden cameras monitoring your movements. I dressed in your gym gear which I stole from your school locker."

Dan remembered this; he was made to wear lost property because he could not find his kit. He assumed he had lost it, a few details from the day made sense. John McAdams must have witnessed or was a direct accomplice to his mother's death.

"I was dressed in your gym kit, tied to a dining room chair in your apartment. I had a hessian bag over my head, which I could see through however from the outside you could not see in. When she entered the apartment, she was confronted with the image; her beloved son tied to a chair with a gun pointing at his head. Looking back the detail was brilliant, I was made to piss myself which was a very convincing touch I thought."

McAdams seemed to swoon at this small piece of detail, admiring his mentor, an assassin, trained in the art form of what he was ultimately to become.

"Your mother was forced to get the research, confessing there were no other copies. She was made to strip, placing much of her clothing on her bed. The remainder was thrown on the floor of the bathroom, she was totally naked. He told her she was going to be put to sleep and her son, Daniel would be left tied until she woke. She was to never attempt the same stupid stunt ever again. She wholeheartedly agreed as long as they never hurt you. Daniel, her last thoughts were of you." He sneered at Dan. "She was injected without a struggle causing no bruising or any other traces. By now I would assume you know what it was with?"

"Potassium chloride." Dan muttered it under his breath.

"A plus, you have been paying attention Daniel, I'm impressed. Potassium chloride, injected under the armpit through a hair follicle. It's a difficult procedure to do but leaves no trace evidence, causing a massive heart attack. Under normal conditions, no toxicology tests are performed and death by natural causes are recorded. Now you know how it happened, does it make it any easier?"

"The pieces were there, I just never understood the full motives until now. I have one last question for you, what happened to the man who murdered my mother?"

"I killed him! He became a threat to my own life knowing who I was and where I came from. I realised that quite early. I took his identity carrying on where he left off. He destroyed my childhood moulding my life. His was the first life I took, it was easy and remorseless and those I have taken since have meant nothing to me." He smiled as if wrapping up the story with a happy ending. "You asked me earlier why I'm here? I've considered my response and ultimately I'd have to say it's for revenge."

McAdams lifted the gun pointing it directly at Dan's forehead who stood motionless, rooted to the spot. This was it. Looking over McAdams' shoulder, Dan locked eyes with a horrified Lizzie, her mouth open.

She looked beautiful, if memories exist after death, hers would always be one to treasure. He closed his eyes, her radiance permeating his mind. The gunshot was deafening. The armadillo walkway pulsed with the gun flash, echoing throughout the habitat reverberating off the metal structure, deafening his ears. He never felt any pain, in fact he felt nothing.

He opened his eyes to see McAdams had moved his weapon and fired off to the side, directly hitting the concertina edging of the armadillo's protective walkway. The first shot simply dented the metal but the second tore through piercing the outer skin, a torrent of water exploded into the walkway, soaking Dan instantly. The pressure of the jet was immense pushing him backwards. Trying to fight the stream of water against him, not understanding what was happening, he momentarily locked eyes with John McAdams who was smiling.

The claxon sounded and screamed into life. With a hiss of hydraulic fluid, the rams gently and smoothly started to close the water tight doors, sealing the compromised compartment.

From behind Matt grabbed him yanking him savagely through the closing gap into the living quarters, he flailed backwards falling to the floor. Matt knelt next to him. Through the closing gap of the water tight doors, the pair watched as their family disappeared from view. McAdams nonchalantly smiled, confidently waving goodbye.

69

Once the hydraulic doors had closed sealing the compartment, the claxon alarm sounded for another thirty seconds, then silence. McAdams took a deep breath; the only sounds were stunted sobs from the girls behind him.

"Now, now girls, don't be silly they'll be fine. I have simply put them out of harms way so neither of them do anything stupid while we sort out the details."

Charlie looked up from comforting his daughter, who was near hysterical. "Details, what details? What do you want from us?"

"Like I said before Charlie, you and your daughter are inconsequential; you happen to have been pulled along for the ride. I don't want or need anything more from you, so I would suggest you keep your mouth shut, unless I specifically address you." Charlie's mouth opened as if in protest. McAdams hand rose pointing the gun to reiterate the point, it promptly closed. "Good boy, now step away."

He spoke to James. "Is all of the research on the data backed up? Are they tucked away in the computer room? Are there any passwords or encryption that need removing before I copy the data onto external drives? That is before I leave you to ponder your future."

Ash, having just watched Matt and Dan cocooned in the living quarters had hardened, her resolve suddenly resolute. She instantly made a decision she was not going to cooperate with a killer. If he managed to escape from the habitat with all the carefully compiled and chronologised research, which her mother had spent years vigilantly documenting and organising, dating back and including her Grandfather's original experiments, plus the entire pod system diagrams from the CAD archives.

What her family had tirelessly worked towards, everything they had sacrificed and died for protecting, would have been for nothing. He was

 any of them survive once he had gotten exactly what
r lives were over. This she was certain of; right now he
a and as long as they had some intrinsic value they might be
uy some time to work out a way to escape.

ave you brought data drives with you?" She tried to make it sound
as though she was helping.

"Yes they're in the chamber where I entered. However, I saw
through the door into the computer room that the backup system is hot
swappable, so I should be able to just remove the drives and be done."

Ash laughed. "If only it were that simple, which it's not." She hastily
added. "I don't even understand how they work as they are encrypted
and coded. Matt set them up; of course if you hadn't stranded him in
the living quarters we could've asked him to decrypt the data."

She said it rather too sarcastically and a little patronising. "I have no
idea how to transfer to and from the drives as they are on their own
individual network. I think the link is through Matt's computer, like an
FTP server because his talks to all the machines in the facility." Pat shot
James a glance. Ash saw it out of the corner of her eye; she just hoped
McAdams had not, for all their sakes.

Pat stepped forward, realising what Ash was doing. "Ash is right, the
data, although completely reworked by myself and written in several
standards for academia and journal publishing, is not set up for normal
archival or retrieval on the backup disks. James and I have a Mac, Ash
uses a PC and Matt's is Linux, I believe?"

"Actually Mom I think Matts's machine dual boots running both
Windows and Linux."

Pat looked grateful for the correction. "Is it, well I'm a Mac girl." She
smiled as if proud of her decision. "Anyway the point is, huge amounts
of data exist on my works drive, a huge amount on James and Ash's,
then the internal systems engineering diagrams and AutoCad drawings,
which consume masses of data on Matt's system. Personally I'd have no
idea what are of relevance to the pod system designs, or to the
underwater habitat itself, which would be of little use to you on the
outside world. The backup data as far as I'm aware is striped across the
drives, so data is spread across all of them, not individually. Matt did it
like that so if there was ever a system failure or drive error we would be
able to rebuild the information. How it works I have no idea. James?"

"Don't look at me, it's all I can do to turn a bloody computer on."
James' shrugging was his way of colluding with them; realising their
situation was desperate and also understanding they were trying to

make it difficult and stall for time. "I'm a Mac fanboy too, give me three buttons on a mouse and I wouldn't know what to do." He laughed.

McAdams visibly darkened, his demeanour soured along with his mood, you could see he was not a patient man. "I don't care how difficult it is to copy the research but we do need to get on with it, now." He barked. "If the easiest way is to attach a hard drive to each individual system then we'll do that and reformat it to match, plus transfer everything from the backup drives. What size is each hard drive?"

Ash looked at her Mom as if defeated. "Mine I think is 1.2 terrabytes. How much of that is used I don't know but that's why we installed the backup system to offload a mass of research data from testing the pod. I've only just started to make a dent and compile the latest test research."

Pat was hoping the combination of the individual systems would be too much for him to download. He seemed unfazed by their break down of the systems. The situation seemed more desperate than they assumed.

The claxon suddenly launched into life again, the noise sounding throughout the lab and operations. McAdams stunned by its abrupt awakening spun on the spot.

"What's going on, what's happening?" When he compromised the exterior structure on the walkway, he expected an alarm or warning, however this was unexpected. The strobe lights burst into archaic life, flashing crimson around the lab.

Ash stepped forward, casually sitting down at her expansive desk looking at her bank of monitors. Closing a few open menus, she peered at the pods maintenance screen, shouting above the noise of the claxon.

"The systems are re-setting, because of tonight's unscheduled demonstration of the pod. The automated flushing protocols are basically trying to catch up with themselves. Everything is out of synch, the system is trying to find an equilibrium and internal pressure, which it will continue doing for several hours yet."

McAdams looked unimpressed, shaking his head disapprovingly, disbelieving her words. "I've already seen this happen tonight, you seem to forget. When I originally tricked you to believe I was entering via the moon pool. Matt showed me the way through the external chamber and I watched him reset the grids along the outside of the habitat as they had been left open. At the time I didn't know what it did but as he paid attention to it, I assumed it did something monumental. I was right!"

He glowered at Ash, but watched mesmerised as the hydro pod filled with sea water, quickly rising to the roof of the chamber, fully submerging the technology within. McAdams spun round wildly, waving the gun at them, shouting orders.

"Stand against the wall, now!" Each of them doing as they were told stood along the wall the opposite end of the lab to the hydro pod. "Move down to the far corner so I can see you, put your hands on your head and face the wall."

They side stepped towards the closed hydraulic doors, separating the now flooded walkway to the living compartment where Dan and Matt were trapped. McAdams walked backwards through the connecting walkway into operations, the gun firmly pointing in their direction. He glanced between his captives and the closed door to the moon pool. The flashing lights turned from red to green and a deathly silence fell as the claxon halted abruptly.

Nothing happened; he cautiously stepped into operations and pushed the manual lock out switch to the hydraulic door. Which slowly opened, sliding back into the wall. Cautiously he stood in the middle of operations, from this view point he could monitor his captives against the wall and cover the moon pool.

Quickly he darted through the door, scanning the walkways for movement. Inside the submarine and the moon pool surface which undulated with air as it was released from the water. There was no movement, no one had entered. He felt slightly foolish, unnerved by the unknown, although he had to check and moved back to the lab.

As he passed the workshop he grabbed several tie wraps from the work bench inside the door. He walked behind Charlie, grabbed his hands, placed them behind his back and cable tied them together. Charlie winced in pain but said nothing. He did the same to James and forcibly pushed them down the other end of the lab. He opened the compartment door to the lock out chamber throwing them both inside. He tied the hands of both Lizzie and Pat and forced them into the chamber next to the pod with Charlie and James.

He glowered at them and said without any remorse in his voice. "Remember I'll be watching. Any of you try anything and I'll snap Ashley's neck like a tooth pick." He closed the door watching as Lizzie slumped to the floor in floods of tears. He smiled and turned to Ash.

"Right then gorgeous, it's just the two of us, where were we?"

"You were going to get the drives and hook up to each system individually and we can then start the transfer. We'll probably have to format each drive to fit."

"Yes you're probably right. I'll go get my stuff, won't be a mo and remember Ashley, don't try anything." He gave her a warning look labouring the last three words. The deadness in his eyes were unnerving but Ash somehow managed to force her most radiant smile.

She sat down at her desk, bringing up several desktops with different data and research on. She watched as he disappeared from view into operations and back into the chamber to retrieve his gear. Pat smiled weakly at her through the glass, she looked sick with worry.

Ash knew she needed to be brave. This was the time for her to be the strong one of the family. She had no idea what else they could do with such a maniacal lunatic down here on the loose, things could turn serious very quickly.

She waited a moment listening intently until she believed he would be out of ear shot, then picked up the microphone from the console, whispering.

"Dad listen to me carefully, don't risk a reply. Use the pod's intercom. See if you can speak to Matt and Dan in living, see if they have a plan. I'll stall him as long as I can while I transfer the data." She let go of the intercom, staring at the four of them, she then pressed the intercom button adding.

"I love you."

70

In those few moments it took for the watertight doors to close, hundreds of gallons cascaded down the walkway into the living quarters. The plush carpets throughout the lounge area were submerged before the water gradually disappeared. Matt slammed his fist into the sodden carpet spraying them both, not that it mattered as they were both still wearing their wetsuits.

"Jesus Dan, why the fuck did you come down here when you knew a man like that was following?"

"Don't you dare take the moral fuckin' high ground with me. If it wasn't for what you and the family have done, we wouldn't be in this situation. Why the hell would anyone build an underwater lab in the first place?"

Matt just shook his head. "It's what I know Dan, it's how I live and I know how to survive down here. I designed this tub, it works, the whole fuckin' underwater system works. We've been down here for years and the pod allows us to survive. You still don't get it do you? Uncle James and Ash see the pod as a way of saving the world, meeting its energy crisis head on. I see it as a way of exploring it! I can build a moveable chamber that can go anywhere, totally self sufficient beneath the waves."

"That's great Matt!" He said sarcastically. "But right now, we're all gonna die if we don't get out of here and do something. The only way out is fuckin' flooded." He lashed out in anger with his bare foot, kicking the sealed hydraulic door.

"Don't be so stupid. You think I'd design something like this without safety protocols in every section."

Dan looked a little confused. "I've seen the plans the only exit was either through the moon pool or the chamber in operations."

Matt smiled. "The plans I left behind for you only show the external dimensions of each habitat, they are not as intricate as the detail needed to build the interiors. Do you honestly think I'd leave them topside? The designs you have don't show the lower decks. They aren't tall but they house many of the essential workings to each individual habitat.

Beneath us is the desalination plant for drinking water, the sewage plant, additional air scrubbers that remove CO_2 and regulate the oxygen levels. The battery units that power the habitat when the pod is inactive are down there and more importantly electric heaters that maintain the ambient temperature. Without them, it would be colder than a meat locker down here. They're so fucking excited about showing the pod to the world; they forget what a monumental achievement the underwater habitat in itself actually is."

"I understand what you're saying, but none of this is important unless we can get the hell out of here, alive. Matt, the guy's a psychopath. He's working outside of his remit. He's like a caged animal. There's no predicting what he'll do. I really thought he was gonna pull the trigger and I was gonna die back there."

"Dan, he's taken my whole fuckin' world from me. That cold hearted bastard owes me three lives, my parents and mine." A tear rolled down his cheek. "He stole my life and destroyed the most important things to me in the world, he doesn't even truly understand why, for absolutely no reason he took ..." He groped morbidly for the name, blurting it out. "... Simon!"

Matt finally broke, his secret in the open. He did not know how to say the words; he had never openly admitted his feelings. "I love ... loved him Dan, with all my heart and he loved me." Dan reached to Matt pulling him into a hug. Matt broke down again for the second time in his arms.

This time the tears he shed were for his lover, for Simon. As his emotions surfaced, his body slumped, wracked with guilt and loss. After a while the tears subsided. He leant back gathering his usual steely machismo, instantly changing the subject as he could easily do deflecting the situation onto Dan.

"So when did you and Lizzie get it on? It's only taken since high school for you to realise you're in love with the girl. You've always been a little slow on the uptake. Lizzie has loved you for bloody years."

Dan knew the moment was over. "Really? Ah shut up." Dan was surprised, however as he thought about their life Lizzie had always been there for him, always. He was foolish not to have realised before. Dan pushed him away. "You mean that?"

"Of course I do. It's the worst kept secret within the family and you know how good we are at keeping them!"

"What you mean like your homosexual tendencies?" Dan raised his eyebrows, mocking him. Matt laughed and pushed him away.

"Dan, how do you think everyone will react? You know, that I'm ..." He had trouble speaking the word out loud.

"Gay? Matt as long as you're okay with who you are. I for one couldn't give a shit and I'm pretty sure I can vouch for the whole family who just wants you to be happy. It's all we've ever wanted and always will. Let's face it though, since your teens you've been a moody bastard. All these years wasted, trying to hide your true self and live a straight life, maybe it's time you moved on and lived an openly gay lifestyle."

"Simon and I worked though Dan. We were both closeted about our sexuality but it worked, it suited us both."

"Maybe it did but maybe too it's time to be totally open about who and what you are? I am sure you'll be happier in the long run. I'm not saying it'll be easy, life never is. You've a lot of emotional stuff to deal with and this time without the support of Simon but I'll be there for you and I am sure Lizzie will be too, every step of the way. Well, maybe not every step!" He laughed again and screwed his face up, Matt did too. They hugged again, like brothers, for the first time in a long time.

There was an electronic crack, a howling whined through the living quarters. Dan winced as the feedback stung his ears, covering them with the palm of his hands. "What the hell is that?"

"It's the tannoy system, someone's in the hydro pod, come on." Matt got up disappearing in to the galley.

"Matt? Dan? Are you there?" The low electronic voice was Charlie's. "Can you hear me?"

James stood with his back to the electronic control panel, looking out across the lab. His hand securely tied but with Pat giving him directions, like a child's amusements, he pushed the correct button to communicate with the galley in living. Charlie was sat on the floor in the corner of the pod looking out across the lab but spoke quietly.

"It's all right Charlie; the hydro pod is soundproof. No one can hear what we are saying outside, especially in the lab. The pod makes a severe high pitched whining noise when working at a high tolerance, which reverberates causing the inner ear irrevocable damage, which is another reason why the system is submerged."

"That would explain William's acute deafness." Charlie said dryly.

"Pardon?" James mocked.

"That would explain ..." Charles glanced up to see James grinning down at him. "Bastard!"

"We fitted the tannoy systems to communicate between all areas, especially if you were working in the hydro pod during maintenance or down times. This lock out chamber between the pod and the lab is totally soundproofed plus the internal systems can control everything if needed. It is the direct link, Ash's control station is simply a remote of the systems in here." As James allayed his fears, Charlie nodded and felt more comfortable talking louder into the mic situated behind James' butt.

"Matt? Dan? Please, are you there?" He almost pleaded for them to reply.

Matt spoke. "Yeah we're here. Where the bloody hell did you think we would be, Sea World?"

Lizzie grimaced at Pat. "You know your family has a real sick sense of humour."

Pat nodded. "I know, it's certainly not from my side Liz. Are you guys okay? What damage have you sustained over there? Is life support still working?"

Matt was sat in the galley watching them on the small LCD screen, two cameras, one in the lock out chamber and the other directly above the pod. "We're fine and the systems are fine, for now. We can see you're in the chamber. Where's Ash, what has he done to her?"

"Don't worry honey, Ash is fine. She is trying to stall him by helping him copy the data from the individual work stations. We convinced him the backup data is set up in such a fashion that it would be useless to remove the drives." Pat glanced across to Ash who was busying herself plugging cables and hard drives into the individual workstations beneath the desks.

Matt was unconcerned about the data. "Listen to me carefully; no one can leave the habitat with the data, in any form whatsoever."

James said patronisingly. "We know this, we've spent fifty years getting to this stage, we bloody realise no one should leave with the data."

"No Uncle James, I've set the system protocols up so no one can leave with any data from any of our drives."

James was concerned by this revelation. "What do you mean no one, not even us?"

"Of course not, I understand that completely which is why I didn't tell any of you how I set the system up, it was for that reason. I introduced secure protocols across every workstation to stop copying any material, that means by foul means or otherwise."

Pat cried into the mic. "What have you done Matt? Have you put Ash in danger?"

"No, she'll be fine but we have to work fast. Listen to me carefully; the individual computer systems are encrypted. I wrote data transfer protocols between our internal systems to only work internally on the network. Anyone attaching an external hard drive to maliciously copy data would believe the transfer is working okay. Basically the underlying program only copies the folder structure and document names, so it looks like you are transferring the data. The only drives that will work are the ones I personally format inserting a flag in the drives index to override the program. Any others that are connected will fall foul to the transfer protocols and effectively be empty."

Pat understood precisely, very recently she had not been able to get a new USB pen drive to work on her laptop. The data, although hierarchically present, would not open. "Like the USB pen drives I've been using, the ones you said you needed to format properly before I could use them?"

"Exactly. Basically anything attached which doesn't have my little exchange protocol in the index will boot fine appearing on the desktop and even look as though it's copying. It will also take the same amount of time to transfer as the real documents because the system truly believes it is copying the data to the drive but it's just going through the motions. Recreating the index, folders and documents from the original material, logging the date stamps, the size of the file and ultimately any other header data within, but its copying nothing of the original data onto the external hard drive. He will in effect take away an empty drive!"

Dan was impressed but he could see a problem. "Tell me then; what happens if McAdams tries to open a document from the drive to check the data is copying correctly."

Matt smiled. "That's the clever bit; it works kind of like a desktop short cut. It links back to the original document on the original hard drive and it will open that."

"But it will fail if he connects it to an external source to check the data, such as a laptop because the link will be broken?"

Matt's smile disappeared. "Well yeah, it will, but I hadn't thought of that. Let's just hope he doesn't."

Dan pressed the pod button on the tannoy and spoke into the mic. "We only have a small timescale, how long do you think it'll take to transfer all the data?"

Pat tried to add up the data across the individual stations. "I don't know, I reckon between my machine, Ash's and James' there has to be at least two terabytes, maybe more, maybe less but I don't know what Matt's would be. How large are some of the CAD engineering prototypes Matt?"

"I don't know, my drive is five terabytes alone. It must have at least three terabytes of system drawings, plus the habitat schematics and pod prototyping. It's got everything engineering wise to recreate the pod, even the dimensioning of the borosilicate glass bulbs are on there."

Dan gave him a look questioning the word borosilicate. Matt knew the look so well, they had all used it on Ash growing up, when she uttered a word none of them understood. "Borosilicate glass has a high temperature load capacity; it is used in micro reactors for viewing inside. Ours is good up to a working temperature in excess of five hundred degrees centigrade, of course being totally submerged it never reaches that kind of working temperature." He rolled his eyes in the manner Ash used to, as if everyone should know that info nugget and they both laughed at the irony.

Matt turned from Dan and spoke back into the mic. "As long as my index system fools him, we have plenty of time. It'll take a while to transfer all the data or at least before he realises it hasn't. It should give us enough time though."

"Enough time for what? What are you planning to do?" Charlie asked, sounding a bit nervous.

"I'm not sure yet but we'll get over to operations somehow, don't worry we'll be fine." Matt paused taking a breath. "Uncle James, tell me, do you know how to operate the manual locking procedures?"

"It's been a while but yeah I think so, I've not done it since we automated it."

Pat suddenly realised what he intended to do. "Matt you can't do that, Ash is still in the lab."

"I know Aunt Pat, but if things look dodgy, you have to lock the doors to the hydro pod and chamber. The plexiglass is bullet proof, you have to get the data out, it has to be protected. Ash and I have our differences but even she would agree with me."

There was silence either end as the words sunk in. The tannoy remained silent. Matt stared into the microphone. He reluctantly pressed the button.

"One final thing, if anything happens to me, the actual backup drives are arranged in a particular fashion and the data is striped across all of them. Any external meddling or removal out of sequence and they will be rendered useless. To remove them from their individual caddy, you have to enter the Oriskany coordinates, follow the touch screen instructions; you've got one attempt and one only to get it right."

71

Matt grabbed the mahogany wooden box abandoned on the breakfast bar. Removing the four knives and dog tag, he stuffed them inside a small Velcro sealed pocket attached to his wetsuit.

He pulled the stools from underneath the breakfast bar, sliding them inside the adjoining bedrooms, his and Ash's. Along the floor of the galley was a trap door almost invisible to the naked eye, the door gap disappearing into the linoleum's engrained pattern. At one end was a handle he depressed and pulled, the counter weighted mechanism easily swung the door open to reveal steps. As the door opened, it automatically illuminated the lower level and Matt descended, motioning for Dan to follow.

The ceilings were a lot lower under the main living quarters; the pair of them had to stoop low beneath structural girders and cross strengthening. Underneath the living quarters was an immense amount of pipe work and hosing, electrical conduit and all manner of systems designed to keep the habitat functioning. The way Matt moved through the inner workings, it was obvious he spent a lot of time down here. Dan however managed to bang his head off every metal and plastic surface and angled corner as he tried to keep up.

Most of the equipment Dan seemed to understand, having seen much of the kit in use over the years through Matt's work. He knew the large acrylic tubes with red neon indicators above them and tiny pellets inside were the CO_2 absorbent, which took the circulating air from the habitat and removed excess carbon dioxide.

He also realised these were quite redundant because the pod produced more than enough oxygen while running to support the habitat, however if there was downtime then they would need a backup system, this was it. Matt had over engineered everything.

At the opposite end of life support from where they entered was a metal dividing wall with a one metre square manually operated watertight door for emergency access. Matt turned the handle and unlocked the hinged door, swinging it effortlessly into life support. He swung his legs over the step as the door was approximately fifty centimetres off the floor, ducking into the room.

Dan stopped and looked back through the maze of pipe work, conduit and electrical cabling they had rapidly navigated, surveying the full extent of life support. There were vast banks of batteries and several UPS - uninterrupted power supply units, providing the habitat's electrical needs during its silent period or when the pod was down for maintenance. There was also a small diesel generator for emergencies.

However his eyes fell on what looked like brown bricks piled along the same wall of the chamber Matt had just entered. Picking one up, it was light, with the crumbly texture of peat; he sniffed the surface which gave off an earthy pungent aroma. It reminded him of the peat logs which he had used to fuel a log burner with Aunt Susan when they had ventured up to Scotland and hired a cottage in the middle of nowhere one winter. It is considered to be an unsustainable natural resource, like coal, because its extraction damages large areas of bog land and wildlife habitats within Scotland, plus elsewhere within the UK.

Matt stuck his head back through the door. "What are you doing?"

"What are these things?" Dan waved one of the brown blocks in front of Matt's face.

"Shit!" Matt laughed.

"What do you mean shit?"

"Exactly what I mean!"

It took a moment to register what he had said; screwing his face up Dan gently replaced it back on the pile along the wall with the others. Matt leant through the door with a big grin on his face.

"Obviously you may have noticed we have full running toilets and showers upstairs. Being down here for so long it was a necessity to have proper amenities, plus we're not in a position for someone to come and empty a cesspit every month. What I installed was an innovative and untested evaporator toilet system. On paper the system had the most effective waste reduction with the least amount of maintenance, which was exactly what I was looking for. What you may have gathered from the name is that the evaporation process reduces the volume of the liquid and produces these shit bricks, for want of a better word, which so far, as you can tell, I've done very little with."

"Does the entire habitat solely rely on this chamber under the living quarters to service its needs?"

"Yes and no. The air scrubbers are operated from here and piped beneath the now flooded walkway, along with drinking water from the desalination plant." Matt motioned to the far end wall of the room.

"The pod operates internally with purified water, mainly because we discovered salt crystallizes under the high operating temperatures and blocks up the pipe work. Kind of like clogged arteries, it would gradually diminish the flow to a point where the power output would dramatically fall."

"What about the power? Could we turn off the electricity and simply stop the data transfer directly from here?"

"No, because each compartment has its own battery store and UPS, so the computer systems can operate non-stop for up to 48 hours continuously without a recharge from the pod. The battery stores under the lab are designed to give enough ampage to jump start the pod to produce the electricity to recharge them. Everything in the habitat is pretty much designed to be self-sustaining."

Matt left the doorway and walked in to an internal lock out chamber which could be flooded to escape the living quarters in an emergency. It was never indicated on any of the drawings left topside, in fact none of the habitat's internal workings were left topside, they were a secret.

Inside mesh fronted lockers hung several dive suits, dry suits, immersions suits and dive tanks, including their gauges and regulators. Matt ignored everything else grabbing two dive masks he had personally designed and had manufactured for emergency use between the compartments.

A unique full face mask, secured at the back enclosing the entire face in a glass dome. The dome was coloured amber, which gave better visibility in low lighting conditions. The main reason for full vision was for inexperienced divers to navigate outside and have full peripheral vision of the environment, hopefully causing less panicking under duress.

On top of the helmet was a set of powerful LEDs which would illuminate the user's vision if compromised, or as in this case, because it would be pitch black outside the habitat. Inserted horizontally above the LEDs, two small gas cylinders stuck out like SodaStream compressed air canisters, feeding the mask with oxygen when activated.

Matt ducked back into the first compartment sealing the manual door. He checked the first mask thoroughly and then thrust it into Dan's hand, who had followed into the escape chamber.

"When I tell you to, put it on and depress the locking button between the LED lights." He pointed to a small button that would sit roughly on the forehead when in situ.

"What are you going to do?" Dan looked concerned.

"In a minute I'm going to flood the chamber and we are going to swim to operations." Dan nodded. "When you press the button, it activates the gas mixture, which allows approximately five minutes of breathable mixture, which'll give plenty of time to flood the chamber, exit and get over to the other chamber in operations. If you shallow breath the mixture will last longer, obviously."

"What's the other button for?" He pointed to a button on the side of the mask just below the right ear.

"It's so we can talk to each other via UQC." Dan gave him the look and Matt sighed before explaining. "Think of it like an underwater telephone, UQC, it's a navy acronym for underwater communication. The transceiver translates your voice into high-frequency sound, which keeps its coherence underwater and then allows it to be translated back. We used them on the rigs all the time. I fitted them to stop anyone from panicking; in an emergency you could calmly talk anyone through a situation."

"Nifty."

Without warning the entire compartment rocked violently sending the pair of them bouncing of the escape chambers walls and crashing to a heap on the floor, scattering the masks across the deck. The water tight door crashed into the wall and slammed against its aperture.

A bloodcurdling and deafening blast of pounded and tearing metal tore through the living department and down into life support. The sound resonated like the innards of an oil drum, relentlessly harangued by an entire steel drum band without any musical prowess. The metal walls reverberated as the concussion and inner shock wave flashed through the compartments.

Dan pushed Matt from his legs groaning, who was partially stunned having smashed his head on the wheel of the escape hatch. Dan spoke, although hardly hearing his own words.

"What the hell was that?" His ears rung and whistled, his inner ear drum screamed in pain from the blast waves which rattled the compartment.

Matt managed to right himself with effort, holding his head which, as a result of bouncing off the metal walls now had a slight graze on the forehead. He hauled himself back through the swinging water tight door weaving his way back to the stairwell. The whole chamber rocked savagely back and forth on the gimbal. Slowly the camber of the habitat reverted back to its original level as the water outside slowed, having spiralled round the hangar bay, moving the habitat with its own inertia, gradually slowing to a halt.

Dan followed him as best he could, staggering behind as the chamber rocked. His legs wobbled like jelly, massaging his ears and purposely yawning, trying to alleviate the pressure on his inner ear. It felt like he had just landed after a long haul flight, the compression on his ears deafening him. The world around him had fallen silent, the electrical equipment no longer hummed, all he could hear was the rush of blood pumping through his inner ears.

Matt ascended the stairs and Dan followed. They were greeted by a torrent of water spilling around the trap hatch edge and cascading down into life support, running like a river through the galley. Matt dashed into the living area, above them in the ceiling a split, no bigger than five inches, had been torn into the metal.

Sea water was falling like an exceptionally powerful shower, cascading around the ceiling mounted projector, which sparked savagely before tripping the electrical circuits. Matt stood there for several moments, trying to gauge the flow of water as it fell from the ceiling. He turned to face Dan, massaging the top of his forehead with his hand where the graze throbbed angrily.

"What's wrong? Are you hurt?"

"No I'm fine, I'm just trying to work out how quickly the water flow is gonna take to fill the compartment. There's about 580 cubic metres, including downstairs, I reckon we have at tops about 20 minutes, maybe 25 before it fills completely."

"Well let's get the hell outta here then."

"You don't understand. The gimbal structure beneath is not designed to take the weight, if the compartment fills; it will destabilise long before that. It'll either fail completely or it'll drag the lab and operations with it, flooding them as well!"

Dan looked at him in disbelief. "What can we do?"

"My welding gear is in operations if I could get to it and back out I could patch the structure from the outside."

"Do we have enough time?"

Matt screwed his face up. "No."

"Well let's get to operations and stop McAdams. He has no intention of letting us leave alive. He obviously set the charge up there that detonated, we have no idea what else he has done, or is intending to do."

An arc of electrical sparks blasted through the galley door well up the stairs, Matt and Dan unconsciously dived for cover. As dramatically as the sparks burst from the galley, they quickly died plunging living momentarily into darkness before the emergency lighting came on.

Matt yanked Dan to his feet from the water. "I think the UPS power supply just fused. Living is effectively dead, we can't save it, we need to get out now."

They both headed back down the stairs. The water was filling the lower level fast. It was already above knee height. Trudging through brown murky water, the shit bricks were gradually dissolving back to their original form, life support smelt more like an open sewer. Matt and Dan dived through the hatch into the escape compartment. The brown water was already at the rim. Matt leant out pulling the door and cranked it shut, sealing them in.

He turned to Dan. "The trouble is as the gimbal starts to give under the additional weight, the whole structure will tilt and the water will shift dramatically inside, causing its own internal wave destabilising the structure completely. When it does this, it will pull the other two habitats out of their correct alignment." He sighed, in his designs he had never factored for this kind of problem. "The added pressure and sideways force could cause the other gimbals to fail under the lab and operations. They aren't designed to take the force."

Matt picked up the discarded masks, which they had both dropped during the explosion and thrust one back into Dan's hand.

"Put this on." Yanking the immersion handle, the escape chamber felt as though the air was constricting, pushing against the flesh of the body as the water poured in to the escape room.

Matt secured his own mask as the water quickly rose around them. Without thinking he struck out at Dan punching the button on the front of Dan's forehead just as the water reached the glass dome. Dan relaxed as the air started to flow into his mask. They were fully immersed.

Unscrewing the escape hatch, Matt motioned for Dan to leave. Dan stepped into the escape hatch which was starting to sink. Locking eyes with each other through the amber glass, they awkwardly tried to hug. Matt pressed the communication button on his own helmet. "You get to operations and find a way to stop him. I'm gonna scout the exterior for more explosives. If he compromises the other compartments, we're all fucked, and not in a good way!"

72

The exterior explosion, which compromised the structure on top of the living compartment, was a directional blast. Comprising a compound thermite underwater explosive, focusing an extremely high temperature on a very small area for a short period of time. The force of which was directed into the steel metal hull of the habitat.

McAdams had designed the charge to create as small outward shock waves as possible. As he was unsure of the exact dimensions of the structure or thickness of the steel, he had guessed how much explosive was needed. Without extensive computational fluid dynamics analysing the water flow in the space surrounding the wet lab, he had no idea how much damage would happen to the surrounding structure after a concentrated blast.

He had been flying blind when he laid the charges but having used them on many operations, had a good idea of their capabilities, hoping that erring on the side of caution would not compromise the hangar in which the wet lab was contained.

Too much and the pressure from the initial blast might have sent a shockwave pushing the delicate walls of the sealed hangar outwards, causing the structure to expand rapidly, which in turn could have fatal repercussions to the Oriskany itself.

Or worse, causing the internal structure to collapse inwards, sealing anyone inside to their demise. Too little explosive and it would have little more effect than denting the metal or swaying the habitat, as if caught in nothing more than a tidal surge, as the explosive shock wave propelled the surrounding water.

Inside the hydro pod, the tied captives occupying the lock out chamber, having little control, bounced around the small chamber mercilessly, watching helplessly as the pits water level unnervingly rose, swirling around the interior of the pod chamber. It circulated the exterior walkway, like a slow moving Mexican wave poking its head through the galvanised mesh as the whole habitat circled.

James, lying on his stomach, watched the water wide eyed as it lapped the internal glass, gradually subsiding and finally levelling out again. The water must have risen by at least eighteen inches; he believed the whole habitat had shifted several feet from the blast. His mind was racing, barely registering the pain in his side. The four of them lay in a heap, Lizzie, Charlie and Pat on top, crushing him, all rather dazed from the sudden unexpected shift. James and Pat had never felt anything like it within the lab, something terrible was happening.

McAdams picked himself from the floor of the lab, smiling. Ashley, caught completely unaware, was thrown sideways from her chair landing awkwardly on her coccyx. She remained sprawled across the floor. The lab undulated on the underwater waves ricocheting around the exterior of the habitat, savagely pulling the structure like invisible hands. The gimbal, as the momentum slowed, gave the whole interior an uneasy spiraling rocking motion.

The tethering to the hangar floor did not allow for the motion to have a familiar pitching and rolling sensation like a boat. Ash gagged, the feeling was seriously unnerving. The metal structure twisted under the duress of the motion, creaking savagely under the unusual pressures. Part of the white plastic PVC sheeting covering the lab's wall fell away revealing the bare steel structure beneath, crashing to the ground and narrowly missing Ash's outstretched hand as she fought to get to her feet.

She could hear the walkway, connected to living, as if it was pushing against the internal water tight door, concerned, expecting any minute for a leak, a trickle or ultimately a barrage of water to break in around the seals. As the motion gradually died, she could hear McAdams laughing. She glared at him from the floor over her shoulder.

McAdams looked very pleased with himself as he waggled a small handheld unit at her. A single illuminated red button on it and a small rubber antenna protruded from the box.

"What a rush! You know if I hadn't become an enforcer I'd probably have gone into explosives work, blowing things up is such fun."

Ash collapsed on her forearms, her lower back in agony. She spoke through clenched teeth, gasping for air, forcing down the contents of her stomach. "What have you done?"

He skipped jovially towards her with an outstretched hand to help her up. "On each chamber I've positioned a directional charge; remotely

I can individually detonate them. Or if anything happens to me they will self detonate under a preordained timescale. Hopefully by now Daniel is taking a little swim, probably his last." He said with such glee.

Ash sucked in a deep breath, staggered to her feet clumsily, holding his hand for stability, with one swift movement she swung her entire body, her right fist intuitively clenched.

McAdams was so jubilant in his reverie; he did not register the movement and failed to act. Ash's small fist caught the side of his temple, his face crumpled under the force, whipping his face and neck sideways. It was a good punch but he was a hard man.

His smile instantly vanished, darkness shadowed his eyes, the venom returned and without so much a secondary chance, his left hand lashed out grabbing Ash round the windpipe. Holding her at arms length and lifting her from the floor, she choked as she tried to force his hand away with her miniscule strength, both hands grasping his for release.

He raised his right hand punching Ash as hard as he could. It did not matter Ash was a woman, she was a threat and she needed to be eliminated. The impact of his knuckles smashed the delicate cartilage of the septum, breaking the top of her nasal bone. Blood sprayed out in an arc. The sudden jolt against Ash's skull caused instant unconsciousness, which was probably a blessing because the pain from her crushed nose would have been excruciating.

From the lock out chamber, her family watched in horror as Ash's limp body flew through the air. Her face in profile was changed dramatically; her bloodied nose was pummelled flat. Her body hit the floor, the momentum and smooth frictionless surface of the lab propelling her several feet across the room before sliding to a halt, unconscious and gurgling bubbled blood through her shattered nose.

McAdams turned and smiled at the disgusted and angry faces staring at him. The look was nothing he had not seen before. As long as he stayed in control, things were looking good. He returned to the screens checking how far the transfer had progressed. It was just a matter of time before he could pack the drives up and get out, absently he caressed the transmitter. His finger felt trigger happy, he wanted this to be over. He wanted to get out of here and return to the surface with the information to return to his life, to return to what he loved doing.

The four had unsteadily one by one got to their feet, which proved difficult in the confined space with bound hands. James was nursing his ribs, bruised or worse, broken. Pat realised something was wrong and lifted his shirt. There was a purple welt about six inches in diameter across the right hand side of his ribs. As she stared at it, she almost imagined it getting bigger before her eyes. She ran her bound hands down gently down the bruise and started to well up with tears.

"It's alright. It only hurts when I breathe." James tried to smile.

For the first time in their marriage, Pat was scared. "He's never going to let us live, look at Ash. Look at our baby girl. This was never worth all of this James."

"I know sweetheart." Pat broke down burying her face into his chest. He wanted to put his arms round her, hold her but they were firmly tied behind his back.

Lizzie pressed herself up against the glass carefully watching Ash. Her chest was rising and falling, so she at least was not dead. She reached for the intercom and pressed the button for living pleading in her voice for him to answer.

"Dan, are you there?"

A feint static drifted back into the chamber, but other than that there was silence.

"Dan please ... are you there?" She looked at her Father with tears in her eyes. Charlie could say nothing, looking over her shoulder towards James who returned the same worried look.

"Liz, they'll be fine." Charlie wanted to caress the back of her head, as he had done all of her life when his little girl was upset, but he could not.

James still felt strong because he honestly felt they had the upper hand. "Of course they will Liz, they'll have already left the emergency exit and be on their way to operations."

Lizzie looked at James, her eyes red and bloodshot, tears streaming down her cheeks. "But what's just happened, what was that?"

James knew exactly what it was, knowing the explosion would have damaged the living compartment beyond repair. He was more concerned that if they had been outside when the explosion had happened, the pressure would have torn them apart; he just prayed they were not but Lizzie need not know his fear.

There was a tap on the glass. All four of them looked up to see McAdams stood outside the door, his smiling face less than an inch from the glass. The tapping was the barrel of his gun, which he held in his right hand, in his left was the foot of Ash. He had dragged her lifeless body across the floor, leaving a sweeping crimson trail in her wake, looking demonic against the crisp white floor. Her hair was matted with clotting blood, her face unrecognisable, they recoiled in horror. He motioned with the tip of the gun, to stand back.

Not taking his eyes off the four of them in the glass room, he opened the door with his left hand while still holding Ash's trouser leg. He hauled Ash through the gap. His eyes unblinking never left James, unceremoniously using his foot to push her the last few inches through the gap.

"Don't move and no one else will get hurt." He slammed the door shut, turned and walked back to the transferring files.

Lizzie dropped to Ash's side, pushing the sodden matted hair from her face, she was unconscious. A rasping sound came from deep within.

"We need to elevate Ash's head, it will help to stop the swelling and blood flow." Pat removed her boots with her feet and Lizzie propped them under Ash's head.

From inside the soundproof chamber, all collectively concerned with the inanimate Ash, they never heard the claxon sounding throughout the lab. The red lights flashing eventually managed to catch James' eye and he stared at McAdams. There was a hydraulic hiss as the safety solenoids automatically locked and sealed the pod doors. The large chamber next to them started to fill quickly.

McAdams was ignoring the automatic vent. He sat with his elbows on the table, resting his chin in his hands staring absently at the computer displays, watching patiently as the copy bar counted down the time to the end of each data transfer.

73

Dan never saw Matt exit the chamber behind him, his mind was focused elsewhere, mainly on Lizzie. He swam harder and faster than he had ever swam in his life, heading beneath the structure.

Underneath living, the light from his mask illuminated the gimbal which was gradually buckling beneath the accumulating weight as living flooded. He wondered if it would jam, locking solid in a level horizontal state, or if Matt's prediction of the monumental swing tilt he described would happen. He swam for the far end of operations, trying to block out the different scenarios, time was something no longer on their side, not that he was sure it ever had been.

He helped Matt exit through the compression chamber earlier to close the bar, it was where McAdams had entered, so he was heading for that. Under operations was a small tube leading to the hatch, fortunately illuminated by the LEDs from his face mask he was able to navigate fairly easily. He grabbed the wheel, it would not budge, which meant the chamber was in use or worse, disabled internally.

Dan slowly lowered himself back down from the tube, he would have to risk the moon pool. It was the only other way in. Swimming back underneath the opening doors, he positioned himself beyond the reach of the water flow during the venting procedure and pulled the knife switch. He waited as the water rushed around him, nowhere near the ferocity in this position he had experienced during his first unexpected entrance.

The V shaped missile doors beneath the moon pool opened and Dan swum through, quickly positioning himself directly in front of the water tight door into operations. He gently landed on the walkway as the water receded. Removing his mask and discarding it to the floor, he waited expecting the door to open, nothing. Breathing a deep sigh of relief, he was in, now what?

He scouted the moon pool for a weapon, it was empty, even the hyper sub secured in its cradle was totally empty. As Dan traversed the edge of the moon pool's walkway, he realised it was far from level. On the far side, the water was a good fifty centimetres above the mesh, rising fast, creeping up the wall. Matt was right, the entire habitat was being pulled sideways as living filled with sea water.

Dan released the water tight door, expecting McAdams to be lying in wait for him. Operation's was empty. Hugging the wall, he crept anticlockwise around the perimeter of the room until he could peer down into the lab. The entire habitat was beginning to lean quite substantially, tools normally hanging flat against the workshop walls were floating gently on their individual hooks. The whole structure was flexing, making incredibly deep throated guttural noises as it twisted in directions it was never intended.

The armadillo tunnel connecting the lab had been contorted in such a way, the adjoining armour had been exposed so you could see through to the outer watertight rubberised plastic skin which was straining against the forces being inflicted on it. It undulated and rippled under the water pressure. The plastic water barrier had been pulled so taut the black plastic was turning white where it was twisting.

The non slip walkway which held the individual compartments at their determined distance, even to the human eye, this strong piece of metal was twisting under the intense stress. Dan could not help but think this was the weakest link.

At least the watertight doors would shield each habitat separately if the walkway broke, how long they would survive without life support though was anyone's guess.

Dan knelt down on his hands and knees to see down into the lab, slowly peering round the corner at floor level. Through the walkway he could see McAdams sat at Ash's desk, although he could not see Ash. McAdams looked very happy with himself, he was busy using the mouse of the computer to check the files. Looking relaxed he was almost smiling, obviously thinking the data transfer was successful. Dan had to hand it to Matt, it was a very clever piece of programming to achieve, he would never have thought of it.

There was a crash from the workshop, something had fallen. Dan ducked behind the wall so as not to be seen. His breathing was heavy, he was still weapon-less and vulnerable. There was another immense thud, this time from inside the lab. The whole habitat gradient was at least ten degrees, maybe more, which did not seem like much but in such a confined space it made an immense difference; equipment was starting to move and fall. He tried to remember what Simon had suggested was the angle before the chambers would touch the floor or outer skin of the hangar.

He was sure it was eighteen degrees, however the Oriskany was already listing by eight, so how much further would the habitat tilt? If it was counter listing towards the Oriskany's then they would have touchdown soon. However if the shift was happening in the opposite direction, it could be catastrophic. The whole structure would tilt savagely catapulting everything and everyone inside. How much time did they truly have before living was full and resting on the hangar floor or worst case scenario, flipped on its gimbal? He pushed the thoughts from his mind.

Peering back round the edge of the water tight door McAdams was not at his seat. He strained further, still unable to see him. Without thinking he jumped from his position and darted into the workshop. The compression chamber's door was wide open, which explained why he could not open the lock out hatch from the outside. Within the chamber was abandoned kit McAdams had brought aboard, he opened a few of the water tight cases.

There were explosives, which he carefully lay aside, data drives and finally, what he was looking for, a gun. He checked it for ammo, it was loaded. Exiting the chamber Dan gently closed the water tight hydraulic door, manually flooding the chamber, with the last of McAdams' gear inside. Matt would be able to gain entry as the lock out door would open externally, plus if McAdams tried to make a hasty retreat he would not be able to.

Listening carefully, he tried to ascertain where McAdams was in the lab. The habitat creaked and groaned with such deep grating sounds it sounded as though the structure was protesting by vocalising its pain. Dan risked it, taking his chance, stepping onto the walkway from operations, stooping low he still could not see McAdams in the lab.

Then he appeared, from under the desk with hard drive cables in hand, having disconnected one of the drives from Ash's machine. He spotted Dan, instantly reaching for his gun which was led on the keyboard.

Dan stood rooted to the spot, like a rabbit in headlights. He tightly gripped both handles of the walkway; his knuckles white, it did not even register his right hand also gripped a gun. He froze. There was a small shudder as the whole habitat unexpectedly swung sideways, just as

McAdams squeezed the trigger. The movement rocked his arm, the bullet sailing past Dan and ricocheting off the wall behind him in operations. McAdams stood there in shock. He had missed, he never missed. He stared deeply into Morris' eyes, he would not miss again.

The lab vibrated savagely, starting to shake, the floor flexed unevenly, buckling as it twisted against the pull of living as it flooded. From above, PVC plastic sheets started raining down from the ceiling as their fixings failed, crashing to the floor, one narrowly missing McAdams. His concentration broke, he looked up nervously looking away from Dan.

A deep resonance started slowly within the metal, building like a crescendo from the percussion section of an orchestra, getting louder, everything vibrated brutally. If not secured or fixed down, equipment started to walk across surfaces and fall to the floor, like a washing machine with an uneven load. The walls and everything around them seemed to be undulating as if creaking to life.

"What the fuck is happening?" For the first time, Dan saw through the hatred and machismo. A glimpse of humanity, he heard panic in McAdams' voice.

Dan stared at him, he had little pity for this monster, he had been there the day his mother died. McAdams had zero feeling towards human life, no more than towards a slug. He respected and admired the man who snuffed the life from his mother, even the methodology used for her murder he held with such high esteem. His humanity had been robbed simply loving what he did, he was inhuman.

Dan shouted above the tearing metal. "You set off the charge in the living compartment, flooding it. It's linked to the lab via the walkway like this one I'm standing on. It's gonna tear us apart and you with it!"

Like a see-saw, the lab quickly tilted inch by inch on its pivot point, then stopped. The shaking and screeching of metal subsided, the lab was silent. Was that it? McAdams glanced towards the hydro pod. James, Pat, Charlie and Lizzie were huddled together cowering on the floor of the lock out chamber. They were weak. The water in the chamber next to them was nearly a metre up the exterior metal wall. He took aim again at Dan and smiled; this time he would have his revenge.

"Goodbye Daniel Morris."

Without warning, accompanied by an amazing crack of failing metal, the whole lab rocked sideways at supersonic speed. Living's umbilical connection below the walkway broke, shearing away from the lab. It felt like a taught bungee rope had been released, acting like a fair ground ride taking off.

Dan had no idea of the G-force inflicted on his body, but his head snapped violently to the left. He hung on to the railing in the walkway like a lifeline, inadvertently dropping the gun from his hand, tightening his grip on the balustrades and prayed they held his weight. He vaguely registered McAdams thrown from his feet, as if hit by an invisible car, disappearing from view in a blur of computer monitors and expensive lab equipment following the same trajectory. Anything not bolted down flew through the air with amazing force and ferocity, smashing the PVC walls and devastating the partition wall into the office.

After the initial momentum surge the lab slowed almost immediately. Once released, the gimbal restricted the movement of the chamber; all the objects in mid air fell to the floor, as if gravity instantly switched on. The water on the outside acted like a buffer, dampening the motion further and slowing the movement. Dan stood gasping for breath, his neck in agony from whiplash, watching in horror as McAdams staggered to his feet. He had lost his faithful gun. He turned to Dan and ran at him, his black eyes wide with rage, arms outstretched to strangle him. His motive was clear, death.

The adrenalin surged through Dan's body, everything was happening in slow motion. He heard the acute rushing of water, long before he felt it. McAdams' expression changed from pure hatred to fear, his eyes widened, trying to halt his onslaught, sliding on the balls of his feet to change direction. It was too late.

Dan had left the moon pools hydraulic door open and as living tore itself away from the lab, the excessive angle had caused the moon pool's water to rise up the exterior wall, as the habitat dropped back to its correct level. A tsunami of epic proportions, propelled by the physical shift, erupted through operations and down the walkway. Dan clung on desperately to stop himself from being swept along. McAdams was too slow and was caught full force by the water, sweeping his feet from under him like a crashing wave on the shoreline; he was tossed backwards into the lab. His battered body bounced off the desk landing hard on the floor winded and in terrible pain.

Dan watched as McAdams' body was tossed effortlessly, bouncing across the desk and disappearing from view before the torrent subsided. He tentatively walked down the walkway. There was a groan from the other side, McAdams was trying to get up, he was on his hands and knees. Dan launched at him, as if taking a field goal, he kicked McAdams' head as hard as he could. For a second time he broke a bone in McAdams' body, the satisfaction was immense. Dan felt McAdams' jaw shatter. He heard the spine tingling bone splinter and McAdams howled in pain, dropping to the floor.

Whether through sheer determination or utter madness McAdams tried to rise a second time, Dan stood momentarily over him astounded at his resolve. He drew back his fist and hit McAdams in the back of his head just above the neck, ricocheting from his punch, head butting the floor, McAdams lay motionless. Dan's whole hand hurt, his knuckles hitting bone but he smiled as he manoeuvred his way through the destroyed lab and equipment.

Computers and monitors lay in several inches of water. The family's work lay shattered all around the room. The walls and internal structure were in tatters as if an explosion had gone off internally. He pulled the X-ray machine away from the lock out chamber opening the door. Lizzie's raised her arms smiling but instantly it vanished as she peered over his shoulder, screaming.

"Look out!"

McAdams hatred drove him, his broken body would kill Morris if it was the last thing he did. He had spotted a gun amongst the debris, the gun Dan had dropped beneath the walkway which the barrage of water had propelled into the lab. Grabbing it, realising it was his trusty Glock, he felt a surge of power propel him.

Staggering to his feet although savagely wounded, he looked like a grotesquely deformed scarecrow. His right arm hung at a strange angle, dislocated from the shoulder socket. His face was distorted as his jaw was pulverised and blood poured from a wound across his forehead. He raged in anger, adrenalin overcoming the intense pain, the venom in his eyes shone the same demonic power they always had.

Lizzie without thinking yanked Dan through the door of the lock out chamber slamming it shut. McAdams held the gun in his left hand, uncoordinated he fired off several rounds, peppering the acrylic glass with spider web-like shots.

74

When the lab was first established, the venting procedures for the hydro pod were done by hand inside the lock out chamber. It was only when the computers were installed that everything started to be controlled remotely. In computer automation mode, only the hydro pods doors were sealed, allowing anyone to enter the lock out chamber to work on the system if there was a remote access problem, or a fault that needed to be diagnosed.

The lock out chamber could also be sealed as well, in case there was a water leak. It was this secondary protocol, installed primarily as a safety precaution that Matt mentioned earlier, James had totally forgotten about. Both locking protocols could be initiated from the chamber.

You could also disable the remote computers or the lock out chambers console could be overridden by a primary console installed in the computer room from operations. This was looked at as emergency use only but was an absolute for any kind of system failure. Checks and balances were paramount to the safety of the pod and those on board.

"Now Pat!" James screamed. Pat viciously punched the buttons on the console attached to the wall. James had explained the buttons to press, he could not do it quickly enough with his hands tied behind his back, coordination was hindered somewhat, so Pat had to.

Pat jabbed the last button, spinning in her bare feet, looking up at the locking mechanism praying she had keyed in the correct sequence. There was a hydraulic hiss as the safety solenoids slid down their internal tubes within the acrylic sheeting, locking into place and sealing the chamber doors. They all sighed with relief; they were safe, for now.

McAdams approached firing in anger. The acrylic sheeting stretching across the room, housing the pod, was nearly two inches thick, the bullets had little effect. Inside, all they heard was a dull metallic thud from the impact, making little if any penetration. McAdams grabbed the door handle trying to open the door. He tugged angrily on the handle, screaming in anger and pain, failing to open it, not even rattling in its aperture, it was sealed tight.

Inside their soundproof cocoon they could hear nothing though it was obvious reading his lips he wanted them to open the door. Dan was unconcerned and stood with his back to McAdams. He hugged Lizzie as hard as he could, tears streamed down her face, only then did he notice.

"What happened to Ash?"

James looked down. "You tell us, I'm assuming an explosion?"

"Yeah McAdams remotely detonated a charge on top of living, punching a hole through the outer skin. Living basically filled up with water until eventually, I'm assuming what Matt predicted would happen."

The group looked at him expectantly to explain. "Matt predicted two scenarios; at some point living would over fill causing it to tilt, in turn causing an internal wave which would basically pull the entire habitat sideways. Or the gimbal underneath failed; one of which is what we felt in here just a few moments ago. As the structure failed it pulled us sideways and then I guess it ripped away, which is why we sprang back upright."

Charlie now understood why Ash punched him. "He must have gloated about the explosions and that was what prompted Ash to punch him."

"Ash punched him." Dan looked at her smiling admirably. "Good girl!"

Lizzie held his hand. "Yeah but he punched her back and then dumped her unconscious body in here."

Dan looked concerned. "She'll be okay though, won't she?"

"If we can get out of here, then yes." Aunt Pat looked gravely at Dan. "After the explosion we tried to get you on the tannoy but we couldn't get you, just static." She was worried Dan was alone. "Is Matt okay?"

"Yeah he's fine." They all collectively sighed in relief. "We both got out together after the blast. He went to see if he could find any more explosives and disarm them. He's outside." Dan looked around the chamber they were in. "How long will the oxygen in here last?"

James backed into the door of the hydro pod, twisting the handle with his hands still tied behind his back, it swung open. "I only let Pat lock the outer chamber door, we'll be fine. We can start the pod up if we need to, excess oxygen vents to the surface, we can remain in here till he leaves."

Charlie cut in. "Let's just pray he does. I don't think he'll go until he kills us all! Not now, look at him, he's gone totally mad. Not that he was ever the full ticket in the first place, from what I can make out."

Outside in the lab, McAdams was screaming at the top of his lungs. He had his back to the pod pushing his dislocated shoulder against the wall trying to get his arm to pop back in place. He slumped down obviously in extraordinary pain, smearing blood down the clear glass, he must have managed to succeed. He tentatively flexed his right arm and waggled his fingers.

Dan motioned at the tannoy system. "Which button talks to the lab?" James pointed at the upper left button, Dan pressed it.

"John, you don't mind if I call you John do you?" He waited for a reaction. McAdams wearily looked round the room for the source of Dan's voice.

"It seems so long ago now John when we had our first chat, just you and I. Do you remember all that time ago in the interview room at Scotland Yard? I advised you that intellectual property remains with the inventor unless someone else has recreated, or eventually surpassed the work and patented the next logical idea, step or product. You remember this conversation John? Do you?" He did not move. "Well, there was another way intellectual property can pass and that's if it's stolen, such as through industrial espionage." McAdams looked at the pod. "You have all of our secrets John, you have all of the plans and designs, you have them downloaded to the hard drives. I suggest you take them and get the fuck out of here and leave us alone. We've had enough, we no longer care, you win, whoever the hell you work for wins. Just get out!"

McAdams staggered to his feet and spoke. They could not hear him from inside the chamber but his speech was obviously monumental as he was animated, he swung the gun around in his left hand. Dan spoke into the tannoy again. "John we can't hear you, use the microphone on the desk."

Staggering to the desk he awkwardly spoke into the mic having to depress the button with his left hand, his wrecked jaw causing him immense pain. In the chamber the speaker uttered his words, which were calculated and to the point. His voice had lost its debonair and confident undertone; he spoke with the harshness of someone issuing their last rites.

"I don't give a fuck about the technology anymore or the British

Government for that matter. I do however intend to kill you all. Call it personal pleasure and an end to this somewhat prolonged sorry and tragic saga." He rasped the last few words from the back of his throat trying to illicit a smile.

McAdams removed the remote detonator from the pocket of his wet suit. Flicking the detonation switch to armed, he dialled in the charge number to correlate to the second explosive. This time as he stared into the acrylic chamber at the occupants within, the smile was unforced and casual. They may not drown inside their water tight acrylic bubble, how ironic they would suffocate instead. He likened it to a fish tank except for a change the fish would be looking in at the humans.

McAdams was in charge again, they thought they were so clever. Milking the uncertainty he could see in their eyes behind the glass, casually picking up the soaked drives. They may be ruined with water damage but more than likely clever technicians could retrieve the data, he may as well take them. He simply did not care anymore.

He wanted out; he wanted soil beneath his feet and blue sky above his head. Holding the fixed desk, throughout all of the carnage befallen to the lab it had remained steadfast, he gripped it tightly.

McAdams fixed eyes with Morris, the rest he ignored, they were inconsequential. Nodding in his direction he calmly pressed the red button. After the detonation it felt like an age before anything happened, although it could have only been milliseconds before the charge exploded. The accompanying noise had been loud when in the next habitat but this was extraordinary.

The metal box of the lab acted like the body of an acoustic guitar, amplifying the sound like a resonating chamber. Standing beneath the blast area was liberating on so many levels, the power, the force and the unadulterated visceral sensation. The inner shock wave from the explosion travelled straight down from the ceiling. McAdams stood, arms outstretched from his sides and face looking at the ceiling in the crucifixion pose. The wave passed over him, grounding him to the spot.

The chamber rocked from the external shock wave. McAdams stood like a grisly visage, the blood from his face trickling gently down his chin. They watched in horror at the twisted appearance he portrayed, like a performer on his final act. The metal walls shook uncontrollably as the concussion and inner shock wave flashed through the compartments. The soundproofing protected them from most of the noise but the shock waves and rolling motion rocked them savagely. The sheer horror of McAdams standing like a crucified profit filled them with dread.

Lowering his head he smiled, just as the outer metal skin sheared, water poured in washing the blood from McAdams face as if cleansing his soul. He shook the water from his face, popping the remote in his pocket, they watched helplessly from the lock out chamber as he grabbed the drives and exited the lab.

McAdams reappeared at brake neck speed, arms flailing landing awkwardly on his back. Matt held him there like a high school hero, his football tackle had lifted McAdams from his feet propelling him backwards, parting the water and broken equipment like the red sea. As McAdams exited the lab he had not expected Matt to be heading down the walkway in the opposite direction and was taken completely unaware.

The claxon screamed again into life, the internal sensors had detected the drop in internal pressure. Matt jumped to his feet glancing across at his family behind the acrylic. They were safe for now but he was not, looking down at the battered body of McAdams, he was a shell of the man he had met only minutes previous. Even that gave little pleasure; he wanted to kill him with his bare hands, personally ending his life, just like he took Simon's and his parents.

There was not time, turning to leave, something made him stop. In his head he could see the mocking face of this killer. His was a face which would always haunt him. He found it unacceptable; there was always time for retribution. As a parting gift he aimed a kick directly in McAdams groin, crushing his testicles under his bare foot. McAdams screamed in unadulterated agony, the kind of chilling scream you never hope to hear, it felt good.

With a hiss of hydraulic fluid behind him, the rams started to close the watertight doors, sealing the lab forever. He glanced at his family, there was nothing he could do. If he stayed he would also be sealed in to his death. He darted back through the closing door disappearing from view, watched by his helpless family in their acrylic tomb.

75

The second watertight door was closing a lot faster than he expected. Matt unceremoniously dived through the closing gap into operations; he only narrowly made it. His left knee grazed the closing sharp metal edge of the door drawing blood, his body crashed savagely to the metal deck.

He lay there winded looking at the metal ceiling; a strange calm came over him. It seemed fate was catching up. There was not a single soul on the surface who knew where they were. It seemed preposterous, he worked in a world where health and safety was paramount, yet no one knew they were down here.

Matt had been outside checking the outer structure when living tore itself away from the lab. Watching the torturous ending to his beloved pet project was heart wrenching, especially knowing his family were still inside. The forces transposed through the structure were astronomical. He was not surprised at how savage the compartments finally broke away from each other; he was however surprised that more of the structure did not rip itself apart in the process.

He had expected the gimbal on living to buckle long before the break, he watched in awe as the gimbal far exceeded the tolerances he originally calculated, although grateful. He strangely wished, during all of the commotion and terror, he could be sat in front of his computer allowing him to calculate and assess the structural compression and stresses of the added load to see how it was reacting. It was quite amazing to watch, right until the point it shifted uncontrollably and dangerously.

Inside he knew livings death throes were caused by an internal tidal wave of water, pulling everything and everyone sideways. He was only a few inches away from the metal structure when it shifted in the opposite direction to his position. He felt the water pull him along with its movement, the suction in such an enclosed space was tremendous, he could not fight it. He had been lucky. If it had shifted in the opposite direction, the impact would have killed him instantly. Curiously he watched the spectacle to see if the structure would right itself after such a massive failure.

He never factored the connecting walkway would break but it was a good job it did. The external structure was designed to allow for uneven movement. This element in the design ultimately became the remaining habitat's saviour. The structural link between each chamber was not the walkway as everyone assumed. It was a single pivoting strut installed beneath the metal walkway; it was this singular steel bar that finally failed. He never designed it with that intention; it was simply another stroke of luck, the weakest point failed.

The problem now facing the lab as it filled was slightly different. The walkway unfortunately was not the only single point of connection between itself and operations. Unlike living, there was also the venting tunnel connecting the hydro pod's water pit to the moon pool and the venting grates. He had no idea how the structure would react as it tried to twist under the added stress. Its exterior was similar to the armadillo walkway, not as wide, but it still had the same connecting strut. There were two struts that would need to sheer, putting twice as much force on the sinking habitat. He prayed they would hold just long enough, to carry out his plan.

From the workshop Matt grabbed the star sockets removing the half inch from the set, carelessly discarding the rest of the box. His workshop was always so immaculate, he knew where everything was. Now was not the time to worry about being tidy and conscientious. In his heart he was rather upset having invested years in the design and gradual fine tuning to prove the habitat would work. He always hoped one day it would be able to have another life and be open to the public, or it could simply stand as an historic landmark in underwater exploration.

Grabbing a ratchet from a sliding drawer he headed through to the moon pool, punching the star socket over the little captive ball bearing and flicking the ratchet mechanism so it only turned anticlockwise. The water was lower than expected; much of it had emptied into the lab as the habitat righted itself.

The hydro pod vent was now visible above the moon pool surface. It would be easier than he anticipated. Usually he had to submerse himself and use diving equipment. Lowering himself into the water by the vent, Matt removed the stainless steel pinch bolts which had to be individually extracted in a specific order, so the intricate valve would not distort in its captive ring. He had discovered on a couple of occasions that ignoring this protocol was at your peril. The vent would twist making it difficult to tilt for inspection. He did not have time to get it stuck, nor did he have the inclination to.

The valve was a left over remnant from the original underground lab beneath the house but the design and ingenuity was perfect for the way the individual chambers worked in conjunction with each other. It allowed the two adjoining water levels, the pit in the hydro pod and the moon pool, to be at completely uneven levels. It was his Grandfather's work which dictated the pit needed to be full of water and the technology permanently submerged. The concept was his Grandfather's but he redesigned and built it from scratch. It was the first thing he ever engineered where he truly felt of use to the family's work.

As far as the actual pod was concerned, it was inconsequential as long as it remained submerged but to the habitat design it was monumental. The biggest teething problem they discovered initially, when the moon pool filled for the hyper sub to access, the external pressure from being so deep would buckle the intricate valve system which was why they originally introduced the venting procedure.

This alleviated the water pressure on the valve by flooding the pod at the same time as the moon pool, levelling the two compartments. They also found it useful to vent, keeping the water circulating because the water in the pit would eventually boil as the pods operating temperature increased. As a matter of protocol they flushed periodically and started each new testing session with fresh water for consistent results.

Matt had planned to install a cooling system to the pit, which would alleviate the need for the venting, except when the moon pool was in operation. Right now though he was grateful it was still on his 'to do list', as the hydro pod venting was what had saved them.

Removing the last of the pinch bolts, Matt pulled the handle at the bottom and pushed at the top, tilting the valve in its captive ring. He was grateful the moon pool's water level was lower than normal, because the pod would have filled, finding the natural equilibrium between the two compartments.

Without the computer controlled valve in place, they would level out at the higher of the two. He had expected he would have to close it and vent the pod, lowering the water level but they were almost the same, luck was on his side for a change. Matt squeezed through the bottom section of the valve, swimming along the vent chamber, directly into the pit beneath the raised pod. He broke the surface of the water, athletically leaping on to the mesh walkway in one swift movement.

Aunt Pat rushed forward and tried to fling her tied arms around him.

"Thank God! We had this horrible feeling you didn't make it through the water tight doors, they closed so fast." He stopped her, cupping her warm hands in his, smiling and winked cheekily. On the wall by the side of them was a small water tight box. He undid the lid and fished a pair of electrical cutters from the spare tools snipping the tie wrap, freeing her. She flung her arms round his neck, pulling him into a hug.

Grabbing the cutters from Matt she removed the tie wraps from James, Charlie and then Lizzie, who gave Dan a proper hug, kissing him passionately. Dan felt a little awkward in front of his family, but everyone just seemed to smile. Matt also winked at him, making him feel even more self conscious.

Lizzie tried to wake Ashley, who was still out cold. "How are we going to move Ash?"

Dan had the solution. "I left my mask in the moon pool. It should still be in there somewhere, as long as it never got washed through into the lab, with the internal tidal wave."

Matt jumped back into the water pit disappearing from view, Lizzie stared after him. "Where does this go?"

James was getting ready to follow. "There's a special valve which maintains the water at a specific level. It's also what vents the pod during the moon pool door activation, which is why the chamber fills to the top. Matt has tilted the valve externally. We can swim through into the moon pool and escape in the hyper sub." As he finished his sentence he sat down and promptly slid into the water, bobbing back to the surface poking his head above the water. "Ladies follow me one by one. I'm going to help Matt find a mask of some description so we can get Ash out through the valve. I'll be back with Matt, it'll take the four of us to do it I reckon."

He held his nose and promptly disappeared underwater. Pat sat down on the side and slid herself down into the water following her husband.

"I want to stay and help Ash. Dad you go, we'll be fine. Once Ash is in the water she'll be okay. I think it'll be harder to navigate the more of us that are down there."

Dan agreed with Liz. "Go now Charlie. McAdams hasn't noticed we are leaving yet, his back is to us. Go before he realises we're escaping.

I'll look after Liz, I promise."

Matt surfaced. Exiting the water he carried one of the face masks he and Dan had used to escape living. Charlie sat on the edge dropping himself in, giving a final concerned glance at Dan and Lizzie before disappearing beneath the water and swimming out through the hydro vent, into the moon pool.

"I had some of the spare oxygen canisters in the workshop, let's get Ash out of here. Once she's in the water, Lizzie and I will swim her through. Stay here Dan, I need you to help me when I get back. I've told James to stay in operations and get the hyper sub ready to go."

Matt unscrewed the spent canisters replacing them, he punched the button on top of the mask breaking the seal and the oxygen began to flow freely, placing it over Ash's face and securing it tightly. "Get in the water Liz, hold her feet as Dan and I lower her in."

As Ash submerged, the blood from her wounds turned the water scarlet, cleansing them in the salt water which had entered through the moon pool. Lizzie took two breathes and pulled Ash under, Matt followed guiding her head and arms. Lizzie reversed down the vent easily sliding through the tilted valve. She fed Ash's motionless body though and single handedly brought her to the surface. Lizzie adopted a life saving side stroke towing Ash under her chin to the walkway. Charlie and James hooked a hand under each armpit and pulled her out, then repeated the procedure on Lizzie.

Matt turned and headed back to Dan. As he surfaced Dan helped him from the water.

"What do you have in mind Matt?"

Matt smiled mischievously. "We have to destroy everything Dan. We planned to leave the habitat intact for the future. However with living destroyed, its usefulness is pretty fucked. Plus with McAdams locked inside we can't leave anything to chance, we just can't afford to leave any trace of the technology. If McAdams has left a trail on the surface, he may inadvertently lead others here, the pod'll still get into the wrong hands and we can't risk that. I never told James what I'm planning."

"What do you want me to do?"

"Talk to McAdams, I need him to do something stupid."

Dan looked at Matt but did not question him. He pressed the tannoy button to talk to the lab. "Hello John, you don't mind if I call you John, do you?"

McAdams turned; until he heard the tannoy he had his back to the hydro pod. You could see as his eyes fell on the empty pod he was stunned and livid. Then he spotted Matt inside.

"I just wanted to say goodbye John, it's been, how shall I say … emotional!"

McAdams managed to grin, contorting his macabre face into a twisted and evil smile, speaking with his controlled, calm and polite manner into the microphone.

"You can't leave Daniel. You're going to die down here, just like me. We're all going to drown, becoming entombed; a part of this wonderful underwater time capsule."

McAdams caressed the remote detonator. He had been looking at it for a while now, he could see no other way, his options had finally run out. He was sealed inside the lab which was slowly flooding. There was no means of escape, he knew that now, he was going to detonate the last of the charges crippling them, killing them all.

Matt stabbed at the control panel to start the pod, fortunately the systems were all still fully functioning, with enough battery power to kick start the system. Within moments the anemometers were swinging inside their respective glass tubes and the swirling vortexes danced.

They started to glow cyan and an eerie low pitched whine started to permeate the pod, not excessive but it was annoying to say the least, like tinnitus. The noise penetrated deep down inside the ear drum, the inner ear feeling like it was burning and itchy.

"Matt?" Dan was staring across the lab, watching the water fall from the ceiling. "Where is the water disappearing to? He detonated the explosive punching the hole in the lab ceiling a while ago and the lab is not filling up yet."

Matt glanced out across the decimated lab from the hydro pod. "The lab is like living, underneath is the pipe work and engineering to control the pod. It's like an iceberg, the pod itself is the tip. Underneath holds all of the energy banks and substations for us to test the system. The water is draining into the subterranean level first."

"So what are you gonna do?"

Matt punched the last few commands into the console. "I'm gonna overload the pod."

"What'll that do?"

"I've no idea. We've never done it before. Think of this as the first trial run, ever!" Matt grabbed the ratchet and smashed it across the console, shattering the dials and delicate controls.

"Right, time to go. You gotta get McAdams to bite now Dan. Now!"

Dan was unsure what he meant. "Well John, I'd love to say it's been a pleasure but that would be a complete lie. It's time for us to leave. So I'll be wishing you a fond farewell and an extremely painful onward journey, to hell."

McAdams jeered at the pair of them through the glass. "If I'm not gonna survive, I'll be fucked if I'm gonna let any of you." Closing his eyes, he pressed the button on the detonator.

The shock in McAdams face was obvious, his eyes shot open, what transpired he certainly did not expect. The force of the downward explosion whisked him off his feet yet again, blasting his ravaged body forty feet across the lab, smashing against the last of the PVC sheets and through into the metal walls. This time, the lab hardly rocked under the force of the explosion mainly because of their delicate placement on top of the lab. The harshest movement was the outside waters explosion induced momentum, causing the lab and operations to sway independently, rocking the individual chambers as if riding several waves.

When Matt left life support after Dan, he surveyed the entire exterior removing three explosives attached to the outside. One on top of operations, one to the moon pool doors and the third was attached to the underside of the labs gimbal. McAdams intended to destroy the habitat if things did not go to plan, which they had not, and that was what Matt bargained for.

Matt had repositioned all three charges on top of the lab, directly above the gimbal. The centre point of the lab marked by a small nipple on the upper most part of the structure. The charges set in a triangle, on detonation punched a hole the size of a fist. Individually they would cause a small tear in the hull but as a group detonation they were far more powerful.

The water cascaded through the hole into the lab, hundreds of gallons a second poured in, filling the lower level in seconds. Before smashing the console, Matt had switched off the lock out protocols, leaving the exterior door unlocked.

He opened the lock out chamber tantalising McAdams for salvation. Seeing his chance, trudging through the rising water, he stumbled and fell, got to his feet, doggedly heading for the lock out chamber to the hydro pod. He did not want to die, that much was obvious.

"What the hell are you doing Matt?" Dan was shocked. Was he going to save him?

Matt screamed above the roar of the falling water. "Get inside the pod now." Dan glared at him but did as he was told, Matt followed, slamming the door shut as McAdams stumbled into the lock out chamber. Pushing the door against the raging torrent sealing himself in, the bubbling water became a distant memory as the soundproof room enveloped him.

As the door seated into its aperture, from above there was a hydraulic hiss. Looking up McAdams watched as the safety solenoids slid down their internal tubes within the acrylic sheeting, locking the door into place and sealing the chamber doors for the last time. The same thing happened top and bottom on the pod door separating him from Matt and Dan. He was locked in.

Matt screamed. "Yes, you bastard, not so fucking cocky now are ya?"

Dan stared through the acrylic glass at McAdams. His body language was different. He was a beaten man, resolved to his fate. He had little sympathy, a snake behind protective glass at the zoo. "What happened, what did you do?"

"To start the pod, I had to disengage the locking protocols, which opened the chamber door. You distracted him long enough so he didn't notice. He detonated the final charges, which he thought were still attached to the outside positions where he left them to destroy the entire habitat, however I placed them all on the roof in a single position punching the hole in the ceiling."

"But why did you open the door for him, why did you not just let him die?"

"Oh he'll die, but he won't die quite so quickly, he'll suffer, just like our parents did."

The pair of them stared unsympathetically at their parent's murderer. Justice was hard to face directly but they had little pity, considering what they had both lost.

"I had to open the door to let some water into the chamber. It was the only way to automatically get the lock out system to engage without access to the console, which I smashed. The sensors detected the rising water inside, however the system failed to realise the water was coming from the lab itself, not the pod. As soon as both doors closed, they automatically locked, sealing us in here and McAdams to his death."

Matt took two large flat headed screwdrivers from the tool box and inserted each of them through the lowering track stopping it from moving. He jumped into the water disappearing into the vent.

McAdams stared into space, his hardened black eyes gave nothing away, he was resigned to his fate. Dan smiled and waved, as if waving farewell to a friend, he turned and jumped into the water. McAdams was alone, the way he had been his entire life, watching listlessly as water filled the lab and gradually entombed his acrylic airtight coffin.

76

Dan exited the valve. Matt tilted it back, seating it correctly and proceeded to replace the individual pinch bolts. When everything was secure, he locked the valve in position, rotating an internal lock and sealing the valves operation completely. The vents were locked tight; nothing could enter or exit, the lab was sealed. James and Charlie were strapping the unconscious Ash into the back seat of the hyper sub.

Pat helped Matt from the pool, looking worried. "What happened? We thought we heard another explosion but nothing like the force of the first two."

"McAdams detonated the last of the charges he deployed."

"My God." Pat looked aghast.

"Don't worry. What he'd not realised is I moved them from the rest of the habitat. I positioned the charges in the dead centre of the lab blasting a hole in the roof. I'm hoping it'll give us chance to get out of here before the lab starts to buckle the gimbal under the additional weight. I was outside when living flipped; the gimbal remained stable under enormous loading. I'm just hoping the lab'll fill evenly and not flip like living did."

Lizzie glanced around the moon pool, it was leaning at an alarming rate, the uneven water surface once more noticeably crept up the exterior wall inch by inch. "Matt, I think we're already starting to lean, look at the water level rising."

They all stared at the moon pool surface, Lizzie was right. This was happening far quicker than Matt had anticipated. "We've gotta hurry, we don't have much time. The lab is filling fast and not level, a lot faster than I assumed. Everyone in the sub, now!" He barked the orders like a drill instructor.

James climbed into the cockpit of the sub, strapping himself into the plush leather. The bucket seats offered luxury but they were also there for comfort and protection. A five point seat belt strapped them to the submarine securing the occupant safely. Dan climbed into the second to last seat and Lizzie jumped in after him, snuggling between his legs, it was cramped but necessary. The sub was supposed to take five passengers but there was going to be seven of them.

James was concentrating as he activated life support and the hyper subs internal systems. "Matt, what is the load capacity? Are we going to be able to carry all of us out of here in the sub?"

Matt shrugged. "I don't know, we're just gonna have to find out. We're two bodies extra and I simply don't know whether the ballast will be enough to bring the sub to the surface."

Aunt Pat ever the optimist. "It'll be fine Matt, get in Charlie, your riding with me, no wandering hands." She giggled like a school girl. "We're the biggest sweetheart, get in the middle, hopefully it'll keep the sub balanced. Tell you what, if we survive we'll both go on a diet."

"Are you calling me rotund Pat?" Charlie mocked.

"Ah no honey, you and me, we're just big boned." Pat smiled her infectious smile.

"I wouldn't want you any other way gorgeous." Charlie said as he lowered himself into the middle seat.

James snapped in a playful way. "Stop bloody flirting you two and get in, we can discuss the merits of obesity and copping a handful when we get to the surface."

Pat hooked her leg over the side and lowered herself onto Charlie. "Mind my bum."

"I don't mind it at all." Charlie said, a little unsure where to place his hands as Pat wiggled her way in, jamming the pair of them into the seat. "At least we won't need the safety harness."

"No you're probably right, although it's certainly gonna take more than a shoe horn and liberal amounts of grease to get us out again." They both started giggling again, like a couple of school kids.

James was getting impatient. "Matt get in, we need to get out of here now, the whole habitat is reaching the point it did before when living broke away. I don't think the cradle will hold the sub in place with the extra weight of us when it shifts again and we'll be screwed if the sub gets damaged."

Charlie and Pat continued to giggle. "I think he means us Pat?"

Lizzie was losing patience, she just wanted to be out of this place. "You two get a room! Matt come on." She screamed at him.

"Hang on, there's something I need to do."

Matt ran through operations into the computer room. Hung on the wall directly in front of the doorway was the remote operations console for the pod. Quickly he scanned the readings of its operational status. There was an error on the console, the lowering track had failed.

The system was going to automatically shut down, as he feared. He manually turned off the safety protocols, setting the output to way beyond the systems known maximum test levels, opening the output as high as he could.

Alongside the console were banks of archive disks, beeping intermittently. The electrical system had failed automatically transferring power to the UPS systems. The high pitched beep was a warning to shut them down before complete power failure, which could cause loss of data or damage a drive. He still had enough time.

From the moon pool he heard the distant voice of Dan. "What are you doing?"

"Hurry up Matt, we've got to get out of here. If we don't get out now, I'm not sure we'll have the clearance between the habitat and the hangar bay floor. It's going to be close to get the sub out whatever we do?" James turned in his seat to Pat. "What is he doing?" Pat shrugged.

Matt stood before the vast array of backup drives, most were redundant. Only five held all of the specialist data from the wet lab. If they were destroyed, everything and everyone, including his parent's death would have been in vain, he could not let that happen.

The array of drives measured ten by ten, one hundred drives exactly. Each held a capacity of a terabyte, one hundred terabytes in total. The array had been a nightmare to install, like so many things in this doomed place.

Ninety five disks seemed excessive if they were to be unused, however they were, and constantly. The supercomputer Ash and James used to compute their masses of data would use the excess disks as virtual memory space; it sped up the lengthy calculations and also helped increase the lead times on data turnover. Installing the supercomputer had increased their operational turnover by nearly six months because they were able to process and analyse the data quicker. That's why they were ready to leave; the system had proved itself way ahead of schedule.

The drives usually blinked their little blue LEDs as it communicated to the lab. As data was being written to and from the drive, the LED would blink faster. All one hundred of the LEDs were lit and static. The only reason Matt could think of was that the link to the computer systems in the lab had been severed. The supercomputer was also beeping a high pitched whine. The power was out, everything was on battery, was that the reason?

Matt pulled open the tiny screen on the disk array, pressing the touch sensitive screen, back lighting itself to reveal a login screen. He entered the password using the onscreen keyboard, USS ORISKANY accessing a systems screen. Scrolling down through the many system menus, he highlighted REMOVE DATA DRIVE and hit return.

ENTER NUMBER:_

Matt fished around in his pocket removing the two tortoiseshell knives, opening the first blade it was Lizzie's knife, he pocketed it again and opened the second which was Ash's. He knew the coordinates off the top of his head but if he got it wrong or made a mistake, the disks were rendered useless and everything would be destroyed. The blade read 30:02.6_87:00.4, he entered the first two numbers from the Oriskany's coordinates, three and then zero.

ENTER NUMBER: 30_

The blue LED on the drive, three columns across from the left, zero down, flashed three times and then extinguished. Matt grabbed the quick release arm of the caddy, lifting it, disengaging the mechanism pulling the drive from its slot. On top of the drive he had written in permanent pen three, zero. He placed the drive on top of the array bank. The display asked if he wanted to remove another drive, YES or NO? Selecting YES, the screen immediately returned ENTER NUMBER, this time he entered zero, two, the third and fourth numbers from the Oriskany coordinates.

ENTER NUMBER: 02_

The blue LED in the first column, two rows down blinked and turned off, Matt removed the drive. Again on top in his own hand was written zero, two. Following the on screen instructions Matt continued entering the coordinates until he removed all five drives, the third from the sixth column, eight rows down, the fourth from the seventh column, zero rows down and the final drive first column, fourth row.

He grabbed one of the large hard shell carrying cases scattered across the computer room, many of which had carried delicate pieces of equipment down into the lab, including the supercomputer which he lovingly rebuilt. Each case was shock and water proof. He inserted the five drives into protective foam inserts, separating the individual drives, stuffing extra foam round the drives so they did not bang against each other in transport.

Matt was so distracted by his endeavours he failed to tune into the structure's resistance. It groaned and strained against the weight of the lab pulling it sideways. The bank of drives and computer room fell silent. The UPS failed, shutting down all the systems.

Matt's focus, suddenly drawn away from his task, realised the lab was at breaking point. Silently it continued to tilt on the gimbal. How much further before something finally broke was unknown. James had been right to ask the question, would the sub be able to get out from under operations if the angle was too great?

Grabbing the case, Matt ran down the incline to the moon pool. Operations hung at a daunting angle as the whole habitat continued to move. They were waiting impatiently for him, the sub, attached in its cradle was also at the same angle making it extremely uncomfortable for the occupants inside. He stepped up, placing the drives into the foot well of the second seat and throwing his left leg into the sub.

Without warning, there was an almighty wrenching noise from below him in the moon pool. Matt knew instinctively what it was. The connecting strut through the hydro vent was giving way. Having no time to react, or hang on, operations lurched violently as the strut broke away. The buoyancy forced the whole habitat to swing upwards, still attached via the strut of the armadillo to living, like a pendulum.

The uniform arced momentum threw Matt backwards landing heavily on his back on the moon pool walkway, he was swept along by the moon pool's water as it surged inwards like a second tsunami. The shifting water's movement caused operations to swing faster on its pivot.

The family watched in horror, helpless as Matt disappeared, carried at great speed back through the door. His body defenceless against the deluge, having nothing to hang on to, he tried to relax with the current. He had learnt during his diving career that fighting strong currents proved more futile than if you rode them, conserving your energy until you could break free. He had seen many a competent diver tragically overcome with fatigue.

The water washed him around operations like a whirlpool, white tops swirling and churning, finally dumping his battered and bruised body in the centre.

The excess twisting and pendulum motion against the hull finally sheared the remaining connecting strut, there was a deafening crack of ripping metal and the lab shot sideways in the opposite direction for the last time. This time the water was less savage but its continuing momentum throughout the rooms dislodged his dive bottles from the workshop.

Finally, not tethered to the lab, operations swung back to its correct level position. The rack holding the dive bottles moved under the surging water, catapulting several from their mountings. Matt rolled out of the way as the rocket shaped projectiles flew through the air, the largest crash landed missing his head by millimetres.

The bouncing missiles dramatically span like yellow Catherine wheels, cart wheeling across the floor, crashing into the acrylic tube on the outside of the moon pool shattering on impact. The tube disintegrated under a cloud of crystalline dust and acrylic shards, exploding around Matt who shielded his face.

"Matt?" There was a chorus of shouts from the moon pool at the noise and the unknown. Matt surveyed the damage of the shattered tube, the sharp plastic had severed the hydraulic hoses, hydraulic fluid spraying outwards like an arterial bleed. The watertight doors were dead; there was no way of mending it quickly, nor did he have the spares to fix the doors and seal the moon pool. Stepping into view in the doorway, Aunt Pat looked relieved.

"Get in Matt, we need to go."

He remained stationary, looking at his family secure in the sub. There was a deathly silence. They stared at him. Crossing to the back of the sub where Dan and Lizzie were squeezed into their seat, hopping on board, he lent in through the canopy and whispered in Dan's ear, so no one else could hear his final wish.

"Bury Simon next to my casket in the family plot, please." Dan could only nod, he mouthed his thanks and then kissed Lizzie goodbye on her cheek. He held Aunt Pat's loving gaze, swallowing hard he whispered. "Look after them, you're the only mother we have left."

Reaching up Aunt Pat touched his cheek, tears streaming down her face. He held her hand in his against his face, slowly letting it slide as he backed away. Grabbing the submarine canopy, he slammed it shut and locked it. Taking a moment with James they locked eyes through the canopy, dropping back onto the walkway he nodded without words.

Matt stood in the water tight doorway, watching them, watching him. He opened the release valves to the moon pool, overriding the safety locks because the doors were completely inoperable.

The pressure started to build as the whole of operations intentionally began to fill with sea water for the last time. It quickly rose, flooding the entire room. He clung to the doorway, taking his final breath, the water submerging him. Matt could no longer see his family in the sub, focus underwater was impossible but he knew they were watching him.

Above his head, he was aware the red light came on. He pushed his hand up into the shattered acrylic tube depressing the micro switch. Usually the inner ball would rise to do this but without the containment tube or the use of the doors, it had to be manually operated. The micro switch released the moon pool's exterior doors, opening them. He slowly waved at no one in particular, saying goodbye.

77

"What's he doing James?" Pat screamed hysterically from behind him.

"Saving us all Pat, I think." James looked at Matt, who grimly nodded, he nodded in return.

"Well stop him. We can't have gone through all this to lose another."

"I don't think we've much of a choice my love." James' voice was low and touching, choking back emotion, Matt was his son too. "Matt is doing this, so we can all live."

Pat stared through the canopy of the sub. Matt for all intents and purposes had been their adopted son for many years. She had promised Susan she would never let anything happen to him and this felt like the ultimate betrayal of trust, both Matt's parents had given their lives for them. She watched him grow into adulthood, becoming the most technically gifted man she ever had the privilege to know.

He had not had the academic intellect or studious nature of Ash, he never applied himself towards academia in the traditional sense and he cared more for the outdoors than books. His intellect was far more hands on and tangible, looking at any given problem; designing, engineering and building a solution from scratch.

He could make the impossible possible, understanding the restraints and instantly creating a solution. His and Dan's general outlook and common sense towards life balanced the scattiness and sheer lunacy which Ash displayed on so many occasions. Between the three of them, they had balanced and grounded each other throughout their childhood and burgeoning adulthood; Lizzie was the glue that bound them together.

Throughout, Matt remained stoically insular about many things in his life, never discussing anything private within the family. She had respected him for it but now felt betrayed that she would never fully know or understand the brave man standing in the doorway. Nor would she be able to see him outgrow the family, which he should have done, making a life for himself outside the fold.

Charlie held Pat's left hand, gripping him tightly, her chubby right palm was placed against the canopy, trying to reach out. Dan held Lizzie tightly in his arms, who buried herself backwards into his chest. A selfish part of her was glad it was not Dan, but equally she could not look, she tightly shut her eyes. She could not bear to see Matt's final moments. They had only just been reunited and having him torn away from her again was more than she could bear. She was grateful Ash was unconscious in the seat behind; this would haunt her for the rest of her life.

She whispered quietly. "What did Matt say to you?"

Dan could not tell her, not yet. It was a private matter he had to deal with for Matt; he respected and understood his wishes. He would tell Liz and the family at the right time, but for now, he simply remained silent. He watched his best friend through the canopy and gripped Lizzie tighter as the flood water crept up his legs and body. Matt clung to the doorway as the water filled the moon pool and the rest of operations.

All of them stared through the fermenting water, they knew the last shift in the structure had destroyed an operational part of the system. Matt would have fixed it if he could; he knew how and would have done so. The water calmed slightly, clearing. The light illuminated above Matt to give the all clear and open the moon pool doors.

Matt stood immortalized in an aura and haze of iridescent colours surrounding his body in saint-like proportions. The occupants of the sub were stunned to silence; Pat stopped crying in amazement. A field of subtle, luminous radiation surrounded his body. He looked as close to God as he could ever get.

Pat smiled through her pain and tears knowing his selflessness would be rewarded in death. What they could see, but did not understand, was the emergency lighting from operations refracted through the water, mixed with hydraulic fluid was highlighting a shifting rainbow halo around his body and head. His visage was beautiful. He waved goodbye, the coloured wisps and clouds gently hung from his hand.

The awe struck silence was broken as James released the cradle holding the hyper sub. The moon pool doors opened beneath them. James gave a final glance to Matt, they all did, even Lizzie. Flooding the trim and ballast tanks, the sub dropped effortlessly, throttling the engines, swinging counter clockwise through ninety degrees, the sub rotated and dropped towards the hangar floor. A proximity warning light illuminated on the dashboard. The hull was as close to the floor as he could get without touching. James turned on the exterior lights, illuminating the bottom of the moon pool's doors, fully retracted to their open position.

Charlie was nervous, he was never a great passenger at the best of times, feeling even   worse knowing he was inside a submarine without a visible route of escape. "Are we going to get under there James? It looks mighty close." The bottom of the moon pool was still in plain view. There was no way the hyper sub could squeeze between the open doors and the hangar floor.

"That it does Charlie, that it does!" James gritted his teeth, rotating the hyper sub back clockwise, through ninety degrees. The lab was resting on the hangar floor directly in front of them. The twisted and mangled structure, was blocking their path.

The gimbal had given way under the added weight of the water as it flooded. He had been outside enough times on dives to check the outer structure to realise a nightmare of epic proportions. The exterior metal plating which should have been snug had obviously twisted and flexed. The welded joints were split and clearly visible. The structure had so many gaps, it was a disaster, they were lucky to have got this far relatively unscathed.

He continued to rotate the sub. The gimbal under operations looked to be holding, considering that too was now flooded, although Matt had reinforced the structure because it needed to withstand more weight as the moon pool was constantly filled and emptied, allowing access, so maybe the structure would hold permanently. It was a shame it was not level, or they would have been able to get out straight away.

"James." Dan shouted from the back of the sub. "Head to the right of the gimbal, go underneath the escape hatch of the compression chamber and then down the side. We may be able to traverse the whole habitat or rise up and go over the top. There should be more than enough clearance with it resting on the hangar floor."

Dan was right; James piloted the sub forward and expertly manoeuvred his way around the gimbal. They looked out of the sub like tourists, Dan could not help but wish Simon was here. After witnessing his excitement over the original plans, Dan knew he would have been blown away to see what Matt achieved in this inhospitable place.

With the lighting from the hyper sub, the exterior of the habitat was actually nothing extraordinary, it was simply a water tight box but what it signified in underwater development was monumental.

It was sad to see its demise, even for Dan who had only been aboard for a few short hours. He could see for the first time what the family had achieved and given their lives for. Matt was right though, their pig headedness about the pod was shadowing another great achievement, the underwater wet lab.

James slowly edged the sub to the back of operations. Adjusting the ballast tanks the hyper sub rose upwards. It was far slower than he expected but he was grateful that it did, it must be the additional weight, with Matt on board they may not have surfaced at all.

He piloted forward over the top of the lab. Directly in front of them was a narrow projection of light, a column shining through the twisted break in the metal surface of the lab where the explosives detonated. Air bubbles pulsed through the blistering bright white light. As they drifted lazily to the hangar roof they widened into circulating dancing doughnuts, twisting and undulating, bursting and scattering along the rust encrusted ceiling above.

James shifted uncomfortably, looking over his shoulder to the back of the cab. "Dan, what did Matt do before you came back through the vent?" He knew the answer long before Dan spoke.

"He activated the pod, setting the output to maximum, also jamming the lowering tracks. He wanted to destroy the pod because he was worried McAdams may have left a trail to the wet lab."

James knew he was right, it had to be destroyed. There was no other way and he would not have been man enough to do it, he knew that. Not hesitating a second longer at the glimmering light, opening the throttle wide on the hyper sub, it surged forward, pushing them back in their seats, it accelerated surprisingly fast. The engines quickly propelled the hyper sub across the top of the twisted broken lab. At the edge, James plunged them downwards at full tilt.

The pod had never reached a pure white light before throughout their entire testing, he knew it was not a good sign and unsure of what would happen, if anything at all. James angrily stabbed the button to a rather mundane looking garage door opener praying it would work in time. The opener was totally out of keeping with the slickness of the rest of the cockpits plush leather interior, it was alien.

In the darkness he could see a small rectangular opening below, getting wider. Thank God it still worked. Light was streaming up the corridor; it was at least daylight outside.

"James." Pat screamed from behind him. "You're going too fast, you can't exit from this angle."

"Fuck!" Pat was right, as ever. There was not enough clearance in the corridor, the sub was too long for this manoeuvre. He would jam it or worse, break it in two.

James panicking, more through luck than judgement, spun the steering wheel managing to level the sub and perform, in essence, an underwater handbrake turn. Perfectly executed like a pro as if intended, he reversed the engines, adjusted the ballast, trimmed and turned the rudder all at the same time, the hyper sub equivalent of patting your head and rubbing your stomach. The sub swung sideways reversing into position above the opening into the corridor, hovering, motionless, facing the habitat one momentous last time.

James opened the ballast tanks and the hyper sub started to lower into the corridor facing the door of the underwater bar at the end of the corridor. All of them watched through the crystal waters, the light show bouncing around on top of the lab. The lighting no longer projected the pinpoint clarity of a laser beam, it bubbled and tormented, flickering on and off as if failing inside the lab. The penultimate flash was the brightest and longest, not blinding but causing considerable discomfort to the eyes. The occupants of the sub could not tear themselves away from the spectacle.

James was too busy exiting the confines of the hangar to be concerned with the lab as its devastating final moments unfolded. Double checking his proximity distances each side, the sub dropped to the corridor floor. It was a small gap to get through, Matt would have done it in his sleep. He stabbed the garage door opener button for the last time and the ceiling started to retract, sealing the wet lab for the final time. Breaking his concentration, he too looked upwards.

Bursting from the top of the lab, reminiscent of a nuclear plume, the five of them watched in awe as an underwater mushroom cloud erupted in the dazzling light, filled with tiny pockets of air, sparkling like a silver confetti cannon. It rose quickly, fanning outwards in concentric circles across the ceiling and down the walls of the hangar.

The entire lab instantaneously inflated like a lung taking its last fateful breath. The walls moved several feet, then imploded, the lab crushed like a beer can.

78

Looking through the acrylic panels, the flooded laboratory's contents floated listlessly around the room. Paper work from endless test runs of the pod, strange clothing including Aunt Pat's amazing knitwear collection, hovered like ghostly apparitions in the water. All seemed calm. The metal structure had long since given up its torturous battle to survive, twisting and protesting, its final death throes were far from subdued.

As the whole lab collapsed to the hangar floor the final spasms had been a rollercoaster ride of epic proportions. Everything had shifted uncontrollably as the gimbal structure had wrenched itself through the floor of the lab, looking like a giant discarded gyroscope. The supporting structure had forced its way through the floor like a rising mountain range as it failed under the excess weight, scattering the work surfaces and the last of the PVC cladding, the lab's technology nestled and formed its own redundant structures around its base.

McAdams nursed his wounds on the floor, staring at the wall of water, an intense illumination pouring from the cubicle next to him. The pod originally was beautiful to watch, the two glass tubes either side danced with such majestic ferocity, it was totally mesmerising. He observed intently as it progressed through cosmic Technicolor, however its beauty had begun to torture his vision.

Intense bursts of light blinded his eyes causing retinal flashes, blazing painfully across his vision like lightning bolts. Its progression through the spectrum had been slow, majestically traversing through the colours.

What interested McAdams, although failing to understand what they were for, was the internal sparks, as if attracted by the vortex, spiralled defiantly into the centrifugal cone and disappearing. They danced within the light display, always a step ahead of their counter- part's colour. If the pod was cyan, the plasma sparks were an electric purple. Like digital colour space, it only had a finite spectrum. Its hue was always intrinsically linked to its base colour.

Inside the chamber itself was one of the most beautiful man made sights McAdams could remember, or had ever seen. Surrounding the pod like a floating aurora borealis was a free forming rainbow cloud. He had seen the Northern Lights, these lights however changed with the same correlating spectrum as the pod. A completely different intensity, unlike the Northern Lights, it could be seen in daylight.

He could only think of one other sight producing a somewhat similar spectacle, when he surfed off the coast of Indonesia in Bali. During his surfing, the spray from the oceans waves caused mini rainbows that encapsulated and moved with the rider, so many concentrated on their surfing without watching the natural phenomenon surrounding them. They were called spray bows and were stunning to behold.

As the pod's intensity increased, the colour ferocity of the light show in the pod proportionately decreased, eventually becoming a pure dancing white light. The pod glowed and the plasma sparked, like lightning bolts. The intensity increased until he could no longer focus on the severe light. It felt like looking into the arc of a welding torch without the necessary eye protection.

Instead McAdams sat staring into the tortured wet lab. The acrylic tomb he found himself in was sealed, airtight and almost watertight. The flexing on the outer skin as it twisted must have put pressure on the joints. A tiny rivulet of water ran down the inside of his chamber. Tracing its constantly changing route, he sat in at least a foot of water, he would suffocate long before drowning.

In his head, he also heard a constant high pitched noise. At first the whine was barely detectable but after a while it started to become unbearable. He believed he had suffered concussion, the blows to the head Morris had given him being the obvious culprit. The sensation was more constant; an itching deep within his inner ear canal, eventually sensing it was burning or maybe reacting to an invisible force or gas within the insular room.

Outside the glass tomb, the red lights started to flash. He was unduly bothered at first as he was sealed in the next chamber. Through the floor, where he was sat he could feel a low resonance in the metal, the water around the edge of the acrylic walls vibrated making miniature ripples.

Holding his hand against the acrylic wall between the pod and his compartment it felt warm. Alarmed, he pushed his hand and instead of a firm resistance the wall slowly indented tracing his imprint like an executive toy pin screen.

Focusing into the bright light, he tried to see past the high intensity light. The test tubes on the pod looked as though they were sagging, could that be happening? Pushing his finger into the acrylic glass, it disappeared to the end of his finger then started to burn.

The plastic was becoming increasingly pliable between the cubicles; the temperature in the other room must have been astronomical. The flood water in the lab against the exterior walls kept the temperature lower, maintaining well below the critical point where it would become malleable, but the acrylic between the pod and lock out chamber was thinner, only three quarters of an inch, would it melt?

The pod changed, the resonance in the metal floor dropped and then restarted. The light stuttered, blinking and then shimmied before resuming, was it burning itself out? His face pressed against the acrylic trying to see, not into the light but through it, at the structure itself beyond the light core. He could see nothing. He blinked, white burned into his retina. Retinal burn is a wound that does not cause pain. He knew what he was doing but had to see.

The pod blinked again, in those milliseconds as the light faded and resumed, he could see the metal core was sagging, glowing red hot. The lowering track had fused its components locking them into position. When the light returned, the acrylic on the inside was charring, turning molten black, studying the interior for the first time, ignoring the technology. The whole room was charred, as if burned, realising too the water pit was empty. The borealis he had seen earlier, which he revered in its beauty, was viewable as the water evaporated into small droplets inside the chamber.

In horror and sheer panic he pressed himself flat against the opposite wall, the acrylic slowly melting. Helplessly he watched as burning molten plastic seeped to the floor, the Perspex dividing the two rooms was spreading a plastic river of flames, thinning his protection. As the wall thickness melted away, the high pitched whine started to penetrate, not just his ears, his mind also screamed in agony, it was excruciating.

The temperature of his tomb was increasing. He felt like he was sweating. Reaching up to wipe the sweat away, the back of his hand was smeared in blood, his ears were bleeding internally, his ear drums had been perforated. The rest happened in silence.

The closest part of the acrylic wall to the pod suddenly drooped, falling away like wax, a hole appeared in the door. McAdams screamed as the temperature increased like a furnace. The moisture in his throat evaporated continuing down into his lungs, the scream turning in to an agonized gargle. The water he was sat in instantly vaporized, the steam scolding his open skin, blistering it, filling instantly with protective fluid. He closed his scolded eyes praying for death, his prayers were unanswered.

His neoprene wetsuit melted away from his skin and ran like boiling tar across his chest and groin, burning his crushed genitals. He clawed at the burning sensation before starting to lose any feeling at all. His skin turned numb and black as the rubber spontaneously combusted across his body, his hair flambéed, disappearing in an instant.

The charred face and body of McAdams was unrecognisable as he writhed on the floor, smelling his own skin barbecuing in the flames. It was the last sense to disappear from his ravaged body. His last sensation was to smell his own burning flesh as he died on the floor of the lock out chamber.

The pod continued to heat. The flames died as the oxygen within was used up. The pod had long since stopped producing excess oxygen because internally the water had evaporated in the heat. With the valve closed it, could no longer feed itself. As the lab collapsed on top of the gimbal breaking through the floor, it severed the pumps and connecting pipe work. The pod was operating without constraint.

The oxygen within the pod finally spent caused a vacuum, the hot sagging thick acrylic wall, pressurised by the sea water externally gave way and thousands of tonnes of sea water fell in filling the void. The force of the water hitting such high temperatures expanded rapidly, causing the pressure to push outwards. The structure started to inflate.

The pod itself imploded, the borosilicate glass bulbs shattered inwards, along with the core, a massive cavitation bubble formed in the surrounding liquid, which rapidly collapsed pulling the lab inwards. Thirty tonnes of steel instantly deflated like a balloon, crushing everything inside.

79

Niles swam back from Hydrous, grabbing the side of Hazletine, the family work boat. She was not pretty but she was the hardest working vessel on the marina.

"We're lucky, the bow is split, but only in the front locker compartment, which contained most of the water. I've managed to push the boards back into alignment with my feet, stemming the water flow. We'll be able to pump most of the water out keeping her afloat to tow her back to the yard. I've also inflated a couple of bags just in case but I can't see her going anywhere now. A lesser construction would have sunk like a stone, she's amazing!"

Joel looked concerned, scouting the dawn horizon. "Is there any sign of them?"

Niles shook his head despondently, hauling himself onto the deck. "None. It looks like Hydrous has been abandoned, but there's no sign of a struggle either."

"Christ, it's almost like when James, Pat and the kids disappeared, except something happened this time that much is obvious." He shouted across to Fools Errand. "J.J. what've you got?"

J.J. was on board the cruiser, reported stolen from the Marina late evening. She was a fine vessel, although as of yet, he could not ascertain why she would not start, even though they had the equipment to overcome the keyless ignition.

"Well there's black paint on the prop, I noticed it when I climbed on board. The power trims still up, she must've collided or reversed into Hydrous somehow. Maybe they damaged the engine and called for help. Where everyone is though could be anyone's guess, there's certainly no one on board."

"I suppose they could've all been picked up by a local fisherman and it's simply not been called in yet? Maybe we should call the coast guard to tell them we found Fools Errand and plan to tow Hydrous in? Fools Errand can be brought in later." He shouted back to J.J. "Are you sure it won't go, have you checked something simple, like the ignition wires?"

J.J. scowled but said nothing as he had not checked them.

Niles looked concerned. "Do you think the Germans were right?" During their evening of merriment at the station, one had spotted the wanted picture of John McAdams shown on the local evening news playing in the bar. Recognising him from earlier, they immediately called the Sheriff.

Aware of Dan, Lizzie and Charlie's plans to dive the Oriskany, they made the joint decision to head out to make sure they were okay. They were shocked to discover a barely floating Hydrous alongside an empty Fools Errand. Whatever happened, it was not a good omen.

"If it was the guy that killed Dan's Aunt and Uncle, there must be a reason why he is after Dan. I'm also beginning to wonder if the tragedies which have befallen the Morris family over the years are actually more sinister than we were led to believe." Niles surmised.

As the Hazles were heading out towards the Oriskany during the night, they were contacted by the Coast Guard. An unregistered E.P.I.R.B. signal had been picked up transmitting in the vicinity. They had been asked to check it out because they were the only vessel with the necessary equipment on board to track the signal. Joel knew it in his bones; the signal was going to be Hydrous. The system was only fitted the day before. They had not had chance to upload the details of Hydrous to the database, thus the carrier unknown.

The E.P.I.R.B. transmitted GPS coordinates as well as an identifier. A GOES (Geostationary Operational Environmental Satellite) weather satellite travelling a geosynchronous orbit would detect the signal. However to pinpoint the E.P.I.R.B. exactly, another set of satellites orbiting the planet in a low polar orbit would be employed, triangulating the exact position. Sometimes unfortunately it took several hours for a satellite to come into range. Rescuers in planes or boats could home in on the E.P.I.R.B. using either the 406-MHz or 121.5-MHz signal, which was exactly how he had found Hydrous, although he knew in his heart exactly where it would be.

"Let's just get a line over and tow Hydrous back. I don't think there's anything we can do out here. J.J. - don't bother with the cruiser. We'll leave Fools Errand to the Coast Guard, our duty is bound to the Morris family."

Niles was staring out to sea. "Dad, what the fuck is that?" He pointed starboard.

Skimming through the water were two thin masts, leaving two tiny V shaped waves in their wake. Slowly rising from the sea, like two connected great white shark fins, the spoiler of the hyper sub broke the surface, racing along at considerable speed, the two thin masts were the individual aerials atop the rear spoiler. Seconds later the cockpit followed, re-emerging from the depths. The hyper sub surfaced like an exploding torpedo through the surf.

Niles and Joel stood aboard Hazeltine in shock. J.J. hearing the noise looked up to see it too. As the hull fully emerged, breaking through the tension of the water surface like a humpback whale, the craft rapidly took to the plane, turning into a stunning speed boat. It headed towards them.

As the distance closed, the back section of the canopy peeled back and two people appeared, as if standing through a sunroof, waving both arms furiously. Niles' heart leapt, he would recognise the person stood at the front anywhere, it was Lizzie.

She clambered from the canopy, followed by Dan, as the craft piloted alongside Hazletine. The engines died and Niles threw Dan a rope, placing protective buoys down the side of the vessel to stop them crashing together. Lizzie jumped aboard hugging Niles, who was still in shock. "What're you doing here?"

"Looking for you guys actually!" He stammered, hugging her in return.

Dan unlocked the front canopy, lifting the entire structure to free its occupants. Joel jumped down on to the deck of the hyper sub, hugging Dan, tears welling up in his eyes. Words failed him, he thought he was dead.

"You better have one of those for me ya big hunk of man?" Aunt Pat struggled in the confines of the cockpit, jammed between Charlie and the seat in front. Joel, still hugging Dan turned to the voice, looking down at Patricia, he thought it was a ghost and burst into tears. "Oh come here you big softie, it's good to see you too!"

She flung her arms round his neck, as he bent down, plucking her from the interior. Charlie breathed a sigh of relief, managing to inhale his first unrestricted breath since leaving the habitat. He made a mental note, must diet.

James, after shutting down the hyper sub systems exited the cockpit. "Hey you, put my wife down. What is it with all the men round here, am I invisible or something?"

Joel looked at James, in a state of shock, one of his best friends whom he had searched the ocean looking for; stood before him, alive. James put his hand out to shake, formally. Instead Joel pulled him into one of his famous bear hugs crushing the wind from his lungs as he so often did.

Lizzie was still concerned about Ash. "Niles you know first aid, Ash is pretty beaten up. Can you take a look?"

"You've got Ash in there too? Where've you been, heaven and back?"

"It's been more like hell to be honest." She uttered under her breath. Niles could tell Lizzie was not joking. "Where's Matt?"

Dan shook his head. "He didn't make it. He saved our lives protecting us against McAdams but it cost him his own life."

"Who's McAdams?" Joel enquired.

"He's the psychopath who killed Aunt Susan and Uncle Mike and Simon Millor. He was after me, it's a long story but I caught him murdering someone in London. He came after the whole family but got far more than he bargained for."

J.J. was listening, he was a man of few words. "Well he almost killed Hydrous too." He motioned to Hydrous which looked slightly sorry for itself, listing in the water.

"Almost, being the operative word. We got out here in time to keep her afloat; we were literally just about to tow her back to the Marina." Joel was happy to see them alive. Pat and James particularly, however he was intrigued as to where they had been, unsure whether he should ask.

James instinctively knew what he was thinking. "The time for secrets has passed Joel, I promise you, but all in good time my friend, all in good time." He patted him on the shoulder, helping Niles lift his daughter from the rear of the hyper sub.

"She'll be fine James, she's banged up pretty good, her nose is broken but she'll be fine." Niles was confident nothing else was broken, just a concussion he believed, which would need to be checked out at the hospital. They carried her on to Hazletine laying her on the deck. She was starting to come round, thankfully.

Ash blinked, staring into a bright light, was she dead? Her eyes took a while, eventually focusing on a blue cloudless sky, the kind she looked at as a kid, laying on her back. Her nose was agony. In her peripheral vision she could see all the faces around, crowding her.

Niles spoke calmly. "Don't get up yet. How do you feel?"

"Stupid fuckin' question!"

"Ash." Pat was motherly and stern. Her tone, even under these circumstances, hinted not to swear.

"Feels like I've been twelve rounds." She spoke with a blocked and strange sound, even to herself. "My dose is agony."

Lizzie leant in smiling. "That's because it's been remodelled for ya, finally."

"Does that mean I can have rhinoplasty? I've always wanted my dose done, I'm thinking slightly more elegant, maybe a bit more regal."

Dan joked. "What so you can look even further down it, at us Neanderthals!" They all laughed.

"Yeah sweetheart, you can have whatever you like." Pat stroked her head. "That was a brave thing you did back there."

"No it wasn't, it was bloody stupid. What was I thinking?"

"It wasn't sweetheart. It was smart because McAdams threw you in the pod with us after he knocked you out. Dan also made it to the pod, before we eventually escaped through the hydro vent. Matt saved us all sweetheart, like always."

Ash looked around. She looked to the concerned faces peering at her; there was Niles and J.J. plus their father Joel. Dan, Lizzie, Charlie, Mom and Dad.

"Where's Matt? I so wanna kick his sorry ass back to the Marina."

Pat compassionately looked at her daughter, tears running down her cheeks. She did not have to speak. Ash instinctively knew, she could feel it. Looking into each of the faces before her, she could feel their unspoken pain. Pat scooped her into her arms, burying her only child to her bosom. James knelt beside them, hugging them both.

Matt was annoyingly gifted, stubbornly lazy, yet always dependable and like a brother, she loved him with all her heart. She burst in to tears, along with the rest of the family and their closest friends.

80

Matt knew exactly how long the moon pool took to fill. The pumps taking exactly one minute and twelve seconds, filling the sealed moon pool when the water level was four inches below the walkway. However with the hydraulic door rendered useless and much of the moon pool's water distributed throughout the habitat, the pumps now had an area twice as large to fill.

If it took the first minute or so to reach his nostrils, with a spot of luck, after taking his last breath, he should have a good three minutes to operate the valves and open the moon pool doors. Three minutes was approximately how long he could hold his breath, would he have time for the sub to exit?

More importantly, would the remaining battery power have enough juice to operate the pumps long enough and open the exterior doors as well?

He could tell they were in shock; Aunt Pat's hand touched the canopy of the sub, tears streamed down her face. His family had lost so much in pursuit of their folly. He followed them, he selfishly had seen what could be achieved and he had proved so much, not just to himself, but to the family as well. One day maybe the realisation that the habitat was as monumental a creation as the pod itself, would dawn on them. Dan understood; he understood many things.

Not until now though had he truly understood why he ran away, the obsession, the family's belligerence and unhealthy corruption of the mind and soul. Dan was the only one who remained true. The only one who kept his principals and because he left to live a life beyond the unhealthy Morris bubble, the family basically cut him off like his own mother. He could see how much Dan had coped with independently; he had lived through many deaths, never fully explained and now the resurrection of a good portion of his family.

Would he forgive? Would the truth quell his anger bringing them closer? Only time would tell.

He was not entirely convinced he wanted to return to the real world. His parents had been murdered and Simon, his lover, was also dead. He was not sure he could return to be alone. A part of him had already died along with the destruction of the wet lab, plus he was also unconvinced he could live an openly gay lifestyle. His real regret was the web of deceit they wove, especially to Dan and Simon. With the help of Lizzie, he truly hoped Dan would finally start living, he deserved that much.

Opening the cover hatch on the dividing wall revealing the valve controls, Matt isolated the water tight doors, eliminating them from the main circuit and releasing the pumps. Unhindered, the system chugged into life. Deep below, the impellers started to turn, pulling water from outside. Within seconds the water started to bubble, rising quickly through the walkway, up his legs. The water continued, as it reached his head he took a final breath, fighting the strong current in the doorway, as the pumps ferociously filled the moon pool and through into operations.

The red light, indicating the water pressure had equalised with the exterior, illuminated. He waved to his family; he could no longer see them. Depressing the micro switch inside the acrylic tube, there was a surge of water around his body which he knew was the sub blowing its ballast tanks. He stood there waiting for a few moments, waiting for his last breath. He never truly believed the sea, which was his friend, would claim his life. He always felt it was his saviour, not his undoing.

Dawning on him like a battering ram, the compression chamber. It did not use power, it manually vented with compressed air. He could use it to escape.

His lungs were bursting, his limbs stung as the lack of oxygen made itself known. Willing his body through operations; the compression chamber was open. Pulling himself inside, he locked the door, which took the last of his strength reserves. Fumbling through the water, like a drunk looking for the light switch, completely uncoordinated, his body was screaming for him to take a breath; his final breath.

He found the handle, more through luck than judgement, and vented the tanks, the water dropping instantly. Matt breathed collapsing to the floor; his entire body ached, shaking through lack of oxygen. He gulped in lungfuls of air, trying to breathe slowly and regulate his heartbeat, his body craved the sustenance.

McAdams' gear lay discarded round the chamber. He rummaged through looking for anything which would be useful. There was no dive equipment stored inside the chamber, everything was kept in the workshop. As operations and living separated, all his equipment had been scattered or destroyed. In his oxygen addled state, his brain had not even registered he should look for diving gear.

There was a discarded floatation bag containing a small oxygen cylinder, unfortunately there were no regulators he could attach. He was going to have to escape without a dive cylinder, would he be able to last that long? He also found his emergency dive mask he had used when he escaped from living, the gas canisters were long since dead but at least he could use the mask to see. Where he was heading was a long route, he just hoped he could make it.

Matt flooded the chamber for the last time, exiting the tube as quickly as he could. He swam to the external edge of operations. Cranking the valve on the floatation bag, it began to rise, dragging him unceremoniously upwards. The bag hit the roof of the hangar, continuing to fill from the canister. Putting his feet in the straps and holding its shape as best he could, he thrust the top part of his body inside. Lifting his mask, he took a final breath and dove back under the water. The floatation bag without any weight attached upended, scattering the gathered oxygen across the ceiling, like tiny crystalline balls.

He headed along the upper most edge of the hangar roof, furthest from the habitat. In the hangar wall was a tube covered with a mesh vent loosely attached. Matt pushed it aside and swam into the tube. Originally the tubes were used as induction fans to extract fumes produced from the machinery in the hangar bays, or the carbon monoxide from plane engines as they were started before being elevated on deck for takeoff.

Matt swam as fast as he could, it was taking much longer than he remembered. Without flippers the distance seemed greater and was far more tiring. Eventually, nearing the end of his lungs, he reached a door. It was small and round like an inverted torpedo hatch, grabbing the hatch handle he swung it inwards, proceeding inside. Using his feet, he pushed the hatch back into position, seating the hatch against a rubber seal and pushing a lever downwards with his foot locking it in position.

Above him was a large bottle of compressed gas inserted into the roof of the tube, turning the valve the tube rapidly filled with oxygen. Matt removed his mask and breathed deeply as the water receded.

Inserted below his back was a small one way valve, as the air filled the chamber, the water was expelled, when empty he shut off the tank.

Matt built the escape tunnel, basing its construction loosely on a submarine torpedo tube, another of his Grandfather's designs. The original valve reincarnated many years later for the hydro pod.

The escape tube was the first thing he designed and built inside the Oriskany, single handedly, long before the contractors arrived on site. It was the only way he believed he could safely escape the occupants if there was a catastrophic failure of the habitat as there was no visible means of escape from a totally contained chamber. No one knew about the escape tunnel. He had hoped it would never be used, however right now he was grateful for his insight.

In the roof of the tube were ten waterproof lockers, each containing an individual SEIE Mk-10, a British designed whole-body suit and one-man life raft, allowing submariners to escape from a stricken submarine. The suit allowed survivors to escape a disabled submarine at depths down to 600 feet (183m), designed to enable a free ascent at a safe speed of approximately two to three meters per second, providing protection for the submariner on reaching the surface, until rescued.

He peeled the orange jumpsuit from its protective enclosure, rolling it out beneath his body. The close proximity of the chamber walls made getting the suit on hard work, but eventually after struggling he was inside and zipped up. Releasing a secondary valve at the top of the tube, water poured back in submerging him again, although this time he could breath.

The constriction of the immersion suit felt unnerving and totally unnatural for a diver. The water pressure equalised and he lifted the lock out handle of the escape hatch in front of him. The escape system was single direction only, maybe the design lacked thought, but it needed to be hidden, which it was.

The escape tunnel opened into a larger tube running horizontal. All of the venting throughout the ship dispensed into the smoke stack, which ran to the top of the island, above the bridge, chart rooms and captains quarters, expelling all the exhaust fumes and other gases directly into the atmosphere above the ship. Matt gently floated upwards, squeezed through the large grate at the top slowly ascending the last eighty feet, to the surface.

81

Hazletine powered effortlessly towards the marina towing Hydrous on a line. Charlie and Pat stood by the helm with Joel. The radio crackled into life, a metallic voice drifted from the mono speaker into the cabin.

"Joel are you still out by the Oriskany dive area? Over."

Joel grabbed the microphone from the cradle and answered. "No we're heading in. We left Fools Errand moored. Hydrous was badly damaged so we've refloated her and are towing her back to the marina. We have the occupants on board, all's good, everyone's fine. Over."

He looked at Pat. "I wasn't really sure whether I should radio in your reappearance. I've just left it for now, what they don't know won't hurt them. You guys can just disappear again if you need to, not without a full explanation first though."

Pat was fine. "It's all right Joel, we need to get a few things sorted before we make ourselves known. We've a lot to sort out, I'm sorry but needs dictated we disappeared, I hope you understand?"

"No, not really but I hope you will fill us in. Well ... eventually."

Pat gave her usual disarming radiant smile. "Of course we will, the time for secrets has past, it's time to show the world."

The radio crackled into life again. *"We're receiving another SOS signal from your area above the Oriskany, have you disabled the transmission signal from Hydrous? If not can you do so, we keep getting SOS alerts. Over."*

Joel looked confused, he was sure Niles had turned the transmitter off. "Okay will check again but I'm sure the signal was disabled. Over."

"Please check, as the signal started retransmitting again in the last twenty minutes or so. There is no information in the signal, so we assume it's the same one having malfunctioned. Better to be safe than sorry. Over."

Joel replaced the mic, reducing the revs to the inboard engine, slowing Hazletine down to a few knots. "Charlie, can you steer please while I check out Hydrous, or at least get Dan to?"

Joel went to the stern and shouted across to Dan, who was sat in the cockpit of Hydrous, along with Ash and Lizzie. "Dan can you do me a favour, can you check the transmitter in the locker please? I've just had a call from the Coast Guard asking if it's still transmitting."

Dan crossed to the front locker opening the trap hatch. "What am I looking for Joel?"

"The E.P.I.R.B., it's a small box with an aerial, is there any LEDs illuminated on it?"

"Nope, it seems to be completely dead, no lights on. I can see Niles disconnected the wires underneath."

"Shit." Joel shook his head. "Sorry people, we're gonna have to head back out. Someone else is in trouble over the dive site at the Oriskany. Christ it never rains, but it pours. Charlie head about, we'll not be long, we'll just go and take a look. I can't see something catastrophic will have happened this quickly. The early morning divers will only just be getting out to the wreck, maybe someone stubbed a toe."

Charlie gunned the engine making a wide arc allowing Hydrous to follow smoothly. Joel shouted back to the guys on Hydrous. "Keep your eyes peeled, we've another emergency by the seems of things. We should take a look and report back while we're out here."

The radio sprung back into life. "What's going on, why are you turning round?" It was James piloting the hyper sub, taking Niles and J.J. for spin having just surfaced after watching them turn while diving underneath.

Pat grabbed the mic. "It's all right hun, there's another emergency SOS above the Oriskany, we're heading back to check. The Coast Guard radioed it in to check it wasn't Hydrous still transmitting."

Niles shouted from three seats back to James. "I disconnected the power feed from the transmitter, the signal can't have come from Hydrous."

James relayed the message. "Niles said he disconnected the transmitter."

"Yeah we know, we checked, which is why we're heading back. Keep your eyes peeled kids. Over." She hung the mic back on the radio. "You know I've always wanted to say that Charlie. I always wanted a CB handle, what do you reckon, Bubbly Mama?"

Charlie laughed. "More like Cuddly Mama!"

"Cheeky!" They laughed.

As they neared the dive site, it was still early; there was no one about. No boats moored with groups of eager dive tourists getting ready. They surveyed the surface, the water was devoid of life.

Lizzie suddenly screamed. "There! To the stern, there's an orange thing floating in the water." They all looked where Lizzie pointed. A good distance from the site was an orange blob on the horizon. Charlie turned Hazletine slowly and headed towards the high visibility fluorescent orange object, clashing violently against the deep blue.

Charlie picked up the mic. "We've spotted something drifting south from the dive site James, where are you? Over."

"We're on the other side of the dive site, slightly North East, we'll head back over to you. Over."

They came alongside the object, killing the engine. Joel leant over the side with a wooden pole, ending with a hook managing to snare the orange material, pulling it towards the back of the boat. Joel jumped down to the platform jutting out the back, Charlie and Pat joined him. They turned the orange suit round in the water. Staring back at them through the clear plastic was a grumpy looking Matt.

"About fuckin' time, you sailed straight by me, what kind of a rescue do you call this?"

Pat lunged at him screaming with joy, bouncing off the suit and ricocheting into the water. She hugged him with all her might, which was difficult with the size of the suit plus the fact he floated a lot higher in the water. Joel and Charlie dragged Pat on board, then managed to pull Matt aboard the swim platform, unzipping the immersion suit.

"I honestly thought you lot were gonna fuck off without me."

They helped him out of the immersion suit, while Dan cuddled Ash and Lizzie both crying tears of joy. All of them stood there in stunned silence, until James pulled alongside in the hyper sub, with the canopy open.

"You know Matt, you never fail to amaze me. I'm really looking forward to hearing how the hell you made it out of there alive."

Matt just grinned. "Come on, let's go home."

The four of them sat along the stern of Hydrous, feet dangling over the edge, down to the water as the bow wake slid by. Sitting in silence, each lost in their own thoughts, contemplating the last 24 hours. Absently they waved to fellow mariners heading to dive the wreck of the USS Oriskany, if only they knew.

The last time all of them sat here along the stern, from left to right,

Lizzie, Dan, Ash, then Matt, was when they were kids. From what they had been through it seemed somewhat surreal to all be together again.

James was navigating the hyper sub with Niles and J.J. excitedly on board. The sub sped along, promptly disappearing beneath the waves and then surfacing spectacularly.

Joel, Charlie and Pat were on board Hazletine, the sensible option which was the consensus held between the three of them, towing the stricken Hydrous back towards the marina.

Dan finally broke the comfortable silence. "Why was I never told about the wet lab?"

Lizzie and Dan both looked down the line at Ash and Matt, far too accusingly for their liking but it was understandable. Ash looked to Matt for support, taking a deep breath to answer, her nose throbbed making speech difficult.

"When you left for England, in fact way before that, after Granddad and Grandma's deaths you changed Dan. You shut down from the entire family. It was like you disowned us. Even Lizzie was unable to get through to you, which was rare. Ever since you came home after your Mother's death, Lizzie was always able to get you to talk and open up. All communication simply stopped; the family duty you once had, or ever felt, disappeared as soon as Granddad's casket was buried."

"That's not fair."

Matt chimed in slightly angry. "You're right Dan, it wasn't fair, it wasn't fair on any of us, especially Ash and I. We never did anything wrong, neither did Lizzie, but it was like you blamed us. Blamed us all for their deaths, and then you ran away. We tried keeping in contact, but you never returned a call, an email or anything, until eventually we just gave up, hoping one day you'd pull yourself together and come home of your own accord.

Aunt Susan kept the lines of communication open, more forced on you I'd imagine but she decided it was necessary plus her duty. After our Grandparents' death, we made a family commitment to finish what Granddad started, all of us, and you never seemed to be part of that. So as a family we decided to continue, without you. I'm sorry Dan, I can see now what we did to you was exactly what Granddad and Grandma did to your Mom."

Ash grabbed Matt's hand squeezing it gently, his anger dissipated. Dan did come back though, when it most mattered. Ash continued. "It may've been harsh Dan but it was also our way of protecting you, we always hoped and prayed no one else would get hurt. None of us ever dreamed things would have ended the way they have …" She looked at Matt, unsure whether to continue, knowing her next few words would still be very raw. "… with Aunt Susan and Uncle Mike murdered." Her voice faltered, she started to cry again, burying her face into Matt.

Matt continued. "It's all right." He comforted Ash. "We really hoped with our disappearance, the people who were watching and waiting would stop. We were right, they did. None of us could've ever second guessed, something completely unrelated, such as a murder in your apartment block four and a half thousand miles away would lead them back.

Maybe if you had known, things would have been different. Maybe you would have come home sooner? Maybe we would never have lost anyone else, especially Mom and Dad? But it's not your fault Dan, none of it, no one's to blame, we were all a part of this charade and I'm sorry."

Dan also put his arm round Ash, who buried her head into him removing herself from Matt. They were right though, he had run away to hide, to conceal his emotions. His world had fallen apart when his grandparents died, everyone he loved was taken from him. No one, not even Lizzie, was able to pick up the pieces. Burying himself in work was his salvation; ultimately his family had seemed less important, especially when he thought he had lost Ash and Matt.

As a family they lost a huge amount but on a personal level, he now understood what happened to his mother and all of the bizarre feelings, the things he had run away from in the first place, had been resolved. Part of his family had been restored, for him it was like rebirth.

"You're right of course, both of you, I'm sorry too."

Lizzie looked aghast. "Wow, this has been a voyage of discovery; did the mighty Dan Morris actually apologise? I can't remember you apologising for anything, ever."

"Oh shut up you, you're not always right you know, well not all the time. There's always a first and this'll probably be the last time I do apologise."

They all laughed, Ash had stopped crying. "So then Liz, did you ever tell Dan what I asked of you the night before I disappeared?" Lizzie turned red.

Dan looked at Lizzie, questioning. "Actually no, she didn't. She started to let it slip when we were out at dinner the other night but after telling me the family was trying to protect me, she clammed up."

Ash looked at Liz accusingly. "I told her to finally spill the beans how she felt about you, maybe it would bring you home, to all of us, we hoped it would. Well Liz, did you tell him?"

She looked at Dan slightly coy. "I've not really had the chance to, although I think he knows."

"Knows what?" Dan sat innocently between the pair, swinging his head back and forth like watching a tennis match.

Lizzie put her hand on his cheek, stopping his head moving, staring into his beautiful eyes. "That I love you, have always loved you, and will always love you."

Dan smiled, looking to Matt, winking. "Oh yeah, I knew that, everybody knew that!"

"You bast ..." Lizzie never quite managed to get the word out, Dan kissed her passionately. As they parted, she sighed, he rested his forehead on hers, locking their eyes.

"You know what, I love you too."

Made in the USA
Charleston, SC
24 June 2014